NECROPOLIS

Santiago Gamboa

NECROPOLIS

*Translated from the Spanish
by Howard Curtis*

Europa
editions

Europa Editions
214 West 29th Street
New York, N.Y. 10001
www.europaeditions.com
info@europaeditions.com

This book is a work of fiction. Any references to historical events,
real people, or real locales are used fictitiously.

Translation by Howard Curtis
Original title: *Necropolis*
Translation copyright © 2012 by Europa Editions

Library of Congress Cataloging in Publication Data is available
ISBN 978-1-60945-073-1

Gamboa, Santiago
Necropolis

Book design by Emanuele Ragnisco
www.mekkanografici.com

Cover photo © Getty Images

Prepress by Grafica Punto Print – Rome

Printed in the USA

CONTENTS

To Analía and Alejandro in Jangpura

Surviving is, in the end, an act as praiseworthy as
searching for the truth until it wears us out.
—SÁNDOR MÁRAI

It's not the history of countries but the lives of men.
—CHARLES BUKOWSKI

NECROPOLIS

PART ONE
THE CONFERENCE

1.

THE INVITATION

The letter inviting me to that strange conference, the International Conference on Biography and Memory (ICBM), arrived along with a whole lot of unimportant mail, which is why I left it on my desk, without opening it, for more than a week, until the cleaning woman, who sometimes takes it upon herself to tidy my things, said, what should I do with this letter? throw it in the wastepaper? It was only then that I had a good look at the stamp, the Hebrew writing, and the ICBM logo. I opened it, thinking it would be something unremarkable, but as soon as I started reading it I was hooked:

> Dear writer, in view of your work, we have the pleasure of inviting you to the International Congress on Biography and Memory (ICBM), to be held in the city of Jerusalem from 18 to 25 May. If you accept, we would ask you to participate in a round table on a topic still to be decided, and to give a talk or lecture either on the vicissitudes of your work and the way you approach it, or on your life or the life of any another person worthy, in your opinion, of being retold. The costs of transport and accommodation, plus your expenses during your stay, will be met by the ICBM, and you will, in addition, receive a fee of 4,000 euros. Please reply to the above address, enclosing as complete a résumé as you see fit, as well as a photograph.
> Yours sincerely,
> Secretary General of the ICBM.

*

I was not only surprised but also, to tell the truth, flattered and euphoric. Questions came flooding into my head: who had given them my name? what kind of conference was this? what was my connection with the world of biography? I've written a number of novels and short stories, a travel book and thousands of pages of journalism, none of which, as far as I know, could be called biographical in nature; what made them think of me? how did they find my address? By the time evening fell, I was still wrestling with the same questions, and not finding any answers.

I should point out that this happened at a time when my life had slowed down completely. The hands of the clock kept turning, but that meant absolutely nothing to me. I would spend hours staring at a photograph in a newspaper, or at the cover of a book without opening it, aware of the emptiness and my own inner sounds, the beating of what Poe calls the "tell-tale heart," the bloodstream, the tension of certain muscles. I had just recovered from a long illness that had separated me from the life I had lived until then, the life of a working writer moderately well known in the small world of letters. What happened was that my lungs had been invaded by a malignant virus, something called a hantavirus, which filled the alveolar sacs with liquid and flooded the capillaries, generating pools of virulent infection, infested with white cells. The illness condemned me to a long stay in hospital, until somebody decided to move me to a sanatorium in the mountains that specialized in respiratory and pneumological diseases, and there I was to remain for just over two years, far from all that had been mine but that, in the end, turned out to be nobody's, since it all faded away the higher up the mountain I climbed (like Hans Castorp).

Illness creates a vacuum, and with time this becomes our only relationship with the world, a relationship that never seems to end. The patient walks along the edge of a crater where there may once have been a lake or even a city, and asks himself questions like, what happened here? why is it so deserted? where did everybody go? Then we are filled with a great stillness, and the past, all that we were before, dissolves like sugar in hot coffee. It is a very strange feeling, but quite a pleasant one, and I really mean that. Some time later, when the pools in my cells dried up and stopped secreting pus, I felt enormously weary. I had invested all my strength into getting well. During that time, I had read a lot, but stopped writing, since it is easier to do without things that do not yet exist, that have not yet taken shape. That was what I had learned in those years of stillness and silent observation.

As we are on the subject—and observing the strict laws of narrative—it might be useful at this point to say something more about myself. I have worked in public radio, especially on nighttime news shows; I have been a newspaper correspondent, written half a dozen novels that have had a modest success in a number of countries; I have taken courses in literary studies and, above all, I have read the classics, not very systematically, as well as my contemporaries, some of whom, of course, should be severely censured, but then it is well known that literature is a barren terrain to which anybody can stake a claim. As I myself did.

As for my private life, there is not much to say. I have been living in Europe for more than twenty years. Currently, I live in Rome, on Via Germanico in the Prati district, not far from the Tiber and Vatican City, in a comfortable apartment that is unfortunately also somewhat noisy, absorbing as it does both the sounds of the street and those from inside the building, which are varied in nature, from the snoring of an elderly alcoholic with cancer of the trachea and six bypasses to his credit, to the moaning of my young upstairs neighbor having sex with her boyfriend, which can be quite maddening, especially when you are trying to read the great Stoic philosopher Epictetus.

But let me get back to the letter.

The next day, at about eleven in the morning, I switched on my computer with the intention of answering the ICBM and accepting their invitation. But first, I went to the window and looked out: that old itch had come back, the itch to put off writing and do all kinds of little tasks that suddenly seemed urgent. Finally, though, I sat down and said, solemnly: the first letter I type will be the first in twenty-seven months, which one shall I start with? I pressed the x three times, by way of a trial, and then the l. I stretched my fingers then contracted them, rubbed my forearms, bounced up and down on the armchair to test the springs, and kicked off my slippers. I was ready. There was nothing to do now but write.

> Dear friends of the ICBM, it is both an honor and a surprise to receive this invitation, which I hasten to accept. I await further details on the logistics of the conference and on whatever procedures need to be followed. In the meantime, I have a small request to make. Perhaps you could clarify for me how it is that such a prestigious institution heard of me and why it has been so gracious as to invite me to its conference, given that I have never written any book that was openly biographical in nature, even though I am a passionate reader of the genre. As that is my one question for the moment, I should like to thank you again, and I look forward to hearing from you at the earliest opportunity.
>
> PS: résumé enclosed.

I went back to the window, to clear my head before rereading the letter, and looked out to see what was happening on Via degli Scipioni. That is one of my main occupations: looking down at the street and watching the people who pass, wondering who they are, what they are doing here, what has driven them to leave their homes, what keeps them going. A pizza delivery boy parked his motorbike near the corner, talking all the while on his cell phone. A girl student crossed the street, went into a building opposite, and slammed the door. At the far end, the owner of the convenience store stood out on the sidewalk, waiting for customers and giving instructions to his son, who was piling crates of mineral water. Things were slowly coming back to life, so I went back to my desk and reread the letter. Then I printed it, put it in an envelope, and walked three blocks to the post office.

On the way back, I dropped by the Caffè Miró on Via Cola di Rienzo, one of the places in the neighborhood that I use as a kind of office, but by the time I was on my second cup of coffee I realized that I could not think of anything but the conference. It was the same on the days that followed. The thing kept growing inside me, like a cry echoing between the walls of a ravine. I started spying on the caretaker as he sorted the post, hoping against hope that I could see all the way from the fourth floor whether one of the envelopes was from the ICBM.

The days passed and I started to resign myself. They must have realized their mistake, I thought. After all, I had, in a way, dissuaded them myself. Well, I would just have to resume doing what I had been doing before, slowly getting my life back, even though I sensed that something surprising was about to happen, which was why I waited at the window or sat on benches in Roman squares, played solitaire on my laptop, or watched old football matches on TV.

But "everyone gets everything he wants" (it's a line from *Apocalypse Now* that I quoted in one of my books), and so, one fine day, the long-awaited envelope arrived. I did actually recognize it from upstairs and rushed to the elevator, convinced that I had to open it before anyone else laid eyes on it: that damned caretaker, for example, whom I had long suspected, not only of being a Fascist, but also of opening the tenants' mail. So I grabbed the bundle of envelopes and hid it under the flap of my jacket, a move to which the caretaker reacted with a disapproving scowl.

I heaved a sigh of relief when I got back inside my apartment, and settled down to look carefully through what had arrived. With a certain morbid curiosity, I put aside the envelope that interested me the most and opened my other mail, which turned out to be an advertisement for a gym and two letters from my agent enclosing royalty payments (one for 26.50 euros and the other for 157 euros). I needed the letter from the ICBM to restore my enthusiasm, even though I was sure they had withdrawn the invitation. I held the envelope up to the light. They're going to apologize, I thought, and tell me they'll send me something by way of consolation, the book with the proceedings of the conference or something like that, so imagine my surprise when I opened the envelope, saw the heading, and read the following:

> Dear Mr.—, thank you for confirming that you are able to attend our conference, please fill in the enclosed forms and send them back to us, specifying if you wish to stay in Jerusalem for the duration of the conference (which we would greatly appreciate) or if you prefer to limit your stay. By return of post, you will receive a code for obtaining your airline tickets, the themes on which we will ask you to speak are in the enclosed booklet, once again we are grateful for your interest.
> Yours sincerely,
> Secretary General of the ICBM.

I felt a kind of primitive joy and my eyes filled with tears (since my illness I have found that I am easily moved to tears, which can be somewhat ridiculous). In gratitude for the letter, I looked out at the turbulent Roman sky. I do not believe in anything apart from the classics of literature, but I felt like shouting out: if anybody up there is listening, thank you! Inside the envelope was a form, with thirty-six questions, so I sat down to answer them. I needed to weigh each word carefully. As it was certain now that I would be going to the conference, I was no longer afraid of saying anything inappropriate, but I did want to give the best, or indeed the most impressive, answers I could.

Firstly, I made it clear that there were no subjects with which I thought I would have any problems or about which I was especially sensitive, from a political, religious, sexual, or moral point of view (questions 1 to 25); then I gave a brief account of my intellectual interests and aesthetic stance (questions 26 to 34), which I found quite useful, as it was something I had never done before; and, finally, I summarized my health problems and physical condition (questions 35 and 36), a subject I was pleased to see on the form, the way a student who knows the answer to a question is pleased when that question comes up, since it allowed me to mention my illness, the one thing that had dominated my life over the past few years. Then I looked at the booklet. I saw that there were going to be a number of round tables dealing with the relationship between language and the past, and that I was invited to take part in one of them, which would focus on "the many forms through which we remember, evaluate, understand, and convey a life." I was also asked for a talk of a biographical nature "on any literary, sociological, human, or archetypal topic that has a connection with the main theme of the conference: *The Soul of Words*." The wording was so vague that I was sure I could use one of my old lectures. That did not worry me, whereas the round table, I thought, might present more of a problem. In my experience, such discussions often throw up a variety of subjects that are not always easy to anticipate.

I started searching for books that dealt with the theme of

memory and the life of words, and spent the afternoon looking through essays by Borges and Adorno and poems by Cavafy, even checking out some of Deleuze's ideas, though I have never quite understood Deleuze, and adding a few ideas of my own, although not many: I have never been strong on theory or abstract thought. During those hours, I would not say I was happy, but I did feel quite content. I was occupied with intellectual labor, and I was making something happen. I had been given a second chance.

Some time later, reading by the light of an old lamp—it must have been three in the morning by now, the hour of the wolf, the hour when hospital patients are most in pain—I realized that there was something basic that I had not yet done, which was to look at the list of the other people invited to the conference. In the past, that had always been the first thing I had done, and it had often been the thing that had determined whether or not I would accept the invitation.

I remembered a fog-shrouded conference in the city of Gothenburg, in the middle of the northern winter, with the eye-catching name *Current Narrative Tendencies, or the Dark Music of Cities*. When I looked at the list and saw that Rodrigo Rey Rosa, Horacio Castellanos Moya, and Roberto Bolaño were among the speakers I immediately accepted, and set off in a Swedish plane that left behind the clear Italian sky to enter the gray atmosphere of the north and had to break through a layer of ice before setting down on a frozen runway. Then there was a hotel called the Osaka, with wooden stairs and striped carpets, and Rey Rosa and Castellanos Moya, their bodies stiff with cold and their faces glum, announcing that Roberto Bolaño had not arrived on the expected flight and that he would not be coming on any other, having cancelled at the last minute, which was very typical of him: he always gave the organizers of such events the jitters. A sense of disappointment settled over us. We felt alone, like three teenagers lost in the inhospitable streets of an industrial zone. The next day, when we had to discuss literature and cities in the fog in front of an audience shrouded in scarves, all we could come up with was a few vague ideas, and I do not know if I am saying this with hindsight because of what happened later, but when we said goodbye to each other in that desolate airport, which was more like a morgue or a gothic cathedral, Castellanos Moya, Rey Rosa, and I had red-rimmed eyes, as you do when you are trying desperately to avoid talking about something tragic, a feeling that, I am sure, was connected with Bolaño and his absence.

But let me return to the list of delegates.

Of course, as was only to be expected, I did not find any of my friends, but I did see a series of names that drew my attention, and I copied them into my notebook:

Leonidas Kosztolányi. Hungary, 62 years old, antiquarian, specialist in 17th-century rolled plate glass and marquetry. Lives in Budapest. His most recent works are *The Life and Achievements of Baron Sarim Bupcka*, *The Calends of Ptolemy*, *Return from Tasmania,* and a *Dictionary of Brevity*.

Edgar Miret Supervielle. France, 64 years old, bibliophile, specializing in Jewish religious texts. Has spent much time in Israel, Lithuania, and New York. A great lover of chess, he is the author of *Life of Boris Alekhine* and *From Nabokov to Stefan Zweig: Writers and Chess*. On other subjects, he has published *The Essential Thought of Ben Yehuda* and a three-volume biography of Herod Antipas.

All of them had sent extensive résumés, full of details of travels and stays abroad. Mine by comparison was fairly concise, just a list of books and the few jobs I had done.

The shortest was the following:

Kevin Lafayette O'Reilly. Island of Santa Lucia. Author of *Memories of the Purple Ghost.* I am black.

And the most eye-catching:

Sabina Vedovelli. Italy. Porn actress and founder of Eve Studios. Among her many films are *The Graveyard of Lost Sex* and the trilogy *Screw Me, Screw Me, I Don't Want This to End!* (sketches for a "Pornography of the Left"). Author of *Kevin McPhee: The Legend, Marcello Deckers or the Modern Priapus* and *Aaron Sigurd, the Twelve-and-a-Half-Inch King.*

I looked her up on the internet and found 320,000 results. There was a website of her production company, which listed her movies, and another that seemed to be her official website, the name of which, translated from Italian, would be something like www.letmesuckit.com. It contained photographs, short videos, and a section for short stories, entitled *Holocaust of the Hymen.* I opened one from Mexico, which read as follows:

I was by the side of the swimming pool, wearing only a tiny G-string that plunged into my shaved cunt and no top because they leave ugly marks on the back. Frank was swimming, taking no notice of me until he came closer and said, what's up, Mireyita? I turned without saying anything, just stuck my ass in his direction, I wanted him to see that I was still a virgin and get the message, the idiot. Frank emerged from the water, opened my legs and thrust it into me, all the way, or as they say in Sinaloa, all the way up to the glottis and back again. It didn't hurt because I was wet, and I'm not referring to the turquoise water of the pool but my own fountain, because with his muscles and his pale skin and his mummy's-boy face he made me sopping wet, and I would have given my life for his wretched cock to be ten or twenty inches longer and reach all the way up to my duodenum. Then, when he came, he shot so much spunk into me that I was dripping for the next three days.

Apart from the writings, there were photographs of Sabina Vedovelli. In one of them a man had his arm up her anus and she was smiling and biting on a white nurse's cap. The man was wearing a white coat with a stethoscope around his neck. It was going to be strange, meeting her at the conference.

Let me continue with the most striking of the delegates. In some cases, this will serve as an introduction to future characters, insofar as time, as in the novels of Balzac, can be measured in pages.

Moisés Kaplan. Colombia, 64 years old. Historian, philatelist, and stamp collector. Divides his time between New York and Tel Aviv. His best known books are: *From Palestine to the Aburrá Valley*, *Biography of Antón Ashverus*, and a book on grammar entitled *Against the Diphthong and the Hiatus*.

José Maturana. Miami, 56 years old, former evangelical pastor, former convict, former drug addict. Served seven prison sentences for armed robbery in Florida and Charleston before finding the light with the help of Reverend Walter de la Salle, founder of the Ministry of Mercy, a church and advice center for drug addicts, alcoholics, prostitutes, depressives, the suicidal, the violent, the antisocial, pedophiles, and other deviants who wish to find redemption through faith. Among his works are *Miracle in Moundsville*, *Christ Stopped on Crack Drive*, and *The Redeemers of South Miami*.

By that point, I had lost all sense of reality. The delegates and their bizarre lives seemed straight out of a play by Tennessee Williams, one of those waterfront dramas where everyone is drunk and desperate, women and men endlessly lust after each other, and everything is profoundly tragic, but I also thought: this is where I belong, when you come down to it, with my illness and my solitude and my novels, what will the former pastor think when he reads my biographical sketch? The ICBM was right to invite me, even though, and there was no doubt about it now, they had made a mistake, a big mistake.

Just before dawn—staring up at the wreaths of smoke from the cigarillo I was forbidden to smoke—I told myself that perhaps the people in the ICBM saw something in my work of which I was unaware, something that did have a connection with biography and exceptional lives and might be about to manifest itself, like so many things we ourselves are unaware of but are obvious to other people: the white whales or Moby Dicks we carry inside us and cannot see, and so I told myself, I will have to be very much on the alert. At that hour of the night, I came to the conclusion that I would not miss the conference for anything in the world, that I would be there from the first day to the last.

The next day I woke up very late, almost noon. On my desk table, next to the telltale ashtray, I found a bottle of gin with almost nothing left in it—I did not think to mention that before—and I realized that much of what I had been thinking (the reference to Moby Dick, for example) was due to that perverse analyst and futurologist to which Malcolm Lowry refers in one of his poems, when he says, "The only hope is the next drink," good old Lowry, but anyway, it was time to continue thinking about the topics to be treated at the conference, so after a light snack I went back to work, and in the course of the next few hours I looked at books by Voltaire, Goethe, Wittgenstein's *Tractatus Logico-Philosophicus*, which I have never read, but which other people have told me about and from which I remembered a quotation I could not find; plus, as always, the diaries of Julio Ramón Ribeyro and his extraordinary *Prosas apátridas*, as well as Cioran and Fernando González, the "philosopher from somewhere else." I read and read, jumping from one book to another, and as often happens to me I ended up rereading poetry by Gil de Biedma and paragraphs from Graham Greene, two or three maxims by Cortázar and verses by León de Greiff, the great León, who had the courage to write the following:

Lady Night, give me Sleep. May my Weariness sleep long
And I with it, (Oh, Night! Let us sleep forever:
Never wake us, tomorrow or ever!)

And so I went on, book by book, phrase by phrase, from Epictetus to Les Murray, from Musil to Panait Istrati, from Bufalino to Malraux, sometimes only a paragraph or a sentence, and then I thought again about the biographical genre and took from the shelf *Primo Levi* by Ian Thomson, and *Charles Bukowski: Locked in the Arms of a Crazy Life*, by Howard Sounes, the life of poor lonely old Bukowski, with his monstrous acne—worse than mine, pitted with craters as my cheeks are—his alcoholism and his love of desperate people and the dark corners of bars. Time passed, and the sky of Rome was filling with dark, terrifying black holes, like something out of a painting by Caravaggio, and I started to wonder if those written lives were real or if their only reality was in the writing itself, the fact that they had been turned into words, into filled pages destined for people almost as desperate as themselves, sadly normal people who populate this world of illusions, clocks, and threatening sunsets like the one that now appeared outside my window, over Via degli Scipioni, and reminded me that it was time to go down and have dinner.

The Cola di Rienzo trattoria is a couple of blocks away, on the corner of Via Pompeo Magno and Via Lepanto. I usually order spaghetti *a la amatriciana*, with an artichoke salad and a bottle of white wine. With that on the table I continued thinking about what lay behind all those books, which were like a trunk containing the fears of so many solitary people who, like me that night, needed to understand something just so that they could tell others that they had no need of it and had never asked for it, or so that they could tell themselves and then find the strength to continue, their brains seething with images and premonitions. And so the days passed, filled with books, dinners at the trattoria, and fierce looks from the caretaker, who had suspected something ever since he had seen that envelope and the writing in Hebrew. The other day, for example, he stopped me at the front door and told me that in one of the booklets put out by his group there was an article on the physical characteristics of the Jews, which made them less potent sexually, or so the article said, but I took no notice of him, just told him that I was expecting a call from my doctor and walked away.

The blank pages were gradually filling up, and, just before I was due to set out in my journey, I finished the first draft of a lecture that I entitled *Words Written in the Cave of Silence*, in which I tried to explain that the literary concept of words is that of an underground stream that runs very deep, dictated by the distant, obscure howling of creation, with extracts from different authors and a Kafkaesque tone reminiscent of *A Report to the Academy*. In the same folder I put three old texts on related themes, knowing that they always come in useful at round tables.

2.

THE MINISTRY OF MERCY (I)
(AS TOLD BY JOSÉ MATURANA)

I'm a Venezuelan and was born in Santo Domingo, in a brothel full of crazy alcoholics hiding under the tables, licking their wounds clean with their tongues. I'm a Panamanian and first saw the light of day on a pile of corpses in Quintana Roo, or was it San Juan? I don't remember. I'm a Cuban and resulted from the coupling of a junkie whore and a blind, mangy stray dog in Tegucigalpa. I was born Latino in Miami and when I opened my eyes three hit men were sodomizing the nurse, who was very drunk and putting powder in her nose. I wasn't born of woman, I was shat out by an animal with three heads who then cleaned himself with a dirty sheet and staggered away between the palms, his three brains befuddled by crack. I'm a Nicaraguan, a Costa Rican, a Dominican, and a Puerto Rican. I'm from Bogotá and Caracas. I'm a punk and a Rasta and a vagrant and a gangbanger and a paramilitary and a drug dealer. I'm black and mixed race and mestizo and Indian and purebred white. I'm sick and I don't know who the hell I am. I don't know if I'm already dead. Maybe I am. I'm a Caribbean. I'm a Latin American.

This was what I told myself every time I opened my eyes and saw the bars of my cell in Moundsville Penitentiary, my dear friends and listeners, before the guard came and hit the bars with his baton and cried, José, wake up! get off the toilet, we're going to change the water! and I'd rack my brains, but all I found was an empty screen, a concrete wall like the towers of the prison, my head was empty, and I'd tell myself, José, you must remember something, search deep down, search, or did you fall from a palm tree like a coconut? even the frogs matter in this world, as the Bible says, and I'd search and search, but it didn't work, all I ever saw was a hill of stones and gravel in the distance, tin houses held up by ropes, a stretch of wasteland in the Latino district, near the Orange Bowl Stadium, with buzzards flying overhead and a wall full of holes. Plus a footbridge strewn with organic waste, empty or near-empty soda bottles, dried dog shit. That was what I had in my mind whenever I woke up and thought of my Latino origins, and the continent I didn't have, the continent that was far from me, as if I was its leprosy. The continent that had abandoned me and expelled me and that I loved, my friends, more than anything I've ever had and loved.

I longed to see a face or remember a voice, because I'd say to myself, somebody must have been pleased to see me some time, even if only for a few minutes, but nothing came, only cold distant images, newspapers blown about on the air raised by trucks passing on the avenue, flies and rotting food, used syringes, sanitary napkins with dried and blackened blood, and when I heard the guard shouting again, "José, thirty seconds!" I would think that somebody must have given birth to me for me to be in this shithole—what did the woman look like?—otherwise, I'd be a stone or a seashell, and so I went out into the corridor and breathed in the fetid air of the cellblock, one, two, three, and then I'd throw myself on the floor and do press-ups, because I had to be strong, and as I did that I'd feel a ball of fire in my guts, the moaning from the cells reminding me of something urgent, the voice of a sick girl saying in my ear, where's today's smack, friend? and I'd reply, when they open the door to the yard, sweetheart, I'll go fetch it, it's in my hiding place though I can't tell you where that is, I have today's supply there and maybe tomorrow's, if the monster trapped in my chest that won't let me breathe doesn't get too upset in the afternoon.

We prisoners would leave the cells and go to the showers and then to the dining hall for breakfast, but by now I was already outside, my friends, I'd swung by my hiding place and had transported myself to the sky, or as they used to say, I was riding the dragon, with the heat of the smack in my veins, which was even nicer than having your cock in the ass of a black female dancer in the province of Oriente, Cuba, or in Maracay or on the island of Guadalupe or in Cartagena de Indias, oh what joy, my friends, and forgive the coarse language, but the fact is, if I don't use that language I won't be able to convey the main gist of my story, which is, and no more beating about the bush now, the piece of lowlife shit I was before the Word of the Lord, of the Man Himself, the Supreme Brother, came into my life in the voice of his missionary on earth, Reverend Walter de la Salle, who was also called Freddy Angel or José de Arimatea, depending on the period or which year his driving license was issued, because without that, and with all the changes of personality, even he himself didn't remember where or how he'd started, and I really mean that, my friends and listeners, and I tell you here and now, Freddy Angel, the original name of that Caribbean Jesus Christ, had the same beginnings as me, in other words, the fucking street, which is what I'm talking about, born like me at the mercy of the elements, under a car fender, and brought up by an angel who was his protector, a cone of light that enveloped him and kept him out of trouble and stood between him and knives and even bullets, and that was why he was called Freddy Angel, because the person who protects us is the one who gives us our name.

The first person in Walter's life was that angel, so that was what he was called, and that was how he explained his origins: that an angel had left him on a bench in Echo Park, under an oak tree, and that only after a few hours did he start to wake up, ah-ha, and open his eyes, and when both of them were wide open he realized what it meant to be a human and not a stellar android, a piece of the sky or a particle of light, so he said, and then Walter or Freddy got up from the bench and started going around the world doing good, because apparently the angel had brought him already fully grown; but doing good isn't the easiest thing, especially if the people who need it don't realize it or don't want it, because anyone who hasn't seen God, my friends, when he does see him he gets a bit scared, and so the young man started to talk to whores and young drug addicts about the Redeemer, to see what they said, and of course, the first person he addressed, a fat black man with eyes as red and bulging as those of a wife-killer, said, God? what's that? and added, I haven't had the pleasure, son, who is he? is he from the block? isn't he the guy in the gray Dodge Polara? and so Walter thought, forgive them, Lord, and talked to them about the origin of life and the origin of love and sadness and problems and how to solve them.

He also started going to the Old Havana Memorial Hospital, the ward for the terminally sick, to be with, and give relief to, people with sunken eyes and pale skin, who were already sitting on the lap of the Grim Reaper, and there he saw a bit of everything, emphysemas, sarcomas, exhausted livers and pancreases, rotten bladders, prostates inflated like blood sausages, he saw the violence of the incurable and the hatred they felt for those left behind, and he talked to them about love and God and tried to bring them relief.

There he was, Freddy Angel, pushing wheelchairs through the gardens so that the old people could breathe the salty, smog-filled air of the parking lot, helping hopeless cases out of their beds, taking them to the washroom and cleaning their asses and groins, he was a true saint, that young man, and gradually the staff of the Old Havana started saying to each other, who is this guy? but they also got used to him, until one day they called him and said, hey, you . . . yes, you, are you somebody's relative? is that why you come here every day? and he replied, yes, I am the father of all these pale-faced men, or the son who takes on their sins and cleans their shit, what does it matter who I am, I come for them, because they're alone and nobody looks them in the eyes or talks to them about God.

They took him to see the director, who said, well, now, young man, what is it you're looking for? a job? do you want to train as a nurse? but he said, no, sir, I don't need any training to care for my children, I come to keep them company, to be with them before they go, that's all.

They continued to let him come, saying to him, you can stay if that's what you like, but . . . you're not one of those damn perverts? to which Freddy said, no sir, let me prove to you that I only want to help, and he kept coming every day; as he was poor he ate what little the patients left on the plates, without thinking about infection, he ate leftover rice and sauce, meat fat, slices of sour tomato, cold dregs of chicken soup, pieces of hardened bread, fruit that had gone soft, he'd collect the old people's trays and take them out in the corridor and there he'd lick the plates and keep little bags of cookies and crusts of bread in his pocket to eat them afterwards, until one day, a few weeks later, they called him again and said, hey, you, come here, would you be interested in working as a night companion for the incurables? and he said, yes, whatever, if it means being with them; the doctors looked at each other in surprise but ended up giving him a paper and telling him he'd be paid a hundred twenty dollars per week.

Reverend Walter de la Salle used to say that contract had been his baptism: the first time his name was printed on a piece of paper, and with that he stopped being a piece of planet that had fallen from God alone knew what skies and started to be human, he now had a name and an employment contract, my friends, and on taking that name it became still clearer that he was like me, a Caribbean and a Latino, a Barranquillan from

Barquisimeto, a Jamaican from Trinidad, and God knows what else, anyway, I think you get my meaning by now, he was the same as me, a Latino adrift in the steel and concrete jungle of Miami, and maybe that's why destiny or the Master, the Big Enchilada, the Man Himself, decided to throw us in the same cesspit so that we could meet and tend each other's wounds, which in the end, my friends, were the festering wounds of life, because the hole where I saw the light was none other than Moundsville Penitentiary, West Virginia, the cruelest factory of human imprisonment in the United States, which today, luckily for humanity and especially for all those guys trying to get by on the streets, is closed and quiet and has even been turned into a tourist attraction, no kidding, the thing just keeps getting more and more ironic, doesn't it? that operating room without anesthetics that they called Moundsville now receives tourists who arrive by bus from Charleston and stroll through the yards and cellblocks eating ice cream and shooting videos, taking photographs of the electric chair or the yard where sometime in the past, in the early years of that hellhole, they hanged eighty-nine inmates, what a contradictory thing, don't you think so, my friends?

You see boys with cell phones immortalizing the punishment cells, those damp terrifying underground places where they gave us only a bit of food a day, in the mornings, but in complete darkness, and you had to eat without knowing what you were putting in your mouth and sometimes you found dead cockroaches or worms still moving about, oh God, my friends, you don't know what's it's like to eat something in the darkness when it's actually moving, and I swear to you by the Big Enchilada, the Man Himself, that yours truly once found a human tooth on his plate, you heard me correctly, a *human tooth*, how does that grab you? but I tell you this, the law of life and the animal factory kicks in and protects you, the body defends itself and the mind defends itself and instead of vomiting I made a pendant out of it and put it around my neck and wore it there for several years, always looking at the people working in the kitchens, as if saying, which filthy cocksucker's mouth did my pearl come from? because that was what I called that yellow tooth, my "pearl," and I have to tell you that the day somebody tore it off my neck I wanted to kill that person and eat him, but that's another story.

Anyway, my dear brothers and listeners, I'm telling you all this not so that you can feel pity for this soul from the sewers but so that you can imagine what that place was like and how incredible it was that being there, in the middle of all that suffering and all those rough specimens of humanity, I didn't come to Christ by myself and that it had to be someone else, my brother in Light, who made me see him with a flick of his wrist, I'll tell you all about it if you're patient, but for now let's continue with the story, because at this point Walter de la Salle or Freddy Angel is eighteen and is in Little Havana and in South Beach, a long way from West Virginia where I met him, because, as I was saying, he devoted himself to the care of the sick, yes sir.

The story goes that Freddy Angel, or the young saint, as they had started calling him, became friends with an old man who had a French surname, de la Salle, a man with skin the color of paper, as if he'd already bought all the tickets for a one-way trip in the arms of the Grim Reaper, as if his death certificate was already written and signed and the only thing missing was the date, I assume you get the picture by now, anyway, the old man, after one of his frequent attacks of hyperventilation, said to Freddy, listen, boy, I'd like to ask you a question, and the young man approached and said, how can I help you, Mr. de la Salle?, are you in pain? and the old man, whose wrinkled face was like a railroad map of the United States, said, come closer, I'm not in any pain, I'd just like to ask you a question, come, and he said, who are your parents? to which Freddy replied, I don't have any, sir, apart from the Eternal Father I don't have anybody, I wasn't fortunate enough to know them, and the old man asked, why don't you know them? and Freddy said, because they must have abandoned me, sir, that's the likeliest thing given the circumstances, and the old man continued, and do you have any brothers or sisters? to which Freddy replied, no, sir, no brothers or sisters or anybody, I'm alone, there's only me.

The old man didn't ask any more questions, but the next day the director of the hospital called the young man to his office and on going up there he discovered to his surprise that the old man, Ebenezer J. de la Salle, who was 87, wanted to adopt him as a son, and that he was being asked to sign a series of documents the old man's lawyers had prepared. The one condition was that he had to change his surname immediately, and Freddy agreed without any hesitation. The lawyers and an attorney-at-law held a simple ceremony, with Freddy and the old man sitting side by side. Then old Ebenezer Jeremiah de la Salle asked, now that you're going to change your surname, would you also like a new first name? and Freddy replied, you choose one, Father, I assume that if you wanted to have a son you must also have thought of a name, and the old man said, yes, you're right, I want your name to be Walter, Walter de la Salle, which was my father's name, and there and then they recorded that and so in that office the young man was baptized for the second time, with the name Walter de la Salle. As those among you more accustomed to stories may already have guessed, three weeks later they put a date on Ebenezer Jeremiah's death certificate, the old man checked out in his sleep, gave up his ID and passport and handed over his soul to the Boss, the Big Enchilada, the Man Himself.

Then the lawyers came back to the hospital and told Walter that his new father had left him an inheritance of seven million dollars, plus a couple of properties: a house by the sea, in Coral

Gables, and another one, a stately home, in the city of Charleston, which was where the de la Salle family came from, and so young Walter, thanks to his natural goodness, turned from being a spawn of the streets into a rich young man with a French surname, how does that grab you, eh? It's the carnival of life, my friends, some people start off with a lot and others gain as they go along, but what's really unusual is to go straight from the sewer to the tearoom with no stops in between. And that was what happened to him.

So begins Freddy's second life, or the appearance on earth of Walter de la Salle, which was the name he used most, as I forgot to say that before going to the hospital, when he was first preaching the Gospels to the underclass, they called him José de Arimatea, or he called himself José de Arimatea, but he'd long since left that name behind, and there aren't or weren't any witnesses, as far as I know. Walter was the name he used most, and how could it be any other way when he'd been so well provided for by old Ebenezer J.? An old man who, by the way and as far as Walter was able to establish some time later, had been the end of his line, the last member of a rich, industrious, and influential family, with important ancestors all painted in oils, and, as is typically the case with dissolute members of the idle classes, had also been a faggot and a cocksucker, which was why all he ever did was cultivate family hatreds and resentments, and also hatreds and resentments among his boyfriends, who did all they could to cheat him out of parts of his fortune, but old Ebenezer J. wasn't stupid and none of the pillow chewers who attacked him managed to get even a cent, quite the opposite, in some cases it was the old man who took them to court and screwed every last penny out of them, taking everything from them, even the dead cells in their foreskins, do you follow me?

Freddy's natural goodness was apparently the determining factor in the old man taking that transcendental decision, as well of course as the very human desire for his name to stay on earth—on the planet Earth, I mean, because obviously he was going to stay in the earth of the cemetery anyway, pushing up daisies—those were the reasons, although it can't be ruled out that Freddy was the old man's last great passion, all concealed behind that wrinkly face, of course, but passion all the same, and maybe even love. Old age loves youth, just as decay and ugliness love beauty. God knows, Freddy was young and beautiful enough.

What happened next, and was only to be expected, my dear friends, is a demonstration of the saying that there's no such thing as a free lunch, which is that one of Ebenezer J.'s gigolos suddenly showed up, an Irishman with straw-colored hair, ears and complexion as pink as a pig, and as big a faggot as you can imagine, and accused Walter of having drugged the old man and made him sign a new will, canceling the previous one that had favored him; to give his petition greater credibility he bribed a doctor to certify that Ebenezer J.'s death had been caused by a cocktail of morphine and stimulants, which was a terrible thing to say. What the Irishman asked in return for calling a halt to the legal proceedings was, of course, the annulment of the will, so that he would end up with everything, claiming that he'd lived with the old guy for more than five years, and so was entitled to seven million dollars and all the properties, he was no idiot, anyway, he threatened Walter with a lawsuit, but young as Walter was, he didn't break a sweat, plus he had a real piece of luck, which was that old Ebenezer J.'s two lawyers, the same ones who had signed the adoption papers, agreed to continue with him and defend him, and that was what saved him, because they were two Italians with thicker hides and colder blood than a regional boss of the Mara Salvatrucha, who could find shit under the cleanest toilet seat. They put their feelers out and discovered that the Irishman had not only had various run-ins with the IRS, but had also once been accused of having sex with underage Asian boys, an accusation that, by one of life's little ironies, had been put on ice thanks to old Ebenezer J.'s money and influence.

The Italians also went to work on the doctor who'd signed the statement about the supposed poisoning, which was the basis of the accusation. To soften him up, they mounted a really spectacular operation and finally managed to photograph him banging a black girl from the Dominican Republic in a highway motel, and then, once the film had been developed and they saw the pictures, which were really artistic to look at, they went to see him in the cafeteria of the hospital, gave him the envelope and said, dear doctor, help us to clarify a few things, does your blonde white wife know that you like it African-style? what do you think your respectable Peggy Sue will say when she sees this photograph, take a good look, where a version of Harry Belafonte, only with tits and cunt, is swallowing your reddened cock to the root? and that little bag of white powder next to the condoms and the Jamaican rum, what is that? such interesting photographs, don't you think? and very successful, really, this one where she's massaging your prostate with a gherkin is my favorite, my God, just like a pre-Raphaelite painting, the photographer's quite a promising talent, don't you think so, doctor? The Italians said all this to the doctor, and although the poor man insulted them and told them their methods were illegal and amounted to entrapment, and threatened to fight back in the courts, in the end he gave in and Walter was able to take possession of his inheritance.

The house in South Beach, Miami, turned out to be a mansion overlooking the sea, with seven bedrooms, its own jetty, and an extensive wooded garden, a real tropical paradise, a miniature Caribbean, if you don't mind me saying so, the kind of house that people look at from the outside and wonder what kind of bastard can afford to live in a mansion like that, and can't even conceive that all that could belong to one person.

And there, in the middle of that luxury and all that space, young Walter de la Salle, who now owned everything, also started receiving an income of two hundred thousand dollars a month, just for pocket money. But he continued working at the hospital, although he'd arrive there in the old man's Cadillac, driven by his Cuban chauffeur, because Walter didn't want to dismiss any of Ebenezer J.'s staff. And that's why they themselves taught him how to give orders and how best to use their services. In those early days, Walter was just like another member of the staff, having coffee and chatting with the cook or the gardener, or with the Filipino maids, and as he didn't know what to do with the money he'd take five-dollar bills and leave the house and hand them out to the people most in need, especially the fraternity of the needle and the rubber knot, if you follow my meaning.

In order not to be alone, he settled on the first floor of the mansion, in the servants' area, but gradually the staff convinced him that he ought to use the upstairs rooms and they taught him how to use the bathrooms with their Italian tiles and the jacuzzi and the best hour of the day to have one of those delicious liqueurs that were kept in the cellar.

Some time later came what he himself described as "the day God showed me the future, showed me what was hidden and beautiful, but above all showed me how to communicate with humanity," and it happened more or less like this, let's see if I can tell it properly: imagine Walter de la Salle waking up very early one Sunday because he thinks he can hear a kind of moaning sound, like the crying of a cat in danger, and goes out to look for it in order to help it. Day has only just broken and the sky is still gray as the young man advances between the bushes toward the jetty. He walks through the reed bed to the sea, and then, in the middle of the reeds, he again hears the moaning but louder this time and he can hear his own heart pounding in his chest, he's breathing with difficulty at each sob he hears and he knows that if he doesn't find the source of that pain he's going to explode, until he sees it, or rather, sees her, because it isn't a cat but a girl of seventeen, with cuts on her arms, and blood around her mouth and nose, covered in grime and mud, with scabs all over her body thanks to untold nights exposed to the elements, and at first the girl bristled like a cat as Walter approached, ready to defend herself, then her eyes met his and it seemed to him that an intense fire was blazing out of those wild ovals, that's what he said, my friends, I'm not exaggerating, real fire, the kind that burns, not the poetic kind, and that's why Walter thought that it was old Satan, Satan the Traitor, Satan the Tempter. His veins turned to tubes of shattered glass and his eyes to the bottoms of Sprite bottles, and he said to himself, this is what you've brought me to, God, this serpent will burn me, but the girl started to come closer without taking her eyes off him and he started to feel something different, not fire now, not streams of frozen light, but a warm air, and he realized that the fire wasn't down to wickedness but fear, or rather, the fear that precedes wickedness, and so he let her come closer with her hand held out and a few seconds later they touched one another, with the fingers outstretched, and ran their hands over each other's bodies as if they were blind, oh yes, my friends, blind with so much fire, but when their cells made contact, his good cells and her tired, sick ones, the good won out, ladies and gentlemen, by a country mile. She stopped spitting out sparks, and in a second her expression was again that of a fragile young girl.

What had happened in Walter's heart was something very strong, that's why he stopped and looked up, and said, and this is very clear in his literature, he said that a cool rain bathed his cheeks and tired eyes, and they joined hands and began walking through the reeds, with an impressive dawn rising over the sea, and at this point, my friends, if you can't see a clear, direct analogy with paradise and the birth of man, then you can't see a damn thing, and I mean that in all sincerity, and they walked hand in hand to the house and once there the girl had a wash and then slept for three days, with young Walter at her side, listening to her pulse to make sure she was still alive and thinking that what was beating in that fragile heart was both their lives.

When she finally opened her eyes he witnessed, in his words, "the beginning of the world," because he sensed that what she was seeing was newly created or that she was creating it. And this was how Walter de la Salle's first acolyte appeared in his life. Her name turned out to be Jessica, Miss Jessica, a young woman who fell out of a strange sky, those skies that in spite of being divine are also, like ours, full of pain and terrible secrets, I don't know if you follow me, my friends, and excuse me if I sometimes wax lyrical in this talk.

Walter installed Miss Jessica in one of the bedrooms on the second floor and from then on they lived together, with the staff, and so the house changed, of course, because the arrival of a woman, however young, always involves bringing good new things to any house, making it into more of a home than a hotel or a temporary stopover.

The young man's court was beginning to form, my friends, do you see that? Jessica was called to be his Mary Magdalene, because according to Walter himself, and this was said in confidence, she was the first person to refer to him in divine terms, seeing him as someone anointed among men, and telling him, you aren't human, there's nothing human in what you do or say or in the way you eat or sleep, you're a Christ even when you wash your hands, that was what Miss Jessica said to him, and God knows what hell she'd come from when he met her, because from this point she converted herself into a slave of the Lord, and I'm not talking about the Lord of the Rings or the Lord of the Flies, but the True Lord, the Boss, the Big Enchilada, the Man Himself, and as incredible as it may seem, her religious conviction set the standard for Walter, because when Miss Jessica revealed to him what he meant to her and how deeply he'd affected her, he himself understood his own path in the world and the task he had ahead of him, and more than that, my friends, and I'm not trying to make myself out to be a philosopher or anything like that, it's just that it seems to me that when Miss Jessica revealed Walter's destiny to him, through her devotion, she also carved out her own path, she found herself, which is the most difficult thing in this life, friends, just ask me, but anyway, having gotten to this point, imagine the scene, a mansion in South Beach with two young people living like brother and sister, like orphans or boarders, with her devoted to contemplating him and him letting himself be worshiped, going out to preach the word and tending to the sick at the hospital and at the same time filling his lungs with the dense air of reality, with the miasma of life, charging himself and charging himself, the way a battery is charged, I don't know how else to put it, charging himself with that message that he then had to go out and convey through the world, and for him it was like an illness slowly taking over his body, whose substance had to be periodically evacuated, seeing as if he didn't do that it would end up choking him, like those snakes you have to extract the venom from, I know the comparison may seem a bit extreme, but the extreme part is what comes now, my friends, because you can't begin to imagine the demands there are on holiness, and I mean that, although compared to Walter I was no more than a go-between or, as he put it, a factotum, a word, by the way, that I'd never heard before, which means, "person trusted by another and who in the name of that other person handles his business," and that was what I was, a real factotum, but we'll come to that soon, my brothers, don't rush me, anyway, the beginning of that newly acquired holiness was that Miss Jessica, once cured of her ills, started going with Walter to look after the elderly and preach the word of God among the terminally sick in the hospitals, the people with AIDS, the drug addicts, the patients with infectious diseases, and so, with their words and their gifts, because they took bottles of Fanta and ice cream with them, the two young people started building a name for themselves among the most disadvantaged people in Miami. I think this was a time when both Walter and Jessica were advancing by trial and error, looking for the path down which they were to go, always together, the definitive path, and so it was that one afternoon Miss Jessica showed up at the house with a young drug addict and said to Walter, he needs help, I picked him up from a garbage dump on Hopalong Avenue, his arms are full of holes, he has hematomas on his neck, his wrists and face are swollen because he's retaining liquid, we have to give him shelter for a time, we have to start with him.

The young man stayed in one of the upstairs bedrooms for nearly two months until he vomited up the last sick cell and recovered, sustained by prayer.

He was the first. From that point on, they started giving shelter to people with problems. It was a time of great changes. One day, Walter sat down with an architect on the terrace overlooking the garden, pointed to a space between two oaks, and said, I want you to build me a chapel there, look, I've already drawn it, this is what it looks like, and he took out that drawing that would later become famous, the first vision of the Chapel of Mercy and the Living God, a concrete dome and colored windows, with a cross on top of it, a cross that, according to him, should be in purple and yellow neon so that it could be seen from a long distance, so that the planes passing over the chapel should know that that distant heart shining in the darkness was the Heart of God, and remember that all those who've been baptized have to cross themselves and say a prayer and forgive somebody or ask for forgiveness, and of course, a cross that size, almost twenty feet high, ended up drawing the attention of the neighbors, who started asking questions like, what kind of church is it? what times do you hold services? As the staff didn't know what to answer the mystery kept on growing until one day, I think it was a Saturday, Miss Jessica was coming back from the market when a woman asked her for the times of services and the name of the church and she replied, it's the Ministry of Mercy, we'll put up the schedule for the services next week.

When she got to the house she found Walter prostrate before a huge red plastic crucifix, with a Christ twice life-size and a green light flashing inside it, and she said, Father—because she already called him Father—Father, the faithful are already asking about the chapel and the times of services, and I told her that we'd put them up on the door next week, so you have to think about that, and he, still prostrate on the floor, listened to her without looking at her, surrounding her with a great silence, as if the church were his body, a temple where the priests officiated from silent cubicles.

Miss Jessica looked at him affectionately, recognizing in him a divine being: his bare chest with the rippling muscles, the trapezoid formed by his back and the back of his neck, his prominent vertebrae, and the long hair cascading over his shoulders like a waterfall; she waited reverently by his side, because she knew that when Walter was at prayer he often reached an extremely deep state, such was his devotion and closeness to God, who without doubt was his father; that was what Miss Jessica was thinking, my friends, she'd already gotten it into her hypothalamus and cerebellum that Walter was none other than the son of the Master, the Big Enchilada, the Man Himself, how does that grab you? and so, after all that silence, seeing him start to move, she said: you're ready, Father, you have to begin and the people are waiting for you, and he replied, we'll put up the schedule on Monday.

With the conviction that Miss Jessica gave him, Walter started holding services at the Ministry of Mercy, which in those early years created quite a stir, my dear brothers, because Walter dispensed with hosannas and had music videos in the background, playing rock and even rap, and invited dancers up on the stage behind the pulpit, because he said that in order to preach in today's world you had to take your inspiration from today's world, the world of the street, with its music and its harsh, sometimes violent but very real images, and he'd say that if his enemies were drugs and violence and promiscuity, which indeed they were, then he had to fight them with the same weapons, turn the lyrics around, you know, those modern urban songs don't exactly inspire the noblest of feelings, they're all about killing blacks and Jews and shooting up and sodomizing your sister and murdering your father, and those are just the gentler ones, but Walter was good at extracting other messages from them and using them to his advantage, because at the end of the day they were what he'd listened to since he was a boy on the streets and in children's homes.

In addition, he'd appear at his services stripped to the waist, his upper body covered in tattoos that depicted Christ, not only in Nazareth but also in the back streets of an industrial slum, preaching to alcoholics and heroin addicts. His back was covered with an image of the crucifixion, but instead of Mount Golgotha, my brothers, the Redeemer was hanging in an old basketball court on Syracuse Drive, surrounded by potholed streets and smog-blackened buildings with God knows what dramas happening inside, young girls raped by their stepfathers, minors having sex for hard drugs, sweaty men in a drug-induced stupor on foul-smelling carpets, old men with prostate cancer groaning with pain, and women trading their anal virginity for doses for their husbands, anyway, my friends, all this could be sensed in those grim tenements surrounding the basketball court where the new Christ was crucified, the Jesus of the slums, the Redeemer of the people sent by the Man Himself to save us from our sins, and that was the central image that Walter had tattooed on his back: the mystery and paradox of evil.

From the pulpit, with rap music in the background, Walter would speak of God and the virtues of suffering and what a great thing it was to be one of Christ's marines and that voice that says to us a second before we fall into the abyss, stop, dammit! what are you doing? be careful of that sharp edge, don't jump into the void, boy, look, they took the net away yesterday, you'll slam straight into a floor dirty with spit and condoms or the roof of some dusty old taxi, don't let your children see that, make sure your blood stays inside your body, my friend, that's the main thing, I know all about that, because if a hole opens everything comes out and doesn't go back in, the body is like a blister and can burst, and the soul is the desire to look after that blister and its aspiration to the stars, so give your hand to the fallen, talk to the lonely, give up your food to the needy and weep for those who are about to sin because your word has not reached them, and for those who do not hear and close the door to your love and repent in sorrow for not having opened it, because that's what handles are for, as was demonstrated by Syriacus the Abogalene in Nineveh, and weep for those who feel a humming in the brain inciting them to open fire in a classroom, and for those who are sweating with cocaine pellets in their stomachs, weep for all the people who long to die because they don't know anything but the smell of poverty and fear, great is their number and great is their fear, all these things Walter said from his musical pulpit, with lighting effects and artificial smoke and shadow play and videos, while Miss Jessica sat like a queen by the side of the altar in religious contemplation, dressed very simply in T-shirt and jeans.

With these spectacles, the Chapel of Mercy and the Living God was soon filled every Saturday evening and Sunday noon, dozens and then hundreds of worshipers grew fond of his direct, plainspoken style, his exalted rhetoric, my friends, which was something to be reckoned with, especially when he attacked the devil, and that was when he really got into his stride, because Walter really hated him, and he would point to the LCD screen at the side that projected a silhouette with horns, and say, go from this place, Satan! do not dare to enter this sacred ground, because we hate you! we will beat you to death, Satan! Then the faithful would rise from their seats and cry out, in fearsome unison, we will beat you to death! we hate you! come no closer, Satan, you scum! and Walter would continue urging them to be ever crueler and more ruthless with Satan, in his own language, which was that of curses, Satan the Foul, the Obscene, the Repugnant! and the people would raise their hands to the clear sky and answer, Satan the Bastard, the Son of a Bitch, the Faggot, God will leave you on some radioactive island with sharks all around, unable to climb to the top because of the snakes, the most poisonous in the oceanic regions, oh Satan, you're done for, your glory days are over, yes sir, now begins the reign of the good, because Walter de la Salle is in town! and someone even cried out, Satan to Guantanamo!

That was Walter's style, my friends, he'd say that you could only be truly yourself, find your own identity, if you talked your own language, the words you lived with every day, the words you used to buy tobacco or quarrel with other people or make love, words of joy or despair, and these were the words he used, which is why the fevered crowd followed his message to the letter, shouting and jumping up and down in their seats, with the colored lights turning in the dimly-lit room, the rap in the background and the smoke and Walter in the middle with his microphone, swaying from side to side, sweat pouring out of him, the veins on his neck inflamed. The people would take up the rhythm in their clapping and echo him and then trip down the street to their houses, and later you would start to hear in the grocery stores some of the things he said like "Get thee behind me, Satan!"

3.
THE JOURNEY

On the day I was due to travel, I searched on the internet for some last-minute information about the ICBM, but, strangely, could not find a thing. Not that I was looking for anything very important, I only wanted to know what kind of clothes I should take to the conference, casual? smart? a couple of designer suits? it was a minor detail but these things can get complicated. I have always felt envious of colleagues like Paco Ignacio Taibo II, the great Mexican writer, who goes to talk to the Pen Club in London in a T-shirt and shabby jeans, and even says he will not attend if they forbid him to smoke, but that is all a question of personality, or extreme shyness in my case, so I try to deal with it as best I can, I hate hearing people clearing their throat and muttering, I like to pass unnoticed, wearing the same clothes as everyone else. I ended up packing a couple of linen jackets, six shirts with their ties, and some casual wear. Most of my clothes were large on me, as I had lost quite a bit of weight during my illness.

The other nightmare is always: which books to take? The first question was if I should take some of mine—those I had written, I mean—and here various hypotheses occurred to me. It might be appropriate to take a few for my hosts and some for any friends I might make there, and as people would be coming from all over the world it would be the ideal opportunity to get rid of a few copies in other languages, which I keep in boxes anyway. But then I thought about how much they would weigh, and it struck me that the best thing to do would be not to take any at all, since arriving with books that nobody has asked for is, when you come down to it, an act of vanity, and a touch unseemly, so I put them back on the shelves.

As for reading matter, now that is another story. To tell the truth, that caused a lot of last-minute problems when I was already ready to go out, with the taxi at the front door and the elevator waiting at my floor. As if, instead of a conference, I was going to a desert island for the rest of my life. Novels by Wiener and Walser, to start with. Three masterpieces of the novella—Truman Capote's *Breakfast at Tiffany's*, *Twenty-Four Hours in a Woman's Life* by Stefan Zweig, and *Hotel Savoy* by Joseph Roth—and a good book of short stories to read on the plane, *The Street of Crocodiles*, by Bruno Schulz, a book with Jewish themes, which I have been reading very slowly for years in a 1972 edition by Barral Editores, and the wonderful *Closely Observed Trains* by Hrabal, and something by Philip K. Dick, perhaps *The Man in the High Castle*, and another SF book, a rare pearl, *We*, by Yevgeny Zamiatin, and *The Elephanta Suite*, the latest by Paul Theroux, the best storyteller of his kind in the United States, and the latest by Thomas Pynchon, the best storyteller of *his* kind in the United States, there are many "best storytellers," and of course, *A Tale of Love and Darkness*, the memoirs of Amos Oz, the best contemporary Israeli story-teller, and the work of St John of the Cross, the father of all poets, and *Lost Illusions* by Balzac, the father of all novelists, and something light, my God, a travel book, yes, that little book by Pierre Loti on the Middle East, where is it? and again the entry phone rang, and the Fascist caretaker cried, signore, if you don't come down now the taxi will leave, hurry up, do you want me to come up for the bags? and I said, no! wait a minute, just a minute, I would never have agreed to that hor-rendous caretaker coming into my apartment, I know he would like nothing better than to spy on me, to sit down and ask me where I am going and for how long and then tell everybody, exercising his panoptic control over the lives of his tenants, so I took a last glance at my library and still found room in my baggage for a book of interviews with famous writers first published in *The Paris Review*, and at last I left, double-locking the door, and ran down to the street, regretting that I had not taken anything by Stifter, which would have been ideal for a journey, although I consoled myself with the thought that you never get time to read at conferences anyway. Apart from the heaps of novels you are given by colleagues, you never get to the hotel early enough or sober enough to read.

Fortunately, my flight left at midnight, which had given me the whole day to solve all these problems. I hate planes that leave at dawn, when you have to set the alarm for four in the morning and leave your bags packed the day before, next to the door, with all the dangers that lie in wait for the man who has slept badly and is not used to going to bed before midnight; in cases like that, it is better to cancel the whole thing, and remember the motto of that castle on the banks of the Danube that Magris talks about, "It is better for the happy to stay at home," and even if you are not happy, or not completely happy, what does happiness matter anyway, it is always better to stay at home.

When I got to the airport, instead of checking in my case and going to the bar for a gin, I found myself trapped in an uncomfortably long line of travelers. The security checks were endless, there were dozens of questions to be answered and I had to subject my baggage to sophisticated detection with liquids and damp cotton. The atmosphere was distinctly hostile, and the nervous-looking soldiers with their submachine guns clearly took the whole thing very seriously.

What can I say about the flight?

Of course, the seat next to me was not filled by any of the pretty young girls of Slav origin or the Italian Jewish women I had seen in the waiting room, oh, no, they all walked past. The person who did sit down beside me was a fat rabbi who had been visiting his family in Italy, or so he said when he saw me looking at him with a certain interest, which I did, of course, not because I was anxious to talk but because I was startled by the foul smell given off by his coat.

Everything was fine until the meal arrived and the rabbi saw normal, that is, non-kosher, food on my plate. Excuse me, he said, aren't you Jewish? I did not know if I had to answer that, but I did anyway, as there were still three hours of the flight left. No, I said. I'm not.

The rabbi insisted: are you Christian, Muslim, Methodist...? I'm an agnostic, I said, but the rabbi ignored my words. You shouldn't eat that, he said, come, I'll give you my tray, leave that garbage alone. He pushed his plate toward my fold-down table, but I stopped him. You're very kind, but I can't accept, I'm an agnostic, this food is fine for me. The man looked at me through his side locks and said, it's been proved that food like that is garbage, take my word, you should think about it.

His attitude was starting to get on my nerves. I've been eating it since I was a child, I said, and here I am, alive and kicking, or don't you think I'm alive? The rabbi turned and looked me in the eyes. Now that you mention it, you are a little pale, have you looked in a mirror lately? it's obvious you've lost weight, you have bags under your eyes and chin, and your clothes are too big on you. It's also obvious that you've been sleeping badly, and that's definitely down to food, believe me, so please accept mine.

I refused again. The rabbi gave a groan and said: if you reject our customs, why are you coming to our country? I was about to ask you the same thing, I said, why do you travel to other countries if you don't accept their customs? There are Jews all over the world, he said. Good for you, I said, and good for me too, there are non-Jewish people in Israel. Don't remind me . . . he said.

If I had had bubonic plague or Ebola, the rabbi would have felt more comfortable beside me. He expressed his displeasure by turning in his seat, which given his size was quite a feat, and every now and again casting withering glances at my plate, as if instead of meat and vegetables it contained the raw, bleeding organs of a pig. I was getting desperate. How much longer before we arrive? I asked a flight attendant who was passing along the aisle, but the answer was the same as always, two and a half hours, sir, we recommend you try and sleep, the DVD system in your seat is out of order but you have your head-phones and there's a varied program of great music to help you relax.

Just before we landed, the rabbi expressed his joy with a lit-tle dance that probably endangered the safety of the plane. Then the light of dawn appeared, and the sheen of Tel Aviv, the white Mediterranean city founded by immigrants at the begin-ning of the past century.

In immigration, I was subjected to more questions. They seemed to be applying, very strictly, an interrogatory method that may perhaps have occasionally given good results, designed as it seemed to be for tired, confused people who have been traveling all night.

Do you know any Arabs?

Do you speak Arabic?

Have you had sexual relations with Arab men or women in the past twelve months?

What kind of novels do you write?

What, in your opinion, is the greatest human tragedy of modern times?

Have you ever tried kibbeh, tabouleh, or hummus?

In what circumstances have you tried kibbeh, tabouleh, or hummus?

Have you had sexual relations with Arab men or women at any time in your life?

Have you ever tried to learn Arab cooking?

What is your opinion of the philosophy of Nietzsche?

How many Steven Spielberg films have you seen?

Do you like the music of Wagner?

If you were given the opportunity to have sexual relations with Arab men or women, would you take it?

Which Steven Spielberg films have you seen and why?

What do names like Adolf or Muhammad evoke for you?

Which countries, in your opinion, make up the Middle East?

What do you think of psychoanalysis?

What do words like "diaspora," "ghetto" or "Shoah" evoke for you?

On reaching question number one hundred or perhaps one thousand, I heard the soldier say, why have you come to our country? to which I replied, I've been invited to a conference, and I handed him the letter from the ICBM.

Then something unexpected happened: the guard's stony face underwent a transformation and he said, you should have told me that from the start, my friend, follow me. As we walked, he said, I'm sure you'll understand that our situation forces us to be cautious, it must be the same in your country, I suppose? I know war is inconvenient, but you have to understand, there are idiots who think they're arriving in Zurich or Monte Carlo and get upset by our methods, but you and I know that there are enemies lying in wait everywhere, there could be a terrorist hiding behind every friendly and apparently innocent face, don't you agree? if you'd like to sit down for a moment while we find your case, would you like a drink?

An orderly approached with a tray. There was lemonade with ice and mint leaves, and there was also coffee. Then they brought my baggage and we went out through a side door and walked to a Mercedes Benz with air conditioning and a mini-bar, which within a few seconds was driving through a modern network of avenues and bridges, accelerating until it reached well over a hundred miles an hour. As we left Tel Aviv behind us, reality hit me. The dawn air was filled with ashes and the smell of fuel. A thick, low-lying fog restricted visibility.

On the road to Jerusalem, the limousine seemed completely out of place, because there was nothing else to be seen but military vehicles. Suddenly a loud noise made me jump. Four army jets had just broken the sound barrier above our heads.

Don't worry, said the driver, they just reached Mach Two, they're ours.

On a big sign pointing to Jerusalem, somebody had sprayed a strange word, *Alqudsville*, which others had tried desperately to erase. I copied the word into my notebook and sat looking at it for a while. It was a powerful, highly suggestive word. As we climbed, we passed military convoys, and I said to myself, this is much more serious than I thought. The years of illness had removed me from the world and its problems, that much was starting to be very clear.

We continued our ascent.

A sign indicated the famous Trappist monastery of Our Lady of the Seven Sorrows at Latrun, but as I searched for it in the hills I saw another military convoy coming in the opposite direction. Dozens of young men with bandages and desperate expressions on their faces peered through the windows. Perhaps they had witnessed atrocities or perhaps they had committed atrocities themselves. I closed my eyes, dazzled by the bright light filtering through the mist and smoke, and fell asleep.

Soon afterwards, the limousine braked suddenly and woke me. I opened my eyes, and froze.

There in front of me was the city.

Dozens of columns of smoke, as black as funnels, rose toward the sky in the eastern area. They were fires. In the distance, sirens could be heard, and a great deal of activity was clearly going on in defense of the city. There were trenches and checkpoints on all sides, armed men, machine gun nests, barbed wire, sandbags on the balconies, walls with holes in them, structures of scorched steel, concrete blackened by the explosions.

If I forget thee, O Jerusalem, let my right hand forget her cunning. If I do not remember thee, may my tongue cleave to the roof of my mouth.

I remembered that prayer from the Psalms as I looked at the thin towers crowned with crescent moons, the gray buildings, the domes, the old walls. I saw the name of the street: Jaffa Road. The storekeepers had lowered their metal shutters and there was not a soul on the sidewalks. The fear was palpable, but that somehow made the sense of life seem even stronger.

At the checkpoint a soldier, clearly Slav in origin, checked my papers and gave the go-ahead with a whistle. A heavy metal bar, kept in balance by a concrete ball, was raised and we were able to enter. Facing us was a labyrinth of asymmetrical streets, pockmarked with holes and filled with steaming garbage. The houses, cubes of stone the color of sand, bore the marks of grenades and mortars on their walls.

A strange place for a conference, I thought, still taken aback by the magnitude of the war.

We now came to a wide avenue, lined with magnificent buildings of the same sandstone color. There were touches of vegetation here, pines and dusty old olive trees. Sycamores. In stark contrast with the general appearance of the city, there were boxes with flowers at the windows. The limousine drove along the avenue and turned in toward a building that in its glory days must have been quite majestic. Over the main entrance was a sign saying *King David Hotel*.

A jovial man who seemed in something of a hurry greeted me at reception, and when I showed him my papers he handed me a folder with information on the conference, a rosette with my name and the word *Writer*, a T-shirt with the letters ICBM, a CD of Israeli music, and a glazed ceramic key ring in the shape of a fish. At seven this evening there will be a cocktail party to welcome the delegates, he said. The bellhop pushed the cart with my baggage to the elevator and I went in after him, but a second before the door closed I read on one of the pillars the following notice:

> *The King David Hotel apologizes to its guests for any inconvenience caused by the state of war.*

When I got to my room I collapsed onto the bed and closed my eyes, which were smarting with fatigue after the uncomfortable journey. I do not know how long I slept, but when I woke up it was already starting to get dark, so I went to the window. The sight startled me. In the late afternoon sun, the walls of the Old City were like a cliff. The towers and minarets glinted like spurs amid the gathering darkness. The whole of Jerusalem might succumb, but the Old City was a pearl surrounded by mud, a melodious voice amid a tumult of inhuman cries, and perhaps that was why everyone respected it. What time was it? Eight minutes after seven. I was going to arrive late at the opening cocktail party.

4.

THE MINISTRY OF MERCY (II)

The Church went from strength to strength. Within a couple of years it had several thousand members. In other words, things were working out. Walter de la Salle, who was starting to think like a businessman, had the idea of going to Charleston and using the other house he'd inherited from old Ebenezer J., which was a spacious villa with extensive grounds. He started going there every week with Miss Jessica, to check out the lay of the land and see how they could extend the Ministry of Mercy to West Virginia. By doing this, my friends, Walter's life and mine started moving closer together, like two planes on a collision course, and we did indeed collide in the end, ladies and gentlemen. That was in Moundsville Penitentiary, but let's take things one at a time.

In Charleston, Walter and Jessica began with the same tactics as in Miami, visiting the wards for terminal patients at the Ancient Ghedarc Hall and the Memorial; at the same time work started on a replica of the Chapel of Mercy and the Living God, to the same plan as the one in Miami but bigger, because by now Walter had great confidence in his word and the finances of the Ministry were growing, thanks to contributions from members, which in spite of being voluntary amounted to tons of greenbacks, and that's putting it mildly, because the rich clean their consciences the way the rest of us clean our you-know-whats, if you get what I mean, my friends, especially if their dough is going toward comforting dangerous people and helps to calm social tensions, that electricity in the air of the streets that makes the lives of the rich so difficult and forces them to hire bodyguards so they can carry on being rich, rich in the middle of shit, which is the most ignoble way to be rich; rich amid the ulcers and pus of the saddest, most desperate cities.

Having started this work, he next began visiting the places favored by the local underclass, places awash with opiates, as you might imagine, until somebody told him about the prison in Moundsville, describing the horrors of the place and the kind of human flotsam it housed, and so he asked permission to pay a visit, which, it should be said in passing, cost him a fair amount, because the chaplain of that hellhole was very corrupt and, above all, fond of dark king-size bananas, applied rectally, in other words: he liked to be sodomized, and picked his boyfriends from among the prison population, because as I'm sure you know, prolonged confinement makes people become very versatile when they get the itch, and most aren't too fussy about the kind of living creature they stick their dicks into; man, woman, or priest, it's all the same, anyway, as I was saying, the chaplain was the master of that hell and of course he refused to allow anyone in who wasn't from his Church, like Walter.

Anyway, a sizeable wad of dollars appeased the faggot, and Walter had access to the cellblocks, introduced and in some cases even assisted by the chaplain, because Walter, with his long hair and his tattoos and his muscles, which were already pretty impressive—he'd had a gym installed in the basement and worked out every day—became very popular among the inmates and there wasn't enough of him to go around, even though most of the time they listened to him in silence and with very deep understanding, as if "downloading files" to use computer language, something the chaplain hadn't managed in twenty years of preaching and holding services and being fucked in the ass. That's how Walter managed after a while to get permission to see the inmates individually, listen to them, forgive them, pray with them, and get them to beg forgiveness of God, the Big Master, so that then they'd go off to reflect on what they'd done and on how life was a beautiful creation that shouldn't be tainted by violence and other evil ways. And it worked, like everything he did, because starting with a dozen people he ended up seeing three hundred a week, that is, almost one whole cellblock.

I hadn't been in Moundsville long when I first heard about him. I was there because of a badly planned drugstore holdup that had ended in lots of shooting and people lying flat on the asphalt. My partner in crime, Teddy, born in Oregon but into a family from Puerto Rico, caught a bullet through one of his nostrils, which were more accustomed to receiving coke or crack or smack. The bullet went through the nasal septum and lodged in his brain, causing what I'd have to call irreparable damage, not that there was anything very much in Teddy's brain to start with, and what there was wasn't worth much, it was more like a room without any furniture, but anyway, there he was, lying on the ground in a pretty unnatural position, with more than half the contents of his cranium spattered on the sidewalk, as if his head had turned into a ketchup dispenser, and I got away with a few bills, but that same night, when I went back to the flea-ridden motel on Cedar Creek where we had our headquarters—in other words, where we kept the drugs and the syringes—hoping I could just get in and out again scot-free, I ran unexpectedly into six police officers who, judging by the way they hit me in the ribs with their batons, had little or no talent for conversation, at least with me, and then they bundled me into a patrol car, saying, your partner had the key to your room with the address and the phone number in his pocket, oh brother, what a bunch of beginners, and that, my friends, is how I ended up in Moundsville.

Once inside, I focused on surviving, which, in that sinister sausage factory with no retail outlet, meant above all avoiding the punishment cells, the so-called Sugar Shack, the cellar of ghosts, which was so dark that if you closed your eyes you could see the insides of your skull, the kind of extreme experience nobody should have to remember, that's how that place was, like being stuffed in the ass of a rhino, because it was hot and smelled like hell, thanks to the pipe that carried filthy water from the bathroom in the third cellblock to the septic tank, and I won't go into details about the animals crawling around on the floor, but they didn't all have four legs, some had a hundred, and feelers too; I was put in that cell twice, because if you're moving about on the edge of the toilet all day you're bound to fall in sometimes, right? but anyway, my friends, my dear listeners, all that suffering also makes a person strong and I survived, of course you turn into an animal, yes sir, but being an animal wasn't the worst of it, and neither was the fear, because, with apologies to the more sensitive, you had to protect yourself from everything, keep a tight hold of your ass, because as I already said there were groups there who grabbed you in the toilets and used you like a woman or a whore, and if you didn't open your mouth to suck their cocks they opened it with a screwdriver and pulled your teeth out; you had to be really good not to be endlessly cauterized with wax in the infirmary.

And so the days passed in Moundsville, getting by as best I could, putting smack in my veins and inventing tricks to stay in my corner, without doing anything, which is the best way to be in a place like that, blotting out everyone else, blotting out the prison, with its guards and its bosses, and there I was, off on one of these trips, when I ran into him; almost on top of me, I saw his athletic figure and those eyes of his, like a lost child's, which was misleading, because they made you think he was just a kid, and I remember saying to myself, what heaven did this angel fall from? I must have said it out loud because he immediately replied, my name isn't Angel, I'm Walter now and I've come to save you, and I replied, no kidding, pleased to hear it, it's about time things started moving upstairs, I've been waiting for years, how long have you had my details, but then I guess the Eternal Commander, the Big Enchilada, sometimes takes his time, right? but well, better late than never, so let's take it one step at a time, if you've really come to save me the first thing you have to do is transfer fifty dollars into my account, and my account is right here in my pocket, the number is zero one, you could make the transfer by telepathy but the machine's out of order, so it'll be better if you do it by hand, which is the most efficient method, and then, when the money's gone in, we'll be able to sit down like two civilized people and talk about God or Muhammad or Madonna's lesbian cousin, whatever you like, and he said, no, my friend, that's not the way it goes, that's not the kind of salvation I came to bring you, we're going to have to understand each other, but I interrupted him irritably and said, is there any other kind? don't come here and get my hopes up, get out of here, you huckster, the Grim Reaper prowls these frozen cellblocks, get out now and don't come back, but he insisted, you don't understand, my friend, the Big Man won't help you if you don't beg forgiveness first, you need Him more than He needs you, remember that, it's your life that's in the mud, or rather, in the shit, but you possess something wonderful, and that's free will, my friend, what did you do with that? and I said, get out of here with your spiel, and I'll pass on this information, the cellblock you want is number nine, plenty of faggots there, all races, put some oil in your ass first, just in case, now leave me alone, goodbye, I don't have time for faggots, and he said, of course you do, and he gave me a punch in the face that by some miracle didn't knock my nose upside down, and I fell to the ground.

My first reaction was to take out my weapon, a fork that I'd sharpened on a stone, but before I could lift it even an inch he hit me three more times, making my head whirl, and smashing me against the wall so that I fell again, unconscious this time. A moment later I opened my eyes and saw his foot, with his huge body attached to it. From down there on the ground, he looked like a giant. I tried to get up but he put his boot on my neck and said, beg God for forgiveness or I'll break your neck right now, you insulted Him, count to ten, and he began, one, two, three, and he pressed down on me with his foot. I felt a sour taste in my mouth, I could hardly breathe, and I fainted, gently drifted away God knows where, and I didn't know anything more until I opened my eyes and found I was lying on a table.

A whole lot of inmates were near me, crying: Dead man walking! Dead man walking!

I sat up and saw him.

I saw the impressive image of Christ tattooed on his back, because as I was recovering consciousness he'd started doing a series of silent exercises, like an animal gearing up for a fight in which it may lose its life. I got down off the table and looked for my fork, thinking to attack quickly, stick it in under his ribs and kill him stone dead, but when I was halfway he turned his eyes on me, my friends, and what can I tell you, they were like two streams of fire, like the swords the Jedi use in *Star Wars*, something you really can't define, and I mean that. I couldn't retreat because the whole cellblock was following the fight and placing bets. If I'd chickened out I'd have lost respect and the consequence, as everyone knows, would have been to suck cocks for the rest of the year in the toilets or be everyone's bitch in the cells, which I don't like because I'm not of that persuasion, apologies if that makes me sound homophobic, so I carried on toward him, forced my way through the lines of fire coming from his eyes and at last drew level with him, but once again he seemed to have about thirty arms and I fell to the floor again, so hard this time I heard a crack, as if I'd broken several bones, which was in fact what had happened, or so the male nurse said later, and there I lay, with my eyes open, conscious but with my brain a thousand miles away, my friends, or as they used to say, in the arms of Morpheus; then he bent down and picked me up by the neck, almost affectionately, and said, beg God for forgiveness right now or you're on a one-way trip to the Land of Oblivion, and, being an animal brought up in the mud, I was about to say to him, you'll be the one going to the Land of the Shit Eaters, I was just about to say that to him when I saw a powerful ray of light behind him, a fiery sunset, and in that sunset a shining city, like the eye of somebody waiting anxiously for something to end, and was dazzled, and said, I beg forgiveness, almighty God, this slave is falling to his knees and begs forgiveness from the bottom of his soul, and I said it not talking to him, in reality, but to that eye shining in the glow of the sunset, and as I said this the man's eyes stopped throwing out fire and started crying, he prostrated himself on the ground, buried his head in my chest and said, forgive me and may God forgive both of us for everything we had to do this afternoon for you to come to Him.

From there, he took me to the infirmary and didn't leave my side for the next three weeks, which was how long I was there, I'd been beaten up so bad, how does that grab you, my friends? it's a miracle I'm alive, but something even worse was to follow, which was that in those same weeks Walter helped me cleanse not only my soul but also my cells, which had been completely colonized by smack, my narcotic love, the serpent of ice that had grabbed me by the balls or, to be more precise, by the inner lining of my balls, apologies to the purists, and what can I tell you about that cleansing, my friends, it was as if I was dead, cut up into pieces, labeled and frozen in the refrigerator of a factory ship, as if I was in flames and tied to a turning post, as if I was falling into the void and drowning in the ocean, I felt cold and lost my teeth from chattering, I saw monsters with hooks ripping my flesh, I saw Satan himself tempting me, disguised as a Puerto Rican transvestite dancing tropipop, but at the end of it, my brothers, when my blood cooled and I got back down to earth I realized that I was full of peace inside, as if the particles of the air had stopped damaging me, and I started prostrating myself and praying, and Walter, who came every morning to read me the Gospels, talked to me about the life of Jesus and made me realize why all of us who live in this filthy highway parking lot called the Earth have to be grateful to Him, and taught me that I could be like him, save others, win over to Him those who didn't have the strength to do it alone.

When I left the infirmary, I said to him, Father Walter, I want to be in your Church, to be one of your people, and he said, you already are, José, it was the eye of God that looked at us and showed you the way, let us give thanks that we met and are both already in His militia, and then he shook my hand and looked at me intensely and I felt life stream into me through all the cavities in my face, as if shot through a powerful hose, as if I had done ten lines of coke in one go, and I think my body started healing at that moment, because I felt this enormous desire to jump up and down and climb the walls and even the ceiling, it was the greatest high I'd ever had and the beginning of my new life, my friends, because with Walter's power and influence and lawyers, after six months I was out again, free and back at work, first in the mansion in Charleston and then in the Ministry of Mercy's house in South Beach, because he said I had to help him in the alma mater, Miami, where heaven and hell lay in wait on the same corner, where Our Lord Jesus Christ, the Big Master, could meet Satan the Traitor in any bar or any grocery store, that was how things were in this city at the end of days, and when I got there and felt the heat of the sun and saw the shiny asphalt and smelled gasoline and frying oil I started crying, my eyes filled with big tears, remembering hard times, the abandonment and the fear, the wish that something happy would happen just once, hazy memories of that life filled with knives and syringes, and I cried because for the first time I felt that I'd be more useful alive than dead, and because I'd found a path I was ready to follow, by the side of Walter and Miss Jessica, by the side of the Everlasting Father, the Big Enchilada, and his son, who were both tattooed on my heart.

At night I would cry again for all the years I had wasted that wonderful thing called life, take note, my friends, especially the younger ones, and sometimes my tears were tears of anger and I would scratch my arms until they bled and bang my head on the floor, because I thought, José Maturana, what a piece of shit you are and what undeserved luck has fallen from the sky, damn it, and I swear to you that in those days I was so angry with myself that I came close to slashing my wrists, which was what I deserved for being scum and an opportunist, but I didn't do it, I took a deep breath and let time pass, and stayed in my corner, in silence, praying and devoted to God.

After a few weeks' training, Walter and I started in earnest, preaching the word in prisons, which was my natural *modus vivendi*, and there I started to realize that the world and each one of us, in reality, were the great stage where a struggle with knives and bullets was taking place between good and evil, because in more than ten years of visiting prisons I saw a bit of everything, the hosts of the Big Enchilada triumphant, of course, but also those of Satan, who seemed to be advancing the fastest, and that's why it was so necessary to go and fight him in the yards and cellblocks, it was there that evil found its raw material, that wickedness was made flesh, Latino flesh, Irish flesh, black and mixed race and oriental flesh, every kind of flesh imbued with wickedness, everywhere distorting faces, turning them into threatening masks, expressions so common they became almost invisible, because disguised as surprise or boredom, but carrying inside them dark, thick water, ladies and gentlemen, have you ever wondered what the souls of the wicked look like? I'll tell you, the souls of the wicked are black, it's a shadow on the faces of those who are afraid.

Apart from the prisons, we opened another front in our campaign to recycle human garbage: the nightclubs, especially those of Little Havana, where everyone was hooked on drugs, liquid or solid, fucking up their brains, and offending God, and there, too, we saw a bit of everything, well, let me tell you a few anecdotes.

One night I went out on one of these field trips with Miss Jessica, who was good to take with me, seeing as how this had been her world, and we went to a club that was very hot at the time, called the Flacuchenta Bar, with good music, the kind that heats the blood of us Latinos and gets us leaping onto the dance floor, do you copy me? rap, tropipop, champeta, and techno-salsa, anyway, we sat down at a table and she asked for a Tom Collins and I ordered a non-alcoholic beer, because after that heavy detox I'd been through I couldn't even look at a drink, and around eleven in the evening, which is the hour when wickedness starts to get in the body and Satan wakes up, Miss Jessica said, José, go take a look in the men's bathrooms, so there I went, fearlessly, dear brothers and sisters, because with my natural authority, a result of my time in prison and these muscles you can see, I started looking in the stalls, and what can I tell you, it was enough to make a man weep, in the first there were two young guys doing lines of coke on the toilet bowl; in the second there were two more young guys and some leftover coke, but one of the two was giving the other a blowjob that could have given Monica Lewinsky a run for her money! it looked like mouth to mouth resuscitation, only through the cock; in the third a black man the size of a refrigerator was vigorously screwing one of the waitresses from the bar, who was kneeling over the toilet, with her back to the action; in the fourth a young guy was smoking freebase with his pants down, and as he inhaled the smoke he was jerking off and his cock was so huge it looked like an escalator, and in the fifth and last, ladies and gentlemen, you'll never guess what I found, the rarest thing of all in a Miami disco, can you guess, my friends? I found a man taking a shit! just that, and as he was taking his shit he was reading an old edition of the *Miami Herald*, the political page, to be more precise. Of course he was the only one who protested, saying, hold on a second, you fucking junkie, I'm already leaving the place warm for you. The last words I didn't hear because the people in the other stalls were already coming out, looking very upset, of course, so I cried, this is your lucky night, this is a police raid, but we're looking for someone in particular, consider yourselves lucky and leave quietly, I said, but the man from the fifth stall said, oh yes? and since when is taking a crap a crime? and he added, don't fuck us around, go back to your town and sell secondhand condoms, if you're a cop then I'm Butch Cassidy's gay grandfather! The guys in the third stall said, listen, you fucking Castro Nazi, what the fuck you got against homosexuality? eh? come out of the closet, homophobe, a good fricassee of cock is what you need, you fucking psycho! The only one who was really scared was the waitress, who came out and said, I'm sorry, officer, he's my boyfriend and we almost never see each other, we're going to get married, I swear we're going to get married; right then and there I left the bathrooms before the black man, who was shaking his dick and wiping it with a Kleenex, could come out and add his opinion to the others.

When I got back to the table I said to Jessica, my friend, we're going to have to do a lot more work in these places, there's a bit of everything here, and she said, I know, José, I went to the women's john and saw what you always see, cocaine, syringes, pills, vibrators with dinosaur tails, and then she said, I've never told you anything about my life, but I used to be on the edge myself and I know what happens in these toilets and what you find in these girls' G-strings, and it isn't only bodily fluids, no sir, but anyway, that's woman's talk, and she raised her glass and said, José, I'm going to tell you my story, so listen, this is how it was.

This will be brief, because she was young when we met and she told me all this. This was what she said: she was born in Los Angeles of a single mother, a Guatemalan with Indian features, so God knows why she turned out blonde, although it's easy to imagine; she had a brother who'd died of typhoid when he was thirteen and her mother, because of that, started hitting the bourbon and vodka, hard, and neglecting her, so she practically grew up alone and of course started hanging out with the neighborhood gang, which was her real school. She started going to discos when she was thirteen and that was when she got laid and did her first line of coke, both at the same time, and so she went from party to party every day of the week, hitting the pills and coke and acid and washing it all down with Four Roses bourbon, which was what the gang members stole, until after a while she became the girlfriend of a Colombian dealer who took her to Miami and kept her like a queen from the age of fifteen until they killed him, which was a really nasty business, apparently they nailed his tongue to a wooden table and left him there for a while, then they released him by slicing through his tongue with a scalpel, took out one eye with a salad spoon, cut off his balls and penis and threw them to his dog, right there in front of him, and when he was almost dead doused him in gasoline, set fire to him, and shot him seven times in the head, and Jessica actually saw the whole gruesome scene, hiding in a closet, and one of the things that most upset her was that the killer was her boyfriend's cousin, the same one who had sprung him from prison in Colombia and brought him to Miami and made him his partner, paying his expenses, anyway, it was obviously Satan pulling the strings. She was alone again, but through her disco contacts she met another Mafioso, Brazilian this time, who took her to his mansion in Coral Gables, complete with a jetty, a yacht, six maids, three cooks (one of them specializing in Thai food, her favorite), and two bodyguards, and she lived there with him for more than a year, although she remembers almost nothing about it because she spent all day by the pool, high on pills and booze, drinking bourbon, gambling in the casinos until the morning, doing coke, and fucking her Brazilian, who was very affectionate. After a while, her boyfriend's brother arrived, who was better looking and who she liked more because he wasn't a drug dealer but an art student, my friends, in other words, he wasn't dealing blow, and so Miss Jessica started seeing him, a fuck here and another there, in secret, but as she was always drugged, she forgot to cover her tracks and the Brazilian ended up catching them in flagrante, dancing the dance of Sensemayá the serpent, and then it was all slamming doors and slaps and out on the fucking street, although luckily the Mafioso didn't shoot them or throw them in the sea with concrete balls on their feet, and he didn't do it because it was his brother and he really loved Jessica, so she went off with the artist, who if I remember correctly was some kind of graffiti artist, a mixture of Keith Jarrett and Basquiat, for those who know about these things and apologies to everyone else, who thought he was a genius destined to change the perception of art forever and, of course, my friends, like all those who aspire to genius he was really smug and self-centered, convinced he had a key role to play in the contemporary world and crap like that, and spoiled by two rich, alcoholic old women, his patrons, who organized parties for him that inflated his ego, though what he gave them in return nobody was quite sure, because the old ladies already had everything, and so time passed and Jessica started to notice that her artist wasn't the same anymore, the young man with a brain boiling over with dreams had turned into a pretentious drunk who wore eccentric clothes and ridiculous silk handkerchiefs and told anyone who would listen, with a glass of whiskey or a joint in his hand, how far he was destined to go in the history of art, even though he'd pretty much stopped painting by now, because he'd get up past noon, always with a hangover, and in the evening would go to parties and society dinners. One night, after they had a fight and Jessica told him he was a loser, he hit her and she ran away without taking anything with her, not even her jewelry, or her clothes, and that was when Walter found her, a raw soul exposed to wickedness but ready to be redeemed.

For Jessica, the hardest part of her new life had been to give some kind of structure to her days, knowing that expanse of time wasn't just a dead space but could be used doing useful, instructive, and even beautiful things, and where many people, for example, went out to work, something that hadn't been part of her world, because her days, as I've already said, were all the same, waking up at two or three in the afternoon, doing the first line of coke and going down to the pool, ordering a burger or a Hawaiian pizza from Harvey's, with a beer to lessen the hangover and a siesta on a floating mat while she called her lover to find out where they were going that night, and then, it being quite late by now, putting on perfume and nail polish and lipstick, doing a few lines of coke while she chose from the closet what she was going to wear that night, and, finally, waiting with a vodka and tonic in her hand for her lover's Hummer, ready to go out and tame that wild tiger called night, and so it went on day after day.

It was hard to get used to a structured life. One night, after she'd been in the house six weeks, she ran away and got drunk in some club somewhere, but that longing gradually disappeared and after a while the prayers and the devotion and being so close to Walter made her strong, they were the armor that protected her from the other Jessica, the handmaiden of Satan. Being with Walter made her believe that life had a meaning, that after the night the sun would come up again and everything would continue in spite of the questions and that strange unreal feeling that things have when you see them in natural light, without alcohol or drugs; every now and again terrifying voices came from the bottom of the mine, the howls of the wolf, my friends, but she was able to contain them, and even ended up the strictest person in the house. It was she who made the Ministry rule that anyone caught high on drink or drugs had to leave, arguing that whoever was in the Ministry should be so close to God that such a thing would be intolerable, and even though Walter, who was very realistic, thought the rule a tad harsh, it was enforced to the letter.

And so, my dear friends and listeners, time passed, just like in a daytime soap, and over the next couple of years the Ministry of Mercy continued its unstoppable rise, becoming a really flourishing institution; the first chapel had become a model and now there were six more in Florida, where we went regularly, always the three of us, by the way, Walter, Jessica, and I. And we were still recruiting friends and followers of Christ in the prisons, which was my area of expertise, and in some counties in Florida we managed to open evangelical prayer rooms financed by us, or rather, by the neighbors in each county through us, which we called workshops, and in many of them I was the one who led prayers.

During a visit to the prison in Sarasota, Walter met a black man from Ohio named Jefferson who struck him as a serious, devout man; after putting him in charge of the workshop there, which he ran for seven months, dealing with the inmates himself, he decided to bring him to the house. The crimes he'd been imprisoned for were minor ones, he wasn't a murderer or a pedophile or anything like that, so it was relatively easy to pay a bond and get him out, and I have to be honest, my friends, when I saw him I almost fell down: he was the ugliest man I'd ever seen in my life, uglier than a farting she-donkey with colitis, I swear, but then the house wasn't a catwalk for male models, so he was accepted, with a rank similar to mine, insofar as our situation vis-à-vis Walter could be compared, or measured in ranks.

I was suspicious of him from the start, and I say that in all honesty, because it was obvious that with the success and growth of the Ministry we were all starting to be possessive of Walter, fearing that his unpredictable passions might remove us from the limelight of his love, and that was why we kept watch on each other, and especially newcomers, seeing as how Miss Jessica and I were, in a way, complementary; we weren't in competition with each other, but Jefferson worried her, too, and I noticed this because from one day to the next she decided to say her afternoon prayers in her room and not in the communal prayer room on the second mezzanine of the house.

Things got more serious when Walter decided that Jefferson was also going to be his physical trainer, and they started to do exercises. They went out jogging in the mornings, lifted weights, did Pilates, and worked out according to the instructions in a book on bodybuilding that Jefferson had bought the first time he got out. To Walter, the obsession with physical strength was the necessary balance between intellect, faith, and reality, the three anchors of life, but for Jefferson it was pure animal vanity, that prison image of the man with thick arms and a chest of steel, anyway, they started talking about exercise all the time, at breakfast, lunch and dinner, and it started to disgust me; it didn't seem to me much of a philosophical topic, but Walter would say that Jesus Christ must have been physically strong, how else could he have held out for forty days and forty nights in the Judean desert, which is close to here, and he'd also say that the struggle between good

and evil could start any day and that was why we had to be prepared, not only with a clean, agile soul, but also with the body,
because it would be a human confrontation, a human battle,
like any of those that man has been waging since his beginnings, and that's why it was necessary to be very well prepared,
and in saying this, Walter would take off his T-shirt and show
us his splendid muscles, his perfectly toned body, it was
incredible, he wasn't a boy anymore but a man, there were
those tattooed worlds that narrated his story and his devotion
and that light that emanated from him and filled all our hearts
with joy and pride, my brothers, and so the disgust and even
the suspicion passed and I gave even more thanks to Our
Lord, the Big Enchilada, the Master, for having led me by the
hand to that house, for taking me out of those foul waters and
putting me in the middle of that group of saints, and my eyes
would fill with tears, my friends, believe it or not, you have to
have lived through something like that to understand it. At
such moments, Miss Jessica would always stand up and say,
Father, you are the principal proof of the existence of God, you
are His son, and she would touch him with devotion, slide to
the floor, get on her knees, and say, Father, show us the way to
life and salvation, I'll follow it with my eyes closed and I'll tell
others, and then Walter would look at her with affection and
say, Jessica, rise, finish your food, I need you to be strong and
robust at morning prayers. Having said that, he'd stand and say
to his new apostle, Jefferson, let's go train for a while in the
gym, and I'd go out and walk along those dark streets winding
between the mansions and think that Walter must indeed be
the son of a God, because until now I hadn't seen anything
human in him, no human reactions or passions, let alone vices.

But this was not to last, my friends and listeners, and it's
here that the story begins to reach its climax, because a few
months later, on one of those nights when I took an after-din-
ner stroll to walk off the meal and think over the events of the

day, I came across a dog that must have been a stray and seemed to be dying of starvation, because it was lying under a bush, howling as if it was injured. Of course I went to it and picked it up, because I don't think there's anything more moving in the world than the look in the eyes of a sick dog, so I lifted it in my arms and walked home, but as I reached the garden I remembered a conversation with Walter in which he'd said how immoral he thought it was that people were always in such a hurry to help animals when the world was filled with desperate human beings, and remembering that, I hesitated, and didn't know what to do, so I took the dog to the kitchen and asked Felicity, our Haitian cook, to give it a plate with some leftover meat and rice, and then went to tell Walter, because I didn't want him bothered the next day, after all he was the owner of the house and the founder of the Ministry.

I went up to his private area and Jessica told me he was in the gym, so I headed there, but when I opened the door I saw a scene that left me horrified, though those of you more accustomed to the plots of novels may already have seen it coming. Walter was lying on one of the weight machines, moving as if he was dancing reggeaton, which was the music they'd put on, as it happens, while Jefferson, his fitness trainer, was supporting his legs or something, but on looking closer I realized that what they were doing was fucking, I didn't look too closely because I didn't want to see it properly, but it seemed obvious to me that they were on the verge of an orgasm, and just at that moment the song finished, imagine the shock, my friends, so I held my breath, closed my eyes and kept quiet until another song started and I was able to get out without them hearing me, as silent as a ninja, calm in the midst of danger and dangerous in the midst of calm, because something deep down, that instinct for self-preservation that doctors say is located in the cerebellum, but for me is somewhere between the prostate and the balls, told me, if they see you, you're in danger.

By the time I got out of there, my heart was pounding irregularly, like an out of order washing machine, and I thought, that's it, it's all up for me, my heart's going to stop, time to check out, goodbye to all this, and I don't know how I managed to get to my bedroom, but I lay down on the bed and cried for a long time, in that harsh, bitter way that grown men cry, and you may wonder if deep down there wasn't a little bit of jealousy involved, but I hasten to say, no, what there was fear, was a fear that chilled me to the bone and made my hair stand on end, that made me think I was at the bottom of a dark abyss, at the bottom of a well, covered with ice-cold water, in other words, I was already dead, because, to me, seeing Walter with Jefferson was irrefutable proof that he wasn't the son of God at all, just a piece of shit like me and everyone else, a man with his human passions and mistakes, and that made me scared, I felt defenseless, I didn't have the voice of something great by my side anymore, just a traveling companion, and so life started going downhill again.

And what if it was a hallucination? could it be that Satan had played a dirty trick on me to confuse me? it was possible, that damn struggle between good and evil was always unpredictable, except that you knew good would win out in the end, but, yes, it must have been that, I said to myself, Jefferson was helping him to train and Satan made me see it as sex in order to create a rift between us, the best thing to do was go to sleep and forget about it.

I pressed my eyelids shut, hoping that by the next day everything would have been blotted out, but it was no use, because when it was time for prayers I saw them arrive at the chapel together, and at breakfast, from the things they were saying, I realized they had been jogging together, early in the morning, so I didn't open my mouth, I just ate my food, my friends, and when I left it was as if I'd been expelled, or maybe I should say, repelled, and I went for a walk by the sea, because there's a kind of conversation with yourself that you can only have in spaces like that, facing the sea or in demolished aircraft hangars, anyway, I tried to calm down, saying, well, you have to understand, José, the man is flesh and blood and he likes to dip his wick like anyone else, surely the Big Enchilada also stops to think from time to time, if He made us in His own image and likeness then it must happen to Him too, because it's one of the things that most troubles the human race down here, and well, my friends, like with the ancient Greeks, there are men who are that way inclined and prefer cock, as you know, we have to accept it because we can't all be the same, just think, the Big Enchilada created things that nobody understands, like mosquitoes or cholesterol, I mean, can you tell me what they're good for, eh? and yet the Man Upstairs invented them so they must be there for some reason, we just have to be patient, and so I said to myself, let's see, when was the last time you fucked a woman? I couldn't even remember, I must have been out of my head on smack at the time, locked inside myself with the key on the outside, but what I did remember was some old affairs, like Susy, for example, a black girl with hair so hard it was like a copper brush, and banging her was like dancing with a porcupine, oh man, I mean it's something you can do but you have to be very careful, and there was another, Serena, who before she gave the green light would put in spermicide capsules so strong she started producing foam that smelled of DDT, anyway, my friends, forgive this very personal digression but it's just that that morning, facing the swelling sea, I had to use everything I could to try to understand what was going on, until I said to myself, that's it, brother, end of story, go on to something else because you're already losing it, and that was what I did, although with tremendous difficulty, because since my arrival at the Ministry I'd gotten used to a collective life, do you get me? we were like a family, like the Waltons, does anyone remember them? we did everything as a community, we commented on each other's work, and everybody was interested in what everybody else did and said and even thought or dreamed, we didn't have secrets and everything was fine, because we were all in it together and we supported each other in doing good in the middle of all that shit, but that image, the way Walter had been moving, Jefferson's proximity to him, broke something, one of the longest and strongest branches, so I started to isolate myself, stopped making comments when we were together, even though I didn't neglect my work, of course not, I threw myself headfirst into what I myself called "pastoral resistance" in prisons and bars, still confronting Satan and fighting vice in his alma mater, the city's nightclubs, the discos where they played tropipop, techno-cumbia and salsa, because there's nothing more beautiful for those hooked on smack to shoot up and then go to hear Caribbean music, "our Latin thing," as sung by Héctor or Ramón or Willie, any of those mega guys, the masters of the dance hall and the stadium, and I'd go there quite early, my dear friends and listeners, and work away at it all day, with enthusiasm, but at night, when I got off the 137 bus on the corner of Sausalito Road and Richmond Street, it was as if a buzzard had come to rest in my heart and was pecking at it, and I was bleeding and bleeding, in the most terrifying solitude, as if the rest of the world was a wasteland laid bare by some catastrophe, a nuclear warhead or something like that, and I was the only son of a bitch still alive on the face of the Earth, the only person in the middle of the ashes and the rubble and the skeletons of smoldering cities in which there was nothing left, not a soul, not even a human sound, nothing to recall this fragile, capricious, crazy species, only the crackling of the hot coals and the twisted girders, wet from a recent shower, and in that fantasy, I suddenly saw a group of hooded men climbing a staircase of rubble and ash to a kind of temple that had survived the conflagration. The group was led by a hooded man who supported himself on a staff, but when they were almost at the top there was a sound of explosions and out of the blackest part of the night came projectiles and warheads that killed all the hooded men, and again I was alone, because the fantasy was over, and I saw the beach again.

It's a well known fact, my friends, that God may grab us by the throat but doesn't choke us, so as a result of that solitude I decided to do something with my life. When you come off hard drugs the first thing you notice is that the days are very long, they're full of unbearably slow hours and minutes and you think the Earth has stopped turning and you're already dead because a nervous calm has invaded your brain, but I'd said to myself, no, go back, and I'd found the Big Enchilada and His son Walter, and devoted myself to filling those capsules of time with evangelical resistance, but now it was different: I had to use my head, but not only the outer part, the one you use for wearing a hat or for head butting someone in a fight, but the other part, and I said to myself, the time has come to explore what's inside that sphere you have on your shoulders, and that, my dear friends, is how I started reading, beginning with books about Jesus Christ, my boss, my immediate superior, picture books for children first, because my mind was still undeveloped, but then I moved on to a study of the Gospels and another of Mary and the apostles, and I realized I was becoming engrossed, and when night came it was great to know that I could immerse myself in those reams of paper, and greater still to confirm that the next day I remembered everything, or almost everything, and so time passed and I continued working hard and reading everything I could, while Walter continued with his bodybuilding and his muscles grew ever more perfect, a sculpture in marble, my friends, and as I was becoming less of an idiot than I'd been before I said to Walter one day that we ought to make a library, which he immediately approved, so I brought up from the cellar the boxes of books that had belonged to old Ebenezer, who being a faggot had been sensitive to literature, and let me tell you this, my brothers and sisters, I didn't have to go back to the library at Kennington school anymore, which was where I used to borrow books from, because now I had all these books to start on, and it was all top quality material, pure dynamite, as the drug dealers say.

In all that ocean of words, I discovered poetry, and set out with enthusiasm to learn its meaning and enjoy the rhymed phrases, something that before then, to tell the truth, had always seemed to me a bit faggoty, and note this, my friends, it was through poetry that I started seriously giving a meaning to my life, in spite of the fact that, obviously, the question of the hairy orifice through which I had come into the world was still a mystery, let me make that clear, but at least I already felt a brotherhood of meaning and solitude through those rhymed words, and that was something I saw in William Carlos Williams or Whitman or Milton, the last of these on a religious theme, which was especially beautiful.

In those words I saw the same stream of light that had blinded me that first day. The same voice coming from on high, but in another format, and sometimes, I confess, a rhyme made me cry because of its perfection, the cleanness and purity it concealed; ever since then, beautiful things have moved me and made me want to cry, beauty touches me deeply, takes my breath away, as if I hadn't expected anything of the world but trash and gruesomeness; the beautiful turns mystical and allows us to regain our belief in appearances, in the possibility of goodness and tranquility, in other words, peace. Beauty, in those days, was synonymous with peace, that space where the spirit, or at least mine, grows wings, launches itself into the air, and sees everything from a long way up. And so I felt grateful to those blocks of printed paper, that black ink, those numbered pages. It was the great revelation of my life after the Eye of the Big Enchilada, and I really mean that, my friends.

A year passed and on my side things improved a lot, because the library in the house had more and more books, so I was able to shut myself in with them and read until late at night in my room. By the way, we called our rooms "cells," just like in a seminary, even though ours had television and Wi-Fi and radio and a thousand things more, including shelves and en-suite bathrooms. For her part, Miss Jessica worshiped Walter more and more every day, and of course he himself was increasingly handsome and conceited, his body so perfect now it was like a sculpture by Bernini, so perfect it seemed untouchable; he still had Jefferson at his side, although with one novelty, which was that at least once a month he brought Walter groups of young men for "evangelical gatherings"; it sounded strange to me, because these young guys weren't thieves or dealers, but did look like faggots.

I could imagine what those gatherings must be like, and from the start I told Walter that I preferred not to take part, no, thanks, I'm teaching myself with Ebenezer's books, ever since I discovered reading I've realized I can become a better person and I think it'll benefit my pastoral work, so please excuse me, I'll join you later, for now I prefer to be alone, and, very theatrically, because he was already wearing made to measure red and yellow tunics, he gave me a kiss on the forehead, closed his eyes and said, José, José de Arimatea, you were my first disciple, you must grow spiritually so that you can bring even greater honor to our Church, follow the path you've found, but don't become a stranger.

So he excused me and, in a way, blessed our separation, with him on one side and me on the other, close but taking different paths, and it's something I really have to thank him for today, yes really, because I studied and read and thought and became, *mutatis mutandi*, an enlightened animal, I joined the world of civilized people, my friends, I'm sure you understand, and I read the poetry of Góngora and Quevedo and Juan

Ramón Jiménez and Pedro Salinas and especially León Felipe, and I read studies on the moral evolution of Jesus by Harold Iridier, S. J. and the three volumes of his monumental work, *Distant Christ*, and I studied the works of St Augustine and St Thomas Aquinas and also Tertullian, father of the Church, who talks about the truth of the impossible, which I think is really beautiful, and in this way my brain started to put forth shoots and show me that the world was something greater than that city of vacant lots and highways and grocery stores with fronts eroded by the wind from the sea; I also discovered history and learned that what we are today is connected with what we were, that we're in a tunnel and can see the end of it but not the beginning, and there in that dark corridor is the philosophy of Hegel and the Punic Wars and that fat man Balzac writing *Old Goriot* and drinking coffee through the night, anyone would think he was Colombian, and you also see the martyrdom of St Lawrence on the grill and old Michelangelo painting his fresco, and even Muhammad's ascent to heaven, which happened quite close to here, and the birth of Jesus and his crucifixion, which is the most painful event of all, and Abraham raising his knife to kill Isaac before the Big Boss stayed his hand, and who knows how many things more that we don't know, my brothers, like the story of the birth of yours truly, your servant and God's, or the birth of Walter de la Salle, which was also a mystery, and remains one, and that's why it seemed that his destiny had to be so elevated, but anyway, let's take our time, let's fly slowly down to the property in South Beach, but take a little pause first, my friends, just two or three minutes before we return for the final part of the story, which is the best part from the spiritual point of view.

5.
The Delegates

When I entered the reception room, which was lit by seven-branched candlesticks, a man in a dark suit was talking from a pulpit. I tried to make sure that nobody saw me, but no sooner had I taken a few steps than the speaker looked up, uttered my name, and bade me welcome. A few of the guests turned, so I said, good evening, I'm sorry I'm late, I'm a bit tired and I lost all sense of time, but nobody said a word or smiled or even nodded, so I added, I've been sick...

From a corner, a waiter emerged with a tray full of glasses of champagne and offered me one, but I did not take it, not because I did not need an aperitif, but because I had been hoping for something stronger. The waiter took no notice and handed me a glass, so I took it and raised it, looking at the speaker, and said, it's a pleasure to be here, cheers to everyone. There was a tumultuous toast and the room cheered up again, as if coming back to life after an anxious moment. The speaker continued with his speech, talking about the tradition of the hotel in difficult times, these walls that had seen fighters firing rifles and patriots falling, sacrificing their lives for a cause, he said, and yet, just as it was now, it had also been a symbol of excellence and refinement, however difficult the times, at other times it had been a barracks and had even been partly destroyed, adding, after a theatrical silence, of course I refer to "that bomb," and when I heard that I was intrigued; only later did I find out that he was referring to the bomb the radical group Irgún had planted in the hotel when it was the headquarters of the British Administration at the time of their mandate in Palestine, an event linked to the name of Menachem Begin, originally considered a terrorist and later prime minister of Israel, that was how it was, it is well known that in the fertile field of History people make astonishing comebacks, as the speaker put it, and he continued talking about these wars of the past, as well as the war outside, which you could breathe in the air and see in the stony, terrified faces of the passers-by, and because of all this, he said, raising his voice, because of what is happening and must be remembered, because of all these select or even simply human things that we must preserve and protect, we have decided to call this conference, whose ultimate aim is to honor memory through memorable lives, those which you, dear delegates, bring us in your notes or in your memories, with no obligation that they should be great lives in the traditional sense, of course not, in no part of the Old Testament are we told that it is obligatory to live great lives or perform heroic deeds, no, gentlemen, man is small and that condition may make him fragile, but it also ennobles him, that is something that all of us here know very well, as we have decided to meet while the world is falling apart, in a chaos of rubble and smoke and ashes, and we are meeting because we believe in the word and in the testimony of life, our most precious gift, and that is why I want to thank you, truly thank you, *shalom*, welcome, the man concluded, raising his arm and making another toast, and the audience rewarded him with applause.

A moment later, a fat man with a nose like a potato approached me and said, you don't know me, my friend, allow me to introduce myself, my name's Leonidas Kosztolányi and I'm a delegate at this conference. He gave a bow, which seemed very appropriate amid all these tapestries and big velvet drapes, and on hearing my name added, yes, yes, I read your résumé, you're the writer, a pleasure to meet you. Then he approached my ear and said, I suspect this champagne is too mild for the complexity of our minds, come, let's go over there, I think they have something more substantial.

At the drinks table, I asked for a double whiskey with two cubes of ice, and when I had it in my hand—I had decided to forget my doctor's warnings for a while—I was ready to listen to Kosztolányi, who asked me if I knew his city, Budapest, to which I replied, yes, I do, and what's more, I said, I consider it one of the most beautiful in the world. In an antique shop in the Jewish ghetto, near the synagogue, I bought a small model plane made of metal, which I still have on my desk, next to my books of poetry. The man responded by striking himself on his stomach, that's good, poets and aviators, of course, Saint-Exupéry and all that, very good, and then he said, you just mentioned an antique shop, which struck a chord with me, my passion is for things of the past, objects created by hands that are no longer with us but are now just ash or earth, anyway, I'm sorry if I'm waxing lyrical, you're a writer and that's why I allow myself such license, my interest is in those things that have a patina on their surface that could be the patina of memory, the air of times gone by, and you must be wondering, listening to me, do objects have a memory? I hasten to say, yes they do, of course they do, you just have to know how to approach them, how to put your hands around a statuette or a piece of porcelain and listen; that is when, suddenly, there appear images, things that were lived, words that echo, souls that are no longer with us, people who once populated this old world and surrounded themselves with beautiful things in order, no doubt, the better to bear the essential tragedy of life, which is its brevity, don't you think so? As I was about to answer he continued speaking—I realized that his questions were rhetorical—and said, you are one of the most interesting people at this conference and I'm going to tell you why, it's because you're new, I mean, new to these biographical debates, many of us have met before on other stages, doubtless less dramatic ones, I'll give you an example, do you see that man over there? he said, pointing to a bald man, that's Edgar Miret Supervielle, the famous bibliophile, you probably saw him on the list, and well, he and I usually meet at antique book fairs, philatelic or antiques trade events; I can tell you he's a thoughtful and highly cultured man, with a keen nose for business and an uncommon ability to spot a lie, but he's a genius, believe me, a real genius. On hearing this I felt a certain unease, realizing the extent to which I was an impostor in this group, so I said, thank you for considering me interesting, I'm here to learn about all of you. Suddenly Kosztolányi, who was clearly not listening, said, come, my friend, I see Supervielle has been left on his own, it'll be a pleasure to introduce you. The man arrived and held out his hand, which I shook firmly; then he repeated my name and said, ah, I know you, you're the writer, the only one among us who writes fiction, isn't that so? a true artist, and I said, well, if we abide by the traditional definition perhaps yes, although I believe that any act of writing has . . . a connection with the shadowy areas where esthetics lie. Kosztolányi got excited and said, very good, shadowy areas! that's what I call speaking, this is the beginning of a true friendship and that deserves another drink, don't you think? of course it does.

With our glasses full, I asked Supervielle if he lived in Israel, and he replied, yes and no, I have a house in the Negev Desert, to the south of Jerusalem, and an apartment in Paris, which is my base for some of my European business, but my family is spread around the world, one son in New York, another in Costa Rica and a daughter in Buenos Aires, can you imagine, you're Colombian, aren't you? Yes, I said, and what does your daughter do in Buenos Aires? and he replied, well, you know, a question of love, she married a colleague of mine, a bibliophile and a treasure hunter, like me, only Argentinean,

I should tell you that of course I was opposed to the marriage and the truth is that even today, seven years later, it makes my blood boil, a young woman of twenty-eight with a man of fifty-six, is that normal? I was not sure what to reply, because age is no impediment to anything, so I shrugged, but he said, any age may have its mitigating points but in this case there's an aggravating circumstance, which is that he was my partner in two bookstores, one in Madrid and the other in Buenos Aires, and to tell the truth, I must say it was and still is strange to know that I am working to build a legacy that, on my death, through my daughter, will pass to my partner, do you see? I try not to think about it when I add to the family capital, because I could very easily argue that he ought to contribute more, but in the end, this is all nonsense, the ramblings of a grumpy old man, what matters is my daughter, not that I'm saying she's exactly happy, because marriage, as I'm sure you know, has the same decaying effect on love that heat and the passing of the days has on meat, turning it into a shapeless and foul-smelling mass, that's why I know that she isn't happy, but never mind, that's life and what's done is done, I've been to visit them a couple of times and I was dazzled by Buenos Aires, its bookstores are like the wreck of a sunken liner, I've found some amazing titles, it's a highly cultured country, a country of immigrants, and there are books in every language, it's magnificent, and I said, I agree with you there, Monsieur Supervielle, I also like books, first editions of authors I admire, and I have one or two important ones myself, like *A Poet in New York*, by Federico García Lorca, Editorial Séneca, Mexico City, 1940, with original drawings and an introduction by José Bergamín. As I said this I noticed that Supervielle was changing, a sharp expression came into his eyes and he nervously raised his thumb to the base of his nose and pushed it up, then said, very interesting title, if you don't mind my asking, did you inherit it? was it a gift perhaps? may I know where you obtained it? I'm sorry, my friend, it's a professional deformation, but I hastened to say, it's not a secret, I bought it in a bookstore in Seville for not much money, I don't remember the name, it wasn't a specialized store and it's possible they didn't know its value, I felt a bit guilty when I bought it, I confess, and Supervielle said, you don't have to justify yourself, my dear colleague, as you can imagine, being a bibliophile I don't have that kind of scruple, I think objects, like people or civilizations, have a destiny, or many destinies, given that they're perennial, that's why it's normal that they should pass from hand to hand, just like antiques; whatever is valuable and beautiful ennobles a life, but then must pass to someone else and then someone else until the cycle is complete, don't you think so, my friend? sometimes the cycle ends with fire or at the bottom of the sea or simply turns into something else, into parts of something greater, anyway, Leonidas, do you agree with my appraisal? Kosztolányi seemed to wake up and said, very much so, Edgar, yes indeed, and as the talk is acquiring the muddy color of profound matters, I suggest we have another drink.

As I walked to the drinks table, my eyes met those of an extremely attractive woman with a wonderfully pure face. I saw her for barely a second, as she turned and put a glass down on a tray. Then she stepped back and our eyes met again, for an even shorter time, before she disappeared in the crowd. After that apparition, Kosztolányi and Supervielle seemed to me like two strange gnomes, wandering jugglers created by a lame, blennorrhagic Shakespeare in a waterfront tavern. I stretched my neck, trying to see her, but in vain. I looked at the waiter's tray and, strangely, it was empty. The glass that the woman had left there a moment before was already gone, so I told myself, it must have been a hallucination due to my tiredness or the alcohol I had consumed, I must have had about five glasses already, my God, my doctor would scream blue murder, it must have been that, something that had emerged from my subconscious; I started to imagine that this narrative might well take an abrupt turn toward the fantasy genre, but Kosztolányi and Supervielle were real enough, and when I focused on their faces both were looking at me, questioningly, and I realized that the last words Supervielle had spoken, don't you think so, my friend? had been directed at me, so I said, I'm sorry, I lost the thread, I'm very tired, I've only just recovered from a long illness, could you please repeat what you were saying.

They looked at me in surprise and Supervielle said, we were talking about the conference, of course, and about the dramatic context of this war, unpleasant and inhuman like all wars; we were saying that people are talking in small groups about those spray-painted notices that have started to appear all over the city and the roads with the word *Alqudsville*, which sounds oddly picturesque, you know that the Arabic name for this city is Al-Quds, so the word is a kind of joke, or worse, something that many fear but that nobody here dares to say out loud, don't you think so, my friend? So I said, I'm not sure what to think, I haven't been following current events for quite a while now because of my convalescence, so it's hard for me to express an opinion, but I'd love to hear yours, it would be enlightening. Kosztolányi made as if to speak, raising his index finger like a conductor about to bring in the percussion or the wind section, except that instead of words we heard a loud explosion that shook the building, cut off the electricity, and turned out the lights.

There were cries, people running blindly, and a couple of glasses fell to the floor and shattered, but the master of ceremonies, helped by the flickering light from the candles, jumped onto the platform and begged for calm; then he ordered the musicians to carry on playing, by heart. The party continued and Kosztolányi said, it was a six-inch shell, I can recognize them, I think it's time for another drink, we don't want to lose the momentum, we're at war and war is men's business, so he moved his bottle closer and filled our glasses. After the conflagration, the second speaker went up to the platform, knocked with his fingers on the microphone and started speaking, thanking the audience for their presence, especially the international delegates, and said, I know this is a strange time to be holding conferences, these fateful years it has befallen us to live through would be more suitable for seclusion and solitude, and that is why we are so grateful to you, the intellect must continue its work in the midst of the most horrifying circumstances, it's always been that way and today more than ever, when the present is growing ever angrier as if to punish us, it is worthwhile looking at the past, turning to memory, which is one of the keys of this international conference, because in memory lies the origin of ourselves and of reality, let us remember that each one of us, or so the novelists tell us, is unique and irreplaceable, but above all it is what each person can tell or remember, what he can tell others, or that other who takes shape in the smooth mirror of writing, and I'm sorry if I speak to you in metaphors, in spite of being a sociologist I have cultivated poetry, where I have found the best of life, its truest consistency, anyway: that thing, so precious and fragile, that is in danger just outside these walls, and not only here but in so many other places, and in so many other wars, that is why we must continue to speak and write and tell stories; I believe in the redeeming power of the word and I know you do too, and that is why I now raise my glass and say, cheers, welcome, *shalom*, and thank you.

I listened to the speech passively, without knowing who the man was, let alone why he was on the platform. I assumed that at the beginning of the party the organizers of the conference had introduced themselves and that was why they were not doing so now, so I asked Kosztolányi, who's the man who just spoke? and he said, ah, you're a dreamer, adrift in reality, it's obvious you're a poet! That man is none other than Shlomo Yehuda, president and director of the ICBM, author of at least fifty books, scholar of language, essayist, teacher, and legal consultant, one of the most distinguished intellectuals in the country, and that's why I advise you, dear friend, when you're introduced to him pretend you know him, say something like: it's an honor to meet you, Mr. Yehuda, I have known your name since I was a boy, I never thought I'd shake your hand, do you see? You have to tell him something flattering because Shlomo is a vain man, an all too common failing in exceptional people, unfortunately, prepare one of those phrases that don't commit you too much and which, above all, don't have to be explained.

Suddenly the door opened and a woman came in. I recognized her immediately. It was Sabina Vedovelli, the Italian diva of the porn industry. I looked at her with great interest and was genuinely captivated by what I saw. Her body and her clothes seemed to say, or even scream, to each man present: "I know how good I am, that on seeing me your cocks stand up like harbor cranes, pulling your underpants to one side; I know you're trying to imagine my boobs jumping over your face and that you're fantasizing about my inflamed cunt and imagining my labia swallowing your penis, and your veins are already as swollen as the muscles of an athlete, and I also know that you're visualizing my anus that you'd like to sodomize, and you want to kiss me like a thirsty dog drinking from a puddle, and bite my tongue, which has sucked so many different cocks, oh, how well I understand you and how sorry I feel for you."

Sabina Vedovelli was wearing a one-piece black leather *tailleur*, like Modesty Blaise in the comic strip (does anybody remember that?), with prominent cleavage, high heels in spite of her height and a silk bow around her neck. She had padded lips, violet eyelids, and intense dark blue eyes, like the doom-laden sky in a painting by Van Gogh, which seemed able to drill holes in anything put in front of her. Of course, seeing her

I thought of the other woman, the one I'd seen not so long before, and I thought, she isn't the same, they were very different although there's something about them, the way you can say about somebody that they have a similar rhythm to somebody else, a certain cadence, even though the first one had a beauty that seemed to have appeared fully grown, pure and uncontaminated.

I remembered the video I had seen on the internet, her ass lifted in that legendary position, immortalized in the drawings of Milo Manara, which some experts on erotica call Looking at Constantinople. It seemed incredible that this was the same woman and yet here she was, before my very eyes. Part of her unattainable air came from the two gorillas who came in with her—and when I say gorillas I do not mean Tarzan's friends, I am using the term in the other sense, meaning bodyguards—two men with dark glasses and earphone leads sticking out of their ears, who cleared a path for her through the crowd. She waved and smiled at the organizers as if these men were not beside her, intimidating everyone, and I thought, she must be used to it, they are her guard dogs and for her they do not even exist.

Supervielle and Kosztolányi were also looking at her.

She's a catlike, dangerous woman, said Kosztolányi before taking a big slug of his whiskey, but you can't imagine the talks she gives, they're real performances, with photographs and animations, I was at a conference similar to this in Stockholm and the fact is, her contribution was fantastic, don't you remember, dear Edgar? Supervielle said, yes, although I must confess that her aggressive style bothers me, without wishing to be critical, I know it corresponds to a way of life that's very widespread in all cultures and it's useful that she's among us, which does not prevent one from feeling somewhat . . . how can I put it? remote from it all, yes, that's the word. Then they remembered an occasion when Sabina Vedovelli (was it in Seattle or

Bucharest?) had appeared with a tiger cub, which had aroused a mixture of admiration and fear in the audience. Listening to them, I realized that most of them had been at other conferences together, and I asked them, do you all know each other? to which Supervielle replied, well, the ICBM is new and this is its first conference, but we've met at similar events. Kosztolányi added, those of us in the trade have periodic meetings, more or less once every two years, I can understand your surprise, I don't know what writers' conferences are like. They both looked at me, so I said, writers' conferences are usually on a specific theme that's sufficiently vague for everyone to fit in, things like *The Writer and the New Century* or *Where is Literature Going?* and, well, once the group is together there's an opening reception similar to this one, and then the round tables start; some people bring written texts and read them and others improvise, depending on their experience, and the members of the audience applaud and get quite excited because the only reason they're there is that they've read the authors' works or have heard of them, and at the end of each session they come up and ask for autographs and dedications, anyway, it's all a bit mechanical. At night, some writers set off on the prowl looking for young female readers or women delegates, and it's normal to see them in the bars and on the terraces, making passionate speeches about themselves or their books, enthusiastically telling anecdotes in which they, with all due modesty, appear as heroes or even superheroes and their books as outstanding masterpieces of modern culture. Others prefer to stay in their hotel rooms watching TV channels like MTV or Discovery so that they can then talk about them with scorn at dinner, when what they're actually saying is, I don't mix with you, you lousy bunch, I'm above all that, thereby creating an aura of respectability and mystery about themselves. There are also those who devote their time to drinking and forging closer ties that will allow them to obtain invitations to other conferences, and so some colleagues are able to go from one conference to another and spend the whole year traveling, giving interviews from which literary matters are usually rather absent, either because they're talking off the tops of their heads or because what they really want to create is some kind of political controversy, and so the writers sound off, taking sides and making accusations, ensuring themselves a great deal of visibility in the press, which records their invectives in banner headlines, and if the writer in question is lucky enough to be contradicted by some political or ecclesiastical authority, things really start to heat up, giving rise to a juicy polemic that increases their fame, and other writers jump on the bandwagon to support that first writer, because if the controversy is big enough there'll be enough left over for them, too, although, of course, the first writer wants to protect the fame he's acquired, he doesn't want to lose it to opportunists, and so, in the end, his books will sell more copies and the polemic will have given the event a contemporary, committed, and cosmopolitan air, which benefits everyone and will undoubtedly ensure that the banks and the financial or political organizations that sponsor them want to continue supporting them, even if one of those organizations was the very one that was being criticized or insulted.

On the last day, the historic achievements of the conference are proclaimed, both from a libertarian point of view, and in generating pure concepts and ideas, and a great final binge is held at which everyone swears friendship and respect and at which traditionally, in spite of the fact that each person knows that he is the best, everyone praises everyone else, saying things like this, "You're the greatest living storyteller since Cervantes, or Borges, or the best poet since César Vallejo," to which the other replies, "Oh no, don't exaggerate, that's going a little bit too far," they exchange quotations from books, and raise their glasses, and usually, by the time dawn breaks, there are already two and even three Nobel Prize winners at each table, depending on the amount of alcohol they've imbibed, including some who swear they'll refuse it if it's offered to them, because it's a disgrace that they never gave it to Borges, which means it's worthless, all these vows made on a great tide of whiskey, before they rush to the bathroom to throw up.

Kosztolányi and Supervielle looked at me in surprise, and Kosztolányi said, my God, you don't have a very high opinion of your colleagues, but I hastened to say, don't take all this literally, one always criticizes one's profession, but the truth is that I've also attended excellent conferences in which people talk seriously; nor did I say I wasn't myself one of the writers I was talking about. For years all I ever did was go to conferences.

After her triumphant entrance, Sabina Vedovelli had settled elegantly in the middle of the room as if she was in her own home. A tray of drinks was brought to her. With two fingers, she picked up a glass of champagne and raised it to her lips slowly and with great relish, as if instead of a glass container it was a fruit or a delicious ice cream or even a penis, and I could not have been the only one to think that, seeing that several men, including the main speaker, cleared their throats and shifted nervously.

Suddenly somebody clapped a hand on my shoulder, and when I turned I almost fell to the floor in surprise, it was my friend Rashid Salman! In the second it took me to open my arms and receive him I remembered evenings in Rome with him and his movie associates, barbecues at a cultural festival in Damascus, and encounters in Berlin and Oslo, as well as his novel *Arab Sunsets*, translated into many languages, in which he recounts his own life as a young Israeli Arab educated in a Jewish school, and the contradictions and humiliations of that situation, and in the same second I thought, how on earth could I have forgotten that Rashid lived in Jerusalem? how come that wasn't the first thing I thought of when I arrived in this city?

My friend, he said, I saw you on the list of delegates and was starting to wonder where on earth you were! I've been in the room for more than an hour thinking, if he hasn't changed, sooner or later he'll come to the bar for a drink, and I was right! I know you've been sick, how are you now? Very well, I said, back on form, as you can see, happy to be here and embarrassed that I didn't look you up earlier, but I only arrived this afternoon.

Our previous encounter had been five years earlier in Vienna, yes, *Literature on the Frontier*, that was it. He had gained weight and his hair was very short, like an adolescent's, an image reinforced by his pink Converse tennis shoes combined with his linen suit and his tie knotted below the second button of his shirt. His face was still the same, a huge smile and two cross eyes, like planets floating in the middle of a storm. I could tell by the way he spoke and waved his hands in the air that he had already drunk quite a bit. This is going to be a really special conference, he said, like nothing you've ever seen before, I can guarantee you that! So I asked, are you referring to the war that's going on outside? and he said, no, that's the least of it, there's always been war here, I'm referring to the helplessness, the profound solitude that infects this region, even though it's in the eye of the hurricane, but come, actually I was referring to something more serious, which is that this hotel has the best bar in the Middle East, let's go fill our glasses, what are you drinking?

Kosztolányi and Supervielle were talking to a couple of venerable-looking old men, so I left them and followed Rashid through the crowd. Listen, I said, what on earth does *Alqudsville* mean? and he said, oh, that's nonsense, don't take any notice, people invent that kind of thing to give the foreign press something to write about, but here it's of no importance, you know wars are fought at every level, including the level of language, we'll see what happens, just forget it for now, better to hit this damn hotel's reserves of alcohol, don't you think? I took a long slug of whiskey and remembered that evening many years earlier, I no longer knew how many, when Rashid and I had gone to an Arab wedding in Tira, his native town, north of Tel Aviv. The bride and groom greeted the guests in the door of the living room, beside a huge strongbox with a slot, into which, after congratulating them, people put envelopes containing cash. Of course, the Arab tradition of not serving any alcohol was being respected, so we sat down at a table at least a hundred yards long that snaked through the living room and waited for dinner. There were bottles of mineral water, Fanta, and Coca-Cola, so Rashid, his father, and I spent the whole time passing each other a bottle of whiskey under the table. Parties without alcohol tend not to last long, so within a couple of hours we were already back in his house, drinking and waving to the neighbors. Rashid's novels were about the people of that town, so that journey was like entering the world of his books. A few years later, we met again in Bremen, at a conference called *Writing in the Midst of Chaos*, at which we were asked to reflect on fiction in countries in conflict, in cities under siege or under pressure, and of course, there were Rashid and I, an Israeli and a Colombian, as well as a couple of Angolans, some poets from Rwanda, and a few Yugoslavs, in addition to the Western Europeans, who theorized about other people's violence and seemed to have the best ideas. As it turned out, the best thing about that conference, as we both remembered, was the night the Belgian professor Céline July burst naked along the corridors of the sixth floor of the hotel, very drunk and a bit drugged, fleeing from the Congolese poet Abedi Lassora, who was following her waving a cock so big it knocked down flowerpots and candlesticks as it swung from side to side. They had been about to have sex when the author of the essay *Postcolonial Metaphor in the Former Zaire* had been startled to see the exaggerated dimensions of the member possessed by one of the leading practitioners in her field.

Something similar could well happen at this conference, given that the presence of Sabina Vedovelli seemed to emit a kind of eroticizing gas into the atmosphere of the hotel, affecting all the men and women gathered there. Would anyone succeed in getting to first base with her? As I thought this, I searched for her with my eyes and spotted her at the far end of the room, just as she was putting her tongue in a glass of martini to extract the olive. A long red tongue that was like a living being. Then Rashid pointed to somebody and said, come, let me introduce you to my publisher, he's the man over there, his name is Ebenezer Lottmann, he runs Tiberias, the largest publishing company in the country, come, you should meet him. We made our way through the human tide until we reached a short, bald man in a tuxedo, who greeted Rashid effusively. After we had been introduced, the little man looked me in the eyes, nodded, and said, it's a pleasure, my friend, a real pleasure, but before we say anything else I need to tell you something: one of your books is being considered by Tiberias, our editorial board is very selective and I haven't heard anything from them yet; I prefer to tell you that now, in order not to raise false hopes. Don't worry, Mr. Lottmann, I hastened to reply, the fact is, I didn't even know my agent had submitted anything to you, but he insisted, I prefer to be honest from the start, I'm surrounded by writers who want to get their friends published, and of course Rashid is no exception, but I want to make it quite clear that if the verdict of the editorial board is a negative one it won't have been through any fault of mine, let alone of your friend Rashid's, don't think that, the board is very selective, as I already said . . .

I turned my back on him and walked away in irritation. His

harangue was starting to ruin the party for me, but Rashid caught up with me and said, wait, he's a good man, just a bit distrustful, as you know, everyone has some stupid flaw in their character, and his is that he's a bit arrogant, but I assure you he's worth it. I thanked Rashid, and said, I know the world is full of rich, arrogant people, but I think it's time I went to bed, I'm tired. Come even if it's only for a minute, he insisted, and the little man, who had heard my words, approached saying, don't worry about Rashid, really, if publication with Tiberias isn't assured it's not because of him, you must try to understand that we're very selective, so I said, I understand that perfectly well, but this scene strikes me as absurd, I have no idea what happens to my books until things actually work out and I have to give my agreement or sign a contract, do you follow me? so I'm not expecting anything at all from you, because until thirty seconds ago I didn't even know you existed, got that?

The little man tilted his head to one side and looked at me gravely, in silence, then, suddenly, he gave a smile that spread all over his face to such an extent that it distorted it, contracting muscles and making his eyes bloodshot, and he said, almost cried, excellent! really excellent, friends, a little masterpiece! Was that prepared or was it an improvisation? At that moment I also laughed and decided to have another whiskey, one last one, because I was starting to like the little man.

You should know, dear friend, that Tiberias has the most demanding editorial board in the publishing world, because it works like an inverted pyramid: at the bottom are the least perceptive, those who can only spot obvious mistakes in construction and characterization, but then, at the second level, the book or manuscript begins its Stations of the Cross, because I want you to know that the same system applies to everyone, even Rashid had to experience this Via Dolorosa, dolorous indeed, if you'll pardon the expression, climbing through every level until it reaches the top of the pyramid, where I sit, the final stone, and I want you to know that just because I've worked my way up from the bottom doesn't mean I'm in any way indulgent toward the candidates, no sir, quite the contrary, when I know perfectly well that I run the best publishing company in my language, how could it be any other way, do you see that?

I told him I did, and, my curiosity aroused now, asked him what Latin American authors he had in his catalog, and he replied, ah, well, that's another matter, it's no secret to anyone that Tiberias publishes the most exclusive products of the human mind, hence the difficulties of selection and, of course, the huge disappointment of those who remain on the outside, which has brought us, believe me, a great deal of criticism, my God, they've said the most horrible things about us, but all that, as you can imagine, is a product of envy and frustration, which is understandable on a human level, I know that a rejection from us is a tragic occurrence to an author and I understand that the natural thing is to search for extra literary reasons, to play the aggrieved victim, or claim that there is some kind of personal vendetta against him, can you imagine, most of those who remain on the outside of what I call the "Tiberias ladder" react with anger and immediately swell the ranks of our most embittered critics and enemies, oh, my friend, you look surprised but I assure you that's the way it is, and that's why I dare to ask you, to beg you, if we reject your book, not to be tempted by hate, antipathy, or resentment, don't do it, I implore you, stay away from those resentful coteries, because in the long run it achieves nothing, none of the more spirited refutees has ever gotten in with subsequent books, while those who choose the stoic path of resignation, with integrity and a vision of the future, always get a second chance, and believe me, we have had notable cases of condemned men who swallowed their pride and persevered and in the end saw their books in the sky blue covers of Tiberias, yes sir! and as he said this, he raised his glass and said, a toast to forbearance and tolerance, and the three of us drank.

Lottmann did not drink alcohol, only soft drinks. Excuse me, Mr. Lottmann, I said, but you haven't answered my question, and he looked at me in surprise, what question? I did answer, you have to be patient and wait for an answer, but I said, no sir, I asked you what Latin American authors you have in your catalog, and he said, ah, yes, well, you see, I'd rather not give you names now, in spite of the fact that our catalog is no secret; I prefer to tell you the type of writer we're interested in publishing, and then you'll be able to think about it, then confirm your ideas by taking a look at our website, tiberias.net.com, do you think you can remember that?

And now, coming to the main subject, what interests us is what we might these days call the "versatile writer," the writer capable of adapting to the tastes of the public without in any way renouncing his own creative magma, his individuality, do you follow me? I'll give you an example: do you remember, a few years ago, there was a great explosion of historical novels about sects and secret societies in the Middle Ages and that kind of thing? I nodded, and he continued: that is the typical situation of which a "versatile writer" will take advantage, putting his own logs on an already blazing fire and making it burn gracefully, while keeping his own identity, of course, which will allow him to defend himself against the accusations and insults heaped on him by old, dyed-in-the-wool writers, who will brand him an opportunist, a sellout, a traitor, a whore, and all those things the resentful say, those who don't sell, the fundamentalists who cling to tradition, you know who I'm talking about, well, anyway, that's my idea of the "versatile writer," the writer who is able to swim in the cloudy waters of popular taste without it being too obvious, without shouting it on the rooftops, without being seen at fashionable parties and getting his face in the papers, because that would be suspicious and counterproductive in the long run, it's good to keep a high profile but not too high, better a two-thirds profile, a three-quarters profile, because anyone who's always at the crest of the wave will fall in the end, I don't know if I'm explaining myself well, number three on the bestseller lists here, a second prize there, a mention somewhere else, do you understand me? Perfectly, I said, and you've made me so curious that bright and early tomorrow morning I'm going to ask at reception for a computer so I can look at your catalog, and he replied, ah, my catalog, the Tiberias catalog! you'll be surprised, the list of guests at the most exclusive council of the human spirit, the great literary party of the century, the one that has now finished and the one just starting; at this point, I raised my glass and said, well, then I propose a toast to the only one of your authors I know, Rashid, and he said, dash it, Rashid is a very special case because, without being really "versatile," seeing as he persists in a confessional vein with touches of drama and humor, a literary stance that, in theory, might appear decadent and suicidal, yet has turned out to be very successful, his books are very popular and we never have any problem in selling the foreign rights, so for me he's the exception that proves the rule, oh, God knows yes, at the end of the day nothing in this business is written in stone and that's why one should feel one's way, or rather, crawl one's way.

Sabina Vedovelli was talking with three weary-looking men. The fattest of them was sweating profusely, his hair stuck to his forehead, as if somebody had thrown a glass of water in his face. Listening from a distance, I thought I caught the music of the Russian language. Suddenly the fat man gave a loud laugh and said, *eta horoshó*, which removed any lingering doubts. I assumed they were partners of hers, the porn industry having flourished in the former Tsarist empire, thanks, among other things, to the great beauty of their young women. I found myself looking at Sabina Vedovelli's cleavage, which was like a maelstrom between her magnificent breasts, and just as I was about to fall into that ravine I saw something really extraordinary emerge from it, nothing less than . . . the head of a small snake! a kind of periscope that appeared for a second, looked right and left, sank back down, and disappeared. Did you see that!!??, I asked Rashid, and he said, what? I felt disoriented, suspecting the wine I was drinking, my tiredness, even my illness. A snake just popped out from between Sabina Vedovelli's breasts! I said.

Ebenezer Lottmann looked at me reprovingly, but said nothing. Rashid, as a way out of the impasse, said, oh, my friend, I see the Jerusalem syndrome has gotten to you, too many prayers create an electricity in the air that causes madness, but don't worry, it passes, the best thing we can do is go as quickly as possible to the bar and get some more whiskey. He took his leave of his publisher with a nod and said in my ear, you're going crazy, friend, when was the last time you had a decent fuck? But as we passed Sabina the little snake popped up again. The three Russians screamed and Rashid stopped dead. Half the room turned to look at Sabina's fleshy promontories, and she, with a smug look on her face, took the thing out, a little rubber toy, which was greeted with shouts and laughter.

This strange bazaar of humanity seemed boundless. On the other side of the room was a mysterious-looking man trying to hide amid the velvet drapes. Seen from a distance, he looked like a medieval warrior from one of those "versatile" novels Lottmann had talked about. He was wearing a black cloak with a hood and only the lower part of his face was visible. His forearms were bare and covered with tattoos, giving them a brocade-like appearance; as I walked toward him, I could make out Roman crosses, the figure of a bloodstained Christ, Latin inscriptions in Gothic writing, an eye that looked like a sun shining over a remote fortified city, and I said to myself, here he is, the Templar, that was all this party needed, and I thought, maybe thanks to him this story will take flight and turn into a resounding bestseller, a Templar of our times! what an extraordinary stroke of luck! I hope he can be part of this narrative, I swear he'll have a leading role, of course he will, the others will have to understand that, we're all in the same boat, oh yes, it was time I became a "versatile writer," and having a Templar on board was the best guarantee.

As I came level with him, these fantasies faded. I saw that one of the tattoos showed the helm of a boat, with the words, in Spanish, "God is my co-pilot," and what I had thought was an armored breastplate turned out to be an elegant gray jacket, so I resigned myself, farewell Templar. This might well be the former evangelical pastor, so I asked him, are you from the Caribbean? and he pulled back his hood, revealing a pair of bulging eyes, and said yes, my brother, from right in the middle of the Caribbean, and how about you, if I'm not being indiscreet? I'm Colombian, I replied, and he said, oh, give me your hand, brother, Walter José Maturana, at God's service and yours, in that order, with the Almighty first, yes indeed, and I replied, pleased to meet you; I turned to introduce him to Rashid, but Rashid was nowhere to be seen, and I thought: he must have gone back to the drinks table, I'll catch up with him later.

The pastor, with his untidy gray beard, raised his index finger and said, I know who you are now, brother, you're the novelist! the first thing I want to tell you is that I haven't read your books, but when I saw your name it sounded familiar, so I started searching for it on the Internet, telling myself, I've heard it before somewhere, and then it came to me, a woman I had dealings with some years ago was a fan of yours, not because of a book but because of an article, something about mature women, she'd stuck it up on the wall and always said,

if ever I meet the man who wrote this I'm going to smother him
with kisses, starting with his dick, those were her exact words,
and having heard your name mentioned so often, I've remembered it ever since, and now I've actually met you! oh God, life
is amazing, isn't it? you can't imagine how important that article of yours was to her, and how it helped her, my God, the
poor woman was trying to get down to two grams and clung to
those words as if they were her last hope. Two grams of what?
I said to him, and he replied, what do you think, my brother?
two grams of smack, horse, don't you get it? heroin, brother,
when I received her into the Church she was on four sachets a
day and she didn't have any veins left, poor thing, she'd lost
her looks because the smack rots your gums and your teeth fall
out like seed from a rotten corncob, poor girl, nobody wanted
to hump her anymore and that's when the drama started, she
was used to giving the dealers blowjobs or sleeping with them
in exchange for coke and horse, but then they got bored with
her and said, that's it, Cinderella, go sell your pussy to junkies
because we don't want you anymore, either bring us money or
the flow dries up, baby, the party's over, can you imagine, the
same guys who got her hooked in the first place just so they
could fuck her when she was nice and pretty now left her in the
trash, oh, brother, this world really is one big shithouse and
stinks like rancid cottage cheese, because to add to that, when
she went with junkies they gangbanged her, three or four of
them at a time, and when she had the smack inside her the
poor woman didn't know what was going on, sometimes they
even crapped on her, and I really mean that, she was like the
living dead when I pulled her out of the garbage, I put Christ
into her nostrils and if you saw her today, my friend, you'd be
knocked out, even her mother who brought her into the world
wouldn't recognize her, she's clean again, and by a miracle of
the Lord, the Big Enchilada, the Man Upstairs, she doesn't
have anything nasty in her blood, because I tell you, with what

they put in her she should have had AIDS the size of a Soviet ship, but anyway, Christ held out his hand to her, and she's the woman who has your article hanging on her wall.

I saw Rashid in the distance. He signaled to me, making a fanlike gesture with his fingers that meant, see you later, so I said to Maturana, listen, all I know about you is what the conference gave us and that's why I'd like to get to know you, I mean, my God, you must have seen some pretty harsh things in your life, I guess? The man twisted the hairs of his beard and said, yes indeed, brother, I've seen the devil in Technicolor and black and white, and I've even seen him in the mirror, brother, because between you and me I can tell you I came out of the garbage truck with the engine on, or when they'd already closed the lid and were throwing earth on top, really, everything's passed through this body, smack, mushrooms, weed, coke, crack, freebase, I was so addicted, brother, I'd lost all sense of shame, until one day I touched bottom and I won't tell you how it was to wake up the day after, man, that was really rough, no kidding, try to imagine the scene, opening your eyes on the sidewalk of an avenue at three in the afternoon, with the sun beating down, pants torn, no shoes on your feet, so thirsty you could have drunk a gallon of gasoline, the syringe still in your forearm and a cop slapping you and saying, hey, hey, wake up, what's your name? and you making an effort to remember something as basic as your name, who the fuck you are and what you're called, that isn't an easy question to answer, brother, and then seeing them almost dying of disgust as they lift you up and put you in the back of a patrol car with the bars around, and hearing them say, this scumbag fell out of the garbage truck, I'd rather clean a dog's vomit with my tongue than touch him again, I'd rather kiss an ass with colitis than smell the breath of this bag of germs, anyway, things like that, and then they put me in jail for destitution, vagrancy, a long way from where I'd grown up because all this happened in the north, in a little town in West Virginia I'd gone to for some business that turned out badly, and I went straight to prison, my friend, I'm not telling you the half of it, but it was there that I met the man who saved me, the Jesus Christ of the Caribbean, anyway, that's the story I'm going to tell, so it's better if I don't tell you the rest now.

Did you see Sabina Vedovelli? he asked. She's going to be the center of attention: there's a rumor around that she's going to tell her life story, and I said, I'm new at this, I don't know what kind of things are being rumored. Maturana continued: may God forgive me if I'm slandering anybody, I'm only repeating what I've heard, but they say she's been the lover of Mafiosi and politicians and all kinds of VIPs, they say Berlusconi, you remember the bald guy who was president of Italy a few years ago and became famous for banging young girls? and I said yes, of course, and he continued, well, they say one night he gave her as a gift to the president of Russia, who was on a state visit, and at dinner Sabina got up on the table and danced and threw plates and glasses on the floor, and then she lifted her skirt and went closer to the men, who must have been drunk and coked-up, and she pulled aside her G-string and peed in their faces, she was aiming streams of urine at them while they sang the balalaika or some crap like that, and they mixed it with champagne and drank it, and then they both screwed her, one from in front and the other from behind, on the table, and they gave her a tremendous fricassee of cock, that's what they say, I don't have any evidence, but what a life, eh? and they also say that she always carries in her suitcase a pair of underpants that belonged to Pope John Paul II and that she worships them as if they were the Turin Shroud and they say she lost her virginity at the age of eighteen, because until then she only took it up the ass, and that the first man who gave it to her from the front and took her virginity was a pilot of the Swedish airline SAS, flying from Rome to Gothenburg,

who came out of the cabin to take a leak in the middle of the
night and found her in the bathroom, with her pants down and
crying with fear, and when the giant, who was probably called
something like Olaf the Bastard, saw her, he closed the door,
took out his cock and impaled her on it as they crossed the
Apennines, and they say that's why she kept the taste for screwing in exotic places, even while parachuting or at the bottom
of the sea, and that she's had sex with various kinds of living
creatures, not all of them human, in fact human isn't necessarily what she likes best, anyway, brother, everybody says something, because it's like this Vedovelli woman is from another
planet.

Suddenly, I heard a voice beside me saying, are you the
writer? It was a young woman with rectangular glasses. Hi, she
said, I'm Marta Joonsdottir, I'm from Iceland, I write for the
Ferhoer Bild in Reykjavik, I'm here to cover the conference, my
readers would be interested to hear about your opinions,
maybe you could grant me an interview, so I said, yes of course,
it would be an honor, although I'm not quite sure how interested your readers would be, and then I said, let me introduce
the ex-Reverend Walter José Maturana, and Maturana looked
at the girl and said, it's nice to see a young woman who's pure
of heart, with her soul shining out of her eyes, and she replied,
thanks for the compliment, Father, but don't be deceived,
these eyes have already seen everything an adult person ought
to see and more, I know about your evangelical work and I'd
like to talk about that as the conference goes on, and he said,
whenever you like, I'll try not to die first.

Just as he said that, there was another *coup de théâtre*, a second bomb going off, even louder than the first, which made
the building shake. A murmur went through the room, there
were a few stifled cries, and the candles flickered. Two seconds
later, the musicians struck up again as loudly as ever and the
guests continued talking, all except Marta Joonsdottir, whose

eyes screwed up like frightened squirrels, how can this be normal? she cried, and I replied, I don't think it is, it isn't normal for anybody, but everyone pretends because they're too embarrassed to say anything or they don't believe it. Marta looked at me gravely and said: one of these days there'll be a flicker of light and a moment later we'll all be dead, and that'll be normal too. Before she walked away she added: I'll look for you.

I moved away from the pastor and went to one of the windows that looked out on the western part of the city. I heard the sound of a siren and the roar of engines and saw an intense blaze creating sinuous shapes and flashes of light. That's where it must have fallen, I thought. But then I saw something strange: below, on King David Street, people were strolling along as if it were a cool summer night, indifferent to what was happening or, at least, what I thought was happening, because by this time, with all those glasses of whiskey and the long journey, I was not the right person to judge the gravity of what was happening, or how much danger we were all in.

Rashid reappeared and said, the smell of the candles is choking us, friend, it's time for a change of scenery, let's go, the city is calling us, it'll be an honor to show you something of this huge coffin that is Jerusalem under siege, a nest of flames whose combustion brings forth monsters, igneous creatures; a fallen burial mound, dressed in funeral clothing; a dolmen brought to its knees but resisting blindly. Let me show you how people enjoy themselves at night in this city.

I walked behind him to the exit and a second later we were walking up King David Street, just like the people I had been so surprised to see from the window. We had gone three blocks when I saw the Icelandic journalist on the opposite sidewalk, so I called her over, so you also wanted to go for an evening stroll? to which she replied, I'm going back to my hotel, did you think I was staying at the King David? no newspaper in Iceland could afford it, I'm in a small hotel on Agrippa Street, the Hotel Agrippa. I introduced her to Rashid, who invited her to have a drink with us, and she accepted.

We could hear explosions in the distance, but Rashid did not slow down at all. We came to a shopping street, Ben Yehuda, and turned into some narrow side streets that were quite lively, couples in the darkness, people on their own enjoying the night. We walked past some old doors until Rashid entered one and said to us, here we are, welcome to the Diwan, the curtain rises!

In my mind, I categorized the bar as noisy postmodern, dark and insalubrious, and its clientele as fringe characters, drunks, drug addicts, mentally unbalanced people addicted to prescription drugs, tranquilizers, and psychoactives, people who had had tough childhoods and had crossed the thin line between reality and the mental hospital, just like in *One Flew over the Cuckoo's Nest*, and in the case of the women, with the addition of being easy lays, not forgetting that some of the *habitués* of these bars usually belong to various high risk groups, people with AIDS or carriers of multiple staphylococcus, pneumocystitis, various kinds of gonorrhea, hepatitis B or C, candida albicans, Kaposi's sarcoma, anyway, all of this might well have been in the Diwan, but I said nothing and walked to the counter with a certain reluctance and a vague feeling that I was crossing a line, until I was able to take my first slug from the glass of whiskey Rashid put in my hand. Then we went to the back of the room, where music was playing loudly, and sat down.

Rashid stopped to say hello to some acquaintances of his, so I asked Marta, do you like the place? and she said, very much, it's the kind of bar I go to in Reykjavik, where I can chill out, a space where nobody looks at anyone and everyone respects everyone else, not like those awful places with leather armchairs and indirect lighting where people go to see and be seen; I have a long history of love affairs and friendships in bars like this, and what about you? do you like it? I forgot what I had thought when I came in, because I had already stopped feeling nervous, so I said, it's a typical bar of our time, when the archeologists of the future want to figure out our civilization they'll find traces of places like this, which are exactly the same in different parts of the world, do you live in Reykjavik? and she said, no, in Paris, I'm their arts correspondent, that's why they sent me to cover the conference, I'm a graduate in philosophy and letters, and philology too.

When I heard that I said, I'm a philologist too, that makes us colleagues. I proposed a toast to the noble science of philology and I said, the only thing I've read from your country is *Paradise Reclaimed* by Halldór Laxness, oh, and *Meek Heritage*, too, but Marta shuddered and said, that novel isn't by Laxness, it's by Frans Sillanpää, who's Finnish, you're confusing them because they're both Northern, just like everyone does, and she added, bitterly: the rest of the world doesn't distinguish between Sweden, Norway, Finland, and Iceland, and yet they're so different! You're right, I said, I confused two writers, but not your countries. She took a sip of her whiskey and said, I'll forgive you if you change this shit for something stronger for me, this is no time to be drinking something that's only forty proof! I stood up and went to the bar. I saw a green bottle with a sinister name, Black Death. I asked for a glass of it and took it to Marta.

She took a sip of it and her cheeks turned very pink, and she cried, Brennivín! they have this at the bar? drinking Brennivín is the most patriotic thing an Icelander can do, and added, I have to confess something, this drink has a connection with the first time I got drunk and also, predictably, lost my virginity, it all happened on the same night. I'd been drinking a bit and dancing in an old disco called Nasa, in the center of Reykjavik, where underground bands played like Björk's Sugarcubes, Juliette and the Licks, Ghostigital, who play really weird rock, and there I was, only fifteen, and I wanted to drink up the world in one go or snort it into my brain with a line of coke; what I did was drink and drink until a guy wearing a helmet with horns and a leather vest took me on the dance floor and whirled me around and around; my feet literally lifted off the ground. From there we went to the men's bathroom to have sex, he was nice and he treated me quite well; it hardly hurt at all. The next day he gave me a couple of aspirins and drove me home on his motorbike. I never saw him again.

Rashid came to the table with more whiskey, and said, what do you think of this bazaar of disturbed lives? It's like a warehouse of humanity, the equivalent of the Museum of Mankind, only with living species that aren't yet completely extinct, don't you find it interesting? I noticed a woman bobbing up and down on the edge of the dance floor. Her head was shaved, and she was wearing an Indian skirt and military boots. I found it strange to see thick hair under her armpits and on her legs, it had been ages since I had last seen a hairy woman. No woman had hair now on any part of her body and I had almost forgotten they had any.

Suddenly Marta cried, hey, I've just had a brilliant idea, how about doing the interview right now? I looked at her and said, my God, you work late, to tell the truth I'm tired, but she insisted, I won't tape anything or make notes, it's just a first approach, I'll use my memory.

And she began: why do you write? The question fell like a stone into water and I was not sure what to say, why do I write? or rather, why did I write before, when I wrote? To tell the truth, I do not have any very clear idea of why I do it, so I said, I don't know, but she insisted, there must be some reason, it may be that you don't see it immediately but there must be one, think and you'll find it, it'll come, we're in no hurry. She asked Rashid the same question, how about you, why do you write? And, although he seemed more distracted than I was, he replied without hesitation: because it would be much worse if I didn't. I was impressed and said to myself, damn it, now that's a convincing answer.

Marta smiled and looked down, a sign that she was pleased with the sentence and wanted to remember it, then continued: and what would be much worse? Rashid, who must have thought he had already won the game, looked surprised, but said, my life would be much worse, and the lives of the people around me, and probably literature.

Marta replied: do you consider yourself a great writer? I'm not the one who thinks that, said Rashid, it's the press and my readers who consider me a great writer, at least that's what they say to my face. They may be lying but that's what they say, and I believe them, because nobody is forcing them; my books are successful in a dozen languages and that must mean something, mustn't it? He took a long slug of whiskey and said, I don't want to appear arrogant, I don't think my books are important, but I like them, that's why I write and publish them. Other people think they're important.

Again Marta looked at me, as if to say, it's your turn, do you have your answer yet?

I can think of a thousand reasons not to write, I said, in fact I haven't written for quite some time now; things like illness or boredom, irritation or fatalism, or remembering that all human enterprises are doomed to disappear, however long they last . . . Thinking that doesn't exactly inspire one to write.

And are you going to start writing again now? she asked, and I said, perhaps I'll try a new genre, biography for example, this conference may be a sign.

And why would you start writing again?

There are things we do without any reason or for the most trivial of reasons, I said: going out and walking along the road during the rush hour and looking at people in their cars; showing up in midafternoon at the box office of a movie theater or

browsing in bookshops or sitting on a balcony watching people on their way home, and repeating to yourself in your mind,
why am I doing all this? why today did I walk to a bookshop
or go to a movie theater and just as I got to the door decide not
to go in? We do things that have no meaning or only acquire
meaning over time, perhaps because deep down we want to
change our lives at the last moment, when everything appears
fixed, like those roulette players who one second before the
close of bets nervously shift a tower of chips, from one number
to another, and then bite their fingers; because we're searching
for some kind of intense experience, or because we want to be
someone else, yes, to be someone else, there you have your
answer: I write to be someone else.

Marta smiled and said, you see, we're making progress
already, I told you we could still get a good article at this hour,
the idea that alcohol and work are incompatible may be correct for dentists or people who perform circumcisions, but not
for those of us who work with words. Of course, provided we
stay a bit horizontal, or support ourselves with the other hand.

I took advantage of our eyes meeting—hers were two blue
fishbowls—to ask her, how about you, Marta, why do you write?

The change of trajectory disconcerted her, but she seemed
to enjoy the game, and said, I write because it's what I do for
the arts pages, that's rather a stupid answer, I know, but it's the
literal truth; if I were on the financial pages or the sports pages
my life would be different, I'd write less, I'd be dictating
results or commentaries by telephone, and that would be all; I
should add that I feel proud when I see my texts printed and
imagine they're going to be seen in railroad stations and tea
rooms and hairdressing salons and the people who read them
will approve or reject them and one in a hundred or a thousand will remember my article that night and make some comment over dinner, that, by and large, is what drives me to write,
don't you feel the same way?

I said yes, I was pleased that what I wrote would be seen by readers unknown to me, but I didn't feel any pride, because to tell the truth the books we leave behind us drift away from us and we end up kind of mutually rejecting each other, as if after a while we did not recognize each other, and that's what's happening to me today, I'm miles from them, I'm not the same person who wrote them; I genuinely think those books are dead.

A loud explosion plunged the bar into silence and darkness. There were a couple of grotesque screams and some laughter. Then somebody struck a light, and I saw that the people were all frozen in their places, even those who were on the dance floor. There was another explosion, and I grabbed Marta's hand and headed for the exit. Where the hell had Rashid gotten to? I found him in the corridor and I said, it's time we got back. The windy night carried the smell of gasoline and scorched tires.

When I got to the hotel I realized how much I had been drinking. The steps were moving like the keys of a pianola and I almost fell. As I walked toward the elevators I heard music on the second floor and decided to go have a look. In the main reception room a waiter was extinguishing the candles and collecting the candlesticks. Another was removing the tablecloths and the remains of food. On one side of the room a few delegates had appropriated a few bottles and gathered around the piano. The person playing turned out to be none other than Leonidas Kosztolányi. They were all singing out of tune and drinking.

When I got to my room, I left my clothes on the armchair and went to take a shower, the only way to clear my head before sleep. I switched out the light and stepped inside the jet of water, which felt really good. I do not know how much time I was in there, but I actually fell asleep and even dreamed. Then I turned off the water, grabbed one of the towels, and stepped out of the shower, shivering as I did so.

It was then that I heard the voices. A woman on the verge of tears and a man trying to console her. Being in the dark, I lost all sense of direction and was not sure where the voices were coming from. I even thought they might be coming from my own room. I did not have the strength to switch on the lamp, so I concentrated all my energies on listening. I love you, the man was saying, you've always known that, why should everything be different now? The words made the woman moan even louder and the man insisted, blaming her. You can't keep returning to that time, he said.

The fact that her moaning did not diminish in intensity made me think that she was hoping for more affection, and I tried to imagine the scene: the two of them on the couch, the man embracing her, the woman with her face in her hands; but his attempts at consoling her, perhaps because they had been repeated too often and had become old and tired, did not convince either of them anymore, and I wondered, what is it that she returns to and reproaches him with? how, out of the many ways you can hurt somebody, has he hurt her? After these questions came others: were they young? middle-aged? The fact that the man was whispering made it hard to determine his age.

He said: I love you and that's all that matters, forget everything else, what does the past matter? life is full of traps; but she continued sighing and crying, and he insisted: if I were lying I wouldn't have brought you here. That phrase produced a special effect, because at last she spoke: I prefer not to believe you, because if it turns out that you're lying I'll slash my wrists and this time I mean it, and it'll all be your fault, listen to me, your fault for making me heartless and false. Now it was the man who paused for a long time, a pause that made me assume they had embraced and the woman had stopped crying, but I was wrong, because the sighs started again: nobody's realized what I've done, but that doesn't mean that I'm ready to keep doing it, do you understand me? let alone for a bastard like you.

Her tone became threatening. Then there was a different sound, which, in my delirium, I associated with a kiss, a long kiss, profoundly desired by the two of them. Finally he spoke, and said, feel how much I love you, you can smell it, touch it, it's no lie. And again the kiss. Don't try to break my heart, she said, you won't succeed this time, I'm strong now, and he said, I don't deserve anything, I know that, what I deserve is for you to spit at me and humiliate me and even pee in my face, if you think it's necessary, I deserve that, you know, I'm not trying to convince you of anything, all I want is to clear the way so that the truth can come out without any shame.

There was a sigh from her, different this time. It wasn't a moan anymore but something more elaborate, and suddenly she said: you know what's going to happen if you keep sucking me there! That's what you want! But he said, I'm doing it because I can sense you want it, it's exactly what you want and I've always been your animal. Again there was a silence, a longer one this time, and a soft creaking sound that suggested a change of position on the couch. Suddenly she said: how can you touch me again after what you made me do? and he said, it was for you, only for you. That was the last thing I heard before falling fast asleep.

6.
THE MINISTRY OF MERCY (III)

Here we are again, my friends, to conclude this story, which I hope you're finding both entertaining and instructive, because that's why we're here. A couple of years had passed since the start of the Ministry when one evening, coming back to the house from an evangelical trip to the penitentiary at Sundance Creek—where, by the way, I'd managed to get three black gorillas, each weighing about two hundred and sixty pounds, to go down on their knees before the Man Himself—I learned that Walter had hired some body-guards, four guys of different races, their muscles developed at the neighborhood gym or in jail, with wires coming out of their ears, who followed him everywhere and kept everyone at bay, including me, because when I went to say hello to them they grabbed me and, as the police say, immobilized me, until he said to them, it's O.K., guys, cool it, this is my partner, he can come to me whenever he likes. All of which struck me as very strange.

The Ministry was doing better than ever. The safes were bursting with dollars, rotten with greenbacks, millions of them. People gave monthly tithes, and Walter's tours to spread the word, with services for up to twenty thousand people, were great for business. All we had to do was fart and we'd be showered with coins. That was how it went. But Walter wasn't the same anymore, for a reason I could well understand, even though I'm no great student of character or anything like that, which is that if you tell a person, from the moment he gets up in the morning until the moment he goes to bed at night, that he's mega, A-number-one, the boss; if everyone who works with him tells him every day that he's the goose that lays the golden egg, and the sun shines out of his ass, well, that person ends up believing it! I mean, that'd be enough to give anyone a swollen head, don't you think, my friends? It's something that's hard to keep in check, like blindness or one of those diseases people have in their blood today, because there comes a moment when that person starts to believe it's all true, that he really is the great Macho Man and all that, and that's where things turn sour, believe me, and I'm not trying to come off as some kind of philosopher or psychologist, but if someone believes something like that about himself it's because he already has one foot and half the other stuck in the shit, one ball and half the other in the wrong orifice, and I'm sorry, brothers and sisters, but this part of the story makes my blood boil, and here I have to make a confession that's very difficult for me, which is that this process of self-canonization that was starting up in Walter's consciousness ran parallel to another process in me, one that went in the opposite direction, which was that I stopped believing in anything, I let go of all those fairly tales and focused on my work on the streets, on the most down-to-earth things, on whatever shit was most recent and smelled the worst, I'm sorry, that turned out a bit scatological, which wasn't my intention; as Walter grew and grew like a balloon, I distanced myself from it all and went out on the street; I discovered that at the center of the world, in the world itself, was goodness, human generosity, what Walter had called in earlier days "the narrative of forgiveness and generosity," which had been his great theme.

Of course I never stopped believing that Walter was somebody special, endowed with an enormous sense of life, with those eyes that seemed like a lighthouse beacon turning very high above our heads, and that's why he was ahead of our thoughts and of reality, because he knew what was coming and was able to adapt himself to it, but also because his voice, his innocence, and his message were a drug to be injected with his word, a verbal substance that made the weak man think he was strong and the cripple a light-footed Achilles, his word had that curious gift of being able to transform things, reality, life itself, to bend circumstances to his will, and that was the source of his success. That was why people went crazy when they heard him and many fainted and felt that the sun was warming their cheeks, that life had stopped being that terrible shithouse it usually is for most people and was transformed into something in Technicolor, like a song by Pedro Infante or Toña la Negra or the great Celia, that's understandable, but I don't think, dear friends, that all that necessarily made him a God, as everyone used to say, as I myself used to say, no sir, and do you know why I say that? it's very easy, because all that he had to give others were human attributes; a man is the best support for another man who's desperate, and to do that he uses human words, which are the only ones we have, and the best, that's the great secret, and now I turn especially to my younger friends here and ask them to listen to this lesson that comes from a distant time, from years already past that were different than today, you can't imagine how different! and not only because there were no cell phones or computers, or because movies were different and people were a bit fatter and women had hair on their vaginas, begging your pardon, I'm not referring only to that, I say it because it was a time when people were scared of life and that's why they felt their way, very slowly, testing everything before making a move, like a blind man who's lost his stick in an inhospitable side street, and that's how things were in those slow, gray years, my dear friends, almost nobody had that self-assurance and that confidence expressed by people today, which demonstrates a complete absence of fear; the fear went out of their lives, and now it's life itself that should take care, and so I tell myself, the story of Walter de la Salle may seem amazing today, it may seem barely credible that somebody could turn into a God like that, a guide to the blind, a beacon to those lost in the fog, but that's what life was like, my friends, and that's why, in those worlds that were hungry for the absolute and the metaphysical, somebody who looked above the clouds and saw beyond the horizon should become a prophet, and then it was only a step for him to become Jesus Christ reborn, and that was what Walter represented to thousands of people.

I would see him getting into his armor-plated limousine, surrounded by Jefferson, Miss Jessica, and the horde of tattooed young men who were always with him now, and I would believe less in him as a demigod, just think of the paradox: the more the world believed in him, the more I saw his human side, in other words, his fallible side, and of course I still loved him and was ready to sacrifice my own life if I thought it would make Walter more real, more magnificent, but life's a very troublesome and contradictory thing, fuck it, sometimes even a suicidal thing, yes, which may be why nobody gets out of it alive; the greater the man's word grew, the higher his image as a Redeemer rose from the ground, the more he seemed to me a false Messiah, full of weaknesses, very attached to trivial things, and increasingly self-centered, which was something that seemed to cover his brain like ivy; it's a complex thing, my friends, but an extremely human thing, and a well-known phenomenon, that people who become famous immediately go a bit crazy! Let me give you an example, when we held services in stadiums, and Jessica went to the dressing room and told him, it's time to make your entrance, there are fifteen thousand people out there, he'd reply, tell me when there are sixteen thousand, that's my number, God woke me with that number in my head. Then he'd sit back in his chair and let Jefferson massage his shoulders while Jessica changed the slices of cucumber he put around his eyes to moisten them. He only drank Vittel water, imported from France.

Let me tell you how things were in a bit more detail. When at last everything was ready and Jessica pretended that sixteen thousand people had come in, he'd withdraw to a portable chapel he had and pray in silence for a minute, and then go out on stage in the middle of a cloud of smoke, with a spotlight following him and loud symphonic music, nothing less than *Zarathustra* by Richard Strauss, do you copy me? The people would rise from their seats and yell and the women would bite their purses and urinate and some would faint, it was completely crazy; the security people would have to contain the crowd, until Walter would turn on the microphone and cry, God is watching you tonight! God is looking at each one of you tonight! God sees what there is in each of your hearts and comes down, slowly, to kiss them! Then he would point to the audience with a powerful finger and cry:

Ooooopen your hearts to Goooooooodddd!!!

The applause would be deafening. His handling of the microphone was excellent, with crescendos and diminuendos that bent the audience to his will, and the rest was a real pop opera, my friends, suddenly he'd say, let's tell sin what we think about it, let's say it loud and clear, I hate you, I hate you! and the hall would be bursting with yells and stamping of feet. Then the lights would go out and there'd be a scary silence. Suddenly, a red light would fall on Walter, presenting himself now as a billy goat in the middle of a witches' Sabbath. He'd take off his chasuble and reveal his tattooed, muscular body. More beams of light would show the illustrations on his tattoos and the people would cry out in admiration and fear, yes, ladies and gentlemen, fear was part of the story. The cripples would jump out of their wheelchairs and the lame would yell with pride, recovering some of their dignity, and later these same little people would go back home along the street, kicking tin cans, poor devils sitting in forgotten parks looking at the world with misty eyes, tangible human idiocy, my friends, but for a few hours these people were happy and that's why Walter was a drug, a kind of crack or coke that was snorted through the ear and maddened the brain for a few days, or only a few hours, I don't know, because it had stopped doing anything to me.

We eventually had more than sixty thousand members, just imagine, and every one of them donated a monthly tithe that could vary between fifty and a thousand dollars, just imagine, and so there were no limits to anything anymore; the house in South Beach was turning into a resort, very different than it had been at the beginning, because Jefferson and the seven samurai, which was what I called that gang of athletic faggots, refurbished the place, knocking down walls, extending the rooms, and building a swanky gym with electronic apparatus and giant LCD screens so that Walter could watch recordings of his own services while he lifted weights or did Pilates. All this coincided with the purchase of the house that adjoined the rear of the property, and as both houses had extensive grounds, a path was laid to join the two gardens.

At that time, my friends and listeners, God put in my devastated brain one of the best ideas I've ever had, which was to move to a cabin on the border between the two gardens, but closer to the newly-purchased house, a cabin that had been used by the children of the previous owners to throw wild parties with alcohol, drugs, and group sex, because during the cleaning I found mineralized condoms, black sanitary napkins, crack pipes and coke papers, colored G-strings with strange stains on them, and dozens of empty tequila bottles and half-empty jars of Vaseline. I even found a box of tampons, because it had been fashionable for girls to wet them in liquor and stick them in their asses so they could get drunk without getting fat or damaging their stomachs. I cleaned the cabin without spending a single dollar of the Ministry's money. I opened the windows, let the air in, and installed some of the old furniture that was piled in the attic of the main house.

Soon I'd constructed a lovely space, with wooden shelves for my books, a comfortable living room, a table, and a few kitchen utensils, very few to be honest, because the one thing Walter asked was that I should continue to have lunch and dinner with the group. From that cabin at the bottom of the garden I devoted myself to observing the life of Walter and the others: Miss Jessica, Jefferson, along with the samurai and other dissonant elements in the life of the Ministry that had become a necessary evil by this time. I also devoted myself to devouring books, poetry and novels, exemplary lives, world history, whatever there was, I was interested in everything because I wanted to make up for lost time, like the time I told you about. I'd read after my Bible-thumping visits to reformatories and crack dens and other places of ill repute in the city, the way Walter had taught me, and the first thing I realized was that real life was poor compared with the lives in books; in books there was harmony and complexity and the most fucked-up things had a sheen of beauty, I noticed that when I read Dostoevsky and Dickens and Böll, and I'm even going to confess something to you, dear friends, which is that with all this reading I found out a little about history and finally learned, at the age of almost forty, that in Europe there'd been an almighty mess called the Second World War, don't laugh, just imagine what a crummy piece of shit I was, because before, whenever anybody mentioned Hitler, I thought he was a Mafia boss or a serial killer, and nothing more; when I read that he'd been chancellor of Germany, or president, or whatever they call it over there, I was completely stunned, and said to myself, I don't understand, is that the same country where writers like Thomas Mann and Musil come from? no way, and I decided to ask Walter if we could hire a teacher of modern history for the young people.

Ask Jessica for whatever money you need and take care of it, said Walter, it's a great idea, as always, so I hired, for a fair amount of money, a guy who wrote historical notes in the *Miami Herald*, a Cuban named Víctor Mendoza, and as it turned out, I wouldn't have missed those classes for anything in the world because I was constantly being surprised, like with that great story of the Cuban revolution and the guys with beards coming to power, I could hardly believe it, or the story of Pinochet, my brothers, it was like being born again every day, discovering that this motherfucking planet was a very complicated place, full of angry people always fighting, shooting each other, throwing nuclear warheads, going in for ethnic cleansing, dissolving each other in acid, running each other through the ass with Belgian rifles and everything, that was the kind of thing Mendoza taught us and I carved them into my brain and then went and repeated them to the young men on my prison visits, guys who, as I've already explained, found it really difficult to concentrate on one complete sentence, by the time you got to the predicate they'd already forgotten the subject and then they didn't remember the verb, but they were my children, what else could I do but love them? I was no different or better than they were, just as damaged by reality and the new psychotropic technologies; I'd tell them over and over: Columbus arrived, Bolívar died, Berlin fell, Tenochtitlan fell, Homer existed, Lenin died, Lindbergh arrived, Che was killed, Allende committed suicide, Trotsky was assassinated, anyway, the prosody of History, my friends, and my boys looked at me with red half-open eyes, their brains working extremely slowly, with smiles that had no connection with the situation, I don't know if you can imagine it; that was my space, alone in the prisons or in the bars with Miss Jessica, almost always in the Flacuchenta.

Walter gave up going out on the streets to spread the word, because he didn't have the time. All those meetings and services and journeys to other cities monopolized his schedule, so he himself said to me, you're going to take charge of the hardest part, you'll be my shepherd of souls, you'll have to bring them from the bottom of the well up to where I can save them, José, gather them together, be strong, it's the greatest responsibility there is in this Ministry and I give it to you, comrade, you're the oldest and most experienced of us, you believe in me and you'd be capable of giving your life blindly for Christ, that I know.

The separation became even greater. I'd observe him from my cabin, and I saw many things.

I saw that the lights in the tower, where Walter had moved his private rooms since the last refurbishment, were on until late, and sometimes I'd see frenzied silhouettes projected on the window. If somebody opened a window you could hear music and laughter. I stayed there in silence by my own window, spying on the movements in the tower, although sometimes I didn't even look; I only thought and thought about what Walter had come to do in the world and how little I understood of his mission, poor wretch that I was, so I said to myself, continue with your education and one day you'll understand, and I went back to my books, the poetry and the religious writings and the biographies, and I started to devour them again, and that way life got back on an even keel.

One evening, one of the Italian lawyers told him that the best way to spread his word nationwide was television, why had he never thought of it before? He ought to build a studio in his house, buy air space and hire a team of communicators to help him, and that was what he did, because Walter was extremely impressionable. He was won over by the idea of expanding, like everyone. Don't you think so, my friends? Doesn't a human being naturally prefer to have two of something rather than one? That was how Walter began his second stage as a businessman and *The Ministry of Mercy in Your Home* went on the air, for which he developed a different method. His advisers persuaded him that the style and esthetics of his concerts, with red lights and bulging muscles, wouldn't work on TV, because all those action series had set the bar really high when it came to convincing the viewers, and what he was doing would look like a children's game. That's why he thought up a kind of spiritual call center, with a theoretical part presented by Walter and another part where he was joined by Miss Jessica and they'd answer questions from viewers, using Biblical passages and other religious examples to get across their points.

Within six months the show was generating more money for the Ministry than all those exhausting national tours, and again there were changes. He didn't entirely stop going out on the streets, because, as he always said, nothing could replace direct contact with reality, grappling at first hand with a person desperate to find a direction in life, and I'd think, oh Walter, you haven't been in touch with reality for a long time now, but I only thought it, I didn't say it. At that time there were a lot of things I didn't dare say.

One night I was alone in my cabin, drinking tonic water and reading Pindar, when I heard heavy breathing in the garden, the noise of footsteps, dead leaves being crushed underfoot, what was it? I went to have a look and was stunned to see that a group of women had climbed over the railings and was heading for the house. I followed them at a distance to see what they were going to do . . . They wanted to see Walter, so they tried to force open a couple of doors, and, when they didn't succeed, they broke a window and got into the house that way. That worried me, so I said to them, hey, ladies, cool it, but they didn't listen to me, they seemed possessed; there was blood on the glass, so now I was really worried, but I didn't know what else to do except follow them, and I said to myself, where the fuck are the bodyguards? now that we need them they're nowhere to be seen, although I also thought, it's better this way, those savages might hurt one of the old ladies and then it'd be goodbye Ministry, big scandal, so we had to be careful. The women realized that Walter might be in the tower, because they saw lights, and looked for the staircase. I ran up the service stairs and got there before they did, to warn Walter. I saw that his apartment was open. I nervously approached the door and half-opened it, and light spilled out into the corridor.

The scene I saw gave me goose bumps

The young athletes and Walter were stark naked on the couches, having sex in a variety of incredible positions, sucking cocks and balls, the whole thing kept afloat with whiskey and gin, and with a smell of grass that knocked you back; as I was trying to recover my composure I heard a loud nasal snort, and looking to the side of the room saw Miss Jessica lifting her face from a mirror covered in coke, and I don't know if I dreamed it, but I had the impression that somebody was fucking her in the ass, because what I do remember is that she was in a G-string and her tits were bobbing up and down. I couldn't speak. I was petrified, I walked to the opposite wall and heard the intruders coming up the main stairs. By a miracle there were already two guards struggling with them, hitting them in the ribs with stun batons, but the women kept coming up. I saw it all unfolding in front of me like someone seeing death, my friends and listeners.

When they heard the women screaming, the guys in the orgy froze and Miss Jessica came to the door, naked. She must have been so zonked out she didn't know what was going on; the guards looked at her in surprise, because in addition to everything else she was smiling and moving her head in time to a tune. My God, I thought, seeing her with her G-string around her ankles, her mound of Venus shaved, a blood-red circle on her buttocks, as if she'd been sitting on the edge of a wall, and completely out of it. I just wanted to jump out the window onto the ground below to blot out those images. My world had shattered into a thousand pieces and, like a shell floating in a whirlpool, I didn't know what to do, how to stop it, I wasn't even sure that all this wasn't one of Satan's dirty tricks, but no, it was quite real; I didn't have the courage to face it, so I went back down the service stairs, without anyone noticing me.

I had to stay away from the house. When, the next day, Walter and Jessica ordered increased security, including electrified fences, I realized that the days of the Ministry were numbered. God would destroy us soon and the only question was, how would he do it? Would He use nuclear warheads, which was the modern way, or would He throw a few thunderbolts? You could smell it in the air. Walter asked me if I'd heard anything the previous night and I said, no, I hadn't, I'd only woken up at the end, after the guards had intervened and the police had arrived. During lunch, he said that love sometimes took on a destructive form and had to be channeled somewhere; that was what had happened in the house, and we had to remember that. I said yes, shrugged, and went back to my cabin.

For Walter it was a hard blow, something that should have started his brain ticking over, because it threw a beam of light on his great contradiction. I would have liked it if he'd come and talked with me honestly about what was happening, because I could have helped him, but he didn't. He became reserved and false. His smile was false, and so were his words of optimism. The falsity of words is obvious from listening to them, my friends, prick up your ears and you'll see, it's like hitting a wooden surface when there's nothing behind, the sound bounces and echoes, that's how hollow words sound. That's what falsity is. And people must have noticed it, not only me, because things started to go downhill, the ratings dropped, went sharply up and down for a while, then flatlined. At this

point, Walter took a couple of decisions that seemed lucid
enough, but actually made matters worse, like giving a gold
casket to a drowning man. In other words, the things might
have been good in themselves, but they didn't do anything to
stop the rot. One of them was the project to spread the word
outside the country, going to meet my people on the brother
continent, the Land of Delight, Latin America.

The idea was to start in Puerto Rico and travel to the
Dominican Republic, Costa Rica, Panama, Venezuela, and
Colombia, sadly skipping over the supreme island, the summit
of greatness and enjoyment, my beautiful Cuba, because my
cousin the Supreme Bearded One wouldn't let anyone preaching the word of Christ come anywhere close, oh, what a pity!
Walter threw himself into the plans for the journey, advised
once again by the Italians, who told him, you have to have a
commercial vision, you have to be managerial, efficient, you
have to set targets, identify strategic objectives and base your
operations on results, you have to optimize and find reliable
indicators; Walter's eyes were opened, and he started to say,
let's decide on objectives, let's lay down strategies, let's find
reliable indicators. Another important question, according to
the Italians, was the question of IMAGE! That was why they
hired a small private jet, a Falcon, I think, and put the name of
the Ministry on both sides, because one of the consultants said,
the Church mustn't convey the idea of poverty, when did you
ever see the Pope traveling economy class? the less you convey
the idea of poverty, the more you'll be listened to, and if anybody criticizes you or talks about ostentation, remember, the
word that lights a fire in people's hearts and cleanses their
souls has an obligation to be universal and efficient, and that's
the main thing, the objective; and Walter said: yes, let's go in
the Falcon, let's be universal, we're going to cleanse souls.
They contacted showbiz promoters in every country and hired
sports stadiums, bought advertising space on radio and TV

and in national newspapers. I helped write the advertising copy and select the photographs, my brothers, which was more amusing than useful.

The advertising read:

He is coming, He is coming . . .
Open your heart to the Supreme Mystery . . .
Become part of the Great Ministry.

For peace, the conjunction of souls, and harmony . . .
Join the Ministry of Mercy.

If you are lost and cannot see the world,
if your eyes do not help you . . .
close them and hear the word
of Reverend Walter de la Salle.

They also had T-shirts, pencils, pamphlets, pennants, posters, and commemorative coins produced, and hired the best lighting, sound, and technical teams that specialized in concerts. Apart from the Italians, Walter invited Jessica and me to travel with him in the Falcon, and sent the samurai in a regular scheduled plane, which they didn't like one bit. To be honest, I'd have preferred to stay in Miami because I could see the Master's punishment coming, but I let myself be persuaded because of my desire to see my Land of Delight, which I couldn't even do in the end because I was too busy organizing the services. The whole thing, as I've already hinted, went badly. In Puerto Rico it wasn't too bad, but in Costa Rica there were three hundred and eight people at the first service and ninety-six at the second. In Panama we didn't even sell six hundred tickets, and as we'd hired a stadium that seated seven thousand Walter preferred to cancel. There was a scandal in the press and we had to refund the money. As you can imagine, my friends, things went from bad to worse, and Walter was once again a soul suffering in the shadows; if the souls of evil people are black, those of fragile people are gray. Jessica and I would say to him: it's normal, nobody knows you here yet, your word will reach them but it's going to take time, and he'd say, where are the management indicators? what did we do wrong? According to the Italians, our calculations for the tour had overestimated the role of the passive element, and he told himself that maybe we should have targeted those strata of society that were more developed from the spiritual point of view. But this was no consolation to Walter, who kept asking himself the same question: why does no one come to me here, whereas they do in the United States, if they're the same people? what accounted for the difference? why did the people up there never speak to the people down here? He was blinding himself, and would have sudden fits of anger; then he'd lock himself away in the suites rented for him for the tour, without anyone coming to the hotel to look for him or to take photographs or even give him their hand or touch him. The security guys spent their time drinking beer in the lobbies and eating peanuts, because there were never any fans to hold back, no screaming, let alone fainting, and that hurt Walter. God, he would say imploringly, where did they all go? why did you take them? what are you trying to tell me? And I'd say, he isn't trying to tell you anything we don't already know, Walter, it's a problem of space and voice, your voice should win people over, we've made a start, more will come, now let's talk about something else.

One of those nights, in Cartagena de Indias, as we were talking on the balcony of his suite in the Hotel Santa Clara, he grabbed me very hard by the arm and said, José, you're a good person and that's why you have to understand that, basically, I'm human, I have human pains and frustrations, nothing makes me different than the others, than any of those that come to hear me; I'm a son of the streets like you, it just so happens that people listen to me. Then he went to the bar and grabbed a quart bottle of Johnnie Walker Black Label, two glasses and a full ice tray, and said, I know you've distanced yourself from all this, but for tonight I want you to think of us as two friends who need to talk, two friends or partners or flesh and blood Latinos who have to level with each other, this won't damage you, you're strong, you have structure in your life; he poured the whiskey and I drank, and in my soul it was as if galleries were collapsing, and a kind of echo rose to the surface from deep inside; a taste of another life or an intense emotion, when you find something that can destroy you the more you long for it, whether love or just obsession. By the third glass, I was confessing my fears to him, saying: you're bringing down what you yourself created with effort, and all for what? What you get from your shitty life in that tower isn't much, compared with what you're putting in danger, but he retorted, you're wrong, José, if it wasn't much I wouldn't do it, I need it, period, I'm like you, I dream of pleasure and things hurt me, don't be deceived about me; I said: be careful, you're riding a tiger and if you dismount you're going to break your legs, and he said, trust me, we're having a downturn, but it'll pass, it'll pass, you have to believe me.

Then we talked about God and life and the distant stars that could be seen over the sea and what hard work it must have been for the Master to create this universal shithouse we live in is only seven days, thing by thing, trees and grains of sand and flies buzzing around shit and the blind fish at the bottom of the sea and the diseases of kangaroos and the flocks of birds, hats off, and we talked about that son of a bitch Satan, who was always interfering in our lives and twisting them around, and the worst thing was that he never tired, we talked about all that until I went to the bathroom and saw that Jessica had returned and was on her iMac chatting or watching videos on YouTube or something like that, because she was dancing with her headphones on: I noticed that beside her, next to a glass filled to the brim with gin, there was a mirror with a considerable quantity of coke, but I walked past and went back on the balcony, where Walter and I continued going over life and the future and the contradictions.

An hour later, with the second bottle of Johnnie Walker half-finished, Jessica came and brought us a tray of coke, and we took turns snorting it, and again something inside me opened my eyes; on top of that Jessica brought a pack of joints and so we smoked then too and inside me I could hear the grunting of an animal that was familiar to me, that had never abandoned me, and so it went on until the black of the night turned ocher and our brains or what remained of them were already bursting; Miss Jessica was jumping like a cricket, she was so high she was climbing the walls, and so, with the last neuron in my brain, I decided to go to my room, just as Jessica was bringing another tray of coke, but I said to myself, if we carry on like this we're going to end up fucking, better if I go.

I went down to my room, put my head under the faucet and said to myself, what a piece of shit you are, José, how can you offend God like that; the grunting of the animal was becoming unbearable, so I said to myself, it's over, there won't be any more crap like that in your life; I grabbed a penknife and made a cut in my right wrist, and then the left, and I swear to you, my friends, it was like a liberation, I saw my blood coming out in the water like a pink ribbon and I felt clean, as if all the poison had gone out of me! I lay down and again saw the light-filled eyes I'd seen that first day, a drop of water glowing in the middle of the night, and I started praying, and I prayed until I was overcome with a great sense of calm and my eyes closed.

To those of you who think I'm going to tell you about my own death and are already making incredulous faces, let me tell you straight away that after what might have been a very long time I opened my eyes again. Mysteriously, instead of the hotel or the fire and brimstone of Hell and the servants of Satan, I saw a white, very white room; I was surrounded by nurses who were all hard at work over me, an injection here, a thermometer there. I was alive, ha ha, like in the movies, the hero is saved at the last moment because the water overflowed and went out under the door, so they called reception and bang! I hadn't checked out after all, I was saved.

Soon afterwards Walter came and said: I understand why you did it, but you must resist. It doesn't matter what you and I do, what matters is them, the thousands of people who believe in us, don't you understand . . . ? Those eyes filled with questions, those people with broken lives who look trustingly to us. It's them, damn it! They will save us and they will give us redemption, because they believe in us! You have to be strong and take care. Yes, I said, and closed my eyes. When I opened them again he was gone.

Two weeks later I left the hospital. Jessica drove me in silence to the airport and from there we flew with two nurses in another Falcon, hired specially for me. I was moved by that, my friends; we traveled in complete silence, with me looking at the clouds that seemed like whirlpools in the air and thinking about what had happened, and forgive me if I wax a little lyrical here, but it's just that wanting your own death is something that calls everything into question, because if life is the most precious gift, how is it possible that a person can choose to throw it away? and so I asked myself the most difficult question of all, my friends, which is, what makes life worth living? Walter's words lodged themselves in my tired brain and from there opened fire: it's them, it's their faith that's going to save us.

When I arrived, Walter held a private service in my honor; he never used the word "suicide" but "accident," and kept repeating the expression "the fragility of life" and also that "life sometimes gets away from us."

Time passed, and I continued to distance myself from the house and stayed in my cabin, and the really paradoxical thing was that Walter started to visit me at night. I can't get to sleep, José, he'd say, tell me what you're reading, and he'd sit down on the floor, and I'd read him poems by St John of the Cross, the greatest of all, and by St Teresa and Sister Juana Inés de la Cruz and of course by Abbot Marchena and Góngora, and he'd listen in complete silence, not saying a word, not breathing, not moving any part of his face, nothing, it was as if he wasn't really there, which at the beginning sent a shiver down my spine but which I eventually got used to. At other times he'd cry, also in silence. The way somebody who's understood something very profound cries, or somebody who's moved by a beautiful or noble gesture, I don't know what exactly Walter understood as he listened to me reading poems, I never asked him, although he must have found something important in it; at the crack of dawn he'd go back to his tower, but his spirit was still tormented, I'd see him pacing back and forth up there, going around and around in circles, as if he was writing a message with his body, the answer to a question I didn't know and neither did he, my dear friends, I know this is all a bit obscure but that's the way it was and that's the only way I can tell it.

One day Walter decided to hire someone to write down his words and the ideas that cropped up in meetings with his parishioners. The idea had come to him one day in the Carruthers Bookstore on Hopalong Street and Quincy Drive downtown, where he saw a book with a blue cover entitled *My Lives*, by L. Ron Hubbard, the founder of Scientology. He looked through it and decided to buy it, not because he believed in Scientology but to see how it was put together, at least that was what he told me, because clearly an idea was going around in his head; then we went to the Big Kahuna on Atlantic Square to have a burger, and after leafing through the book for a while he said, don't you think my ideas on life and salvation ought to be written down?

that way they'll survive if the Father decides to take me, what do you think? My feet turned cold when I heard him. It was the first time I'd heard him talk about his own death.

The idea was a good one, so I made a few inquires and found an unemployed writer, a guy from the north of Colombia who wrote essays for the students at the Faculty of Letters at the university; his name was Estiven Jaramillo and his job would be to go with Walter when he met the people and write down what he said. Miss Jessica and Jefferson looked at him incredulously and didn't seem at all pleased, among other things because this poor Estiven, I have to say, had a few problems, including one particularly bad one of a physical nature, a spectacular disproportion between the huge size of his head and the limbs of his body, like those human dolls you see at the entrance to toy shops with pumpkins or watermelons on their shoulders, but this was on the physical level, because on the intellectual level Estiven was tremendously tough and he demonstrated as much right from the start in the quality of the notes he made.

In this way, he was also helping himself, because from what he said he'd had to leave Colombia in a hurry. As a result of a series of articles on the laboratories maintained by the guerrillas in a number of areas of that long-suffering country, they put a bomb in his car, to be detonated when he started it, but as so often happens in movies, it was his wife and two children who were blown up.

The first day Walter brought Estiven's notes to my cabin and we read them out loud, and they were really good! The next day we did the same and so on for several nights until Walter asked me to be the official editor, the one who would take a chisel or a fountain pen to Estiven's notes, O.K.? That was the start, my friends, of what we might call "my vocation" for writing books; at the same time a kind of mystique about the affairs of the Ministry was reborn, something I'd almost completely lost. I threw myself into the work. The texts were good, they convincingly conveyed the greatness of the message in a few words; each section had a narrative thread that made it both easy to follow and educational. Imagine what that meant for me, I'd only recently tried to slit my wrists, and now I was writing a book. Christ must really be great, no kidding. It was like an award for my fascination with books, because after the Big Enchilada and His son books were what I loved the most, those parallelepipeds of paper that had given me a past and even a future. So I asked Walter, how much freedom do I have to rewrite and interpret? and he said, complete freedom, a hundred percent, you were my first disciple and you know what I do better than anyone, the only reason I didn't ask you to make the notes was because I didn't think I had the right to do so, and I think I made the correct decision, because this book has to be the work of at least three heads, Estiven's and yours being more cultivated and mine the one that advances blindly, like a submarine without lights at the bottom of the sea, following the inspiration that the Big Boss whispers in my ear when I encounter a wretched soul, like a mystical Doppler effect, an impulse that comes and goes, indicating distance, but when it returns is enriched by the space it has traveled, the speed of whoever hears it, and, who knows, even by its own ideas; let's make a great book that'll be a summary of our work, the final achievement of the Ministry and both our lives, friend, that was what he said and again I sensed a cloud laden with dark premonitions. He clenched his fist, raised it and knocked it against mine, which is the way people greet each other in the Caribbean, fist to fist and fist to the heart, that was how Walter said goodbye before going to his tower, and outside it was raining, just like in a movie, and as he was happy he raised his arms into the lines of water and let them hit him for a while, maybe with the idea of purifying himself; it was very beautiful to see him there, with the water streaming down his armpits, falling from his jaw and his fingers. That night, my friends, I almost believed in him again.

Jessica and Jefferson still regarded Estiven with suspicion. To them he was an intruder who had Walter's full attention with something they were excluded from, and in addition, I insist on this, there was the whole physical thing, not only that big head due to water on the brain, but also a lack of carburation in one of his digestive organs, because every time he opened his mouth his breath absolutely reeked, it was like lifting the lid off a container of organic waste, which was why Jefferson, who was sensitive to men's smells, him being a faggot and all that, and Jessica, who in spite of her religious dedication had already given signs that she was still a hundred per-cent woman when it came to sex, despised him and found him disgusting and made passing comments to win over the others against him, which must have been quite hard to bear, but Estiven must have been really needy because he stood all the joking in spite of the fact that nobody ever offered him a glass of Coke or a meat pie or a piece of the cake made by Felicity, the black cook. He seemed used to all that kind of thing, as if he'd seen it all before. On one occasion he went into a drugstore at night and as he approached the cash desk the owner was waiting for him with a sawn-off shotgun, aiming it at his chest and saying, get out of here, you fucking thief, and don't come back! and other people shouted, can't you read? no pets allowed, out! But I liked him and admired his work, and apart from that, as he was from Magangué he talked like us, the friends of the immortal Caribbean, a man from the land of reggaeton and champeta and vallenato, a man who, like me, had been overtaken by life but was still pedaling, with the wind and everything else against him, the wind and life and the world in general, and there he was, floating like a turd or a log in this Babylon of the Caribbean.

As I've already said, he had a good ear for getting convincing phrases out of Walter's words. He was able to put in prose what he said in his dialogues; at the end of the afternoon he'd tell me what he'd done and then I'd take over and make a fair copy, correcting and adding, intensifying this effect or polishing that idea so that the whole thing was harmonious and the basic message shone through even more, which really opened my eyes, until one day, going over the text, I had the brilliant idea of turning it back into dialogues, a traditional way of conveying knowledge; when that idea came to me my eyes filled with tears and I said to myself, José, you son of a bitch, you've just given birth, for the first time in your damned life, to a good idea, a fucking brilliant idea! you're going to be the Plato to the new Socrates! What an opportunity!

With Walter's approval, I set to work. I gave each section a separate heading, like *Conversation with an Angel on 47th Street*, or *Answers to a Disciple with AIDS*, a kind of mixture of the classical and the contemporary; and I organized everything by theme: drugs, poverty, violence, abuse, prostitution . . . My head started flying like a falcon that's been let loose: a dialogue with three Caribbean girls selling their bodies I entitled *The Open Legs of Latin America*, and a conversation with a black neighborhood leader *Sad Song for the Great-Grandchildren of Kunta Kinte*. I was overcome with lyricism, my friends, and as I worked I became aware of how technically complex the whole process was, and so one evening, after getting the go-ahead from our financial controller, in other words, Miss Jessica, I set off with a couple thousand dollars to buy a computer, an Apple Mac that I installed in my cabin, a big screen, and as a screensaver I of course chose a sunset over the Caribbean, and I began to pound the keyboard, convinced that I was dealing with something really big.

I soon came to one of the greatest dilemmas: the title. I thought and thought for several days until it came to me: *Encounters with Amazingly Normal People*, and so I put it on the draft. As was to be expected, Walter approved it, and I continued with the process. Later I had to deal with the question of what I call "hot and cold writing," in other words, the way you perceive the writing as you're doing it and the way you see it after being away from it for a few hours, when the words get cold and you can look calmly at what you did, and think about the distance between that result and the impression you had as you were doing it in the heat of the moment. It's like the casting of the metal in the making of bells, as you see in the film *Andrei Rublev*, by old Tarkovsky: the tone and appearance of a cast when you put the molten steel in the mold is very different than its final form, when it's cooled down, and the same goes for words: when they're a flow of lava descending from the cerebral cortex to the fingers they have an shiny appearance that blinds and flatters, but their true face is the one they acquire hours later, when the smoke clears and you can see them by the light of day; they're never as radiant as they were before, and you dither and feel lost and go back to the beginning, you stand back and redo it or give it all up and are left with the empty space that's the silence of writing and which, as in music, has its own value, that's the way it is, my brothers, but anyway, let's carry on with the story.

Walter started having highs and lows again, sometimes he was euphoric and then he'd plunge into a deep depression and wouldn't come down from his tower for three or four days. Those were the years that biographies dismiss in a couple of lines, but as you know, life happens every day and we can't always be on the crest of the wave, until we come to that chapter in which lives rush through a gorge that quickly leads to the void, sometimes to death and very rarely to happiness, in fact almost never.

Oh, my friends, my dear friends, maybe we need a little fresh air here, so let's remember the story of that man who made himself wings with feathers stuck on with wax and started to fly, higher each time, and having seen the world so much from above cherished the fantasy of dominating it, because from up there it looked like something he could hold in his hands, a loose stone, a bottle top, and he dreamed of reaching the gods, he continued rising and rising, friends, and when he got to the top of the sky his wings went all to hell, the wax melted and down he plummeted, free fall without a net. Let this serve as an introduction to what follows, in metaphorical terms, even though the beginning of the end for the Ministry of Mercy was an unexpected visit, a man in suit and tie who came to the gate and asked, does the Reverend Walter de la Salle live here?

Jefferson looked him up and down curiously and said, meetings with parishioners are over for the day, and he turned away, but the guy stopped him and said, wait, that's not why I'm here, come closer, and took out a shiny police badge, I'd like you to tell me your name, seeing as we're here; Jefferson turned pale and said, my name's Jefferson, I haven't done anything. The officer adopted a forceful tone and said, cool it, nigger, I'm not saying you've done anything, I was only asking for your name, O.K.? and he said again, Jefferson Lafayette, I work here; O.K., Jefferson, we're doing fine, the next thing I'm going to ask is even simpler, open the fucking door and call Reverend Walter right now! you think you can do that, nigger? Jefferson let him through and ran to the house.

The detective had come for information. They'd arrested a minor with six thousand dollars in bills buying crack on Meridien Island and when they questioned him he'd mentioned the Ministry. Then he'd retracted his statement and his parents were adamant that the boy was being rehabilitated thanks to the Ministry, but the whole thing sounded fishy. In the course of his investigation, the detective had heard a rumor that Walter hired minors for private parties. There was no actual accusation, but he wanted to take a look around and see if he could figure out how these rumors had started.

Tall stories, detective, said Walter on receiving him, you can't imagine the number of people who envy my success; more than one jealous pastor would love to see my Ministry in ruins, but they won't, detective, because the work we do doesn't belong to me but to all the people who believe in it, and nobody will ever able to bring it down, do you understand me?

Absolutely, said the detective, that's what I'm trying to avoid with this visit, I've seen your TV show and I'll tell you something, my wife believes you're the son of God, and she really believes it, is it true? I mean, are you really the son of God? Walter looked straight at him and replied: I'm a son of the God of those who believe in me, officer, will that do? No, replied the man, unfortunately not, I'd like to see your property, may I? it isn't an inspection, only a visit. Go ahead, said Walter, we don't have anything to hide.

They went to the communal rooms and the refectory, the kitchen and the garage. Then they came to my cabin and when he saw me the detective asked, is this one of your apostles? Nobody laughed at the joke and I showed him my papers. He took them to the window to look at them in the light and said: former inmate of Moundsville, eh? you're certainly living in style now . . . He looked through the bookshelves, grabbed *The Odyssey* and said, very good book, yes sir, which of you has read it? He flipped through the pages, as if shuffling cards, and put it back in its place. He was looking for something, that was obvious. Returning to the garden, he looked up and said, what's in that tower?

Jessica, alerted by Jefferson, had already cleaned the place.

My God, reverend, what luxury, he said when he saw the white leather couches, the LCD screen, the Jacuzzi with the piped music, the paintings with 3-D images of Christ. I didn't know sons of God lived such a . . . He stopped to think of a word, but it didn't come, so he said, do your followers know you live like this? Walter looked at him and said, do you think there's something reprehensible or inappropriate about that? No, reverend, not in the eyes of the law, but I seem to remember Jesus saying something about the rich and the kingdom of the Lord, I don't remember exactly, I'll have to ask my wife.

You've surprised me, said the detective, as they went back down to the garden, to be honest, your wealth raises a lot of questions in my mind. They walked along the paved path to the street and Walter said, when I feel I need to know what those questions are I'll call you, but for now give my very best regards to your wife. I don't think you're really interested in my questions, replied the detective, but if I were you I'd get a lawyer, I'd hate my wife to miss her favorite show, if you get my meaning, my visit is over, the Miami police department thanks you for your cooperation; then he left without shaking anyone's hand.

That's how things were, my friends, and of course I thought, shit, the hurricane is heading straight for the living room of our house, no doubt about it. The next night, when Walter came to my cabin, I said, what about that thing with the detective? but he dismissed it, it's nothing, José, accusations by the envious, it's that son of a bitch Malik McPercy of the Church of Juliana the Redeemer, because nobody goes to his prayer meetings, or the people at Crisostom Abogalene just around the corner, whose hall is always empty, and I said, that's as may be, but you have to be careful about what you do, Walter, they have us in their sights and we mustn't give them ammunition; but he said, if something happens I'll know how to defend the Ministry and everyone, don't worry, how's our book going?

A few days later Walter asked me a strange question: do you have a bank account? I looked at him in surprise and said, of course not, why would I want something like that? I have everything I need right here, and he said, go with Jessica and open an account, I'll give you instructions, don't contradict me, I want you to be paid for the work you've done on the book, which is really excellent; Estiven has already had something and I want you to have the same as him, it's only fair, don't refuse, I won't take no for an answer. I opened the account and Jessica put in two thousand dollars, but I said to her, I'll never touch that money, never, and she replied, do whatever you like, it's yours, I'm just following Walter's suggestions.

I sent the book to a publishing house with a financial proposition, and three months later we received the galley proofs, which Walter and Estiven and I read out loud in my cabin. There were 987 pages, to which I decided to add a very brief history of the Ministry and a basic chronology of Walter's life. Then came the question of the cover. My first suggestion, my friends, was a photograph of Walter during one of his services, showing him kneeling, bare-chested, and the congregation making the sign of the cross, but he said, no, José, I don't want the book to be about me, I'm only an emissary, I communicate with something that's already in the people, the nest where God resides; I know you mean well, but it can't be a photograph of me. Miss Jessica suggested a photograph of the Chapel of Mercy the Living God and, with all the crosses in the vault lit up and looking really beautiful, but again he said no, we mustn't ape the vanity of the church of Rome, and he opted for a photograph of a slum neighborhood with a group of black teenagers playing basketball, a Dodge Dart with flat tires, a drugstore on a corner, and three people sitting on the sidewalk in an expectant attitude; to one side of the picture a man in a sweater is talking to a woman who's been beaten up, and in spite of the fact that the man has his back to us and is wearing a hood we sense that he's somebody special and that he's giving solace to the woman, who's only just stopped crying and is starting to give a timid smile in spite of her bruised cheeks and the dried blood on her nose. Her expression is what the cover is all about, my friends, and finally we came to the last subject, which was how to distribute it among the parishioners, whether or not we should charge them, because obviously the Ministry was buying twenty thousand copies from the publisher, which was why they'd agreed to publish it immediately.

Again Miss Jessica gave her opinion, saying, we have to charge something to cover our costs; if we give it away people won't attach the same value to it, after all, they buy Bibles, don't they? In the end it was decided to give it away free to those members who contributed more than five hundred dollars a month, and we all agreed. To everyone else, it would sell for thirteen dollars, and I won't even tell you how much of a fuss it caused. The book had to be reprinted several times because we didn't have enough copies, and Walter was reborn. Excellent reviews appeared in the *Miami Herald* and other local newspapers, he gave long interviews on radio and TV, and we reached a hundred thousand copies, which was incredible; I was prouder than I'd ever been in my life, it was as if that object of a thousand pages was a child that other people appreciated and read, and that gained widespread recognition, but that I'd modestly helped to create.

Every joy has its danger, my friends, believe me, because after this resounding success those who were against us now took our good fortune personally and brought out the heavy artillery; I don't know what he'd been paid, but one of the black faggots who came to Walter's parties started spilling the beans, describing those parties to a newspaper, without skipping anything: the lines of coke, the poppers, the whiskey, and of course the sex, and the problem was that the boy was a minor.

Soon the detective showed up again, this time with a search warrant and six of his colleagues, but we were able to get out of things thanks to the Italian lawyers. A large check is a great help, a small check is a small help, so we settled for half, O.K.? The boy's mother withdrew her complaint and everybody went home happy, but the next month there were two more accusations, one of them with recordings and cell phone photographs where you could see everything. The family told the Sicilians they'd drop everything for two million dollars, but Walter wouldn't agree, going into one of his trances, which I'd once thought were mystical but now didn't know what the hell they were or where they came from, and saying, I'll protect everyone, there's nothing to fear. Three days later, the next accusations fell like a meteor shower. The parents of six boys asked for millions in compensation for the abuse to their minors, presenting sworn statements, photographs, and videos. There was nothing we could do about it and the scandal blew up in the press.

The police came to take Walter away. It was a massive operation, they closed the neighboring streets, a helicopter flew over the house, and of course there were TV crews outside to film the arrest live. Large numbers of police officers took shelter behind the wall and the one who seemed to be in charge took out a loud-hailer and said, Reverend Walter de la Salle, please come out with your hands up, along with everyone else in the house.

I was watching it all that from my cabin, thinking, what a ridiculous spectacle! it isn't as if we're murderers! I opened the door to go toward where the police were, but at that moment I heard a series of shots, and I cried out, don't shoot, they're coming out! Much to my surprise, dear friends, the shots were coming from the top of the tower and one of the police officers was writhing wounded on the asphalt.

I threw myself on the ground and closed my eyes, and my head turned into a swarm of questions, or rather dilemmas or aporias, shall I go to where Walter is, stand by his side and resist until they shoot us down? should I go out and try to negotiate with the police, act as a mediator? go back to my cabin until the commotion dies down? Another burst of shots distracted me, and in a second I saw destruction hovering over us. My vision had come back, my brothers, my listeners, the one I'd dreamed some time earlier: the image of a monk leading a group of hooded men through a destroyed city; rubble, dead bodies, twisted metal, ash in the air, tongues of fire.

I crawled back to the cabin, because by now it was impossible to get near the house. The shots were tearing up the tiled floor of the patio and making holes in the walls; there was a shower of glass, tiles, red stone. The firing was concentrated on the tower, where there was fierce resistance, and I thought, what fools, there's no way they can win, they ought to come out; I was still thinking that when I saw one of the gates of the garden open. Jessica was waving a white flag and coming out with a group: Felicity, two gardeners, and a driver; then Jefferson came out, wounded in one arm, and finally the bodyguards, but Walter wasn't among them. They were all handcuffed and bundled into a van, but as the police moved toward the house more shots came from the tower.

He wants to die, I thought, he wants them to kill him like Christ; the response from outside was a violent one, and a minute later the first floor was in flames, with tongues of fire coming out through the windows and rising toward the tower. A SWAT team got in the house and a tanker truck put out the fire. By now, the shooting had stopped. After a while they signaled that they'd searched everywhere, but hadn't found him, so the alert continued; and now comes the strangest part, my friends, which is that after the search not a trace of Walter's body was found, not a cell or a print, nothing at all. He'd vanished into thin air.

That was when I finally left my cabin, with my hands behind my head. Before they could throw me to the ground, the detective stopped them, and said, let him go, he can help us. He put his arm around my shoulders and said, now then, José, your name is José, isn't it, now why don't you tell me where the hell the secret passages and hiding places are in this house, I don't want to have to pull it to pieces but that's exactly what I'll do if I don't find him in, let's say, an hour, do I make myself clear? Yes, detective, but believe me, I don't know any passages or hiding places, this house was built long before the Ministry took it over.

They put me in the van with the others and sat me down next to Jessica. Where is he? I whispered, and she said in my ear, I don't know, he ordered us to leave and said, I'll stay here and pray to the Lord, you go, and that was the last I saw of him.

This happened twelve years ago, my dear friends. The police never found Walter, dead or alive, despite a thorough search that involved the blueprints of the complex, scanning devices, drills, and so on. All the furniture was carefully taken to pieces, but nothing was found. They questioned Jessica and me for weeks, but in the end they had to let us go; the body-guards and Jefferson, on the other hand, they put back in prison.

So it was that one day Jessica and I met on Sylvester Road, soon after we were released, and I said, what do we do now? She replied that she wouldn't do anything. I know Walter's alive and will look for me, so I'll wait for him. I looked her in the eyes and saw again the young woman from all those years earlier. I gave her a kiss on the cheek and walked away, saying: if he comes back, he'll make sure we all get together again.

I didn't know what to do or where to go, but then remembered the bank account, so I went to the branch to withdraw a few dollars and have a bite to eat while I cleared my mind. At the window a surprise was waiting for me: the balance was three million dollars! Walter, what a fucking bastard you are, what a piece of shit. I took out five thousand bills. A little way along the street there was a not too dirty hotel, the Stardust

Inn. I went in and took a room. I asked for a chicken sandwich and a Diet Coke, what could I hope for? I looked at the scars on my veins and thought, now would be the perfect time to do it, but maybe it'd be better to wait until morning. Besides, the sandwich was good. I took out the bills and laid them out on the bedspread, took my clothes off and filled the bathtub. I immersed myself in the water with the can of Coke and took a few sips. Outside, night was falling. Then I closed my eyes and went to sleep.

7.
THE MAN WHO GOT AWAY

J osé Maturana slumped forward across the table, with tears in his eyes, and was immediately buried beneath an avalanche of applause. It was strange to see him with his long gray mane of hair, his unkempt beard and his tough guy tattoos, so moved by his own words; he stood up, took a few steps toward the proscenium and gave a simple bow that earned him more applause, in fact a standing ovation. I was impressed and, to say the least, inhibited; could my text hope to arouse a fraction of this enthusiasm? of course not . . . mine was supposed to last no more than twenty minutes, the time that, according to the form, every speaker was allotted, but Maturana had spoken for nearly an hour, although I had not kept count. What was more, his talk had not been read but improvised, which was an amazing feat, something only a real professional could have achieved. I again looked for his biography in the form that the ICBM had given out at the door, but the information was the same, and extremely concise: nothing on his childhood and nothing on the years since the end of the Ministry of Mercy. There was not even any mention of something as simple as his country of residence, was he still living in Miami or somewhere else in the United States? The dossier mentioned that he had published other books under a variety of pseudonyms, and there was no photograph.

I left the lecture hall trying to digest what I had heard and saw that there were other activities going on in the side rooms. In one, the poet from Benin and president of the Circle of

African Poets, Joseph Olalababa Jay, was speaking; at the end of the corridor, in an adjoining hall, the round table *Concentric Circles of Modernity* was in progress, chaired by Professor Aparajit Chattoppadhyay from Jawaharlal Nehru University in Delhi. But I kept going. What with the ravages of the previous night's alcohol and Maturana's words, my head was overloaded; better to look for a place to be alone, in silence, so I went down to one of the inner gardens of the hotel.

It was like stepping back in time.

The path that wound past the bushes was of sandstone, like many of the buildings in this part of the city. I sat down on a bench and watched a robin peck at a puddle of water, then a dragonfly. I remembered my days in the mountains, my long, long soliloquies with the stones, the dragonflies, and the robins. There was a certain language in things, a language that had spoken to me in those days. Now I tried to hear it again, but my ears were as hard as stone. Standing by one of the ornamental fountains was a short man with a gray beard. As I passed him, he turned and said, are you the writer? His accent sounded familiar so I asked, Kaplan? Yes, he said, I'm Kaplan, pleased to meet you, it's nice to find a fellow countryman in such a remote place, come, let's walk together for a while, I think there are orchids along that path.

The war that is destroying this place has deep roots, he said, so unlike our sad war. I told him that I had been outside the country for a long time and that I had been ill, but Kaplan replied, it isn't necessary to keep up to date, it's the same war that's been going on for forty years, or is it fifty? Things never change: boundless ambition, rivers of blood, hatred, ignorance; I wanted to know if he had been a direct victim, and he said, come, let's carry on as far as that fountain and I'll tell you the story.

My family is from the city of Armenia, in the department of Quindío. We're Jews. For a hundred years we've been in the clothing and wholesale fabric business, and we've done well, with branches in Medellín, Pereira, Cali, and Bogotá. Kaplan's Tailors, maybe you've seen some of our advertisements. Three hundred employees and a seven-story building in Armenia. A hundred stores throughout the country. The work of four generations, because the first Kaplan arrived in Colombia in 1894, from Polish Galicia; he escaped to avoid military service and got on a ship he was told was going to America. South America, as it turned out. Seven years later, he went back to Poland to fetch his wife, and with her he opened his first tailor's shop. Three generations have passed since then, we're Colombians. The problem started in the middle of the year 2001. The paramilitaries of Quindío started sending us messages: we had to pay them a large sum of money every month in return for protection; we said no, no thanks, we're peaceful people, we provide work and progress, we don't have enemies. We told them we didn't think it was right to give money to murderers. We're Jews and we can't deal with murderers. A family meeting was called, us three brothers and our brother-in-law, and we confirmed our decision; there will be consequences, we said, but we just have to keep firm; they asked for money again and again we said no. What they were asking us for we spent on bodyguards and bulletproof cars. A couple of months went by until they put a bomb in one of our stores in Pereira, an assistant was killed, and three loaders were seriously wounded. That night they called again and said, you see? you need protection, but we refused. The following month, they attacked my brother Azriel on the highway to Medellín, fortunately he was in a bulletproof car with three bodyguards. One of the paras died, and that was the start of the war. The family met again and we said, we need to be stronger, redouble our security, buy weapons, be prepared. Our brother-in-law went farther: I have contacts in Israel, they can help us, but I said: let's wait.

It was distressing not knowing where the next blow would come from, like protecting yourself from a mosquito in the dark. We spoke to the police but they couldn't do anything; they said they'd increase their patrols, tap our phones, have people followed. They didn't do a thing and one day the attack came. A car bomb on the building in Armenia; it destroyed the first three floors and left nine people dead, innocent people who were just passing by. We met again and took the decision: part of the family would go to New York and Tel Aviv, and we brothers would stay in Armenia and fight. Reason was on our side, we thought, God would have to help us. I made inquiries and found out the names of some politicians who were friends of the paras. I summoned them to a restaurant and said to them, why are the paras treating us like this? don't we pay taxes and create work? don't we deserve respect? But the politicians said: you're businessmen, hardworking and honest, you should support them; the paras are defending the businessmen and the hardworking families of this country. I said: we don't need that kind of protection, we have to respect our history, haven't you ever heard of the Holocaust? we can't negotiate with murderers, we're Jews. The politicians looked at us gravely and said, we'll study the case and pass it on, of course all that comes at a price, but you can pay it, you're wealthy; I said: aren't you elected by the people? you already have salaries, that's your income, why should I pay you? They looked at me in surprise and their expressions gradually began to decompose; first a soft laugh, then a noisy peal of laughter that distorted their faces, turned their cheeks red, inflamed their eyes. One of them said, you're funny, you know, do all Jews have such a good sense of humor? You really are very funny, said another, wiping away his tears of laughter. They took a few seconds to recover their composure. Good, said the one who seemed to be their leader, now seriously, the day after tomorrow we'll tell you how much our mediation is worth and then you can decide, but I can tell you right now that it's advisable to accept because this country is becoming very unsafe, with all those guerrillas everywhere, cooperate with the country in which you've made money, show some solidarity. The other politicians stood up saying, yes, it's highly advisable, give that to Colombia, be patriots even though you're foreigners, don't be such bastards. Before they went out, they threw a piece of paper on the table. We've left you the check, to accustom you to being friendly: a bottle of Buchanan's and some meat snacks, you kept us waiting a long time; and six Absolut with tonic because the fat man is well-bred and only drinks vodka, not much for you, Mr. Kaplan. But I stood up and left without paying.

A week later, they asked for thirty million pesos. I didn't even gather the family but said, we won't pay a single peso, you have salaries, the State pays you. Oh, you're a foreigner, you don't understand, but I interrupted and said, no, señor, I'm not a foreigner, and I do understand, I'm not going to pay you a single peso, you or your bosses. The politicians said, oh, then you'll have to face the consequences, and I replied, that's what we plan to do, but you'll also have to take the consequences. I was filled with rage, I had to pray to calm down; then I called my brother-in-law in Tel Aviv, and told him the moment had come; no problem, Moisés, he replied, I'll send somebody. Six people arrived from Israel, bought weapons, and followed the trail from the last messenger all the way up to one of the bosses of Armenia. They grabbed him one night when he was out painting the town red with some girls from Cali, they took him out naked and left him lying in the center with a note that said: *Beware of the Kaplans, get out of town, you have three days.* I thought it would be the last thing I did in the country, when it was over I would go to New York, where I had quite a bit of capital invested. We put the business in the hands of administrators. Colombia was expelling us. We had to get our help from Israel, can you imagine? The one thing worse than losing your country is losing your dignity, and I said, we're going to see this fight through to the end! Four days later, our people grabbed two of the politicians and said, you have a week to leave the Congress and the Senate, whether you like it or not, if not we'll bring you down like rotten fruit.

Two days later, we gathered them together. They weren't so proud now, they wanted to know if we were declaring war on them, but I said: you already declared it, being strong with the weak and weak with the strong. Another asked if the group that had threatened them was ours, and I said, you don't deserve a reply, they're soldiers of God, aren't you believers? A third one tried to reconcile us: Señor Kaplan, we understand your case and we could intercede without charging you, but you have to assure us of your goodwill; I replied: we don't want your understanding or your clemency, you had the chance and missed it . . . Get out of here, you sons of bitches!

That evening, my brother and I left the country. I felt angry and very sad. God willing I can go back some day, I dream of the mountains of Quindío, the smell of the coffee plantations and the wet earth. From that moment I devoted myself first to reading biographies, and then to writing them.

He approached an orchid, sniffed it and said: hmm, it's the smell of the country we've just been talking about. I moved my nose closer but could not smell anything. Then I asked him: and what happened to the politicians? He looked at me slyly and said, well, that's another story, I'll tell it the next time we meet, which I hope will be very soon. He walked to the gate of the garden, stopped, turned, and said: of course you know that tomorrow I give my talk, did you see it on the program? I hadn't seen it, but I said, of course, Señor Kaplan, are you going to tell your story? No, he said. I'm going to tell a similar story.

On returning to the coffee shop, I saw Marta. Although she was talking on her cell phone, I assume to her newspaper, because she was taking notes, she signaled to me to come over. She hung up and said, hi, speak of the devil, I was just talking about you to the arts editor and we're in luck, he doesn't know you but he's agreed to an article about you, his idea is for a long article that illustrates the current situation of midrange writers, the moderately successful ones compared with the bestsellers, what do you think? it would come out in the Saturday supplement as one of the items connected with the ICBM.

I thought about it, then said, are you sure that's a literary subject? publishers would have much more to say on the subject, they're the ones who classify their authors depending on their sales, why don't you ask Ebenezer Lottmann, from Tiberias? I think that would make for a better article. She sat there for a moment, staring out at something in the garden, and said: O.K., I suggest another, the situation of the writer in Latin America, how about that? Oh, that's been done to death, I said, but she retorted, you don't think that in Iceland we spend our lives reading Latin American novels, do you? you may think it's been done to death, but I have to think of my readers. I was not very convinced, so I said, and what does your editor think about that? She looked at me very gravely, looked through her notes and said: for him any subject is fine, provided it reflects the current situation of the committed writer. As I listened to her, I remembered the Icelandic writer Arnaldur Indridason, the author of *Jar City*, and asked her whether in Iceland, mystery novelists were committed to the depiction of reality? She nodded but did not speak. I prefer not to say anything in order not to influence you, what's your opinion? I have opinions on what happens around me and I suppose that shows through in what I write, I said. Marta hesitated, wondering whether or not to take out her recorder, finally decided against it, and said, no, wait . . . I know! It'll be better if I do a article in a literary style, a piece of "new journalism" about the impossibility of interviewing a writer in the middle of a city under siege, how about that? It depends, I said, what's the cause of that impossibility? is it the war or is it you? I don't know, I hope to answer with the article. Do you want to start now? I said, and she said, not really, or maybe yes, but as an exercise, in fact we've already started, let me take a few notes.

I turned my attention to the garden and, right at the end, beyond a stone wall, the image of some distant buildings reminded me of what was happening outside. In all this time I had not heard any explosions, but I assumed that even in wars people do not shoot all the time. I went to one of the balconies and looked at the city—the cube-like sandstone houses, the acacias and jacarandas, the wall, the minarets, the sky filled with crescent moons and towers—through the evening mist.

On the other side of the garden, between the bushes, I saw José Maturana. He was waving his arms in the middle of a group of people. It stuck me that it was going to be very difficult for the next speaker. I noticed that Marta was also watching him and thought: now there's a good subject for her newspaper. I told her that and she asked, do you think it's all true? I don't see any reason to doubt it, it's a story that may seem unusual to us, but in Miami, in those neighborhoods that are like a jungle, it may be the most normal thing in the world, a life like any other. She studied him for a few moments and said, there's something about the way he moves that confuses me, but I still don't know what it is; as I listened to him I had the feeling it must all been have a dream, but I don't know, don't pay any attention to me. I looked again, but Maturana had already gone. Don't you think his scars and tattoos are real? the proof of his story is on his body . . . Marta had already stopped listening to me, she was now taking notes, with great concentration, so I went back to the garden in search of dragonflies and robins.

It was getting toward evening and the delegates were chatting and laughing, some drinking coffee, and others already warming their engines with white wine or beer. I caught the fact that the round table *Tendencies in Autofictional Narrative*, chaired by the Congolese Theophilus Obenga, professor at the Sorbonne, had been a great success. I saw him on the way to the bar and heard him say: "Life is above all a narrative, the truths of reality create very clear links of language, which are then stored in the memory and are transformed into experience." I looked for José Maturana again, but he was not there. Marta, holding a cup of coffee, said to me: I have to get straight down to writing but I don't want to miss dinner, they say there'll be a few words by the honorary president of the ICBM, would it disturb you if I work in your room? Of course not, it's Room 1109, here's the key.

When I was alone, I looked around the throng and spotted Supervielle, so I went up to him and asked him about the afternoon's debate. It was really good, friend, weren't you there? I said no and he started to tell me about it: you know, there's a sentence in Dostoevsky's *Notes from Underground*, which says: "Man is a fickle creature of doubtful reputation, and perhaps, like a chess player, he is more interested in the process of reaching his objective than in the objective itself," I don't know if you remember it . . . I shook my head and Supervielle continued: that's what we were discussing, my friend, that simple yet profound way of reading experience, what drives a person to make one decision and not another at a specific moment? to get off a train, get on a boat, cross the street? What there is at the end of a life is irrelevant, it isn't the result that makes a life exceptional, but the path trodden, am I being excessively obscure? There are great lives that don't get anywhere, but what does it matter? That's not a paradox. I'm reminded of a text by a twelfth-century Persian poet, *The Conference of the Birds,* I assume you don't know it? I did know it, but I preferred not to contradict him. Anyway, it's all about Simorgh, King of the Birds; everyone's looking for him, everyone would like to find him because they believe that when they do they will be better and happier. A group of birds decides to leave for the mountain where the king has his home. They meet with many obstacles along the way and many turn back or die; only a group of thirty noble birds reaches the summit where Simorgh lives, but when they get there they realize that the throne is empty, the King of the Birds doesn't live there but within each one of them, he has their face, his soul is that of a bird wearied by flight, the flight of a bird searching for Simorgh. The story I'm going to tell in my talk is about chess and that kind of life, that's why I don't want to go deeper into this, I don't want to spoil the surprise for you, I assume you'll be there? Of course, Monsieur Supervielle, it will be an honor.

I drank two more coffees as I walked up and down the corridors, hoping that José Maturana would appear, I wanted to congratulate him on his story that morning, about which, of course, I had already made a few notes. To tell the truth, it had overwhelmed me.

Not meeting anybody, I realized I was in one of those pockets of time that are typical of conferences, moments when nothing is happening, so I decided to go up to my room to rest and see what Marta was doing. I knocked at the door several times but nobody opened. Had she left? was she asleep? I asked the cleaner to open it for me. Just as I was about to lie down on the bed, I heard the bathroom door open and Marta came out, stark naked, wrapped in nothing but a cloud of steam. She had a nice body, with smooth white skin, pear-shaped breasts, a shaved pubic area, and a piercing in her vagina, a silver ring through one of her labia.

I thought you'd gone, I said, I knocked but you didn't hear me, wait a minute, I'll go out so you can get dressed in peace. Marta walked past me and bent over her heaped clothes. Don't worry, it doesn't bother me if you see me, does it bother you?

I shook my head. She sat down and lit a cigarette. I asked her about the article, have you written it yet? No, she replied, to tell the truth, I only had a few notes, and I don't know what it was, but they suddenly seemed empty and meaningless, or rather: they didn't have the force I think a true story should have.

She took the towel from her hair and went and hung it on the handle of the bathroom door. Her breasts bobbed up and down as she passed me and I found myself with an erection, which I managed to conceal. From the bathroom she said, and what do you think about this war? I did not reply immediately, not sure of what to say, but she went straight on: or are you one of those pacifists? So I said: it's just one more war, although it could well be a metaphor for all wars, the frustration, the discord, the hatred, the separation; but that's just words, whereas bullets are quite real, they pierce the skin and damage organs, they puncture and maim. The most absurd wars are those that aren't even of any benefit to those who win them, although that doesn't mean there aren't times when it's necessary to fight them. Even knowing full well that nobody will win. There's a perverse logic, a human destiny, that leads to war, and individuals can do nothing to stop it.

As I said this, I recalled images I had seen of the bombing of a church in Colombia with shrapnel-filled gas cylinders, a bombing carried out by the guerillas; I saw the mutilated bodies, the ground soaked with blood, the kind of thing that has been happening for centuries, although you never get used to it; I suddenly found it hard to breathe, and my eyes filled with tears, I was falling into one of those hypersensitive states all too common in convalescents, so I said, I'm sorry, but she came to me and said, cry as much as you want, there's nothing more touching than a man crying; naked as she still was, she embraced me. I was afraid she would become aware of my erection, which was still there, but she did not seem to notice it, only hugged me tighter. One of my tears dripped onto her shoulder, trickled down her back and lodged between her marmoreal buttocks. The scene was like a Pietà, and was interrupted by some cries coming from the corridor; I thought at first that it was my neighbors, embroiled in another argument, but it was not them; these cries were more urgent and desperate, so I broke free of Marta and ran to the door.

A group of male nurses was shouting at the end of the corridor, outside the last room. The cleaner was crying and somebody was consoling her. What was all this? what was happening? Before long, a stretcher appeared. I went closer and saw the blood-drenched bathroom, the body emerging from the tub, lifted by four strong arms. On the pale skin with its ocher reflections I recognized the tattoos, the sun like eye on the inert forearm, the town in the background. It was José Maturana.

I looked at him, incredulous, as they tipped him onto the stretcher, a bag of bones that seemed to have emptied, the skin like a damp cloth, that mysterious diminishing process that operates on lifeless bodies. They had tried to resuscitate him, but to no avail, which was understandable, judging by the vertical gashes on his forearms: anyone who slashes himself like that means business.

I moved aside to let the stretcher pass, then just stood there, unable to move. Marta came out a second after the elevator closed its doors and only saw the end of the funeral cortege. Who was it? what happened? Maturana, I said, he slashed his wrists. Marta opened her eyes wide, what?! She took a couple of steps along the corridor, then turned back and said, this is a bombshell! I have to call my newspaper. She placed a collect call from my room and, by the time she had hung up, her hands were shaking. I only have forty minutes to write an article! I told her what I had seen but she was so busy with the table lamp, switching on her laptop, plugging in the adaptor, that she did not seem to hear me. Then she said, what title should I give it? Let me see, how about something like *Blood at the Conference*? No, she said, don't be so sensationalistic, that'd be fine for a crime report, this is for the arts section, it has to be a bit more poetic. Go ahead and write the article, I said, and then we'll think of something, in the meantime I'm going to have a look around and maybe grab a bite to eat as well. You're lucky, she said, I have to stay here, bring me a chicken sandwich and a Diet Coke. If you see or find out anything call me, O.K.?

As I left the room, I was overcome with an intense feeling of danger. A strange wind was pushing me toward that room at the end of the corridor, the dead man's room. Everyone seemed to have gone. I tapped nervously at the door and went in. The carpet was soaked in water and blood that had overflowed from the bathtub; I saw towels, tiles glowing red, a bathrobe with the hotel's emblem. The bed still bore the imprint of a body. On the table were papers with notes for his talk, and some open books. I picked up one at random and it turned out to be *Encounters with Amazingly Normal People*, by Walter de la Salle. It was dedicated to José: "How absurd, me dedicating your book to you. With love, Walter." There were penciled annotations. On page 267, for example: "The death of the fetus is an invention, a way of talking about the formation of life." On page 347: "The addict is Millie, I changed her age from twenty-five to sixteen to make it more dramatic." On page 560: "Complete passage from an astrological discussion between L. Ron Hubbard and Kaspar Hauser." Maturana was the true author of the book. It was his magnum opus.

Among the other books on the table were works by St John of the Cross, with more scribbled notes in the margins (one said: "This is about the eye I saw"), the complete works of Feijóo, and *The Life of Bartolomé de las Casas* (another annotation at random: "He licked the Indians' sores, why?"). I opened his briefcase and found a folder containing photographs; in one of them, two well-built young men were raising a crucifix in a garden, and on the side someone had written: "Sammy and Jairo in Oakland Road." I shuffled through them quickly until I found one that had the word "Walter" on it: it showed a tall, well-built man, bare-chested, with powerful dorsal muscles and long hair gathered in a ponytail, just like José; in one hand, a crucifix covered in diamonds, and in the other, a microphone; tattoos depicting man's quest for God. I thought of Marta writing in my room, a long way from the real story.

I stood there, looking at Walter's photograph, because there was something in it that held me spellbound; after a while I noticed in the background, in the middle of a group of people standing behind him, a face that looked familiar, a woman, where had I seen her before? I was thinking about this when I heard a noise in the corridor and was immediately on the alert. Somebody had died in this room and sooner or later the police would have to come, so I rushed to the door, and looked out. A police officer was standing there with his back to me, talking on a cell phone, so I slipped out without making a noise.

Downstairs, in the lobby, there was a great deal of agitation. Some police officers were taking notes and the director of the ICBM was making a statement to a TV channel. I caught him saying: ". . . suicide is a mysterious, multifaceted, and very profound choice, an act of supreme freedom whose reasons, of course, we do not know; for the ICBM this is a great loss, and I can announce right now that we will take care of everything, the transportation, the funeral, etc., wherever his nearest and dearest decide."

I went to the dining room, wanting to be alone. In the rush to get out, I forgot to say that I still had the photograph of Walter and the book, *Encounters*, in my jacket. I sat down at one of the tables at the far end, ordered an omelet and a beer, and settled down to read, but as I took out the book a sheet of paper fell out, it was a message on headed hotel notepaper saying: *José, we've found you.* I was stunned, and read it several times. The words boomed in my head like an echo in a cave: *We've fooouuund yooouuu, oouund yoouuu, yoouu!*

The message bore the time, 19:38 that same day. Everything was clear now: Maturana had decided to kill himself after reading it, perhaps because of it, who was it who had found him? I gulped my food down and went back to my room. Marta was drinking a Coke and chatting on Facebook. Seeing me, she cried, did you forget my sandwich? I can't concentrate, damn it, I have less than ten minutes left and I don't even have a title, this is a disaster, I'm just telling a Spanish friend I met on Erasmus all about it . . . Don't write any more, I said, Maturana didn't kill himself.

Marta looked at me incredulously, why do you say that? Look at this, I said, he received it today. Marta looked at the message with intensity and said, and what does this prove? It proves this is all very strange, don't you think? At that moment the telephone rang and Marta said, it's my newspaper, can you answer for me? tell them I'm doing an interview, and that I need more time. I lifted the receiver and gave the excuse, but they said, we're getting the news on the wire, so it's covered, just tell her to write us a good article for tomorrow. That solved everything. I showed her the book and the photograph and Marta said, good, let's get to work, where do we start? I'll help you on one condition, which is that you let me tell the story. I accepted and said: we have to start with the message, find out who sent it, the operator who gave it to Maturana may know.

We went down to the lobby, where, in spite of the fact that it was one in the morning, the agitation continued. We went to the offices where the switchboard operator worked, and found a young woman there. I asked her if she had been on duty at

19:38, and she said no, she had started at 21:00. Are you the only people who take messages for the guests? No, she said, another guest or a visitor can leave messages at reception, in which case it doesn't go through the switchboard. Who distributes the messages to the rooms? One of the bellhops from the main lobby, she said. And is there a register of those messages? Yes, there's a book with the destination and time of each one. I looked at her, pleased. Good, then you may be able to help me, was there any message at 19:38? The woman asked for my name and room number, then she took out a book and, making sure we did not sneak a look, turned the page. Can you confirm your room number? 1109, I said. She hesitated. There was a message at that time, but it wasn't for you, you could ask my colleague tomorrow, were you expecting an urgent message? Yes, I said, very urgent, there may have been a mix-up over the room number, can't you call your colleague? The woman was silent for a moment then said: I can't call him, he's working right now. If it's very urgent you can find him at the Bamboo, near Rehavia. His name is Mordechai but everyone calls him Momo.

We thanked her and went out onto the street.

The Bamboo was a modern-looking bar, full of mirrors, indirect lighting, wooden recesses. We sat down at the counter to be close to the staff; it was really strange to see a place like this in the middle of a siege. Three young men were serving: one making cocktails, another taking them to the tables and bringing the orders, and the third taking the money. Put your intuition to work, I said to Marta, which one do you think is our man? She asked for a Herradura tequila, downed it in one, asked for a second tequila, and said: give me ten minutes, if I'm wrong you can ask me for anything you want. Anything I want? Yes, a blow job, money, whatever you want, just let me concentrate.

When the ten minutes were over, she said: that one over

there. She pointed to a young man of about twenty-five, Caucasian in appearance, perhaps of Slav descent. She went to the other end of the counter to talk to him and came back after a while. I'm never wrong, she said, he's Momo. How did you know? It's something I've had since I was a child, I look at people for a while and suddenly I know who they are, as simple as that. I was amazed: I didn't know you had powers, what else can you do? She gave a wicked laugh and said: many things, but you lost your bet. I ordered another double whiskey and said, did you tell him what we want? should I go and talk to him? Marta smiled smugly. He'll come to us, but he's already given me a lead: the message was left by a woman of about thirty-five in a long distance call, he doesn't know where from, because he didn't look at the caller ID. I wanted to know what her method was for obtaining so much information in such a short time and she said, the oldest and most traditional method of all, I asked him and he told me, and I'll tell you something else, he'll answer every question I ask him, I could smell his pheromones, he wants to fuck me and because of that he'll tell the truth. I was stunned and said, can you always smell that smell? and she replied: always. It's another of my powers.

Within a short time, most of the tables were empty and Momo came over to talk to us. The man you took the message to killed himself, I said immediately, just to see his reaction. He became nervous and said, I didn't take it to him, there's a bellhop who slips the messages under the doors, do you know why he did it? did he leave a note or anything? was it because of the message? who are you? I told him I was a friend of the dead man and a delegate at the conference, and asked him, could you describe the woman who left the message from her voice? Momo closed his eyes for a moment and said: I know enough about women to assume she's thirty-five, single, an only child or maybe the eldest child . . . Marta interrupted him, an only child or maybe the eldest child? how do you know that? It's easy, replied Momo, she doesn't hesitate, she has a naturally authoritarian manner; when I asked her to dictate the message she did it in a very sharp way, as if she was saying it to me: "We've found you." I can still hear the words in my head, my God, I'm not surprised he killed himself, who was he, another delegate? Yes, I said, it's strange that somebody should decide to do that so suddenly, after a success like the one he had with his talk in the morning. Momo shrugged and said, it's sudden for us, but maybe not for him; by the way, I almost forgot to tell you that the woman had called before, three times, she seemed really desperate to speak to him; she even asked to have the call transferred to the restaurant, it's strange, she had to speak to him as soon as possible but she didn't want to leave her name; when I asked her she said, that's all you need, write it down just as I say it, thank you, and hung up. What Momo was giving us was worth its weight in gold. I asked: how did you know it was a long-distance call if you didn't look at the caller ID? She told me herself when she called the first time, she wanted me to know how urgent it was and she said: this is a long-distance call, please try to find him; you could look at the caller ID, which has a memory, but that's confidential information and we aren't authorized to give it out to guests.

Somebody called Momo and he excused himself. Marta said to me, do you still think somebody killed him? It's a possibility, I said, that phrase "we've found you," could be taken several ways: we've been looking for you, you've been running away, you owe us something, you have to pay, why did you do it, all that time ago, you betrayed us, you hid from us, all kinds of things. But the basic question is a simple one, who are "we"? Marta polished off her drink in one go and said, well, after hearing his story it seems pretty obvious that "we" are the people from that Ministry, don't you think? maybe the guru didn't die, maybe things were very different than the way Maturana told it. It's possible, Marta, it's very possible, the next thing we have to do is gain access to the caller ID and see the memory, the number must have been recorded. As we were about to leave, Momo came and said, I've just remembered something else: the guest in that room, the one who killed himself, called the operator twice during the afternoon and asked if there'd been any messages for him, and when he was told there hadn't he insisted, not even any calls without a message? and I told, him, no sir, not even without a message, so it's obvious the poor man knew they were looking for him and was expecting to hear from them.

Another notable thing happened that night.

As we were on our way out of the Bamboo, we heard a voice from an inside table, somebody calling out Marta's name; she turned and cried: Bryndis! It was Bryndis Kiljan, the war correspondent for her newspaper in Iceland. When we were introduced, Bryndis said: I know and love your country, oh, Colombia! it has the most cruel and unnecessary war of any I've seen in the world and therefore the stupidest, I'm sorry if I say it as I see it . . . If it wasn't for the number of people killed, it would be laughable. She was with other journalists, they were drinking iced vodka. Bryndis had just come back from the front and was exhausted. She said: all I want to do is drink and cause a great scandal. They obviously had a lot to talk about, so I preferred to leave them to it and went back to the hotel.

The next day, I went to the switchboard operator's office. At that hour the person on duty was an older man who looked at me with great reluctance when I asked to check the caller ID. I'm a delegate at the conference, I said, and I need to check something quickly, can I? The caller ID isn't at the disposal of the guests, if you give me your room number I can tell you the source of the calls you've received, and I'll send you a message about it, that's all I can do. I thought to give him Maturana's number, but the deception would be obvious immediately, he did not look stupid and he must have heard about what had happened the night before. The man was waiting for my answer, so I said, can you please check the calls from the United States, it's code one, the person who was supposed to call didn't know my room number, so that's irrelevant, could you have a look yesterday between 19:00 and 20:00? I'll be back in half an hour, thanks. As I got to the door he said, you don't need to wait half an hour, at that hour there weren't any calls from the United States, for you or anybody, is there anything else I can help you with?

I went to the coffee shop thinking: if the call was not from the United States, where the Ministry had been located, well, that was understandable, I would cross check this with Momo later. It was time to make a few notes. This was what I wrote:

> The message (we've found you) raises one basic question: who are "we"? Hypothesis: Walter de la Salle and Miss Jessica. They are looking for José for a reason we don't know, something he concealed in the story he told, because it may be assumed that the death, if it really was a suicide, was a way of escaping. If it wasn't a suicide—which is what I think—then the death was a punishment. What had he done? This poses another question: how did Walter de la Salle escape the fire? What really happened at the Ministry? The fact that José Maturana used pseudonyms for his books reinforces the theory that he was running away. For all we know, he may have only ever used his real name at this conference, but why?
>
> One thing that argues in favor of the suicide hypothesis is that in the story told by Maturana he himself said that he had already tried to kill himself at least once, using the same method of slashing his wrists in a hotel bathroom. It was something he carried inside him, it was on his mind.
>
> As for the telephone call, what to make of it? If it didn't

come from the United States, where was it from? Anything's possible, even that it came from inside the hotel. It's also possible it wasn't Walter but Jefferson, why not? Or that it was the detective, or a blackmailer, or simply somebody who has no connection with the Ministry. The fact is, I know very little about Maturana's life. Do we ever know much about a life, even after it's been well told?

I closed my notebook and left the coffee shop. From a window in the corridor I looked out at the city. Over it there hung a heavy curtain of fog, the smoke from fires, the smell of fuel, the thick air of war. In the distance, on a flat roof, I saw an old lady moving about, taking clothes off a line and putting them in a basket. At that exact moment a voice echoed in my brain: it's time to start writing again. I went to my room, ordered a Diet Coke and a chicken sandwich and started writing, quickly, not rough notes now but a narrative, everything I had lived through since I had received that invitation from the ICBM.

I had been scribbling away for just over an hour when there was a knock at the door. It was easy to guess who it was, and in fact, when I opened it, Marta gave me a hug and said: I need something strong, and I'm referring to alcohol. What happened? I asked, and she said, wait, wait, let me catch my breath, or rather, let me drink this, and she drank a miniature bottle of vodka in two gulps, and, having recovered her breath, muttered a few words of Icelandic, then said, you'll never guess what I saw this morning, something really heavy, really heavy, and I said, what did you see, Marta? and she said, I saw Maturana's body! I was in the morgue of the hospital, the Notre Dame de France, and I saw it, his arms with the cuts on them, his skin like a parchment, his mouth in a fixed grin, his face all sunken and expressionless, as if the flesh had been sucked in to his cheeks, I'd never seen a dead body before, do you think the bodies of people who've killed themselves are the same as those of other dead people? I don't know, I said, perhaps they have an expression of relief or sadness, but what made you think to go there, and how on earth did you manage to get in? Oh, my friend, we journalists have ways we can't reveal, even more if you're a woman journalist, so I said, I respect your reticence, would you like some more vodka? I opened the minibar, took out another little bottle and she said, you're a friend, I really don't mind if you know, so here's the story:

I found out that some bodies qualified as "select," those that have nothing to do with the war, go to the morgue at the makeshift Notre Dame de France hospital, and so I went there this morning, on foot, because it's not far from Agrippa Street. I arrived, walked all around the outside of the building, and when I saw it was a bunker I realized it wouldn't be easy to get in the normal way; I was just pondering this when I saw a doctor walking toward one of the side entrances and had a brainwave, something that came to me out of the blue: I screamed as if something had happened to me and the doctor rushed to me and said, what's the matter, miss, and I said, I'm in great pain, I'm sorry, and started to collapse and of course he immediately caught me, and then I said, I have pains in my uterus, doctor, I can't move, I'm a journalist, I write for a newspaper in Iceland. I pretended to faint, which provoked an even stronger reaction, and he said, calm down, take deep breaths, come with me; he helped me walk to the door, and we went inside and along a corridor until we came to an empty office. He sat me down on a chair, but I said, do something, please; I pulled my jeans and my panties down to my knees, and the man, who was about forty, came closer, touched me, and said, take a deep breath, hold it, then let it out slowly, I'll see if you have any lesions . . .

He put his head between my thighs and discreetly explored the area; after a while he said: superficially at least, I can't see anything unusual, apart from that silver ring, are you feeling any better? It's easing off a bit but it's still there, like a stitch that keeps coming back, a dormant pain, and he said, I'll give you a pill, come, but I insisted, how can you prescribe something if you haven't even touched me? His face changed and he said, what is it you want? The moment had come to take the plunge, and I said: what I want most, only you can give me. He blushed, gave a smile, and said, well, you're in luck, ask me what you like, and he laid his hand on my belly. You may think that what I'm going to ask you is a bit strange and you may refuse, but he insisted, tell me, remember I'm a doctor, I live with the dark side of things, with life and death, pleasure and pain; then I raised my pelvis a little and said, I want you to take me to the morgue to see the body of the man who killed himself at the conference, I know you have him here.

He was surprised when he heard that, of course, and drew back a bit. I had already realized that the doctor wanted to fuck me, I told you I can smell pheromones, didn't I? and in fact, there was frustration all over his face, but he pulled himself together and said, I don't know if I can do that, remember this is a military hospital and the deaths are confidential, but I moved again and my mound of Venus sent him a signal, so he said, I could try, I'd do anything to ease the pain of a beautiful Icelandic woman; we went back out into the corridor and walked for a while, up and down stairs, until we came to an iron door. It's through here. We entered a dark, damp room, with a kind of spooky atmosphere, all tiled, and with a slight smell of formaldehyde. He gave me a mask and said, put this on, you're going to need it, and it's compulsory anyway. We came to another door, and there was a fat male nurse there who must have been guarding it, reading a magazine. They said something to each other and we went through. There were huge concrete tables and other tables of iron where they did autopsies.

That was when I saw him, from a distance. They'd pulled

back the cloth covering him and I recognized his face, his white beard; we had to wait so as not to bother the people who were with him, but they soon left, so we went closer. I saw his open forearms, two violet colored wounds, his expression of calm or indifference, anyway, it was heavy, really heavy, that's the only word I can find to describe it.

Marta fell silent, looking at the wall. And what about the doctor? Ah, the doctor, his name is Amos Roth, he's a very well-mannered and attractive man. He's invited me to dinner tonight.

Then she asked, were you writing? Yes, I said. She seemed a bit disconcerted. I'm sorry, she said, I was thinking to ask you the same favor as yesterday, that you let me work here, to tell the truth, I prefer to be close to the conference and the people in it, I may have to go out and check some information, you don't mind, do you? I could put my laptop under the bed, but I said, it's no problem, I can go out and work on the balcony, I write by hand. By hand? she cried, wow, I'll never understand you writers, all that spiel about the manuscript and being close to the text, my God, I'll never understand it, and she took out her Dell Inspiron, switched it on, and started typing.

I went out on the terrace, thinking about Marta's visit to the morgue, and suddenly something occurred to me, so I went back and asked: you said there was somebody with the body, who was it? I don't know, she said, two people, maybe three, it was very dark, the only light was over Maturana's body and I was concentrating on that, why do you ask? It just seems odd to me, did they look like people from the hospital, from the police or something like that? but she said, I couldn't say, they were wearing masks. Would you say they were a woman and a man? two women? two men? Let me see, wait, I need to concentrate, she said, and closed her eyes. One of them was definitely a woman, I remember the noise of high heels, I heard them long after she'd gone out, they were echoing in the distance, what are you thinking? Well, I said, it's odd that José Maturana should have visitors in the morgue, don't you think? It could have been somebody from the hotel, said Marta, or from his embassy, or the police, or from the conference. Did you notice what language they spoke? They didn't speak, said Marta, they were just looking at him in silence. Would you say it was a sad scene? Yes, it was: a dead body, not much light, the smell of formaldehyde, that's a pretty sad scene, wouldn't you say?

I went back out on the balcony, thinking, it's them, they're here. My head was seething with ideas and I started writing again. They're in Jerusalem, they came for him, perhaps they heard his talk at the conference, but the reason they left him that message is that they preferred not to approach him, they must have been waiting for the right moment, they wanted to announce themselves through a message to see his reaction, and he was unable to bear it. Perhaps he did kill himself after all.

I heard the telephone and went back in the room. Marta was lying on the bed, smoking. She had taken her clothes off. I'm sorry, she said, it's hot and I feel more comfortable like this, I wouldn't do it if things weren't so clear between you and me. Don't worry, I said, and I lifted the receiver. It was Momo. I have news, sir, the woman who left the message has just called the hotel again, to Room 1209, just above yours, and something more, sir, the caller ID gives me a number in Tel Aviv, would you like it? He dictated it to me. Then I said, Momo, please, can you check if the call yesterday was from the same number, and he said, yes, sir, exactly the same, I already looked. I hesitated, then asked him, in whose name is Room 1209 registered? William Cummings, he said.

Momo, I'm sorry to ask this, but . . . do you know if Cummings is black? That's hard to say, sir, the register with the photocopy of his passport is in reception, and I don't have access to it. Thanks, Momo, anything else you hear, let me know immediately. Of course, sir, how's the young lady? Fine, Momo, she's working. Give her my regards. I will.

I dialed the Tel Aviv number, with my hand shaking, and to my surprise it turned out to be a branch of the Universal Coptic Church. I had never even imagined an eventuality like that, so I decided to ask, is Miss Jessica there? There was a silence and then they said, there's nobody here of that name, Jessica who? I thanked them and asked for their address, because I wanted to visit them. Aaron Pater Street, number 19, near Allenby Street, sir, we're open from eight in the morning to seven-thirty in the evening. Then I dialed the number of Room 1209 but nobody replied. I had an idea. I went down to reception and asked the receptionist if it was possible to be moved to the room directly above mine, Number 1209, is it occupied? The man typed on his keyboard and said, yes, it's occupied until Tuesday of next week, sir, I'm sorry, by that date you'll already have left the hotel, won't you? Yes, I said, it's a pity, is the person occupying it at the conference? No, sir, no.

I walked away, thinking that I had to go to Tel Aviv to pay a visit to the Coptic Church. At six there was Supervielle's lecture, and early the next day the much-awaited talk by Sabina Vedovelli, one of the high points of the ICBM, because according to gossip she was going to tell her life story. I had just over an hour to rest.

With all the demands of this conference, my recovery was taking longer than expected.

Going back to my room I found Marta in the same position, wearing nothing but a white G-string. I asked her about her work and she said, I haven't been able to start, I checked my e-mail and then I started chatting with an old friend, and the time just went, my God, and how about you? I'm tired, I said, I'd like to sleep a while before Supervielle's talk. Good idea, she said, I'll do the same, yesterday I drank like a prostitute from Minsk. I could really do with a nap.

She closed the curtains and lay down beside me. Her closeness and her smell gave me an erection, which I tried to conceal, but she put her arm on my hip and finally noticed it. What about this? I was silent at first and then said, it's only an erection, leave it, it'll pass. Is it me who's causing it or are you thinking of somebody? I told her it didn't matter. It had not happened to me in a while, and it was like meeting an old friend; but she insisted: you won't be able to rest, let me help you. She lowered the zipper of my pants and took out my penis, which grew even harder at the touch of her hand. Yes, you're very hard, you must really like the woman you're thinking about, let me help you, I think you need it. She started caressing it and squeezing it in her hand. Close your eyes, she said, I'm good at this. Imagine someone you like, a naked woman you'd like to fuck, O.K.? I looked at her out of the corner of my eye. She had gotten on her knees, with her legs half open; where the pubic hair should have been there was a soft furrow of golden dots, on the verge of sprouting. She moved her arm rhythmically and I felt I was about to ejaculate; she also must have felt it, because she said, wait a moment. She got up and ran to the bathroom. Her ass and breasts bounced up and down and I had to make an effort to contain myself. A second later she came back with a towel and said, leave it to me, just tell me when, O.K.? She continued rubbing my penis with increasing force until I felt myself coming, and I told her, so, still rubbing, she put the towel around it. When I had come, she got up and went and left it in the bathroom. I heard her sitting on the toilet and tearing off pieces of paper, had she become aroused? It was quite likely.

When she came back she said, all right, now you can rest, and she lay down again by my side. You didn't have to do that, I said, by the way, there's a drop left on your arm, clean it off. Instead of which, she raised her arm to her mouth and licked it. Your semen tastes of iron, I like it. Then she knocked back what was left of the vodka and said, don't talk anymore, we only have an hour's sleep.

PART TWO
THE BOOK OF TRIBULATIONS

1.

THE OSLOVSKI & FLØ VARIATION
(AS TOLD BY EDGAR MIRET SUPERVIELLE)

This story begins one night in a bar in Tel Aviv, the Blue Parrot, and its main characters are two elderly immigrants, one from Wadowice, Poland, and the other from Gothenburg in Sweden. Their names are Ferenck Oslovski and Gunard Fl ø. I shan't say which is which, as I assume a certain degree of education in my listeners and have no wish to insult them. As I was saying, Oslovski and Fl ø were in the Blue Parrot, it was already very late, and between them on the table was a chessboard.

The Pole was drinking Smirnoff vodka and the Swede a nauseating apricot schnapps, one of those Nordic digestives that is sure to rot your stomach if you were not born somewhere several degrees below freezing point. The two men were both staring into the distance, and neither said a word, which means that they were good friends, friends who did not need to talk in order to feel together.

Suddenly Fl ø struck the table with his hand and said, I have it, I think I have it!

Oslovski, who was familiar with these outbursts, looked at him and said: All right, show me.

Fl ø arranged the pieces with three pawns on either side, king, knight, and bishop. Look, he said: pawn advances and blocks the king behind the rook. Oslovski sat looking at the chessboard for a while. He looked up and cried, waitress, another round! Then he looked down at the chessboard again, silent once more. The drinks were brought, he took a sip, then continued sitting there with his nose very close to the pieces. After two more sips of his vodka, he at last looked up again and said, no, Gunard: there's a way out in bishop four, and no way to stop it.

Fløstared at the board and took his head in his hands. It's true, he murmured, it's true.

It was a position from the 1971 Interzonal in Buenos Aires, in which Petrosian and Fischer had drawn. Flø always maintained that Fischer could have won and had been trying to demonstrate that for some time now. It was not a totally irrational belief, but he felt it in the way that grand masters are aware of positions: as a series of luminous lines traced across the chessboard, like the routes of bombers flying across the Atlantic, trajectories that at first are merely flashing lights but then take on a shape and turn into known positions that have previously been played or studied.

To Oslovski, too, the rhythm of a combination was important. It might be a march rhythm, a concerto, a minuet, or a rondo, not to mention the effect of the silences, that beautiful instrument called silence, which means so much in both music and chess.

Oslovski recalled the epitaph of the composer Alfred Schnittke in Novodevichy cemetery in Moscow, a pentagram carved in marble with the words *silencio fortissimo prolongado*, equivalent to the moment when a player moves away from the chessboard and comes out of himself so rapidly that he is left depressed and alone, feeling lost in the world, and longing desperately, as Spassky used to say, "for another chess player." And so it was with Oslovski.

But let us continue with the story.

Oslovski and Flø had met in difficult circumstances, behind a wall riddled with bullets and shrapnel. Oslovski was a lieutenant and Flø a captain, although in different companies, and both had been involved in an operation to take a refugee camp where the ringleaders of a rebel group were apparently hiding, an operation that had meant advancing a few feet at a time, knocking down houses as they went, under covering fire from their own tanks and artillery.

During the advance, Oslovski had jumped through a window and fallen into a courtyard filled with broken glass. Blinded by the smoke of the artillery fire, he ran toward a doorway and did not see a huge hole right in the middle of the courtyard. He stumbled, tried in vain to hold on to the sides, and fell some fifteen or twenty feet, making a great deal of noise as he did so. It was a clandestine well, quite small in diameter, which was why when he fell in the water at the bottom, which did not cover him, he found it difficult to turn and aim the barrel of his rifle upwards.

He crouched and waited a few seconds, cursing his luck or his lack of foresight, until he saw a head appear at the top, wrapped in one of those colorful cloths that made the enemy so easy to recognize, so he fired several shots, then said to himself, I'm defenseless, in a few seconds I'm going to join my ancestors. He took out his torch and shone it at the walls of the well, and his spirits lifted when he saw that there was a side gallery. He retreated into it, the water around his waist. As he did so, he heard voices at the mouth of the well. Seeing some rocks and bricks, he piled them in front of him to protect himself. As he finished, he heard a whistle, followed by a gurgling sound. They had thrown a grenade down, but it had fallen in the water and the fuse had not exploded.

What luck, he thought, but it would not last, they would soon think of something, so he retreated farther into the side channel, realizing after a while, to his horror, that it was getting ever narrower. It doesn't lead anywhere, I'm a dead man. He heard a loud explosion, and the gallery filled with gunpowder and smoke. To protect himself, he got down on his knees and put his head in the water, but was unable to keep it under for

186 · SANTIAGO GAMBOA

long without breathing. He was getting very anxious now. On the other side of the stones, he saw beams of light and heard voices. The echo of voices he could not understand. The air was full of smoke and brick dust, provoking a coughing fit that must have been heard by those above, because a hail of bullets immediately lashed the water.

He retreated, and saw this time that, a few feet farther along, the passage widened again and the water was colder, which might mean something. He washed his face and tried to think. He remembered that before he had fallen he had been walking ahead of a group of men, but had advanced very rapidly and had found himself alone. The enemy were here, but it was possible his own side would arrive soon. He just had to hold out. There was another huge explosion, and he felt the earth tremble. The stones that had fallen with the first explosion, plus those he had piled up, protected him, but then it occurred to him that the enemy were trying to bury him alive. Would they do that? In wondering this, he was not thinking about whether they could bury a human being alive, everybody did that kind of thing in war, but whether they would fill in a well from which they drew water, which was one of the most precious commodities in the region.

Where the hell were his comrades? Even way down here, he could hear the sounds of fighting. According to his calculations, they should not be long now.

With luck, he might be able to survive, so he tried to retreat along the channel, and found that he could, except that as he moved the level of the water kept rising and was already up to his chest. In a strange way, he felt safe, even though he was in the bowels of the earth, and in complete darkness. Another explosion made him think that they were indeed preparing to fill in the well. Too bad for him.

After all, they could always clear it later, if there was a "later." His legs were numb, but he tried to walk as best he could, because the last explosion had again filled the narrow chamber with dust and smoke.

There won't be a "later" for me, that's for sure. He recalled a chess position that had no way out, and concentrated on that. As he did so, he had to touch his eyes to be sure if they were open or closed, such was the state he was in. He did not think he was seriously wounded. All he had was a graze he had received when he had knocked down a wall to enter a house, and the blow to his shoulder when he had fallen in the well. Not much if you took into account the magnitude of this war and all the bullets fired and all the bodies he had seen fall since he had first pressed the trigger.

He heard cries again, and it seemed to him that he could understand a few words. Somebody was saying something in Russian or Hebrew or even Polish. He went back along the passage, groping his way, and when he reached the open part he noticed that the cave-in had raised the level of the ground and the water. He saw the gleam of a torch, and a rope hanging down in the middle, and again heard the voice. He realized they were saying to him, grab the rope, and that was what he did. As they hoisted him up, he could not see what was happening, as not only was he blinded by the light, but his pupils were also filled with dust.

When he got to the top, he had an unpleasant surprise. Instead of his comrades, he found the courtyard filled with the enemy and a man speaking to him in broken Hebrew. They tied his hands, threatening him with rifles pressed to the back of his neck. Then they took him into a room off the courtyard, and he asked himself, why don't they execute me immediately? and also, where are my men? The fighting seemed to have moved farther east, and he was alone. He was a prisoner. He said to himself: I was better off down there, in the darkness and the cold water and the all-embracing earth. That was the way he was.

They laid him naked on a rusty, rickety table full of holes, and started asking him questions. How many of you are there? What's your objective? Which rebel chief are you after? What are your plans of deployment? How far are you planning to go?

The man who was asking the questions spoke Hebrew, and the first thing he did was to put out his cigarette on Oslovski's stomach. Oslovski screamed in pain. Then came something rather more unpleasant with his nails. They removed the nail from his little finger with wooden splinters. Then from his ring finger and index finger. Oslovski writhed and twisted, but did not answer their questions, partly out of pride and partly because most of the things they asked him about he did not know. As long as he did not answer, he would stay alive. If he told them what they wanted, they would shoot him in the back of the head and throw him down a well. Not his nice, cool, maternal well, but a dry one full of dust.

One of the men stared at his testicles, then grabbed them with his hand and seemed for a moment to be weighing them. What was he going to do? The light glinted on a razor, black with dried blood, and Oslovski thought, the end is near, my comrades aren't coming and it's all over for me, and he felt a pain in his thigh.

Still holding his testicles, the torturer had made the first cut, a clean deep fissure in the thigh that made Oslovski see stars, although he was so tired, his body forgot it immediately. He was still alive, still had a few seconds left. He did not understand what they were saying around him, only what the man asking him questions said. He wanted to pee, but contained himself. He did not want to call attention to his member. What was coming next? The man with the razor let go of his testicles and a hand pulled his head back. The same man as before was now holding a pair of garden shears and moving them closer to his toes. The man asking the questions said: I'm going to repeat what I want to know and if you don't tell me you're going to lose your toes.

A young man who had been watching all this with a certain horror put a plastic bag under his feet. Oslovski made a calculation, if they're going to cut off my toes one by one, that means they're in no hurry. Where the hell were his comrades? They must have been repulsed and now he was alone. That was the situation.

At the far end of the room, a pregnant young woman was knitting a sweater. The image seemed completely out of place here, but he looked at the wool and remembered something. What was it? His grandmother had used the same stitch, three knits with one of the needles and six with the other, knitted back to front, and then, with his forehead bathed in sweat and his body anesthetized by the pain, he noticed that the woman was getting the sequence wrong, she wasn't knitting the complete series and one of the sides would come out too long.

Without thinking, he said in a thin voice: you're getting it wrong, it should be six with the right needle, otherwise one of the sides will be too long and your son will be uncomfortable. She stopped her knitting. One of the men hit him in the mouth but she made a placatory gesture, came toward him with her huge belly, and said, how do you know it's a boy? Because of the color blue, he replied. Then she said, you think the knitting is wrong? He told her what he remembered and the woman compared the sides. You're right, this one's turning out narrower. I can still undo it and save the wool. Thank you. She turned and walked out.

They let him rest and gave him water, and later, with the sounds of fighting apparently getting closer, a man came into the room, untied him and said, your things are over there, your weapons stay here, now go.

Oslovski went out, feeling very confused. He walked through the shadows, one more shadow himself, lingering in the ruined houses and foul-smelling trenches, and thinking, trying to understand what had happened, afraid of advancing and being seen. He had no weapons. He decided to wait until nightfall, and when it came started retracing his steps. As he passed the well, he considered hiding in it, because they had left the rope, but it was better to take a risk, so he continued walking, treading carefully over the broken glass and the rubble, and was wandering through part of a field when he saw a tank coming. He fell to his knees, took off his combat jacket and waved it above his head, crying: save me.

The hatch opened and a fair-haired man emerged and said, come on, get in, you must be wounded.

It was Gunard Flø.

Later, in the mobile hospital behind the lines, after they had sewed Oslovski's wounds and told him he would have to be immobile for a while, Flø said to him, I know what to do when we can't sleep at night, and took out a chess set. They hit it off, and after a few games realized that they already knew each other. They had taken part in some of the same tournaments, and although they had never played against one another, they remembered each other's names.

That was how the heroes of my story met.

I will add one more thing, which is that Oslovski had a curious experience some years later, in Berlin,. He was at a crossing, waiting for the lights to turn green, when he saw on the other side of the street the woman from the torture room. She had an absent look on her face, and of course she was a bit older. She was holding a little boy by the hand. When the lights changed, they met in the middle of the street and he said to her, do you remember me? you saved my life in the refugee camp. She looked at him in surprise, uncomprehendingly. He insisted, remember, the knitting stitches that were wrong, it's me, I owe you my life! The woman looked at him in terror, picked up the little boy, and broke into a run. Both of them disappeared into the crowd.

Now, in order to continue the story of my characters, it has become necessary to give a brief account of their lives.

I shall begin with Ferenck Oslovski.

His birth and early childhood are fairly irrelevant. Knowing that he was the son of a Jewish notary in Wadowice and a woman who had studied philosophy does not help us to understand very much about his gifts. Hundreds of human beings have had similar childhoods, just as anodyne or interesting, or even brilliant, and none of them, none at all, became champion of Poland.

He himself says that the first time he saw a chessboard was in a local tailor's shop, Roth's, where he had gone to collect a suit for his father. The tailor was playing a game with one of his employees, and let him stay for a moment to watch. Oslovski would always remember how glossy the polished ebony and boxwood of the classic Staunton pieces seemed. He looked at them with such rapt attention that the tailor, a friend of the family, said, would you like to touch them? go on, reach out your hand, move one. The boy chose a knight and slid it across the board.

What he felt in his fingers was so agreeable, so soft, that he was overwhelmed, conquered forever by a pleasure that he would soon learn all about, because the tailor invited him to come whenever he was free to watch him play, and between one game and the next started teaching him. This pawn moves like this, the knight jumps there, the queen can move forwards, backwards, and diagonally.

The boy would watch him in silence, not telling him that he had already watched enough times to know the moves perfectly and absorb all the different openings. One day, after a few months had passed, the tailor said, sit down and start with white, and so that we're evenly matched, I'll play without the queen, and that was what they did. After twenty moves, the tailor performed a classic checkmate, which left young Ferenck

192 · SANTIAGO GAMBOA

on the verge of tears. Then the boy ventured to say: Mr. Roth, can we play another game with all the pieces? The tailor was touched, and said, of course, if you prefer I won't give you any advantage, but it's going to be more difficult.

The game began well, and after thirty-one moves the boy delivered an astonishing checkmate, much to the surprise of the tailor, who had not seen it coming, and when he tried to figure out what had happened, the boy said, Mr. Roth, you were already done for six moves ago, look, and he started manipulating the pieces at great speed, explaining the position. They played four more games and the result was always the same: the tailor, who was not a bad player and had even taken part in tournaments, was checkmated every time. Never again was he able to beat the boy, which convinced him that he was dealing with a case of precociousness that was worth investigating. So he took him, with his father's permission, to the chess club run by Ozer Miller, an experienced player who had been local champion and who gave classes and played with other former players and enthusiasts.

Ferenck's appearance in Miller's club was quite a milestone, because in the eleven months he was there he never lost a game, not even with Ozer Miller himself. Miller decided to take matters in hand and introduce him into other clubs, of greater standing and quality, such as the one run by Sam Edenbaum, where the boy at last found his level.

Sam Edenbaum earned his living selling fabrics, a profession close to that of the tailor Shlomo Roth. They were two links in the same chain, which had created a bond between them that verged on the fraternal. But there was more to the long-standing relationship between these two men, Edenbaum and Roth, than a business connection, and here I hope you will allow me a short digression, because I think it is true to say that they owed their lives to chess.

They were both part of that much-reduced Jewish community in Poland that had survived the Holocaust, and in their case it was thanks to chess that they had survived. Both had been deported to Auschwitz but had been saved by the fact that one of the section commandants in the camp was a lover of chess and organized tournaments. For a prisoner, to lose a game could result in death. That indeed had happened to a number of Jews and one political prisoner, a Communist, whereas when an officer lost the penalty was typical of the military, like having to drink five glasses of brandy or walk between the huts in their underwear, the kind of drunken revel that bore no relation to the tragic outcome with which the others were faced.

Roth and Edenbaum always won, and although that exasperated the officers, it also kept them alive, because they would never send to his death a man they wanted to beat at chess, a consideration that only chess players would understand. The officers did not dare touch them. What they did was make them play against each other, which was somewhat macabre, because they had no idea what would happen to the loser. But to avoid trouble, they played a real game to the death, which Edenbaum won in fifty-six moves, to much acclaim from the officers. In fact, the officers were so pleased that both men were treated to canned chicken and brandy.

As they told it to Oslovski, Roth and Edenbaum never allowed themselves to lose a game. The system they concocted consisted of thinking about chess all the time, closing their eyes, imagining moves and analyzing final positions as they dug holes for fencing in the snow and rain. Thinking about chess and nothing but chess, conceiving the world as a succession of pieces moving across the board according to their own hierarchies, the ignominious reality in which they were immersed being merely the canvas on which they projected moves and planned unexpected advances: that was why, whenever the officers came into their huts and took them away to play, they were always ready, they already knew which openings they would use and how they would develop them, just like the protagonist of Stefan Zweig's novella *The Royal Game*, which I am sure you will remember, whose life is saved by chess but who is later driven mad by it. Well, something like that happened in Auschwitz, although neither Edenbaum nor Roth went mad, only concentrated their energies in the brain and switched off everything else. Their survival depended on that one organ, the brain, and on their skill at playing chess.

This situation continued until the camp was liberated, and caused them a few problems afterwards. Edenbaum and Roth, who were in better physical condition than the others because of the food they had been given by the officers, were now denounced to the authorities, accused of having been collaborators or even spies. These malicious stories went no farther, however, because in those days of horror there were better and more useful things to do than try to pursue two Jewish chess players who had not only survived but even prospered.

But let us return to the education of young Ferenck at a time when Poland was slowly recovering from the war.

Edenbaum took his education in hand and, for a small amount of money, hired a former regional champion to train him in openings, which, according to Edenbaum, were the pillars on which the outcome of a game depended, and so Ferenck started devoting himself increasingly to chess. His father gave him special permission to leave school at noon and spend three hours on chess, a time judged sufficient to deepen his knowledge without taking him away for too long from the world and the things a boy his age needed to do, because, as is well known, most young prodigies develop a distance from reality that sooner or later destroys them, look at Bobby Fischer, a genius but quite awkward and even unpleasant when it came to other human activities, or Gary Kasparov, the prodigy from Baku, who never had a real adolescence and who, as an adult, had the same mental age he had had when his childhood was snatched from him. This did not happen to other grand masters and champions, such as Boris Spassky or Tigran Petrosian, who continued to be human beings as well as great chess brains, so it was important to his new mentor that young Ferenck should be a child like any other, and he made it a condition that his apprenticeship should not take precedence over his life. And he was successful, because Ferenck Oslovski spent his teenage years just like his classmates, going to the river to bathe and trying to win the love of girls—mostly without success, by the way, which contributed to his somewhat melancholy temperament—but by and large leading a healthy life and even developing another great passion: music. He learned musical notation and piano, both major tasks, which helped him to keep his eyes on the horizon and molded his spirit in the clay of the artist.

But the passion for chess is so strong that it may wipe out other vocations. Remember Marcel Duchamp, the man who destroyed the traditional concept of art when he presented an upturned urinal at the Salon des Artistes as his magnum opus. Duchamp gave it all up for the infinite spaces of chess, never again creating anything but combinations of pawns and bishops and kings on a chessboard.

And Oslovski was the same.

Before long, young Ferenck gave up the piano and musical notation to devote himself exclusively to the study of combinations and variations. In his first tournaments, he obtained some surprising results. At the Municipal Tournament in Wadowice he came third, but did not lose a single game, claiming 16 victories and 38 draws, which in points put him below two of his rivals, one of whom he had actually beaten. These small tournaments provided the young man with a great incentive to continue. What a chess player longs for above all is to confront a rival of his own, or greater, stature. The desire to follow an ascending curve kept him awake at night, studying variations, reproducing games by grand masters such as Tal, Capablanca, and Larsen, making notes and coming up with new ideas that he would discuss daily with Edenbaum, until something happened that would completely change his life, which was that in the middle of studying a position, as he was writing down his possible moves, Sam Edenbaum's head tipped forward onto the chessboard, before his whole body collapsed noisily on the floor. An aneurism had burst in his brain, killing him outright, the expression on his face one of concentration rather than pain. As they say of Archimedes, death interrupted him in mid-thought.

So Ferenck found himself without a teacher, because although the tailor, Roth, was still a good companion and pleasant to talk to, he was not at the requisite level to train Oslovski. The young man drifted for nearly a year without a guide, until someone at last appeared to pick up the torch from Edenbaum, a Russian named Vasily Andrescovich, who had heard about the young man and his achievements and was looking for a pupil out of whom to carve his masterpiece. To him, Oslovski was like the block of marble to Da Vinci. The raw material for his great art.

The first thing Andrescovich did, when summer came and the school vacations began, was to apply for permission to go to Moscow, which he managed easily thanks to his contacts and an invitation from the Russian Federation. When he arrived, young Oslovski was stunned. Moscow was not only the capital of the Socialist world, but also a mythical city to chess players. Ever since Alexander Alekhine had snatched the championship from the Cuban, Capablanca, Russian predominance had been unquestioned: Mikhail Botvinnik, Vasily Smyslov, Tigran Petrosian, Boris Spassky, and even Viktor Korchnoi, who despite his talent never became world champion, as well as young hopefuls such as Anatoly Karpov and

Gary Kasparov. Moscow was the cradle of chess, and he, a shy young Pole from one of the most obscure and forgotten corners of the world, was there to devour it.

With his hands in his pockets, sweating with the emotion and the heat, young Ferenck turned on to the tree-lined Boulevard Gogol, passed the huge bronze stature of the author, and a little farther along, on the left hand side, came to the great temple itself, the headquarters of the Russian Chess Federation. When he entered the hall on the second floor, he thought he was going to faint at the sight of the mirrors and the stucco and the meticulously lined-up tables.

Andrescovich told him that a series of games were being played that afternoon between Grand Masters in honor of Botvinnik, the so-called "Dialectic of Iron," three times world champion and second longest holder of the title after Alekhine. Young Oslovski sat down in the room on the first floor where the games were commented on and waited for the beginning. With trembling lips he saw the white, cold figure of Karpov come in through reception and start up the stairs toward the hall where the tables were. The games began and Oslovski listened to the commentators, old players and Grand Masters, and after what seemed to him only a moment, although nearly two hours had passed, he asked if he might be allowed to make a comment. He left his chair and went to the chessboard where the positions were analyzed and there gave a rapid demonstration of a better play. The old men listened to his explanation, given in fairly correct Russian, thought about it and approved his hypothesis. Later, during a second game, they asked his opinion about another complex position and again the young man gave a brave and highly original analysis. By now, the wise old men were murmuring among themselves.

The next day, Oslovski played for the first time at the Russian Chess Federation. He felt his fingers tremble as they touched the pieces and slid them over the board and the afternoon sun made slanting lines across the floor. A week later, he played in a youth championship and came second. Then he took part in a number of amateur tournaments and won four of them.

From here things began to move fast, as often happens in the lives of chess players. He played in Leningrad, Prague, Kiev, and Odessa, won a tournament in Budapest and another in Athens. He was runner-up in the all-Poland championship and finally, at the age of seventeen, became national champion, which earned him honors and the possibility of traveling around the world.

Now begins a new chapter in the trajectory of Oslovski. By now he was twenty-three and many things had happened in his life. One of them was the death of his father, and another the illness of his mother, for whom, thanks to his position as Grand Master, he was able to secure the best possible care at Warsaw's Central Hospital, in the ward for patients suffering from terminal illnesses, which in her case was nothing less than leukemia. In spite of these setbacks, Ferenck concentrated on chess, which was now no longer just a passion but a way of rising through the social ranks in Gomulka's Poland, in pursuit of which he doubled his concentration and efforts.

He continued to work with his Russian teacher, Andrescovich, but something had started to go wrong with the mechanism. The young Polish master stopped winning tournaments. Instead, he would always come second or third. These were anxious years, and the history of Poland, which had always been sad, seemed to be somehow embodied in this young man full of dreams. And what happens to young men like Ferenck, when they gain a certain fame and their personal lives get in a mess? They generally start to develop a weakness for hard liquor, which they justify by stress, or nerves, or those baleful dusks when the sky of Warsaw fills with a purple light, as if tongues of fire were swallowing the city and the souls of its citizens, and then the glasses succeed one another on the bar counters, filled with transparent, highly concentrated liquids intended to counteract that complicated sense of abandonment in which the mind can find no rest, a glass, knocked back in one go, is followed by a second, then a third, and so Oslovski's hours started to darken and black clouds covered his soul, presaging bad weather.

The storm lost no time in breaking, in the form of a wire from Warsaw announcing the news he had so feared, "Mother died during night, in her sleep. Come ASAP." It had been sent by the director of the hospital and Ferenck received it six days later while he was in Odessa, in an elimination heat for a place in the Interzonal, a step on the road to the World Championship.

When he got to Warsaw, he had to go straight from the airport to the morgue, together with his teacher Andrescovich, to identify a body that was indeed his mother's, although he could no longer recognize her. She was buried in a ceremony attended by only six people: two directors of the Polish Chess Federation, a nurse from the hospital, the doctor, his teacher, and himself.

It was after the funeral that Oslovski ran away for the first time.

He disappeared from the streets of Warsaw for three months, as if swept away by one of those icy winds from the far north that lash the squares of the city, or as so many friends and enemies of the government died, without anyone ever finding their bodies, and both Andrescovich and the directors of the Polish Federation searched everywhere for him, especially in the cities he most liked to visit: Moscow, Kiev, Prague. They checked the hospitals and the police stations, all to no avail, and remember that I am talking about the Communist era in Central Europe, when it was not so easy to disappear, because everything was under such strict control, and yet Oslovski managed it. After three months, in desperation, Andrescovich decided to make the disappearance public, which he had preferred not to do before in order to avoid a scandal.

And what he had hoped for happened. As soon as it was announced in the newspapers and on television that the chess master Ferenck Oslovski had disappeared, a call came in from the central police station in the seaside resort of Międzyzdroje to say that the player was staying in a hotel there. Andrescovich immediately traveled to the town and found Ferenck, looking gaunt, haggard, and sad. "I was taking a cure of silence," was the only explanation he gave his teacher before setting off for the airfield and getting on a Tupolev to Wadowice, where everyone expected the former young prodigy to regain his spirits and return to the chessboard.

He did in fact manage to do so, although slowly, because the game suffers when it is abandoned for too long and the first moves are like those of a sportsman who has spent a whole season out of action. Timid, erratic steps, exaggerated calculations. That was how it was for Oslovski.

Three months later, he tried again and to everyone's surprise won an international tournament in Athens, taking a substantial prize of ten thousand dollars, which made it possible for him to replenish his depleted savings, because those were still the days when chess players in Eastern Europe had certain privileges but did not earn very much unless they played in the West. He and Andrescovich returned to Wadowice feeling very pleased, but this vein of good luck was short-lived and soon afterwards Oslovski again reverted to his cruise speed, which meant he would always come third or fourth, or occasionally second. That seemed to be his level, and at least it guaranteed him a salary of three hundred zlotys a month, fairly high in comparison with the two hundred and fifty earned by a university professor or the five hundred earned by a highly placed Party official. From that position, he watched the history of the world and chess pass by. He saw the arrival of Spassky and his rise to the heights, he saw the coming of that young devil, the American Bobby Fischer, performing amazing feats and defeating everyone, including Spassky, and he felt angry at himself for admiring such a mean, self-centered character. From his room, following the championship in Reykjavik, he came to the conclusion that chess did not make people better, which again depressed him, so he closed the curtains and did not come out again for a long time.

There were further crises, and during those years he disappeared four more times, only now neither Andrescovich nor anyone else bothered to look for him. They knew that all they had to do was wait.

By now, fifteen years of work had passed and Andrescovich was starting to grow old. The list of misfortunes that had befallen him during that time, by the side of his disciple, included the following: his parents died, his son defected to the West on a journey to Sydney, he underwent three hernia operations, and his hair started falling out, leaving a smooth ball in the middle and wisps of gray at the sides. After a careful reading of all these signs, he decided to return to Moscow and live on his chess player's pension, so one fine day he announced to Ferenck that he was leaving, which brought about yet another attack in the younger man.

After this, Oslovski woke up one day and saw that General Jaruzelski had been appointed prime minister of Poland. He also saw, from his window, that the street was covered in dirty snow streaked with weak black prints, and so he decided to close the curtains and carry on sleeping. He woke up again and now Jaruzelski was president, but the snow and the ice continued making the streets dirty, so he again shut himself away. When Lech Walesa was elected, Oslovski thought: they don't deceive me, and again closed the curtains, until one day he had a brainwave and decided to go outside.

The trees were green and there were flowers everywhere. The sun was shining into every corner. People were singing and whistling, but it was too late for him, so he went and bought an airline ticket and a few days later arrived in Tel Aviv claiming *aliyah*, which would ensure him a modest but cozy apartment, Israeli citizenship, and help with finding work.

And so it was. He had an apartment on Allenby Street, not far from the beach, and a monthly salary that allowed him to cover the basics. Most afternoons, he went to look at the sea. He loved the outline of the old port of Jaffa to his left, and beyond it the horizon of the Mediterranean, that sea that had given and taken so much from the peoples of the Middle East and was so strange to someone from Central Europe. He would spend the hours making marks in the sand and analyzing positions on a little portable chess set, until he met Gael, a woman of thirty who had lost her husband in the Yom Kippur War. Gael served pizzas and fast food in a restaurant near his apartment called the Nightingale of Odessa, run by a Russian. Oslovski went there every day for dinner, and one night he asked the waitress, what time do you finish work? She looked at him angrily and said, I know what you're thinking and I'll only go with you if you're serious, that's not too much to ask of a Pole who's as alone as his sad country.

Ferenck looked at her in surprise and said, I'm alone because I want to be, it's my way of life, you mustn't deduce from it that I'm desperate, or that I'm special in any way, to which Gael retorted, nobody likes living alone and if you do then you're crazy, and Oslovski said, I'm not crazy, I carry my love in my pocket, and he took out the little wooden box with the chess set, but Gael, who was of Lebanese origin, said, if your only company is inside that little box then things are worse than I thought, and went to the counter to serve some beers. Then she approached and said, it was a joke, I know chess is something bigger than the two of us put together and bigger than the Nightingale of Odessa and the whole of Allenby Street and this little strip of land where someday we will all be free. Those words sufficed for Gael and Ferenck to make love that same night in the apartment where, three months later, they decided to set up home together.

Here I shall leave the story of Oslovski.

I leave him with Gael, in the apartment on Allenby Street, to head north, far north, to that mysterious North that is home to so many legends and was home, too, to Gunard Flø, born in Gothenburg into a rich Lutheran family, mine owners and shareholders in a number of shipping companies, who learned to play chess in a very exclusive club in the city, the Barajó, after being enrolled by his father, a lover of the game who had never reached more than a modest amateur level, but who sensed in the chessboard a kind of greatness that neither his money nor his political contacts could give him, nothing to do with fame or success, but with a certain indestructible solitude, a temple that would allow his son to undertake elevated enterprises of the spirit without stooping, daily, to the banality of human affairs.

So Gunard, as a small boy, received as an inheritance his father's frustrated desire to be a chess player, and received it gratefully. From the age of nine, he devoted himself body and soul to chess, with results that went far beyond what his rich family expected of him. He won youth tournaments in Gothenburg and by thirteen he was the Olympic champion, which would be his greatest prize in chess. He would never again get that far, but that never bothered him. Quite the contrary. Unlike other chess players, defeat or the idea that his talent was a modest one never seemed to bother him. Rather, it gave him a great feeling of harmony, as if knowing that he was not called to great enterprises allowed him to enjoy the game more intensely.

And so it was. In whatever tournament he played, from the age of fifteen, he always achieved decent results, but never genius, never an ovation, never victory. His father was not worried, because with great wisdom he said to himself, I wanted a son who was a chess player and that's what I have, aspiring in addition to his being a champion would be to tempt fate, may God bless him. In the Lutheran church, people do not long for things, and greed is punished. The only thing his father did for the young man was to give him the best teachers so that he could get as much enjoyment from the game as possible, while playing at a high level. One of them, Theodor Momsen, had even trained the Master Bent Larsen, although we should point out, for the sake of the truth, that the reason Momsen agreed to take care of young Gunard was not that he had seen a huge talent in him, but because Mr. Flø put in front of him a check with many zeros on the right hand side, which is where they count the most, at a time when Momsen's career was entering what might be described as the final stage of a long, slow decline.

So young Gunard studied openings and variations. He fell in love with the more romantic aspects of chess and started using obsolete combinations such as the King's Gambit, the Vienna Game, or the Bishop's Opening, common at the time of Morphy and Anderssen, classic players whom Gunard admired and whose games he studied with delight. During his hours of study with Momsen, Gunard enjoyed the beautiful precision of the game and its rhetorical figures, the prosody of those pieces sliding across the board and, of course, he was especially delighted to play blitz chess with his teacher. Every time he achieved a good position, or indeed won, he celebrated it with a few flamenco or tango steps and a burst of wild laughter. He was a cheerful young man, and for his father that was the main thing.

He must have been about eighteen the first time he dressed in women's clothes. The whole family was vacationing on the island of Capri, where they had a beautiful house, and that was where it happened. One afternoon, without making any particular decision, Gunard put on a green suit, with a degree of cleavage but with the skirt covering the knees. It was a formal outfit that belonged to an aunt who was with them on their vacation and was much loved by Gunard. His mother's clothes, which were thicker, were excessively baggy on him, not to mention the fact that, although she was his mother, he had no very strong feelings for her. Gunard's great love was his father.

It was actually his father who found him in the room, and on seeing him asked, what are you doing with that, Guny? The young man replied, I don't know, daddy, I felt a irresistible urge to put it on, and now, with it on, I look at the horizon and the lights of the distant boats and feel as if my spirit had taken flight, and then his father said, well, I'll leave you with your spirit, but don't even think of going down to the living room like that. When you've finished put everything back where you found it, is it your aunt Adelaide's? The young man nodded and turned again toward the sea, and a while later came down in his normal clothes. His father saw him and gave a sigh of relief.

Soon afterwards, while still on Capri, Gunard met Renate Schlink, a young Swiss woman who was spending her summer vacation there. They chatted one afternoon on the beach and she showed great interest in his stories about chess, which were the young man's whole life. When night fell, as in a scene from a novel, they entered the sea holding hands, watched the stars come out, and kissed each other in the warm waters of the Tyrrhenian Sea. Renate had already had some experiences with men, and she it was who threw aside her bikini and rummaged in Gunard's swimming trunks. Going with the flow, he penetrated her, stunned by the revelation of what a conversation with a woman could lead to. Then he felt a trembling in his pelvis and was about to withdraw, but she stopped him and received his seed, which much to the surprise of both of them reached its target. One afternoon three months later, as Gunard was analyzing a position in a game between Mikhail Tal and Botvinnik, he received a call from Zurich in which Renate said to him in an anguished voice, listen, you want to hear something strange? You're going to be a father!

Soon afterwards, there was a hastily arranged civil wedding in Monte Carlo, and the two families, who knew each other from Capri, showed great understanding toward the two young people and were even happy, in spite of the suddenness of the whole thing and the fact that it had all come about by accident. Gunard's father had an additional reason to feel happy. He was relieved to have this proof of his son's masculinity.

After the wedding, Renate and Gunard settled in Gothenburg, in an apartment owned by the Flø family in the Ulmbjorg district—in a building that today houses the Hotel Osaka—but in spite of the rich, cushioned life they led, Renate Schlink, thanks to the dark, oppressive atmosphere of those far regions of the world and its obvious effects on the psyche of anyone born in more southern latitudes, went through a crisis and said, I don't know what you think or want to do, but I'm going to have my child in Switzerland. Gunard, who had a conciliatory personality, left with her and soon afterwards their son was born in Zurich and christened Ebenezer.

Two months later, Theodor Momsen joined him and settled into an apartment on Heinestrasse, very close to the Schlink residence, so that he could continue the young man's chess training.

Gunard would spend the day in his study facing the Lindenhof, studying games with Momsen, while Renate remained in her parents' house with little Ebenezer. One night, coming back later than usual, the young woman went up to the study to say hello to her husband and gave a cry of horror. Gunard was sitting by the window, with the light off. He had put on one of her dresses and a blonde wig. What are you doing? she asked, on the verge of tears, switching the light on, but he said, please turn that off, I prefer the dark, I'm looking at the moon.

Obviously I'm not talking about that! she said, I want to know what you're doing in those clothes! Oh, he said, it's just that I feel freer this way, as if my spirit could fly all the way to the moon and sit down in one of its craters and think in solitude or think about how strange and miraculous it is to be alive while I travel those lunar valleys and linger before the vast depths, and Renate wept bitterly, and said, you're going crazy, darling, chess is driving you crazy, you have to stop playing and live like other people, go shopping, look at what's in the windows, meet friends, have a few beers, that's what you need. Her tears turned into a nervous breakdown.

She tore the wig and the dress off him, which only made things worse, because she saw with horror that he had also put on her underwear—bra and panties—and Gunard said, you want me to be somebody else and go to bars, but I'm fine just staying here by the window, looking at the moon, don't you see? I'm not harming anyone, not you, not little Ebenezer, and when he said this she replied, be grateful that he's just a baby and doesn't know anything, how do you think he'd feel if he saw his father dressed as a woman? Gunard looked at her and replied, he'd be curious and would ask me why I do it, and I'd answer the same way I answered you, I'd tell him the truth, and he'd have to understand, Renate, because he's my son and he'd be happy to see his father at peace.

The next day Renate called her father-in-law in Gothenburg and told him what she had seen, and he asked, but do you have normal relations? She said yes, many times, she had no complaints about that side of things. Then Gunard's father replied: it'll pass, it's something he's had since he was a child and finds it hard to let go of, but it'll pass, believe me, and by the time she put the phone down she was feeling somewhat reassured.

From that night Gunard's father and Renate sealed a secret alliance based on fear of something they did not dare name, which was the possibility that Gunard was a homosexual and was hiding it, or refusing to accept it.

Renate started taking precautions, like keeping her closet locked and collecting her used clothes every day. She also, very reluctantly, started not coming home at nights. The routine had been that she would spend the day with little Ebenezer in her mother's country house outside Zurich and come back late in the afternoon. But now when the time came for her to leave, she would feel a great sense of unease, so she would call Gunard and say, I'm staying here, Eby has a cough and I don't want him to be in the cold air, and he would reply, don't worry, darling, I'm going to miss you, but I'll see you tomorrow.

During this period, Gunard usually stayed up late studying games, alone or with Momsen, and now that Renate was staying away more frequently, three or even four times a week, he would sleep in the study and the next day the maids or even Renate would find him asleep over the chess table, a cup of cold coffee beside him. He has to give up this evil game, she would say, the damn thing will be the death of him.

She immediately launched a campaign against chess, deciding that she would never leave him alone but constantly create things they urgently had to do together, always involving little Ebenezer. When it was his time to study with Momsen, Renate would press him to go with her on some errand or other that, according to her, could not be postponed, and he would obey. But one night he said, Renate, I want to get back to chess, so don't schedule any activities between nine in the morning and five in the afternoon. She lost her temper and said, it's obvious you don't care about our life, it's obvious what happens to your son doesn't interest you, it's obvious I don't matter to you. When she saw him looking at her in silence, without contradicting her or arguing, she lost her temper and said: what you want is to be alone so you can wear my clothes and my underwear! And she added, beside herself, God knows what you get up to with Mr. Momsen when I don't see the two of you, do you act like a woman? does he like my panties? was he the one who taught you to dress like that?

Gunard said nothing, unable to think up any answer to such accusations. He merely shrugged his shoulders and looked at her curiously, until she burst into tears, struck her chest, and head and said, admit you're having an affair with him, admit you're a lousy queer and you love him, admit you'd give your life to be with him all the time and sleep with him and spend Christmas with him, admit it, monster, admit it now!

Gunard replied: I don't know why you're saying that, Theodor and I do nothing but study chess, that's all I have to say, and he opened the front door. Before he could go out, Renate ran and threw herself in front of him. She traced an imaginary line on the floor and said, if you cross this you can't come back, you'll be gone forever and little Ebenezer and I will be on our own. Gunard hesitated for a moment, looked down at the line, and strode across it. Then he said: the field is clear, when you calm down you can come back, I'll be waiting for you with the same love and concern I've always had for you and our child.

Then he turned and went out, and she watched him walk along Lindenhofstrasse and turn toward the Limmat. What hurt her most was that Gunard did not look back or give any indication that he was interested in what he was leaving behind. Quite the contrary. From the way he was walking, which she knew well, he seemed lost in thought, the kind of thoughts she had never been privy to, connected with that evil game, so she closed the door with dignity and, remembering an old movie, said to herself, he'll be back in a few hours begging my forgiveness, groveling on the floor wanting to come in, an image that gave her back her pride. And she went upstairs to wait for him in one of his rooms.

The wait was in vain. Gunard did not appear that evening or night, or the next day, or any of the days that followed, so Renate, feeling desperate and guilty, decided to call Mr. Flø in Gothenburg and tell him everything. Gunard's father was very worried and said to his daughter-in-law, leave everything to me, I'm on my way.

The next day he landed in Zurich, booked into the Hotel Eden au Lac, facing the lake formed by the River Limmat, and there he met with Renate, who explained the situation with tears in her eyes, all the while embracing little Ebenezer.

Stellan Flø, who knew a lot about domestic disputes, said, if I've understood correctly it was you who forbade him to come back, wasn't it? and she replied, that was what I said that day to stop him walking out, to which Stellan Flø replied, it's no good putting somebody as fragile as Gunard to the test and hoping he'll react like any other human being, it was a mistake and we're going to try to rectify it, that's why I'm here, I'm on your side. The reason he hasn't come back is that he agreed to your request not to do so, but I doubt that's what he wants. Let me talk to him.

He went to see his son and found him in his study, analyzing a game with his teacher, Momsen. Gunard was very happy to see his father and asked him if he would like a cup of tea; then he said, look at this position, do you think there's any way the whites can get anything more than a draw? His father looked at the pieces for a while and said, I don't know, I have no way of knowing, but to be honest I can't concentrate on chess right now, and the young man asked, is something wrong, father? Stellan Flø, with a mixture of indignation and affection, said, yes, what's wrong is that my son is throwing his life away and that worries me, doesn't it worry you?

Realizing that father and son were about to start a serious

conversation, Mr. Momsen excused himself and left, and Gunard said, did Renate call you? His father told him the reason for his visit and asked him what he was planning to do, go back to her or separate and leave his son? Gunard avoided looking him in the eyes and said, Father, everything has been very complicated, she doesn't understand my way of life, in fact she rejects it, she feels threatened by it. I can't understand why, my desires are harmless and concern only me, they're solitary pleasures that change nothing on the face of the earth, don't you see that, Father? and Stellan Flø said, yes, I do, but you have to realize that to her it seems as if something isn't working when she comes home and finds her husband in her clothes and underwear, can you at least understand that?

Gunard insisted that he was not harming anyone. Nevertheless, his father managed to persuade him to put on his coat and go out to the house, where Renate and little Ebenezer were waiting for him. Nothing especially unusual happened at the reunion. Renate acted with dignity, waiting for words of repentance that did not come, but in the end they gave each other an embrace that left Stellan Flø feeling very relieved, and he invited them to dinner at the restaurant of his hotel.

What happened later you can all imagine. The reconciliation was the first crack in a dam that was about to break, but the final impulse did not come, as many of you may already be thinking, from another of Gunard's transvestite episodes, but from the entrance onto the scene of a Norwegian collector, Edvard Gynt, who was in Zurich to handle some financial matters and ended up seducing Renate. This time, it was Gunard who was forced to witness an awkward scene, coming back from his study one day and passing a car parked near the house. Purely as a reflex action, he glanced inside the car and recognized Edvard, with his pants down around his knees. Renate was leaning over him, her blonde hair bobbing up and down at a frenetic rhythm while the collector, with his eyes closed, was sighing and gripping the wheel tightly.

Gunard waited on a nearby bench and when he saw her get out he approached and said: I saw what you were doing. Renate burst into tears and rebuked him, it's your fault, you abandoned me. He did not reply, not even with a gesture of anger or sorrow. This exasperated Renate, who said, you're a closet queen, how do you think that makes a woman feel? He looked at her and said nothing, and she continued: you have sex with me, but only to conceal your true nature, you're Momsen's lover, I know you are, so don't look at me like that, what you saw in Edvard's car is normal in a woman whose husband has left her, and the judges will understand that if you're planning to sue me for a divorce, what will they say when they find out you dress like a woman?

Gunard remained silent, looking at her without malice, and she said, don't try to take the boy away from me in the courts, if you do I'll report you as a homosexual and a pederast, and who do you think they're going to believe? you or me? do you dare to find out? If that's what you want, you just have to go and tell your lawyer what you saw in that car, and you'll see how things will turn against you. If what you want is a court case you'll lose everything and will even have to give me your damn chess sets.

Having said this, Renate calmed down and went to bed, and he shrugged, turned, and went back to his study.

Weeks later, attending, as an observer, a tournament at Zurich town hall involving Grand Masters such as Elmor Topkin and Constantino Reina, he met a 32-year-old woman named Cécile Roth, who came from a Lithuanian Jewish family and was married to the great Swiss banker and chess enthusiast Seymour W. Maeterlinck. Gunard had that absent expression that took possession of him whenever there were pieces moving across a chessboard, and that was why it took him a while to notice that Cécile could not take her eyes off him. When the games were over (ending in Topkin's entirely predictable victory) there was a cocktail party thrown by the town council, at which the players were able to talk with the public. It was there that Cécile approached the young Swede.

They talked about the tournament, and Topkin's victory (his fourth successive one in Zurich), and the strange final position, with two knights crossed and a bishop in the middle. By the second glass of champagne, Cécile's cobalt-blue eyes had done the trick, and Gunard, with the same innocence with which he did everything, said, it's a pity you're married, I'd love to spend the night with you. Cécile replied, it's true I'm married, but there are exceptions to everything. Then she handed him a piece of paper and said, write down the address of the place where I have to go so that you can have what you want, and then she returned to her husband's arm.

Gunard went back to his studio feeling somewhat confused and without holding out any hope, but just before midnight there was a knock at his door, and there she was. She kissed him and said, quick now, this first time will have to be very quick. They made love on the carpet and when they had finished she leaped to her feet, adjusted her clothes and went to the door. I'm taking your telephone number, she said, I'll be in touch very soon, goodbye. And she left.

Gunard sat on the couch in the studio, naked, unable to believe what had happened and with an angel in his throat, to quote Rilke.

For the first time, he felt there was something that could distract him completely from the world, from his own world, and so he sat naked on the couch for the next two days, waiting for Cécile, unwilling to get her smell off him.

She did not come. Instead, Renate showed up. Gunard opened the door without putting anything on, like some mad satyr. Renate looked at him with contempt and said, well, you're making progress, at least you aren't dressed like a woman, and he said, you don't know who I am, and sank into complete silence. He refused to tell her if he was coming home or if he wanted to ask for a divorce. Nor did he speak when she asked him, as tactfully as she could, what exactly did you see that night in Edvard's car? At last Renate left and he was able to return to his couch and his thoughts, which were all of Cécile's body and her smell and the way she pronounced every syllable before she had left. He went over and over her words, "I'll be in touch very soon"; he made an effort to see her as she had said it, analyzing her facial muscles, the way she pushed her lips forward in a smile, the kiss she blew him on her index finger, the noise of the door as it closed.

Two more days passed and Momsen, who until now had never given him any advice on anything other than chess, decided to help him, saying: Gunard, a man sitting on a couch waiting for a woman is a classic situation, what you're doing now has been done at least once by most of our fellows, that's why I understand you, that feeling of being at the bottom of an abyss, the rapid heartbeats, the loss of appetite, and the conviction that if that person doesn't return, a slab of granite will fall on our head and we'll be buried in a wave of grief and solitude, I know that, it stops us breathing and puts us in a highly sensitive state, any story reduces us to tears, the words of every song hurt us, we can't go to the movies and concentrate, the whole universe is a metaphor for that person we're yearning for, who doesn't come, that's the way it is, you're experiencing something tremendously human that has inspired a great deal of poetry and art, because although it's unpleasant to live through, once we've overcome it, it becomes a source of ideas, esthetic ideas, even scientific ones, and it's the best inheritance we can leave ourselves, always remember, there's nothing worse than the frivolity and foolishness of those who have never suffered, those whose fears are abstract concepts, no, my friend, what truly moves us men, what drives us to dig in the magma where what doesn't yet exist can be found, what makes us search for what we lack or what we are not, is the fear of going back to those solitary hours, the fear of being unable to breathe, the fear of losing the certainty that the world, after a night in darkness, will return to the light because there is somebody close: all that is at the origin of creation, don't forget that chess is an esthetic, use this experience to make yourself strong.

When Momsen had finished, Gunard said, I'm sinking, Theodor, I can't help sinking, farther and farther down, I don't want to avoid it, I'm not the one who chose to be like this, it's the situation and it's Cécile and it's what grew in me after being with her, something inside me that's alien, like an illness we can only cure with waiting and silence, because there's no substance or bacteria that needs to be cured, the organism is healthy, I don't want to do anything to stop the fig tree growing and choking me, why should I? the idea of death through love is something we only understand when we're on the verge of dying for love, Theodor, thank you for your advice and experience, they've been very useful to me today.

After the talk with Mr. Momsen came the longed-for prize. There was a rap at the door, and when he opened it the world starting turning again, the planets resumed their orbits and their muffled noise, and night and day stopped being the two faces of a frozen sphere. Gunard's heart swelled to the bursting point when he heard Cécile say, forgive me, my husband forced me to go with him on a ridiculous journey to Venice, but all I did was think about you, the surge of the canals brought me your voice, I demanded a separate room in the Hôtel des Bains to think about you in the middle of that vast ontological lagoon, I couldn't stand being with him, I don't want to be touched by anyone but you, touch me, kiss me, come inside me.

They rolled on the floor and made love as they had the first time, until night fell and they phoned out for something to eat, and sat on the couch, eating pizza and drinking Burgundy.

They stayed like this for three days until there was another knock at the door and Gunard heard Renate's voice through the air vent, but he did not let her in. She wanted to know if he was planning to come back home, if he was planning to leave little Ebenezer, if he thought his marriage wasn't worth the bother of an explanation, and added: I haven't the slightest idea what you thought you saw that night in Edvard's car, but it must have been a hallucination, the product of your obsession, don't you think?

Gunard opened wide the door of his study, pointed to Cécile lying naked on the cushions, and said, let me introduce the new woman in my life. Then, turning to Cécile, he said, this is my ex-wife, I hope you get along well. Renate looked at him with eyes full of hatred and said, how long have you been screwing this whore? Cécile got in ahead of Gunard—although he had not in fact planned to answer—and said, madam, I've been here for three days and we've made love twenty-two times. Before these three days, only once, last week. Don't worry, this is new, believe me.

Renate glared at her, turned to Gunard, and said, I don't know how you're going to justify this to your father, and then, much to everyone's surprise, Gunard said, he already knows, my father already knows, and he fell silent again. Renate was terrified when she heard that and only managed to say: now I understand. Then she walked out, slamming the door, and Cécile and Gunard embraced.

The next person to arrive was the banker Seymour W. Maeterlinck. He had learned Gunard's address by bribing his wife's chauffeur and now here he was, in front of the two of them, accompanied by his lawyer. Maeterlinck came straight to the point, and said, very well, I see you've decided to make a new life for yourself, I shan't stand in your way, I will only ask you to sign a few papers, Mr. Heep? The lawyer, Uriah Heep, handed her a folder of documents and said, madam, please sign here, at the bottom, next to your name. Cécile looked through the documents, nodded in agreement, and signed them, until she came to one particular document, and said, don't be cynical, Seymour, the house in Amalfi was chosen and decorated by me, to which the banker replied, indeed it was, my dear, but I paid for it, so sign, Mr. Heep thinks a monthly allowance of 25,000 euros will be sufficient, and she said, if Mr. Heep thinks that, then it must be right, although I would be inclined to go for double that figure myself. Then the lawyer Heep said, I understand, madam, but there is a problem, which is that if you don't agree I'll have to accuse you of adultery, there are many witnesses, not to mention the fact that you are here today, in front of us, half-naked. You'd also have to pay the legal fees, which seems rather pointless, so my advice to you is to stop arguing and accept the 25,000. Cécile thought it over for a moment or two and signed. Before he left, the lawyer Heep said, I wish you all the best in your new life, madam, and if at any time you have legal problems don't hesitate to call me. Heep held out his hand to Gunard. It was damp and cold to the touch, like a reptile's. That was the image he kept of the lawyer Uriah Heep.

Three months later, Renate and Gunard agreed on a divorce and the young Swede was able to devote himself to Cécile. But Switzerland, and in particular Zurich, was hostile territory. There were unexploded bombs beneath those sidewalks and squares and they contained too many disturbing memories. Where to go? Gunard would go to the ends of the earth in order not to be separated for a single moment from the woman he loved. Cécile, whose family had emigrated to Switzerland during the Nazi era, had never seen it as her country, the fact that she had been born in Zurich was purely fortuitous. What she dreamed of was a thin strip of land in the Middle East, a fragile space of which she had heard thousands of stories and to whose defense she always sprang with passion: Israel, the land of the Jews. That was the place Cécile suggested, and Gunard, who was not himself Jewish, said, all right, we'll go where you say, the best thing is to get away from this city, and the shadow of these clouds and these mountains, and that was what they did. They sent their belongings by sea and flew to Tel Aviv and then to Haifa, the city of the gardens of Bahaullah, and settled in an apartment with a view of the port and of Acre, and there they began a new life, she as a rich immigrant receiving visits from a multitude of relatives and friends, and he devoted to chess, sitting on the balcony, breathing in the air of the Mediterranean and bathed in the golden reflections of the sun, because it was still September.

One afternoon when Cécile was out and he was contemplating the vague outline of Acre and the bay from his table, he felt something very deep, as if inside him a little goblin had opened a door and switched on the light of a grotto where antique objects and old masks lay, dusty and twisted but still there, intact. He went into the bedroom and opened Cécile's closet. Twenty minutes later, he was wearing a purple dress and a pair of nylon stockings. He made up his eyes and lips and put a pin in his hair, which gave it a strangely volcanic effect, and sat down on the balcony in that costume to observe the swell of the sea, the slow movements of the boats and the clear air that appeared to shine on the water. He felt a disturbing happiness, a hurricane that was born in his chest and was struggling to come out, and so he gripped the iron bars of the balcony and cried out loudly, until the veins rose in his neck, and he cried not a word but a brazen lament, a song that was to split his life in two, this side, the side of the balcony in Haifa and Cécile and the view of Acre, being the part where he planned to stay for the rest of his life, leaving everything else behind. He was conscious that there were people he loved, like little Ebenezer, but that's life, at times it can be cruel and incomprehensible.

Imbued in these thoughts, he continued observing the landscape, and a moment later what he saw had stopped being the horizon of the Middle East or the profile of Acre or the gardens of Bahaullah. His imagination had taken him to Orplid, the distant city of stalactites, but as he walked along one of its avenues, there came a tremor, and the air filled with smoke and dust, and when he looked at the ground he discovered that it was covered in rubble and the remains of corpses, with mutilated arms and legs and faces frozen by death in a desperate attitude, the infinite solitude of a corpse, and then, as he walked up the main street, lined with demolished palaces, he realized that he was not alone, that behind him a group of shadows was beginning to climb. He was at the head of a silent retinue of people dressed in cloaks and hoods, carrying long sticks and advancing with difficulty, and he continued his march, seeing the highest hills in the middle of the city, where a dome still glittered in spite of the fires. With great effort, he led the group and began the last ascent up a blackened staircase that crossed the remains of a garden of charred birches and a layer of ash where there should have been grass and flowers. As he reached the top and sighted the palace, and the group caught their breath before entering the temple to register its destruction, a deafening bust of gunfire coming from the darkest part of the night decimated them, and Gunard, faced with such sorrow, fell to his knees and raised his arms and looked down at his own body now torn to pieces, destroyed by shrapnel, and then heard a voice saying, what are you doing? why are you kneeling?

Cécile covered her face with one hand, hiding an expression of surprise. Her eyes filled with tears, she let out a fierce laugh, and said, what the hell are you doing with my clothes?

Gunard was still recovering from his terrible daydream and could only reply, I'm sorry, it's the way I have of getting close to certain things, ideas or premonitions, it's the only way I can unravel them, and she said, you look very pretty, come help me make dinner, my God, the wind is starting to get cooler, don't you feel cold? Cécile did not make any kind of scene on learning of his clandestine enthusiasm. It seemed not to bother her, in fact she found it amusing, so they continued their life in Haifa, she devoted to her visits and he joining a local chess club, starting to play again and, much to his surprise, winning tournaments, because the general level was lower than his.

He began to feel again that in order to enjoy life he did not need to go far, to be a Grand Master or gain prizes or anything like that. In the little chess club in the harbor area of Haifa he learned that, apart from Cécile, the one really important thing was to have time for his whims, a comfortable space in which to live quietly and privately, and a clean environment where he could breathe freely. Greatness, as it was traditionally understood, seemed to him a prison. So he devoted himself to simple things, which is another way of saying that he led a happy life.

Four years later, he applied for Israeli nationality, in order to join his destiny to that of this strip of land and to be even closer to Cécile. One condition, though, was that he undergo military training, which he accepted immediately. A year and eight months later, he was another man, weathered by the sun, with well-toned muscles, a strong man always to be seen on the beaches of Haifa or in the restaurants of the harbor area. He started to play in tournaments in Tel Aviv as an Israeli, because it gave him pleasure to think that he was sharing the life of six million people who had come from the four corners of the earth with the idea of a country of their own, such as he had found in Cécile and they both had in Haifa.

But happiness rarely lasts forever, as Gunard was to discover in the most brutal manner. In a fairly succinct e-mail,

Renate informed him that little Ebenezer had died of meningitis. When she got home that evening, Cécile found him sitting in front of his Mac, as motionless as if a distant sniper had planted a bullet between his eyebrows. When she touched him she noted that he was freezing cold. In the emergency department of Beth Israel hospital, they said he had had a nervous shock, and when he recovered his first words were, my little Ebenezer is gone, I've been punished for leaving him alone.

They flew to Zurich and attended the funeral. Renate was cordial enough, although she looked at him with accusing eyes. She had been living for some time now with the Norwegian Edvard, which was only logical, and was devoting herself to non-figurative art and artistic happenings, in the style of Paul Hayse and Miriam Cunningham. She announced that she was planning to operate on herself, in order to create a work of sculpture out of her own body, as a way of expressing her grief over Ebenezer's death in a permanent form.

They talked about this over a beer in the café attached to the funeral parlor, minutes before the cortege set off for the cemetery. Outside, it was raining. Gunard was surprised that Renate could use the death of their child for artistic purposes, however noble the idea; he found it hard to believe that her grief was not as strong as his and that she could only think about herself. But he said nothing, only listened to her and then stood up, paid for the beer, and went back to the room where the coffin lay.

His father had come from Gothenburg for the occasion. They embarked, which gave Gunard back his strength. Then they went for a walk and his father said, the death of a child is the worst pain a human being can suffer, but you mustn't look for reasons and you mustn't try to assign blame, any more than you can deny that it's a terrible injustice and demonstrates that this world is not ruled by a superior being but by a murderous, drunk little tyrant who gloats over his creatures. Above all, don't try to understand, be strong and wait, the pain will pass, remember the Chinese proverb, we have to be like the bamboo, which bends when there's a storm and then rises again, let the storm pass, the noise of it will thunder in your head, but don't do anything. It's like the rain. You can't stop it falling, you can only wait until it's over.

He spent all night with his father and Cécile. The next day they buried Ebenezer in the Friedhof Fluntern in Zurich, in a grave on which Renate had had the following phrase carved: *The rest of my life is written on the stones that lie at the bottom of the Limmat.* Gunard made no objection, even though Renate's need to transform the child's death into something distinctive struck him as vain and ridiculous. The symbolism and metaphors concealed her imperious desire to play a leading role in the tragedy, to appropriate it for herself, thus demonstrating her extraordinary crassness and egotism. Gunard said nothing, and looked absent during the ceremony. Some of those present claimed they felt a great sense of cold when they gave him their condolences, as if something of that frozen North from which he came was in his eyes.

Ebenezer's death marked the final break with Renate, and that gave him a feeling of calm. On the flight back to Tel Aviv, he looked out the window at the glistening blue expanse of the sea and remembered the night with Renate in Capri. My God, he said to himself, what begins so romantically, between two human beings, has a tendency to become corrupted and end tragically, in contempt and insults and humiliation, is it always like that? The proof of the contrary was Cécile, but he also said to himself, it's too soon to draw conclusions. We'll have to wait a few more years.

Some time later, when Gunard was on the point of abandoning chess, he was called into the army. His new country was getting ready to launch a military action outside its borders and needed all its reserves. Gunard joined a tank company

whose mission was to transport the wounded as well as sup-
plies. Cécile enlisted in a mobile hospital unit.

The combat began and Gunard became accustomed to
advancing amid dust and rubble, lifting bloodstained and
mutilated bodies full of holes. He became accustomed to
shrieks of pain and the sharp crack of ampoules of morphine
opened with the teeth, and other things too: the smell of
charred flesh and the smell of gangrene and the bulging eyes of
young men who were dying and knew it and having to stop
bleeding by plunging his hand into hot wounds, yes, Gunard's
fingers, accustomed to moving delicate pieces of wood or
ivory, were now exploring the insides of shattered bodies,
suturing broken veins, and occasionally, only occasionally,
finding bodies that emerged from the rubble and started to
run, propelled by the force of life, an image that made him cry
and forced him to hide his face, because the simplest actions
had turned into something precious.

So it was that one afternoon, after a thunderous combat in
a village, he saw a body emerge out of nowhere, and a man lifting his hands and saying, save me. Ferenck Oslovski.

They met at the moment of salvation.

Later, in the mobile hospital behind the lines, where they
sewed Ferenck's wounds and announced a slow recovery,
Gunard said: I know how to spend the sleepless nights, and he
took out a chess set. After a few games, they realized that they
knew each other. They had both taken part in a tournament in
Austria two decades earlier and although they had never played
against each other, they remembered each other's names.

When the war ended, they continued to meet.

Gunard would come to Tel Aviv and they would play on the
beach until the orange sphere of the sun descended below the
surface of the sea, seeming to sink in the water. The two men
would talk and move the pieces rapidly. The lives of both men
had drifted to that coast like a school of fish moving to warmer

224 · SANTIAGO GAMBOA

waters. Oslovski would say to Gunard: look at the sand, it's made of tiny stones and crystals. When one of these particles sinks it's covered by another, by ten more, a hundred or a thousand, and the same thing happens to us, don't you think? When we sink others will come, hundreds of thousands, and the Earth will always be populated by people who will feel alone, but a hundred years may pass before two men again play chess on this beach, do you think chess will still exist? Yes, said Gunard, chess is deeper and more mysterious than all of us put together; it'll exist until somebody manages to master it completely, and that'll never happen, Ferenck, it's impossible for that to happen. Oslovski looked at him in surprise, and said, at the end of the day it's a question of statistics: we'll keep getting better, more intelligent, more gifted, we'll keep going farther. Soon the great men of the 21st century will be born, or rather, they'll turn into adults, because many may already have been born, and then we'll know about them. The Freuds and Marxes and Einsteins and Nietzsches of the 21st century must be going to school right now, or still playing with toy cars, or watching the fall of a leaf in a park, who knows? And apart from them, there'll also be a young Kafka suffering then turning to literature as therapy, and there'll be an aristocratic Proust, who'll portray the decadent bourgeoisie of the early 21st century from within, and of course the new Rimbaud must already be walking the streets, a young man with his fists clenched with hate, struggling against the social forms, and the Bukowski of the 21st century receiving a thrashing from his father and discovering that alcohol dulls the pain, and of course some boy of seven or eight must be on the verge of checkmating an adult on a chessboard, because in humanity's infinite pack, the cards are equal only on one side; when we turn them over we find that there are many twos and threes and sixes of spades, but far fewer aces of diamonds, do you see what I mean?

Gunard listened to him, looked again at the chessboard, and said, you're right, not all of them are aces, but being an ace doesn't always ensure a happy life; the six of spades may end up much happier. Ah, great lives! Usually they're people who suffer, maladjusted creatures; some because their vocation was so overwhelming that it put an end to anything that didn't serve its purposes, others because their longings were never satisfied; others because they pursued the vanity of fame and success fruitlessly; others because sometimes talent is associated with terrible defects and vices, serious shortcomings . . .

Then the two men would fall silent and finish their game, and then spend a while analyzing the positions. When they could barely see their pieces, they would gather everything up and go off to a bar on the beach, near the walls of the port of Jaffa, and drink a few beers and continue talking about life and its curious variations, until at dinner hour they would walk to the Nightingale of Odessa where Gael would serve them pizzas with vodka and herrings in vinegar.

Sometimes Cécile came with Gunard and the four of them had dinner on the second floor of the restaurant, which was an uncomfortable space, a low-ceilinged mezzanine that filled with steam from the kitchen, but there they could sit down alone and chat: all this in spite of the fact that Gunard and Cécile were rich, rich in the best meaning of the word, that is, they did not have to work in order to live and enjoyed a comfortable lifestyle, but that did not mean that they closed the door to people of lower financial status, which was why they always preferred to meet in that cramped space and not in fashionable restaurants or hotels.

Although Gael and Cécile only knew each other through their husbands and were not obliged to become friends, they, too, developed a friendship that grew and put down roots. After a time, Gunard and Cécile decided to rent an apartment in Tel Aviv that would allow them to spend the weekends with their friends, a beautiful penthouse on Rothschild Boulevard, not far from the Allenby district.

The lives of these four friends went on like this, placidly, for six years until, once again, the fates got angry, or else grew bored and turned their gaze to them, and something very sad happened, which was that Cécile found a lump in her breast, a little ball just under her right nipple, and the subsequent tests determined that the cancer had spread to sensitive areas like the pancreas and the liver and that a swelling of the tissue of the lung was in fact emphysema. Radiation treatment began immediately and Cécile foundered, in spite of the efforts of Gunard, Gael, and Ferenck, who constantly invented new and extravagant ways to distract her, to make her feel happy and lucky.

Every human being has his limits, and seven months later Cécile lay dying. She weighed eighty-five pounds, her skin was the color of linen, and Gunard prayed for a quick, painless death. The gods heard him and a few hours later Cécile's heart stopped. Oslovski and Gael were at the hospital and they were the first people to receive the news from the doctors. Gunard was so absent, it was as if he was under the effects of a drug. Of the following seventy-two hours, he retained only chaotic, disjointed memories. A sumptuous funeral, with Cécile's family present, meetings with rabbis and lawyers to settle the inheritance, and then it was all over and Gunard decided to settle in Tel Aviv, near the only friends he had in the world.

Oslovski and Gael looked after Gunard as if he were their son. They took turns being with him, making him lunch and dinner, or going out for walks with him. Ferenck's company was more beneficial, because with him he could descend into that deep cave that was chess, which took him away from the surface, where all the pain and absurdity was, where the memory of Cécile waited for him with its daggers and its hot irons, and so the two friends grew closer than ever, to the point where Ferenck would spend the weekend in Gunard's apartment, and Gael would come there to sleep and be with both of them. On one of these weekends, Ferenck and Gael told Gunard that it was time to throw out Cécile's things, and that they had found a charitable association that took used clothes and sent them to less fortunate countries. Gunard liked the sound of the association, but refused to allow Cécile's things out of the apartment. They were his and he wanted to keep them. Ferenck and Gael shrugged, and that same night, after dinner, Gunard appeared in a striped dress, green nylon stocking, high-heeled shoes, and jewelry. Don't worry, he said to them, I do it to find a bit of peace, I've always done it; Ferenck, who had already drunk a few vodkas, said, if you have to confess to us that you're a fucking queer, do it now, nothing will happen, but he said, it isn't that, Ferenck, this calms me down, not many people understand, but Cécile did.

Gael intervened to say, that's enough, don't say anything more, just let me tell you, that color really doesn't suit you, you look like a madwoman in a beauty parlor; Ferenck, overcoming his initial rejection, finally said, it's O.K., forget it happened. That settled the matter, and every night, after dinner, Gunard performed his ritual with Cécile's clothes and chatted with them for a while, before going to the window of his room to look out at the night, which from there was mostly lights on roofs and buildings rising in the darkness, and ask it his many questions, his sad, disconsolate questions.

His participation in local tournaments, although increasingly sporadic, led a chess correspondent from the United States to take an interest in the case of these two players who had decided to live in anonymity. He researched who they were, and what struck him most was that neither of them had striven to reach the heights. They had both been content to break off careers that could have led farther. The journalist wrote for the *Chicago Tribune* and his name was Earl Coltodino.

One afternoon, after a couple of fruitless calls, Coltodino went to the beach to look for them and found them near a terrace. They had a roll-up chessboard held down by stones and were analyzing a position, with bottles of Diet Coke that they kept cold in a bag filled with ice, plus chicken sandwiches that Gael had made for them that morning. In another bag was a thermos of hot coffee and a bar of chocolate. They were well prepared. At the bottom, ready for the end of the afternoon, was a quart of Smirnoff vodka.

Coltodino observed them from a distance and concluded, from the way they joked, that they were kindred souls. They reminded him of the uncomplicated friendships he had had as a child, back in the old neighborhood. He went closer, feigning interest in their game, and saw a complicated position from which his own knowledge offered no way out. He ventured to speak to them, saying he could not understand why the whites had given up.

Are you interested in chess? they asked, and Coltodino said, yes, very much, it's my favorite game.

Gunard sipped at his drink and said, look, the next move is this, and then this, and that way you get to this. He explained it very quickly, and Coltodino did not even understand, but did not say so. He asked them if they always played on Sundays. Oslovski looked at him and said, we come to the beach to play in peace. Coltodino begged their pardon, I'm sorry, I didn't want to disturb you, to which Oslovski replied, I'm not saying that because of you, if you're interested in chess you have something in common with us, come, sit down, and so Coltodino was accepted that Sunday afternoon and was able to chat with them and ask them things, until he said, you both play really well, you must have won a few tournaments in your time, I guess? Ferenck and Gunard looked at each other and nodded, but Oslovski added, all that happened a long time ago, it isn't worth remembering.

Coltodino drank his beer as he listened to them, and said, how is it that the two of you, who not only have a passion for chess, but also play it brilliantly, never wanted to take it farther? and Gunard said, there's too much pressure to deal with. Oslovski confirmed his friend's words, and added, what prize in the world is greater then this? Watching the sun set over the sea, playing with a friend, eating and drinking, eh? That's life, friend, what a privilege it is to be alive, would you like a sandwich?

Eric Coltodino took many notes in the three days he was with them. Before leaving he confessed to them who he was and what he was planning to do with their story. Gunard shrugged and Oslovski said, at least offer us a few drinks, and that resolved the matter, much to Coltodino's relief. He took photographs of them with different backgrounds, the port, the sea, and the walls of Jaffa.

The article was published two months later in the *Chicago Tribune*, under the title *The Oslovski & Flø Variation*, the name Coltodino chose to describe their approach to the game. It was a great success. Never before had he received so many letters or comments from readers.

I was one of those readers, my dear listeners, and I want to tell you, by way of conclusion, that until a very short time ago you could still see that couple of old men moving the chess pieces on the sand, drinking vodka and waving their hands as a sign of disagreement over some game, which was the greatest thing in their lives.

And that is the end of my story.

2.
THE SURVIVOR
(AS TOLD BY MOISÉS KAPLAN)

The events I am about to relate all happened to a man named Ramón Melo García, who lived in the town of La Cascada, in the department of Meta, in the Plains region of Colombia. Ramón was a good man, hardworking and honest. By the time he was twenty-nine, he already owned three auto repair shops, two in the town and another on the road to Granada, where he also sold soda, coffee, meat pies, and donuts. He had a total of twelve employees, working for minimum salary but with a percentage on outside repairs, Christmas bonuses, paid vacations, and health insurance. They all liked Ramón, because he wasn't a boss who gave orders from his office, but a worker like them, with his greasy uniform and his fingers covered in cuts and blisters. The little finger on his left hand was missing: at the age of fifteen he had caught it in a fan on a bus. As he would say, God cut off the finger I used for cleaning my ear, which must have been a message to stop listening to so much crap. And he would get back to work.

In the evenings, after work, he would go to see his girl-friend, Soraya Mora, who was twenty-six, had studied IT and secretarial skills, and worked in an internet café called La Maporita at the corner of Calle Tercera and the Parque Boyacá. He would sit down at one of the computers, look at his messages, check his Facebook account, and sit there for a while, chatting, drinking soda, and showing her photographs of his friends. At eight o'clock they would both go to Soraya's house for dinner; her mother, Doña Matilde, would make fish soup and pork and sometimes corn pancakes, because she was a peasant woman from Santa Fe de Antioquia. After dinner, they would sit in the doorway and watch the people passing by, and Soraya would say, when are you going to ask for my hand, Ramón? you're putting me to sleep with all this waiting, and he would say, calm down, Sorayita, you know I will. Of course I know, but when, next year? my mother asked me the other day, and so did my brother. Is your brother back? Yes, he just got back from Medellín, he's working in an office. And what kind of work does he do? What kind of work do you think? office work, I don't know, but it's well paid, about a million and a half pesos, maybe even more, yesterday he brought Mamá a gold necklace, and some earrings for me. Tell him I'd like to see him, tell him to drop by the shop whenever he likes, and we'll go have a few beers. Then Ramón would go home to sleep. He lived with his mother and an aunt, who were both seventy years old. At weekends, he and Soraya would go out dancing and drinking, almost always with his best friend, Jacinto Gómez Estupiñán, and Jacinto's wife Araceli Ramos. Most times, they went to a nightclub called the Rey de la Pachanga, on the road to Cubarral, next to the bridge over the River Ariari, and there they would drink and dance until it was time to spend a while at the Llano Grande motel. Jacinto and he had studied at the teacher training college in Cubarral and then taken their higher certificate in Villavicencio. As both were only sons and their mothers close friends, they had grown up together. Jacinto had a farm near Lejanías and raised cattle.

But the situation in the region was becoming complicated.

The 39th Front of the FARC operated around La Cascada, under the command of Mono Jojoy, and in 2004 the Héroes de los Llanos, an urban paramilitary militia, arrived, led by a man known as Dagoberto, a former lieutenant in the army who had worked as a foreman on a farm growing African palms before taking up arms again. La Cascada had become a strategic route in the drug trade and the paramilitaries began extorting money from local businesses and asking for information about FARC members. About a week after they arrived, the first bodies appeared in ditches. One of them was the body of Braulio Suárez Acevedo, a waiter from the Brisas restaurant, and the other, Alfredo Mora Cañizares, an assistant at the Don Saludero drugstore. They had been tortured with candles, their testicles had been cut off, and each had been shot three times. They had signs pinned to their backs that said: *I am a traitor to my country.* The people who saw them did not dare approach, and the bodies lay there almost the whole day. Just after nightfall, the police arrived in a van, identified them, and took them to the morgue at the local hospital.

Ramón did not see the bodies, but he had known Braulio Suárez Acevedo, who, as far as he was aware, had no connections with the FARC. One of his employees said to him, no, Don Ramón, of course he didn't have anything to do with the FARC, what happened was that he didn't want to pay the paras, that's all, anyone who doesn't pay them, they say he's with the guerrillas and they take him away, yesterday apparently they took Jesús Torres, the guy who works at the La Ceiba pool hall, who didn't have anything to pay them with and didn't want to give them the deeds to some land he owned, so they took him away, he'll show up in a ditch, that's for sure, nobody escapes those guys.

They hadn't yet come to Ramón's auto repair shop to ask for money, but he knew it was only a matter of time. A few days later, they did come, not to ask for money but to leave him two vans to be repaired. One had a blocked carburetor and the relay was missing; with the other one, he repaired the starting mechanism and the spark plugs and changed the brake pads. When they came back for the vehicles, Ramón handed the bill to the man known as Dagoberto, who looked at it, put it in his pocket, and said, thanks, I hope you did a good job, I've been told you're the only reliable mechanic around here. Ramón looked at him without saying a word, turned, and continued with his work, which involved stripping a camshaft on a Chevrolet dump truck.

More or less once a week, they left him vehicles to fix. One day they brought him a Cherokee with seven bullet holes in it, and said, Ramón, let's see if you can do a job on this piece of shit, look what a mess they made of it. Come back in a week, I'll get rid of those nasty holes, it's a nice car. They did not come for it after a week, but one of the men said to him, Dagoberto told me to tell you that he's selling it, so keep it and you can pay him later. But I don't know if I can afford it, it must be worth about thirty million, right? better if you take it away, I don't have the money. The chief said we should leave it, if you don't want it, talk to him about it. They went away and Ramón left it parked in back of the shop.

As it was Saturday, he went to La Ceiba to meet Jacinto, because Soraya had to stay at home to look after her mother. They had a few glasses of aguardiente and he told his friend about the car. This Dagoberto guy told me I should keep it and pay him later, but I don't have the money, a pity, it's a great car. But Jacinto said: if I were you I'd hold on to it, these guys have a lot of money, they might get themselves killed, and you end up with a car, so don't be stupid, tell them yes, they haven't even told you when you have to pay, so do it, if the worst comes to the worst you can pay them off by doing more repairs for them. No, Jacinto, I don't like these people, I prefer to have things I bought with my own money, not like that.

The next day he told Soraya about it, and said he was going to give back the car that evening, but she said, oh, Ramón, you really are an idiot, why give it back if they're giving it to you? I love that car, it's really classy, it looks great, keep it, you won't be sorry, you'll see, in fact, why don't you take me out now for a drive? No, Sorayita, if I use that car and something happens I'll be in trouble. What's going to happen? If something does happen, you can fix it, you're a mechanic, aren't you? go on, give me a ride, Ramoncito. O.K., darling, but only a short ride, come on.

On the Wednesday of the following week, one of the paramilitaries came to the shop and said to Ramón: Dagoberto wants to know when you're going to pay him the thirty million you owe him, he needs it by the end of the month. I don't owe him any money, I already told him I can't buy the car, I don't have that kind of money. What do you mean you're not going to buy it? you already took your girlfriend out for a drive, didn't you? Dagoberto wants the money by the end of the month. No, look, this is a misunderstanding, the only reason I took it out was to test drive it, because I also had to fix the electrical system, that's why I gave it a spin, to charge the battery and leave it ready, it's parked out there, you can take it away with you now if you like.

Another week passed, and nobody came until one day the police from Villavicencio showed up. They gave the Cherokee the once-over, checked the serial number of the engine, and told Ramón that the car had been stolen in Bogotá, was it his, if not, whose was it? Ramón said it belonged to a man he didn't know, he didn't even know the name. And what kind of work did you do on it? We fixed the ignition, the starting mechanism, and the condenser. I have it parked out there to see if they come for it, but I don't know who it belongs to. The police towed away the Cherokee and took Ramón with them. As they left town he saw two of the paramilitaries in the Caleñita store. They both watched him until the police car disappeared around the bend.

He was kept in Villavicencio for three days, until it became clear that he was not to blame. He did not give them the name of Dagoberto or anyone else. About a hundred times they asked him who the car belonged to, and a hundred times he said, a man who isn't from La Cascada, they left it with me and I repaired it, but I don't know the man's name, that's the way I work. When he returned home, Jacinto and Soraya came to see him, looking worried, and he said, you see what a gift they gave me, the car was stolen, didn't I tell you it's better to have your own things honestly?

Three days later, a messenger came from Dagoberto, with two other guys. They arrived in a Toyota 4x4. Ramón was partly underneath a Hyundai taxi and did not bother to come out. He said to them: what kind of trouble have you gotten me into? the Cherokee was stolen. I didn't tell the police anything, I didn't give them any names, you can sleep easy, there won't be any problems. But the guys said to him: what Dagoberto wants to know is when you're going to pay him the thirty million you owe him, and if you don't pay him, then give back the car.

Ramón took his head out from under the Hyundai and said, don't you get it or what? the police in Villavicencio took the car away and they're holding on to it because it was stolen, I don't have anything to do with that and I don't owe anything to anyone. The police took it away? The guys looked at each other. Well, what happened to the car is your problem, but you still have to pay the chief. We'll be back for the money next Monday, got that?

Ramón watched them go. He felt very angry, but he didn't say anything. That night, he said to Soraya: they got me into trouble and now they want me to pay for the car, can you imagine, and there was I, protecting them from the police, like an idiot, what I should have done was name names and let them go fuck themselves. Don't talk like that, Ramoncito, the best thing to do is sort it out once and for all. Can't you see, these people are really dangerous. Yes, that's why it's better to do things legally, Sorayita. On Saturday I'll go to Villavicencio and talk to the police again and tell them everything, let these guys go to jail and leave me alone.

That Friday night, over a beer, he said to Jacinto, no, brother, I can't go to the Rey de la Pachanga tonight because I'm getting up early tomorrow to go to Villavicencio. He told him this in a low voice. I'm going to talk to the police, can you believe it, those sons of bitches want to rob me, after I protected them, idiot that I was. Careful, brother, these people are tough. Yes, but the bastards aren't going to bring me down, all I ever did was do them favors and this is how they repay me, it's not right, it's not how things should be done.

The next day Ramón got in his Land Rover at six in the morning, filled his tank at the Texaco station, and drove out toward Granada in order to come out onto the road that would take him to Acacías and Villavicencio. The same guys who had come to the shop stopped him on the bridge over the River Ariari, and said to him, where are you going so early, Ramoncho? I'm going to Granada to buy equipment. And to go to Granada, you had to fill her up? I thought you were going farther than that, Ramoncho. The thing is, I always like to have her well filled, you never know. Good, we were waiting for you here because we need you to come with us, Dagoberto wants to talk to you. Is it about the Cherokee? I don't know, Ramoncho, I don't know, I imagine it is, come with us and work it out with him yourself, that's the best thing, come on now, Miguelito will drive your car, come on, get out.

He was tempted to accelerate suddenly and leave them in the lurch, but their Toyota was faster than his Land Rover and they would soon catch up with him and pump him full of lead. The best thing to do was gain time and go with them. He got out of the Land Rover and into the Toyota. So, Ramoncho, why are you up so early? The driver of the Toyota was Dagoberto's bodyguard, whose name was Nelson. I'm not sleeping too well these days, that's why I take advantage of the morning and do my errands early, but what about you, what's the hurry? No hurry, the chief just wants to talk to you and as he's an early riser, too, we decided to wait for you here.

Ramón preferred not to ask the question that was aching to get out. How did they know he was going to leave early? why were they waiting for him that particular day? who had told them? They had gone a couple of miles when one of the men in the back seat, who was well armed, said to him, Ramoncho, from here on, we're going to do the journey in the dark, O.K.? They blindfolded him and tied his hands with wire. Why are you tying me up, I'm not going to run away, I just want to get this whole thing sorted out properly, you know I have money, there are my shops and my things, if you like we can sort it out here among ourselves, once and for all, what's the point of making things worse, what do you think, guys? But the men said to him, shut your mouth, son of a bitch, stop talking crap, go to sleep, try to get some rest, you're going to need it later, and so Ramón fell silent, still thinking, over and over, how did they know? how did they know? He had only told Jacinto and Soraya, and it was impossible, what could have betrayed him? impossible, impossible.

They drove for about five hours until they came to a farm-house, where they at last removed the blindfold. It was one of those big old houses, surrounded by shady trees. They were received by a group of uniformed men who were playing *parqués*. He didn't know anybody, but one of them stood up and said, take him to three-ten, downstairs. Without giving him any explanation, they shoved him into a cell in the basement of the house and left. It was a room about fifteen feet by fifteen feet, with a bed and a chamber pot. From the ceiling hung a bare lightbulb surrounded by insects. The walls were not plastered but were of pure stone, it was obvious that the house was an extension of an older one. There he spent the rest of the day, or what he thought was the day, because there were no windows and the lightbulb was never switched off.

He did not know how long he slept, but suddenly the door opened and they said, get up, come with us, the chief wants to see you. They took him to what must have been the kitchen, because it had white tiles on the walls and concrete tables. There they tied him up, and after a while Dagoberto came in. Ramoncho, I'm sorry I had to bring you here in these conditions, but you do have my money, right? Ramón looked at him without any fear. That car wasn't yours, it was stolen, the police in Villavicencio kept me locked up for four days and I didn't tell them anything, I didn't give them any of your names, in order not to get you into trouble, didn't they tell you that? Yes, Ramoncho, and that was a good thing to do, but I also found out that in order not to pay me for the car you were planning to report me to the police, you were going to Villavicencio to do that, am I right? Ramón never told a lie, so he said, it's because you were very unfair, I protected you and you tried to ruin me, apparently I had to pay you for the car, but that car was never mine! Calm down, Ramoncho, let's not get all excited now. The problem is, the price has gone up now, and I think you're going to have to sign over the deeds to your shops, they're drawing the papers up now and they'll bring them in a couple of days, but there's no hurry. We'll talk when they arrive, O.K.?

Dagoberto went out and one of the three guys said to Ramón, oh brother, you're really in the shit now and all because you've been mean, meanness never pays, here you are, in this shithole, instead of banging your woman at the Llano Grande, nice and hard, you must be very stupid and a real snitch. Ramón spat in his face and the guy punched him, twice, three times, threw him to the ground, still tied up, and kept kicking him and shouting, you're a dead man, we're going to kill you, understand? take this scum away before I kill him.

After two weeks, Ramón looked really haggard. They had hit him with rifle butts and tortured him and showed him photographs of the way they cut up FARC members into pieces to avoid making a noise shooting them. That's the way we're going to leave you for being a snitch. We're going to cut you in little pieces so even your mother wouldn't recognize you, we're going to tear off your dick and send it to your girlfriend to eat.

After about a month, they arrived with some papers and Dagoberto appeared again and said, how have they been treating you, Ramoncho? well? Now the time has come to behave like a man because the deeds are ready to transfer your three shops, you see, here are the papers from the new owner, all you have to do is sign here, and here, and here, and the notary will do the rest.

Do you really think I'm going to give up the fruits of my labors, the only thing I can leave my children, to you people, no way, it isn't fair, maybe I could give up one shop, but not all three, you'd be leaving me with nothing. The thing is, Ramoncho, debts have to be paid, and if a person doesn't pay his debts he's punished, haven't you read the Bible? the man who does something pays, and the man who snitches gets fucked, that's in the Bible, yes or no? and they all said, yes, chief, of course, the snitch dies squashed, the scum dies disemboweled, and Ramón said, no, you're going to kill me anyway, so go ahead and kill me, but I'm not signing that thing, and so they hit him with their rifle butts in the balls and the penis, making him throw up several times because of the pain and because the air was sucked out of him. Take him away and let him think it over. Think about it, Ramoncho, sign this thing and you can go, of course you'll have to leave La Cascada because nobody in the town likes snitches, that's worse than being in the FARC, but I'll let you go, I give you my word. There's no hurry, man, in town they're saying you went to Villavicencio to sell what you had in order to move to Antioquia, and there's the testimony of Gil the guy at the gas pump who says you filled the tank of the Land Rover because

you were going to Villavicencio. Nobody's looking for you in
La Cascada. There's no hurry, Ramoncho, go back to your cell
and think over what I just said.

A couple of days went by and Ramón said, what I have to
do is see how I can get out of here. With a knife, he started to
file around one of the stones in the wall, and he could see that
the earth was falling and that it was more or less easy to open.
When he hit it, it sounded hollow, which he thought was
strange, because this was a cellar, so after his meal he continued using the knife on the stone until he felt it move. Am I
dreaming? The stone moved until he was able to remove it
from the wall, and much to his surprise, instead of more wall
what he found was a kind of tunnel, a very narrow passage that
a man could only just fit into, so he said to himself, this is for
me, and he stuck himself into it, and moved like a snake
through the passage until he found another stone that was
loose. Light could be seen around the edges and he said, shit,
I can't shift it. He listened, but could not hear a thing, so he
gave two little blows with the knife, to see what happened.
After a while he heard, knock knock. Someone was answering
him. So he said in a whisper, who's there? There was a long
silence. I'm Father Benito Cubillos, who's that? Ramón Melo
García, from La Cascada. He heard the stone move and the
passage was filled with light. A hand pulled him through to the
other side. Come on, man, come, nobody will look in at this
hour.

When he saw the man, he was almost scared. His hair and
beard came down to his belly, he had no teeth, and he was
deathly pale. His eye sockets revealed the skull beneath the
skin and his eyes themselves were the color of bone. I'm Benito
Cubillos, parish priest of Usiacurí. Where's that? Near
Barranquilla. The paras took me four years ago and have been
keeping me ever since, for helping the guerrillas, they say, but
that's not true, I was helping the Indians, which is different, I

tried to protect them but I was kidnapped, are you from the police, Ramón? have you come to get me out? No, Father, if only! They had their eye on me, too, they want to steal my auto repair shops and my money, I'm from La Cascada. And where is that? Here in Meta, Father, don't tell me you don't know we're in the Plains! How should I know that, they drugged me before they brought me here, they gave me burundanga.

Can I ask you something, Father, did you make this tunnel? Yes, of course, only when I saw it led to another cell I thought I'd leave it open to see if there was a way to escape, but it's very difficult, I hollowed out a bit of space on the other sides, too, but there's only gravel there, no way out. They heard a noise and Ramón rushed back to the tunnel, crawled to his cell and put the stone back in its place, smoothing the earth in such a way that nothing was visible. After a while one of the paramilitaries came in and threw him a bag. These things are yours, aren't they? There was a photograph of Soraya in a picture frame, a notebook, a memory stick, a digital camera, a white iPod, the earphones for the iPod, a pack of Pielroja with two twisted cigarettes, a credit card wallet, a box with his own business cards that said, *Ramón Melo García, Mechanic, La Mariposa, The repair shop you can trust.* It was all the things he had had in the desk drawer in his office. Had they already taken over the shop? The paramilitary stood there looking at him and said, don't be ungrateful, I brought you this without my partner knowing, to keep you amused, but if you like, I can take it away. No, leave it, leave it. Thanks, man, very kind of you . . .

The guy left and Ramón started thinking. These bastards are clever, what they want to do is wear me down, they think I'll see the photos and be even more determined to get out of here, but as soon as I sign those papers, bang bang, they'll kill me, you can't believe a word these people say. The noises had stopped, so he went back along the tunnel. He showed Father

242 · SANTIAGO GAMBOA

Cubillos the photographs of Soraya, Jacinto, his mother, a
stroll along the banks of the Ariari, a trip to Bogotá. Then he
told his story, in minute detail, and said, Father, you know people, who betrayed me? was it Soraya or Jacinto? it had to be
one of the two, only they knew. Don't torment yourself thinking about that now, Ramón, you mustn't let yourself be consumed with hate, that's the worst thing you could do. Think
deeply about life and you won't lose it, the Lord is not going
to leave you in this hole, not if you're good, that's why it's better not to be filled with hate. The thing is, Father, I've never
been a believer, I have to admit that. They killed my father by
mistake in Villavicencio. Then they apologized and tried to
give money to my mother, but I said, there can't be a God if
such things happen. I used to go to church before that, Father,
I'd always take communion with my mother. She also stopped
believing for the same reason. My father was the most devout.
He gave a tenth of what the shop made to the Church, and
look what happened, they killed him, they thought he was
someone else, someone who was giving money to a Mafioso,
they shot him seven times in the back of the head. He was just
coming out of the bank where he'd paid in the weekend's tak-
ings, because he was a good man and didn't spend his money
on drink or women, nobody could have been more sensible
than him, and look how God repaid him.

Oh, Ramón, there are things about God that we don't
understand all at once, but why should we understand, sometimes a person spends his whole trying to understand himself,
doesn't he? Yes, Father, he does. What happens, Ramón, is that
God sees a person in the context of his whole life, whereas that
person, when something happens to him, only sees the thing
that happened, but God sees the whole person, from all sides,
never forget that, and He knows why He does what He does,
you'll see, sooner or later you'll understand.

Back in his cell, Ramón started thinking over every moment

of the last few days before the kidnapping. On the Thursday night he had told Soraya that they had come by and asked him to pay for the car and that he had decided to talk to the police in Villavicencio. She had told him not to do it. On the Friday, he had worked until seven, when Jacinto had called him on his cell phone and told him they were going to the Rey de la Pachanga. He had refused and had suggested an early beer at La Ceiba. There, he had told him that he was planning to go to Villavicencio early the next morning. He remembered they had been at a table on the balcony, nobody could have overheard them there. Could Sorayita, in her desire to resolve things, have possibly said something to somebody, without intending any harm? or had Jacinto gotten drunk after that and, when they asked after me, said I was going to get up early to go to Villavicencio? That by itself doesn't mean anything. The paras knew he was going to report them. With this he fell asleep, although the light from the naked bulb was like a skewer in the brain.

The next day, they took him from his cell and interrogated him in the kitchen. He had heard moans earlier, and now he saw blood on the tiles. They must have been putting the screws on someone, he thought, and it made his hair stand on end. Let's see now, Ramoncho, are you going to cooperate with us today? It wasn't Dagoberto interrogating him, but one of his lieutenants. Tell Dagoberto I want to see him, I'd like to talk to him personally and sort things out. Ah, it looks like Ramoncho has seen reason, all right, call the chief.

An hour later, Dagoberto arrived. He was wearing a combat jacket and boots and carrying an Uzi. What's up, Ramoncho, are we signing or what? I'll sign if you tell me one thing, who told you I was going to Villavicencio to talk to the police? There was a silence. Dagoberto looked at his men and burst out laughing. Oh, this Ramoncho really is a scream! Setting conditions now, are we? Ramón remained impassive.

I'll sign the deeds to all three shops, he said, if you tell me who betrayed me. Dagoberto walked in a circle around him, like a fly turning around the light, and said, I'm going to confess something, Ramoncho, you know what? I like you, you're a good guy, a bright guy, ready to do anything to find out who snitched on you, that's what I call a man, damn it. I'm exactly the same, which is how I found out you were going to snitch on me to the police, you see? I did the same, Ramoncho, that makes us equal. Ramón looked at him, as impassive as ever. It isn't the same because you were robbing me and I'm not robbing you, and because you're a murderer and I'm a hardworking man, so it isn't the same; tell me who informed on me and then kill me, but don't say we're equal. Dagoberto looked at him furiously. We aren't equal, I'm not a snitch like you, and I don't have to tell you anything. Around here, nobody so much as farts without my knowing it, do you hear? I know all about you. I know you used to bang your girlfriend in Room 312 of the Llano Grande because from there you can see the church in Cubarral and she likes the reflection of the dome, and you like that room, not because of the church but because the TV has a big screen that's better for watching porn movies, like the ones with that Italian actress who acts as if she has gunpowder in her crotch, you see how well I know the lives of everyone around here? What you don't know, Ramoncho, is that Soraya also went to the motel with another man, I'm not going to tell you who, because I'm not a snitch. Oh yes, life is just one big shithouse, nobody has any principles, there are nothing but bad people. I'll give you another week to think it over, I'm in no hurry. And he walked out.

Back in his cell, he thought about what he had just heard. It was all lies, Soraya couldn't have had someone else, when would she have had the time? When he was in the shop they talked all the time, and then he went to La Maporita in the evenings. Impossible. If this was a TV soap opera, he thought, then Soraya would definitely have been making out with Jacinto, but this isn't TV, a pity, he said to himself, because it means I'm going to be pushing daisies soon, but before that I want to know, I really want to know! There's nothing sadder than dying without knowing.

That night he went to Father Cubillos's cell, but was unable to tell him anything because he found him feverish and delirious. The old man was seventy years old and seemed to have reached his limit. In that damp cell, his lungs must have been affected. Ramoncito, the Lord already has my service record in his hand and is looking through it now. He's already taken the decision to free the two of us, yes: a while ago, as I was dozing, I seemed to hear Him, He came to see me and said, get ready, we're going to get out of here, you and your neighbor, I'm going to free both of you, and then He showed me an image of Usiacurí; I think it was Usiacurí, but in reality it could have been any of those sad little towns in Colombia, the houses had been razed to the ground, the central square was a sea of ash and rubble, the church was like a burning torch, the general store had been turned to smoke, and He or somebody like Him was there, in a tunic, walking in the ruins of Usiacurí or Bellavista or even La Cascada, the name of the town doesn't matter, He had His head covered and He was leading a group of friars who were praying in silence, walking toward a hill where there was a cross, the only one not yet burned, and they started climbing, treading on rubble and the charred bodies of peasants and children, and when they had almost reached the cross there was an explosion and bullets came flying out of the coffee plantations or the orange groves or somewhere, and they all fell, riddled with bullets, and there was nobody left, and then everything went black; and then I saw His hand, Ramoncito, saying to me, let's go, I'm taking you out of here, and your neighbor too. You must both leave.

He was delirious, and Ramón said, Father Cubillos, you're

leaving here for eternal life, how I envy you, but the priest looked at him and said, we're both going, He told me how, come closer, bend your ear to me, and I'll explain, He's going to help us.

After the explanation, the priest said: help me take out this piece of cloth that's sewed into the cuffs of my pants, let's see, can you find it? on it are the directions to a chapel on the outskirts of Barranquilla, the place is marked, and there's a key, can you see it? Yes, father, here it is, a small key, yes, I have it. Then the priest said: take everything you see there, take out the case that's there and throw away the key and take everything and go. You will find out what to do. What's in that case is yours, He told me to tell you so you'd understand, do you see, this life is very confusing, Ramón.

The old man was burning up with fever, and coughing so much he could barely speak. They said goodbye and Ramón went back to his cell, taking the piece of cloth with the map and the key. With Father Cubillos's thread, he sewed it in his pants and started waiting. A couple of hours later he went back in the tunnel and, without moving the stone, heard voices saying, ugh, this guy kicked off a while ago, bring a bag and we'll put him in it, and tonight Arnulfo's men can take him and throw him in the river.

Later, they came and asked him if he was ready to sign the deeds and he said, almost, when the time Dagoberto gave me is over, I'll sign what you want, I've had it up to here with all this crap. One of the paramilitaries said to another: this corpse is getting skinny, what he needs is rice, we'll give him rice! Then Ramón asked them, who did you kill in the kitchen? I noticed it was covered in blood. Nobody, they brought someone in who was already dead but we had to remove his scars, so that he couldn't be identified. We'll do the same for you if you behave yourself, Ramoncho, we'll make sure your corpse looks nice and pretty, how about that?

When he calculated that it was already dark, he got in the tunnel and crawled to the Father's cell. They had put him in a waterproof black canvas bag with a zipper. He opened the bag, took out the priest and put him in the tunnel, pushed him with some difficulty all the way to his own cell, laid him down and covered him with the sheet, with his back to the door. Then he cut off a lock of white hair, went back to the Father's cell with his things, closed up the tunnel, and got inside the bag. He left the ropes loosely knotted and within reach of his hand, and placed the lock of hair close to the zipper.

Soon afterwards, the door opened and he felt them loading him, first onto a handcart, and then onto the bed of a truck. He was worried they would discover Father Cubillos's body before too long, but as it was nighttime that would probably not happen until the next day. What river were they going to throw him in? Hopefully a deep one, otherwise the impact when he hit the bottom might kill him. But he was also thinking, is it true that Soraya was cheating on me? who ratted me out? was it Jacinto? Three hours later the truck stopped and he heard them say: right, in the water with him, let's weigh it down with those bricks, we want this dummy to stay at the bottom. Shall we shoot when he falls in the water, chief? Don't be so dumb, can't you see we can't make any noise? Just throw him in and let's get out of here, I don't like being around here too late, my friend's been waiting for me at the Tinieblas for half an hour now.

I'm in the Ariari, Ramón thought as he went in the water: the Tinieblas is the brothel in Puerto Lleras!

As he fell, he felt the coldness of the water. He sank slowly. The bricks were heavy but two of the four came loose from the ropes as the bag fell. He had taken a deep breath, and he was a good swimmer, so he put his hand out, untied the knot, and the bricks sank to the bottom. The bag rose to the surface a hundred yards farther along the river, filled with air, and served as a life preserver to help him reach the bank.

He stood up with his heart pounding and the adrenaline surging through his blood, and said to himself, what a good idea of God to get him out, maybe he would start believing in Him again. Now he had to get away quickly, because as soon as they realized they would be back. He walked and walked until he came to a shack that looked uninhabited. He looked through one of the windows and did not see anybody, so he entered cautiously; he found clothes, and a piece of bread. He changed and slowly ate, until he had calmed down. His heart stopped pounding and he went out again. He followed the path until he found a bigger one and then a road.

He was in Puerto Lleras.

At dawn he got in the undergrowth and started drying out what he had in the billfold: his Bancolombia card, a couple of cell phone recharging cards, his ID card, his driving license, his judicial certificate, he had all that. The only thing they had taken was his cell phone. They had never imagined he would escape so easily, that was why they had left everything in his pockets. He looked up and prayed a bit. For the soul of the priest who had helped him escape and for God, who had paid him back for his father's death with this. Of course, he still had to get out of the area, but that now depended on his wits. He would have to find money, or steal a car, but he was not sure how he could do either, and he did not want to leave any trace, because they must have realized by now that he was gone. They could well be looking for him on the banks of the river: fortunately he had gotten rid of the bag, burying it in the undergrowth. But once again Father Cubillos performed a miracle for him, because as he walked, he came to a fence and saw that it was the airport of Puerto Lleras. He made up his mind to go in, he saw that a Cessna belonging to the Satena company was leaving for Villavicencio in forty minutes.

He decided to take a risk. He went to the Banco Popular ATM, and put his card in, and it worked, so he took out a million pesos. With that he bought a ticket and then went to the bathroom to wait until it was time to board the plane, because it was possible that the paramilitaries might think to check the airport. Again he was in luck: he got on the plane and as it rose into the air he felt a wave of tiredness come over him from all his aches and pains, but at the same time he realized that he was alive, and that he was not going to die as soon as he had thought.

In Villavicencio, he did not even leave the airport but got on an Avianca flight to Barranquilla, via Bogotá, and by nightfall he was getting off at Ernesto Cortissoz Airport, beside the Caribbean, thanks to the help and inspiration of Father Cubillos, may God keep him at His right hand. He took a room in a hotel in the Abajo district. He got in the bathtub and let the water stream over his shoulders, head, and chest, and closed his eyes. He had the map and the key in his pants, and he thought: tomorrow I'm going to see what kind of gift the father left for me in that case.

The next day he went out and walked to a shopping mall. He bought clothes, shoes, dark glasses, and a watch, and had a haircut. He went to Telecom and dialed Soraya's number several times, but hung up when he heard her mother's voice. Should he talk to Jacinto? call his shop? He did not trust anyone and if he dialed a cell phone they would know he was in Barranquilla, so it was better to wait. He called home and heard his mother's voice, but decided not to talk, the paramilitaries were sure to question her and it was better if she knew nothing. He would call her or send for her later.

The map on the piece of cloth was half erased, but he knew it by heart, so he went to look for the little chapel, which was in the same district, Abajo. He would have to figure out a way to get into the sacristy, which was where the hiding place was located. For the moment he went in and huddled on one of the benches. It was a simple chapel, with an altar at the front, two

250 · SANTIAGO GAMBOA

prayer rooms at the sides and two rows of benches. A young man was sweeping the corridor and three women were praying. He looked around and saw a half-open door on the right, between the two confessionals. He walked toward it, but just as he was a few feet away, somebody closed it. Never mind, he would come back the next day. He went back over the next four days, studying the chapel. He found out that there was a fairly young priest, a sacristan, three altar boys who came in the mornings, and a woman cleaner who lived at the back. The priest did not live in the sacristy but in a residence.

He hatched a plan. It was quite simple: he would stay in the chapel after the noon service, get into the sacristy and go down to the cellar. This was what he did two days later. The door was locked, but he had a penknife and opened it without any difficulty. He ran down the stairs and came to a first room, which was a kind of prop room for the things used in the mass, and then a second, with a closet at the far end. Inside it was a smaller closet. He took out the key and opened it. The map said: below the closet, second tile. He stuck the penknife in at the side and saw that the tile was loose. He lifted it and saw a plastic bag with another one inside, then a third one, and finally, inside that one, a leather billfold. He put it in his belt, put the tile back in its place and closed the closet. On the way out he tried to conceal the fact that he had forced the lock, but it was impossible, because the wood was split. It was possible they would not realize, because they would not notice anything missing. He got back to the hotel with his heart pounding because of what he had done and had to lie on top of the bed for a while, before opening the billfold. He finally did so and found a couple of envelopes. In one of them was a sheet of paper that said:

"Father cubillos I know you dont aprove the way I earn my living but I am very grateful to you, and that's why I want to give you this. you brought me up and the little education I have you gave me and when I was young I got in trouble and you helped me to get out of prison. thank you father cubillos. I prefer not to go and see you because maybe you will pull me by the hair and we will fall out and thats why I am sending you this with my little sister ester. I am leaving you fifty bills of a hundred dollars and a key with a number. that number is the number of a safety depozit box in the banco central of panama, in panama city, where you will find everything you need any time you have a problem or want to help somebody. its the way I want to give back to you all I got from you. thank you, father cubillos, you were the father I never had. Edwin."

Ramón read the letter several times, then counted the money. There was five thousand dollars. Who was this Edwin? another para? a local drug dealer? It must have been something like that, although Father Cubillos had not gotten around to telling him. Almost certainly a para, well, with that five thousand dollars they were starting to pay him back for what they had taken from him. The next day he went to Bogotá and presented himself at the offices on Calle Cien, showed his ID card and asked for a passport. As he stood in line, he kept looking around. By the afternoon, he had his passport and he went to buy his ticket to Panama. He really wanted to call Soraya but he restrained himself, and what he did instead was say to a taxi driver, take me where the girls are, where are the girls here? Jacinto had been to Bogotá once and had told him that the brothels there were the best, that you could find women of all races, really amazing, gorgeous women, oh boy. The flight was not until the next day, so he wanted to go out for a few drinks anyway. The taxi driver looked at him in the mirror and said, how much do you want to pay? I want one that's good, but not too expensive either. Right, boss, I know where. He took him to a place on Primero de Mayo called

Luceros, he paid four hundred thousand pesos for a 22-year-old brunette and took her to the Paracaídas motel, near the airport. Everything was perfect. He could eat there, have a few glasses of aguardiente and enjoy the girl, who was really good. Jacinto was right, the girls in Bogotá were the best, even though this one was from Cali. That son of a bitch Jacinto, could it have been him? Better not to think about it.

The next day he gave the girl a hundred dollars as a tip and at eleven in the morning he set off for the airport. He had a feeling he was being watched, that somebody was walking behind him, but it was pure paranoia. Who could have followed his trail if he hadn't dared to speak to anybody? Then something occurred to him that got him really worried: if his mother had reported his disappearance, then there was a strong possibility that the agents of the Security Service would grab him when he tried to leave the country. He walked anxiously to immigration and got in line. When it was his turn, he went to the window and, with his heart skipping a beat, handed his passport to the official. Of course he was from the Plains, which meant he was good at keeping a cool head, so he looked the official in the eyes and said, I'm going on vacation, one week, no more. The man put his name in the computer and a shiver went through Ramón. He had heard that the Security Service people were in league with the paras. But once again Father Cubillos protected him, because the official handed him back his passport and said, have a nice trip, next. He got on the plane and as it taxied along the runway it struck him once again that the kidnapping and all that violence were taking him toward something new, and he remembered the words of the priest when he had said, a person cannot understand the actions of God, because when God does what He does, He is taking into account the totality of a life. It was the first time he had left Colombia and he felt a mixture of euphoria and fear. Would Panama be safe?

In Panama City he took a taxi and as he only had a small case he went straight to the Banco Central. He looked at the avenue, the buildings, the cars, and the people. Just like Colombia, he thought, nothing special. The key had the number B-367. He went to the window marked *Customer Service* and when it was his turn he said, thank you, I need to see this box. One moment, somebody will go with you. A tall, sophisticated woman said to him, follow me, this way. They walked up and down stairs, past a reinforced door and then another and then an elevator to the second basement. B-367? this is it. She opened the cubicle for him and then left him alone and he took out an attaché case something like an airline pilot's. He was stunned: brand new bundles of dollars. How much was there? A note on the bills, dated five years earlier, said: "Dear Father, by order of my client Señor Edwin I hereby deposit the sum of three million dollars. If you wish to open an account go to the Balboa Investment Bank and ask to speak with Señor Emilio Granada, who is in charge of offshore accounts. He will not ask you any awkward questions if you say you are a friend of Edwin's."

He took the case and went out on the street. To his surprise, the Balboa Bank was just opposite, on a corner. This must be the financial district, he thought. Señor Emilio Granada opened a numbered account for him and issued him with a card for taking out cash and making payments, and said, were you very close to Don Edwin? Ramón did not know what to reply, and said, I'm close to a priest he was fond of. If that's the case, said the banker, let me give you my condolences, maybe you did not know that Don Edwin passed away last year, four bullets in the back. He crossed some men, and you know how dangerous that can be.

He still had about three thousand dollars left from what he had brought with him, so he did not make a withdrawal, but went to look for a hotel. He chose a Holiday Inn facing the beach, and that same night he sat looking at the ocean and telling himself, what a contradictory life this is, a few days ago I was dead and now I'm a millionaire, I'm here by the sea, I can do what I like . . . But I'm alone. Which of the two was it? or was it both of them? or neither? were they bugging my phone? That could have been it, those sons of bitches have their noses in everything.

This is where the story of Ramón Melo García really takes off, because with that money he stayed on in Panama, first one week and then another, until he felt safe. When, after three months, he finally decided to call his mother, it was his aunt who picked up the phone and gave him the bad news. She said, your mother died, or rather, she let herself die, being left alone like that, and people here saying the guerrillas had kidnapped you and that you'd died on the road. Who said that? I don't know, Ramoncito, that was what people started saying. That Señor Dagoberto came around a few times to talk to your mother. He told her he was going to do what he could to get you back but that she had to help him, keep him informed. Oh, Aunt, don't tell anyone about this conversation, do you swear? Yes, sweetie, I swear, but where are you? A long way away, Aunt, a very long way away, but don't worry, I'll be back.

He preferred not to ask after Soraya, let alone Jacinto. The less he stirred things up, the better. He would have time to find out what had happened. Something had hardened inside him. He felt sorry about his mother but that was all. No tears came out. That was one more thing Dagoberto owed him. They had not seen the last of him.

The director of the Balboa Bank helped him to obtain a residence permit, as he had decided to settle in Panama City and invest. He rented an apartment in Paitilla and looked for premises to set up an auto repair shop, which was his line of work. He found it in the same neighborhood and started setting it up. When he had everything ready, he sat down to wait and the first customer turned out to be a Colombian in a Pontiac. Ramón got down under the car and changed the brake pads and by the time the man had gone, his hands were shaking, the fear had come back, would they come all the way to Panama? did he have to go farther? But he stayed and worked hard, and before the year was out, he already had two shops in the city. He was good at his job, and very reliable. None of his customers could have imagined that he had a fortune in the bank, but his life was here, surrounded by screws and camshafts and carburetors. He didn't want to have a girl-friend who would ask too many questions, so every Friday he would go to a bar called the Púrpuras, where they had a show, and pick up whichever girl he liked the best, making sure she was not a Colombian.

He lived like this for more than four years, until one day he read in the newspapers that the paramilitaries in Colombia were demobilizing, that they were negotiating to hand over their arms and surrender to the authorities. He searched and searched but did not see any reference anywhere to Dagoberto or La Cascada, so he waited a little longer.

By that time Ramón already had a chain of auto repair shops. Six in Panama City and three outside, on the highways. He invented a slogan: *Drive slowly and travel safely, why not?* He was the one who introduced into Panama the culture of having one's car serviced before going on a journey. It is a small country, and people travel a lot by car, which was lucky for him. By now he had already doubled the inheritance from Father Cubillos and had bought a better apartment, in Bella Vista, which was more like La Cascada, even though it was very different, starting with the climate, but he got used to it. He'd also gotten used to the solitude, to not having any friends or girlfriends. In his dreams, he would be back in the cell, feeling the fear when he heard the footsteps coming closer, seeing Dagoberto and the paramilitaries who were always with him, saying, you're going to die, scum, you look like a corpse already. Sometimes, out on the streets, he thought he recognized them. His hands would start sweating, his heart would start pounding, and he would forget where he was. But he was a man of the Plains and all that psychiatric stuff was not for him. So he finally summoned up courage and picked up a Colombian girl from the bar and asked her where she was from. I'm a country girl, from Pereira. And how old are you, sweetheart? 22, how about you? Me? I'm already old, and how did such a pretty girl end up in Panama? I came here for work, because there was no work in Pereira, and in Bogotá it's very cold, and besides, they pay better here. But you're Colombian too, aren't you, darling? His jaw trembled, but he said, yes, I'm Colombian. Where from? Villavicencio. Oh, a man from the Plains? that's why you ride me so well, ha, ha, don't worry, just my sense of humor. And why did you come to Panama? To work. What kind of work? My kind of work, girl, don't ask so many questions. No, don't tell me, are you a trafficker? don't worry, darling, I love traffickers. No, girl, I'm not, come on, I'll get you a taxi. That was how things were when he went out with these girls, but this one, this country girl, was one he chose several times and in the end she became a friend and he would call her on her cell phone or pick her up from her apartment. One time, he took her to the beach. Her name was Daisy. Let's go to the beach, but no questions, O.K.? O.K., darling, but you're funny, you know? what's with all the secrecy? did you kill somebody or what? why all this hiding? No, Daisy, I never killed anybody, how can you even think that? It's just that you aren't normal, with such a nice face and all that money and living alone the way you do . . . Where did you leave your wife? Look, sweetheart, I said no questions, why don't you sing me a song instead, you have such a nice voice. Oh, you're such a liar! but I feel good with you, you know, and that was how they spent their Sunday afternoons.

Every day he read the news from Colombia: that the paramilitaries were going, that they were not going, that they had already gone, that they were still there in the mountains, that they were rearming in the cities, that everything was a lie, that they had handed over their arms, that they were being extradited, but he never found any mention of his story, so he decided on a strategy. He started letting his beard grow and cut his hair very short and dyed it. As he could not make himself any taller or shorter than he was, he decided to fatten up a bit; every day, even though it disgusted him, he ate two or even three McDonald's burgers; at first they gave him diarrhea and made him vomit but in the end it worked and he started to develop a paunch. He put on glasses with flat lenses, and bought himself some casual clothes and some smart office clothes. For about four months he prepared his return journey to La Cascada. The time had come. He had to know what had happened.

His friend, the director of the Balboa Bank, helped him to obtain Panamanian papers so that he could enter Colombia as a foreigner. The riskiest part of his plan was that he had decided to take Daisy with him, as a man on his own attracts more attention to himself. He said to her, look, sweetheart, you're coming with me on a little trip to Colombia and I'll pay you well, the only thing you have to do is be with me and keep quiet, we're going to Villavicencio, do you know it? no? it's nice there, I'll put you in a really good hotel and you can spend your time in the swimming pool and go with me wherever I have to go, and the more you keep your mouth shut the more I pay you, O.K.? Daisy was really pleased and said, fantastic, I'm going to Colombia, I love my country, you are a trafficker, aren't you? obviously you're going there for that, but like I told you, don't worry, darling, I won't say a word, I grew up among those people, I'll go with you and keep my mouth shut, I'm not stupid. It struck Ramón that it was better this way, with her thinking he was a drug trafficker, so he went along with her.

They arrived at El Dorado airport in Bogotá and waited for the shuttle to Villavicencio. They landed just after seven at night and went straight to the Hotel del Llano. In order not to attract attention, he did not ask for a suite, just a really good room with a view of the swimming pool. Daisy told him they should go down to the bar to dance and he said, okay, let's go and have an aguardiente, but we won't stay too late because we have to go out early tomorrow.

The next day he hired a car from the hotel, an Opel station wagon, and drove straight to Acacías, in the high Ariari. There was a good breeze and the smell of the Plains brought tears to his eyes. He held them back as his childhood passed in front of his eyes: those palms, those ceiba trees, that earth, and that air were his, or rather, he belonged to the water and the land and the trees and the grazing cattle. Daisy must have heard him breathing heavily but did not say anything. She kept her mouth shut. In Acacías, they had a bite to eat and Ramón kept looking around to see if he could spot anything strange. They drove farther into the Plains. They had lunch in Guaymaral and Ramón started to feel an itch in his neck, a tightness in his lungs, so much so that he left half the roast veal he had ordered. They carried on. The smell of the Ariari reached him as they turned off toward Cubarral, and he thought: I learned to swim in that river, and that was what saved me. Snapshots of that night came back to him and beads of sweat broke out on his upper lip. Very soon he caught sight of Cubarral, the church with its dome, the clouds behind it like cotton wings. He remembered Soraya and his stomach lurched. They came to the bridge over the Ariari and, with his T-shirt bathed in sweat, he saw the Rey de la Pachanga and, at the bend in the road behind it, the lights of the Llano Grande motel. Everything was the same as ever.

At four in the afternoon, they reached La Cascada and went straight to the Parque Bolívar. Let's have a beer, Daisy, and I don't want you to look at anything except me. He had told her to dress like a tourist, in sweatshirt and tennis shoes. He was dressed in the same style, in T-shirt and jeans. They had the beer and Ramón, behind his semi-opaque glasses, sought inspiration in Father Cubillos. Here I am, Father, I need you more than ever now, help me to solve this difficult dilemma, that's the only thing I want. After the beer, calmer now, he got up and walked to the internet café, La Maporita, but when he got there he saw that it was not called that anymore. Now it was called Café Hilton and had better computers and decent furniture. He turned, grabbed Daisy's hand, and went in.

A popular reggaeton tune was playing. Ramón asked for a computer and sat down. Daisy did not say a word for a second and only opened her mouth to say, darling, can I go on Facebook for a bit? There were three young girls working there but Soraya was nowhere to be seen. His fingers trembled as he tried to work the mouse. Daisy chatted for a while, then he paid and they left. He went back to the car and drove around the town. He passed his main repair shop, where he had had his office, and saw it open, and working. It did not look any better or worse than it had before. He slowed down a bit, hoping to catch sight of somebody, and there, at the far end, he thought he recognized Demetrio, one of his workers, but then a car came up behind him and hooted its horn and he had to drive on. He approached Jacinto's house and did not see anything unusual, it was all closed up, as was Soraya's. He could not do anything more for now, so he decided to go back to Villavicencio. It had been a bad tactic to show his face here like that, without a plan, and it was dangerous. He had to think.

The next day, he had a look around the center of Villavicencio and suddenly, on the opposite sidewalk, he saw a sign that showed him the way: *Delta Agency, private investigations*, and a telephone number. He took out a ballpoint pen and wrote it down at the top of a bill. That was the solution! Come on, let's go back to the hotel, girl, I just had a brainwave. Aren't you going to take me shopping? there are some nice things here . . . Later, sweetheart, later, I have work to do now, let's go, you can use the pool.

They got back to the hotel and he called the number. When they answered, he said: hello, I'd like to know something about the service you offer. Well, if it's for a matrimonial matter there's one rate; if it's a work-related problem another; if it's a family thing or something like that, we look at it on a case by case basis, may I ask why you're calling us? To ask if you take on work outside Villavicencio. Of course, boss, we're global-ized, we go from Puerto Gaitán to the Guaviare, tell me where we have to go? I need a little job done in La Cascada, is that possible? Say no more . . . what kind of case are we talking about? matrimonial? an affair of the heart? work-related? we also issue Facebook and Hotmail passwords, but they're more expensive, are you interested? Not for now. I'll send you a let-ter with the information and an advance. Then I'll call you again. Sure, boss, and what's your name? I'm the Poor Friend, remember that, the Poor Friend. O.K., boss, I hope when you say poor that's just a metaphor, right? Ha, ha. I say that because if the case turns out to be complicated it'll cost you. Don't worry, it's a metaphor, and what about you, detective? what's your name? Oh yes, of course, I'm Marcos Ebenezer Giraldo, boss, at your service.

He mailed him the details that afternoon and called him the next day. This is the Poor Friend, did you receive my package? No, my friend, nothing at all. I sent it by mail yes-terday. Ah, no . . . That won't arrive for another two or three days, the mail here is terrible! Never mind, we can wait, are you in a hurry? Only to help you, boss. Well, you'll get the chance and I can assure you, if you're discreet and do a good job you won't be sorry. All right, boss, don't worry, my motto is, *our pleasure is in discretion*. Or this one: *our profession is an inside job*. Seriously, friend, discretion is my middle name, I'm so professional they call me the invisible man, I make less noise than an Alka-Seltzer in a pot of yogurt, nobody even knows I'm there. Call me the day after tomorrow and I'll let you know.

He spent two more days at the hotel, going out very little, like a businessman on vacation with his girlfriend. Daisy was as good as her word, she was cautious and kept her promise not to speak or attract attention, even with that terrific body of hers and everything, she was discreet. Ramón was starting to feel nervous about being there, as he assumed that the para-militaries, who knew everything, might easily discover his presence. After two days he called the detective again. Did you receive it? Yes, boss, over and out. Perfect, I have the names of the two people, the address of the auto repair shop that has to be investigated, and the money arrived, too, by a miracle nobody robbed the mailman. And is it enough? Of course, boss, it's enough to start the investigation, no problems, if it turns out I need more I'll submit it and then you pay me, all fully invoiced, obviously. And how long do you think these enquiries will take? Two weeks maximum, boss, and everything will be sorted and ready. Good, then I'll call you again in two weeks. Sure, boss, write down my cell phone number, in case you have any questions.

That day he went back to Panama, and to be honest, leaving the airport and driving to his house, he began to breathe more easily, and he felt free. His stay in the Plains had been an emotional experience, but it had revived the fear. He paid Daisy and thanked her. Without her, everything would have been more dangerous; he decided that, when he went back, he would take her again, as she gave him the perfect front. He tried to analyze his feelings and realized that what he had inside him was not pain, or anger, or even regret, but above all curiosity. His heart had become hardened. So much solitude and so many questions had led him to consider his misfortunes as if they had happened to someone else.

Two weeks later he called the detective on Skype, which was good because the call could not be traced, and asked him about his report. It's almost ready, my friend, I just need to copy a final piece of information that I already have, of course as I said it's a first step, if you want to carry on we'll have to do another contract, won't we? Yes, of course, said Ramón. Good, my friend, now when can you come for the report? No, I don't have time to collect it, can you do me a favor and scan it and send it to me at this address, write it down, poor-friend21@hotmail.com, and for anything else contact me that way. All right, my friend, do you mind if I ask a question? Ramón did not say either yes or no. Is it because of the girl that you're doing all this? There followed a silence. Ah, I thought so, I'll send someone to the corner right now to scan it and then I'll send it to you, boss, glad to be of service.

It was afternoon by the time the mail arrived from the detective with the document attached, and the photographs. Seeing all that, Ramón closed the shop, and sat down in the office with a bottle of rum. He drank five glasses, one after the other, before even daring to open the files. He left the photographs and started with the text, it would be easier to read first. There it all was:

Soraya Mora has been married to Jacinto Gómez Estupiñán for three years and they have a daughter, Gloria Soraya, who is eighteen months old. Soraya is a housewife and Jacinto is the owner of the restaurant Luna Roja, the bar El Feliz, and two auto repair shops, Su Motor, which he took over after his former partner Ramón Melo García was kidnapped and later killed by the FARC. Señor and Señora Gómez live in the exclusive residential community of El Paraíso, in the new part of La Cascada, and have a farm near Lejanías where they grow African palm and raise cattle.

Señor Jacinto Gómez Estupiñán is divorced from Señora Araceli Ramos, to whom he pays seven hundred thousand pesos a month in alimony. At the divorce hearing, she accused him of adultery and physical violence. After the divorce, Señora Ramos went to live with her mother in Villavicencio, claiming to have been threatened with death if she stayed in La Cascada.

Soraya Mora spends the day with her mother looking after the little girl, Gloria Soraya. In the morning, from nine to twelve, they go together to the kindergarten in the residential community where they live, then they have lunch and in the afternoon go shopping and visit the Häagen-Dazs ice cream parlor on Plaza de Bolívar or simply stay at home and cook, which is their hobby. The mother goes on Thursday afternoons to a choral group and Señora Soraya plays *parqués* with her friends from the gym on Fridays at the Escrúpulos tearooms.

Jacinto Gómez Estupiñán leaves home at seven in the morning and goes to the restaurant, then to the market to supervise the purchases of meat for the day, the specialty of his establishment being fresh meat, straight from the farm. At noon he drops by the main branch of Su Motor, on Calle Acacias, and talks with his partner, Arnulfo Solano Arango. Then he has lunch at home with his wife and mother-in-law, but takes his siesta at the house of Señorita Fernanda Osorio Timoco, in the Antioquia district, a young woman of twenty-seven with whom Jacinto Gómez has a relationship of a sexual nature, and for whom he pays the rent on her house, which is 280,000 pesos. Señor Gómez has his account in the Banco Ganadero.

He read the report several times in quick succession, one after

264 - SANTIAGO GAMBOA

the other, and one word surged up inside him: Revenge . . .
Revenge!

Religion says that we should forgive, but Ramón was not
ready for that. Let the bastards beg for forgiveness! If they
come to me humbly I may forgive them, but first I want my
revenge. He was overcome with rage and something unexpected: a strange happiness within the rage, a dizziness that
gave him a tingling in his fingers. In losing his illusions, he had
become free. He drank the rest of the bottle and wept, of
course, but also felt a kind of pleasure in imagining how it
would be when he had taken his revenge. He did not feel up to
looking at the photographs yet. He would leave them for later.

The next day he wrote to the detective:

> Excellent work. Now I need you to find out a few more
> little things. Firstly, what is a paramilitary known as
> Dagoberto doing now, tell me if he is still operating in the
> area or if he is cooperating with the authorities. Tell me
> when you think you will be able to give me that information
> and how much it will cost. I will send you the money wher-
> ever you tell me to, without asking questions. Secondly, I
> need to know what connection there was between Jacinto
> Gómez and that Dagoberto and when it started. Thirdly, I
> want to know if Soraya Mora was already involved with
> Jacinto before his divorce, and when that started too. I need
> dates. I want you to find out how long Soraya had known
> Dagoberto and why she did what she did and in return for
> what. Fourthly, find out what happened to that ex-partner,
> Ramón Melo García, if it is known where he is, and since
> when Jacinto has been a partner in those repair shops.

The next day the detective replied:

> Oh, my friend, what you are asking me is definitely

going to cost a bit more, especially as asking questions about the paras in this region is more dangerous than shaving your testicles with a knife when you're drunk, ha ha, sorry, I joke about everything. This is embarrassing, but I need to ask you for three million pesos, friend's rate, of course. Send it to me by Western Union, made out to the Agency, and addressed to our office in the central market in Villavicencio. As soon as I receive the money, I'll get down to work, boss, over and out, and one last thing, I know this is all very hush-hush, so I want to assure you, now that I'm on the case, you can trust me absolutely. Best wishes, XY.

He sent the money from a numbered account and waited, more taciturn than ever before, brooding on his plans, completely given over to his one obsession: revenge, revenge. He was gradually putting it together, one element at a time, like a bird building a nest branch by branch with its beak, confined to his apartment and his office, supervising his workers almost without speaking to them, without calling Daisy at all, given over body and soul to the task of hating, feeling anger, knowing that very soon he was going to feel that thunderclap that meant his revenge was complete.

Until he read the next report:

What I am able to tell you is that Dagoberto gave himself up to the authorities seven months ago as part of the new government accords; they have in him in custody in the prison of Cómbita, Boyacá. He admitted to six murders in La Cascada, Puerto Lleras, and Lejanías, which weren't massacres, but said, in order to avoid being put on the list for extradition, that neither he nor his group had ever been involved in drug trafficking. Of course, there are witnesses in the town who say that the man was indeed a trafficker and was smuggling cocaine to Venezuela; that there are a number of mass graves filled with his victims and that he's a major criminal. He's represented by a very good lawyer here in Villavicencio who is advising him to stay and do his time in Colombia. They're plea bargaining for a lenient sentence, six years maximum, which means he'll be able to keep the business going through front men while he's inside and reestablish himself in no time at all when he gets out.

Jacinto met Dagoberto through Soraya Mora's brother Hernán Mora. It's important to note that Jacinto was already having an affair with Soraya while married to his former wife, Araceli, and that was how he got to know Hernán Mora. Her boyfriend, Ramón Melo García, was a good friend of Jacinto's, and the rumor in town is that the FARC took him away to protect him, because he was a Communist, but as he was also a small businessman and owned auto repair shops in La Cascada they ended up extorting money from him and then killing him. Jacinto was a good friend of the family and took over the shops, but then Ramón Melo García's mother died, so that Jacinto was left with everything, in partnership with Arnulfo, Ramón Melo García's chief mechanic. That's the official version, boss, but as I'm good at my job I dug a bit deeper to find what really happened, and it's this: Jacinto was giving it to Soraya Mora every time Ramón Melo went off to Villavicencio to buy equipment for his shops, and through that relationship he became friends with Hernán Mora, who had just come back from Medellín and had contacts with the paras. As soon as he got back to La Cascada, Hernán Mora starting working for Dagoberto, and one fine day, after both of them had been drinking aguardiente, Jacinto told Hernán he loved his sister Soraya and the one thing stopping them becoming brothers-in-law was that Communist Ramón Melo García, who had been a Communist since he was small because his dad had fought with the guerrillas in the Plains, and so Hernán Mora said, don't worry, I'll talk to my sister and then we'll ask Dagoberto to get that Communist bastard off our backs, Jacinto, I'll take care of everything, the bastard deserves what's coming to him.

Jacinto talked with Arnulfo, the man who managed Ramón Melo's shops, and asked him to let him know about Ramón Melo's calls and movements, and told him that if he didn't they might kill him too, because his boss was a Communist and hated Colombia and our president and that was why they were keeping an eye on the people he worked with. Arnulfo Solano let himself be won over, partly out of fear, and partly because if he did what they asked him they told him they would make him a partner in the shops. He said yes without thinking twice.

With Soraya Mora, from what I've been able to establish, things were more difficult, because she was in love with Ramón Melo and they had to work on her a bit more. Obviously she was also in love with Jacinto and that was why she let him have sex with her, but although I'm not a student of character or anything, I do think women feel attracted to their boyfriends' friends, and so the woman ended up sharing herself between the two of them at the same time, although she was officialy involved with Ramón Melo García. Hernán Mora won her over by telling her that Ramón was a member of the FARC, but they themselves were patriots so it was better if she forgot him. It took him a week to win her over.

Ramón was reading and weeping at the same time. They had all betrayed him. Not just one of them, all of them. His head was seething. He took a bottle of rum and went out onto the balcony of his apartment and looked at the lights of the bay and racked his brain for memories. He remembered one time when he had asked Soraya to come with him to Villavicencio, and she had said, no, Ramón, it's better if I stay here and chat for a while with a friend on Facebook and then I'll go to see my mother, it's better if you go alone and come back quickly. He had given her a goodbye kiss—she was still wearing the uniform from La Maporita—and he had set off, listening to songs by Carlos Vives; he imagined her fucking Jacinto, an hour later, as he was driving along the highway. He heard the voice of the man known as Dagoberto saying to him, someone else is banging her, Ramoncho, they all like a bit of cock, what can we do?

His revenge should not be ordinary. No bullets in the back of the neck, no throwing bodies off a cliff. He would do things properly. He would not get his hands dirty: they were not worth it. He would lift the curtain and make the whole horrible affair visible to everyone. That was what he had to do. First he would deal with Dagoberto, then with Jacinto and Soraya, and finally with Arnulfo, his rat of an assistant, who was now part owner of his auto repair shop.

He wrote to the detective as follows:

Things are getting more and more complicated, but your fees will rise in proportion. This time you will need to hire people you trust. I want you to locate a farmhouse belonging to Dagoberto, an old house about four hours' drive from La Cascada and another four hours from Puerto Lleras. They killed people in that house. I don't know what it looks like from the outside, but it has a cellar with a number of rooms and stone walls, and a kind of kitchen with big concrete and tile counters where they tortured and killed people and cut up the bodies. If you find that farm for me, take some photographs of it, send them to me and I'll recognize the place, your payment will go up to 10,000,000 pesos, how does that grab you? I also need you to find a connection between Jacinto and Dagoberto, a photocopy of a check, a signature, anything that shows that they were together, that they had a common interest, that they were protecting each other.

Three weeks passed before the detective sent his next message, which said:

Well, friend, let me tell you I have really good news. Brace yourself, because it really is good. It's better than good, it's brilliant. Get a grip on yourself before you download the photographs I'm sending you, because they show Dagoberto's house, the one where people were killed. Don't just take my word for it, have a look. It's near Lejanías in a village called Palestina. It's abandoned now, or rather, with a peasant looking after it with orders not to let anyone in, only this guy is hungrier than a piranha in a glass of water and doesn't give a damn about orders. As soon as my colleague gave him a whiff of a fifty thousand peso bill, he opened his legs, or rather, he opened the doors wide and said, I'll give you half an hour, I'm not responsible for what you find inside, I don't know anything and I never saw anything. My colleague took some really artistic photographs. There's a cellar just as you described it, with bloodstains. Take a good look at photograph number three. But the best of all is in another of the rooms: some metal trays and some drawers full of chemicals, enough to make a mountain of cocaine, how does that grab you? And there's more, boss, pure gold: my colleague found a drawer with a padlock on it. He opened it and, to his surprise, there was a small laptop inside, clearly those guys hotfooted it out of there very quickly, or maybe just took the bigger things, in any case I have the machine here and on it there are names and photographs and everything, really sweet. My partner, who always has his eyes open for his big chance, says we could sell it for fifty million, but I told him that as you're a friend we should let you have it for twenty million, because all the information you're looking for is in it, and don't faint dead away when you hear this: there are even photographs of Señor Jacinto and Señora Soraya actually in the act, a real delight, I can tell you. Those guys must be really depraved, to go around taking photographs like that and then keeping them, or maybe they were taken with a hidden camera. Well, friend, I await your reply, because what my partner wants to do is sell the computer to Dagoberto, but I keep telling him no, that's not the way to proceed, which is why the best thing to do is for you to answer me quickly and leave the matter settled, and for my partner, who's really short of money and whose daughter is getting married, to stop getting ideas like that.

Ramón read and reread the message. Then he decided to look at the photographs, and recognized the corridor and the narrow walls. It was the house, there was no doubt about it. The detective was really good, how had he managed it? had he bribed a former paramilitary? It was possible. Seeing those images, he remembered Father Cubillos and the confidence with which he had said to him, "we're both going to get out of here, it's God's will," and in fact they had both gotten out. There was no more room for doubt. He had to buy that computer because in it lay his revenge, which would now have to include them all. Maybe Father Cubillos was still helping him from on high. Only when it was over would he be able to feel clean and dignified again.

My friend, I congratulate you. You are one of the most professional people I have ever met, and I mean that. The photographs are good, that is the place. I really can't imag-

ine what you did to find it, but it's better if you don't tell
me. There are things it's better not to know. Now, let's talk
about money. I'll give you the twenty million you're asking,
and five more if you let me have a signed paper assuring me
that you did not make any copies of the material you're
handing over to me and that you will not be using any of it
in the future. If you send me that, I'll immediately send the
twenty-five million, and I'll send somebody to pick up the
computer, placed carefully in a case and locked. But let's
take things one at a time.

Less than two hours later the detective's answer arrived.

Ah, my friend, I already knew the name Poor Friend was
a metaphor, and that you were a gentleman. Well, everything is confirmed, boss. You can send me the money and I
will hand over the things. How could you even think I'd
keep hold of any of it? And I'm sending you the paper you
ask for, scanned, so that you can be reassured, my friend,
and I'm already starting to feel sad that when our contract
comes to an end so will our friendship, because I don't
mind telling you I've really gotten to like you.

That same night he called Daisy and said, well now, sweetheart, how would you like to go back to Colombia? Sure, darling, just tell me when. First thing tomorrow, to make sure
everything's fine, I'll send for you now and we'll leave together.
Oh, that's really wonderful, and are we going somewhere hot
or somewhere cold? The same place as last time, you told me
you liked it.

The next day, after transferring the detective's money, they
took the first plane and by noon they were once again at the
Hotel del Llano in Villavicencio. Ramón told Daisy: now then,
darling, I need you to do me a favor. I'm going to dial a num-

ber, I want you to say you're calling on behalf of Poor Friend and you want them to hand over the package, which they should leave, addressed to Daisy, at the reception desk in the Hotel del Llano, O.K.? O.K., darling, as long as you swear to me it isn't dangerous. I swear, and anyway we're going to Bogotá today and after that if you like I'll send you to Medellín, at my expense, for a few days, O.K.? Now then, dial the number, and say it's from Poor Friend.

Ramón dialed the detective's number and Daisy said exactly what he had told her to say. She asked the detective to bring the package in a case to the hotel before three that afternoon. The detective said O.K. and they hung up. Ramón started pacing the room nervously. Daisy called reception and said that someone was going to bring a case in her name, and would they please let her know, and they sat down and waited. Ramón hired a taxi and asked the driver to wait outside. At 2:40 the telephone rang. The package was downstairs. Ramón went down to the street, got in the taxi and made sure that there was nobody or nothing unusual. Daisy came down a few minutes later, picked up the package and walked out of the hotel. She joined Ramón in the taxi and they set off for the airport. That evening they were in Bogotá, at the Hotel Suites Jones in Chapinero Alto.

Daisy said: as you can see, darling, I make a good trafficker. That isn't what this is, sweetheart, I already told you a dozen times. Oh really? why all the mystery, then? Because it's something important. Remember what I said, no questions, now do you want to go to Medellín? Daisy said of course and the next day, very early, Ramón sent her by taxi to catch the shuttle with a ticket and two million pesos in cash.

As soon as Daisy had left, Ramón went downstairs, paid the bill, and changed hotels. This time he went to the Bogotá Plaza, on Calle Cien, near the freeway. As soon as he had settled in, he sat down and switched on the computer. It was only then that it occurred to him that he should have checked everything in Villavicencio. He had been concentrating so much on his security measures that he had forgotten the most important thing, but anyway, he would soon see. Once he had switched on, he had direct access to all the files, but there were others that were encrypted. He looked at the photographs and saw things that filled him with horror: Soraya naked, with Jacinto taking her from behind, Soraya giving Jacinto a blowjob, Jacinto sticking his finger into her anus, who had taken these photographs? He saw that they were all from the same angle and he assumed there must have been a camera hidden in the room, maybe the paras used the photographs for blackmail. In the other files, there were hundreds of photographs of other naked people, even others of Jacinto with a woman who was a friend of Soraya's and worked in the same internet café, clearly he had been screwing both of them.

He kept looking at the photographs, his heart on the verge of breaking, and then opened another file that really knocked him sideways: Soraya and himself, naked in the motel, ten, twenty, thirty photographs, all from the same angle. He huddled on the floor, in a fetal position, and wept bitterly. He did not want to see any more and shut down the computer. He took a quarter bottle of aguardiente from the minibar and started drinking slowly. Outside, night was falling but he did not feel any desire to go out. He was alone and felt like shit, with a hatred in him that kept him awake, like a glass of cold water thrown in his face. He called room service, ordered a chicken sandwich and a Diet Coke, and waited, sitting on the floor. Then he got in the bathtub and filled it with hot water. The sandwich was good. They had all deceived him and now the Grim Reaper was coming for them. The next day he would think about what to do and see what else was on that damn laptop.

He spent two days looking at files and found many things

that filled him with ideas. There were Excel pages containing details of drug consignments, drugs, prices, weights, and routes, the dates were recent, after Dagoberto had supposedly volunteered for the demobilization process. There were photographs of a grave with nine bodies, with faces taken from close up so that they could be recognized, and other photographs showing corpses being cut up to make them unrecognizable.

And there was the connection with his friend Jacinto. He had been buying, at a knockdown price, the cattle the paramilitaries had confiscated from other farms. Then, when Jacinto had become a major auto repair shop owner—with *his* shops—he had become the one who fixed the cars for them, cleaning off the blood and human remains. After every job Dagoberto handed the vehicles over to Jacinto and he handed them back as good as new, repainted, and with new plates. Jacinto never invoiced him, but in the accounts there were all the payments to his shop, each with a description: *Toyota van, seven bullet holes and traces of bodies. Fixing, repainting, and cleaning of traces. 1,500,000 pesos to Jacinto,* or *Chevrolet Suburban after Operation Mayor of Fresno. Chassis cleaned and repainted. 1,200,000 pesos. Jacinto.* And there was a file of more than a hundred and twenty pages, with invoices attached, which demonstrated that the cocaine was cut on Jacinto's farm!

Another file detailed the cleansing operations by area, such as: *32 executed by Hernán Mora in Operation Lejanías. Buried in seven pits, cut up, does not count as massacre. List:* followed by the names and the approximate ages. This Hernán was the brother of Soraya, so they were all there. The only one missing was Soraya, how could he take his revenge on her? It was Soraya he felt angriest at because nobody had forced her, she had done it even though she loved him. The photographs of her and Jacinto in the motel and the fact that she had married him, even though he would never have asked her mother for her hand: all that was more than sufficient proof that she was involved in the thing right from the start. All of them had been against him, and what had he done to them? Nothing, nothing. He had loved her, and he had loved Jacinto, who had been his friend since they were children. They had paid him back for that love and friendship with death and ruin. As he thought this, his breathing grew heavier and hatred filled his blood-stream, giving him even more strength. He would destroy them, that was clear.

And he was going to start with her.

He copied all the photographs in which she was with him, naked, and even with Jacinto, and erased the faces, leaving only her face. He chose five in which she was seen on all fours and with her face turned towards the camera, and two in which she was sucking Jacinto's cock. Then he e-mailed them to the town hall of La Cascada, the Community Center, the kinder-garten her daughter Gloria Soraya attended, the restaurant Luna Roja, the bar El Feliz, and Jacinto's auto repair shops. Also to the Häagen-Dazs ice cream parlor and the Escrúpulos tearooms, where she spent her afternoons. Also to the people of the El Paraíso residential community, wherever he could find the addresses. Everybody and everything with a more or less public e-mail address in La Cascada received the photo-graphs, and to make it even worse, he opened an account on Facebook in her name and added the rest of the photographs from the computer, including those of Jacinto with other women so that he could see it and know he had been found out. This Facebook idea was a brilliant one, he thought, which he could also use for Dagoberto. But he preferred to wait and see the reactions. His idea was to hand over the computer to the Public Prosecutor's Office or the newspapers or the Human Rights Commission and that was why he decided to stay a little longer in Bogotá.

After five days he moved to the Hotel Charleston, on Calle 85 near Carrera 15. He was so nervous, he found it impossible to leave the hotel, even for a short walk; all the same, he did go a couple of times to have a drink in the Zona Rosa and walk around the Centro Andino. Finally, after three days, he received a message on Facebook that said:

Let's see if you're brave enough to come out and show your face, you son of a bitch, do you have something against my family or what? We're already on your trail and we'll soon find out where you got all those fucking photographs that you've been putting on the Internet. We're going to cut your balls off and eat them fried, with chopped onions, you bastard.

The message was not signed but was obviously from Jacinto. It came from a Facebook account called The Executioner. So Ramón decided to have a bit of fun and replied: "Your wife is indeed a very elegant woman, what nobody can understand is what she's doing with a para." He waited nervously and that same night the answer came: "Son of a bitch, you're still hiding, feeling pleased with yourself, but you'll see, we're on your trail, we may be coming for you right now, as you read this, so start shaking."

The next day he made copies of the computer's hard disk and went to the Human Rights Commission. There, he had to identify himself and they listened to his story. A lawyer from the Commission went with him to the Public Prosecutor's Office to lodge a major complaint against Dagoberto, Hernán Mora, and Jacinto Gómez for kidnapping, torture, extortion, and theft. He handed over a copy of the hard disk and the prosecutors immediately started running and making calls. Ramón realized that his days as a fugitive were over, that he had to regain his true identity now, go back to being Ramón

Melo García. It was the only way he could accomplish his revenge.

After a long statement in the Public Prosecutor's Office about how he had gotten hold of the computer, Ramón was able to return to his hotel. It was late by now, but he had the feeling that he had achieved something. The next day he called the political desk at *El Espectador* and announced that he had information about paramilitarism in the eastern Plains. Somebody came to pick up a copy and that same night he was able to return to Panama City.

When he got home, he said to himself: the die is cast, now the one thing I have to do is make sure they don't kill me, or don't find me so easily. Dagoberto was confined to a high security prison at Cómbita, but many of his men were still on the outside, doing all they could to get him out as quickly and cheaply as possible. He did not know if Hernán Mora was also being detained.

A week later, *El Espectador* splashed all over its pages a lengthy article accusing Dagoberto, with photographs of the torture house in Lejanías, and information on the mass graves and the laboratories that were still functioning. There were also charges against a whole series of elected members of the senate who had been friendly with Dagoberto, and had received votes and money from him.

Ramón had not even known about that, as he had not checked the whole of the hard disk. The article quoted sources within the Public Prosecutor's Office and the Human Rights Commission, which were investigating and had asked the National Institute for Prisons to separate Dagoberto from the other demobilized paras, since in his case there were enough elements to bring more serious charges.

Less than a week later *El Espectador* reported the arrest of Hernán Mora and Jacinto Gómez, both accused of paramilitary activity in the region. The traitor Arnulfo Solano, his trusted former employee, was also detained, although on lesser charges. Everything came from the same computer, and Ramón felt a light inside him. He knew it was not good to take pleasure from hatred and revenge, but he had not been the one who had started all this. Then he wondered if now might be the time to take the step he so much desired, and decided it was. Now that his identity was obvious, he could make a frontal attack.

He took out his cell phone and looked at it for quite a while. Then he put it back in his pocket and took a good swig of aguardiente to give himself courage. Maybe the number had changed? Finally he dialed, with his heart standing still, and heard the rings. One, two, three . . . At the fifth ring the automatic message came on and he hung up. He went out on the balcony and drank another aguardiente, and was standing there looking at the bay, lost in thought, when the cell phone started ringing. He looked at the screen and froze. It was Soraya. Hello? There was a silence, it was her, she had recognized him. He hung up. Again unsure what to do, he waited. He imagined Soraya with the telephone in her hand, cursing or crying, he could not know which. The voice was the same, with a slight quiver because of the years; he remembered her husky tone, which had always sounded both erotic and comforting. But now everything was different: she had given him up to the paras! Nothing could make up for that. There was no excuse, and apart from that there was the fact of his mother's death.

He checked the Facebook address and found a message from Jacinto from four days earlier, before his arrest, which said: "We know who you are and we're going to kill you, you son of a bitch, wait and see." He reread the text with a smile and thought, this bastard doesn't know a damn thing, he has no idea what's in store for him. The fool.

An hour later his cell phone rang again and he made up his

mind to answer. It was her. Was it you who took those pictures? was the first thing she asked, but instead of answering that, he said, were you in on their plan to kill me? There was a silence; then she said, they told me you were in the FARC and wanted to kill my brother. That's nonsense, how could you believe such garbage? The thing is, Soraya, you were cheating on me with Jacinto and any excuse would have been all right. She was unable to respond immediately. She thought about it for a second and said: it's your fault, Ramón, I told you to ask for my hand and you did nothing, just waited and waited, and when you wait too long the soup gets cold, doesn't it? Oh, Soraya, you don't kill a person for that, the fact of it is, you knew they were going to kill me and you didn't care, and later my mother died because you didn't even go to see her; she died of sadness, or rather, you all killed her; you killed her, Soraya; so don't ask me to respect you or understand you, the only thing I want is to see you crawling on the floor, because you're a bitch, a cheat, a traitor, and a murderer.

There were sobs, but his anger did not abate: You cry now that my mother's dead and they took away my life's work and almost killed me, and all because of you, so go on, cry until the blood comes out of your eyes. There was another silence, then she said: I'm already weeping blood, Ramón, you can say whatever you like to me, you can even tell me I'm a whore, you haven't said it yet but you're thinking it, so say it, filthy whore, lowdown whore, don't hesitate to say it because it's true, it's what everyone is saying here in La Cascada since you came out with those photographs . . . The whole town has seen me naked with a guy they don't even know is my husband, and with you, but as nobody remembers you they think it's somebody new, and so I've become the whore of the community, the whore of the club and the tearooms, the whore of La Cascada, and now they've put Jacinto in jail and things are really difficult. I already threw him out of the house because of the photographs on Facebook with other whores who aren't his whore of a wife, oh God.

Ramón was getting impatient and said: tell me why you slept with Jacinto, what were you missing with me? I missed the risk, Ramón, I missed that great sensation of hanging from a thread . . . I missed feeling more of a woman or more of a person or maybe even more of a whore, I don't know, I liked him and I wanted him and you see, I even gave him a daughter who maybe he didn't deserve, but what can we do, that's how it was, we can't change it.

No, but we can make sure the bad people appear bad and the murderers appear murderers, and that's what I came to do, Soraya; the worst that could have happened to you, to all of you, was that I escaped from the paras and stayed alive, because now you're fucked. Soraya had stopped crying, her voice was neutral and relatively steady. She said: and what more are you going to do, they're already going to take everything away from us, they're going to extradite Dagoberto, and they're going to give my brother Hernán the maximum sentence because the bastard didn't get involved with the demobilization, so you see, Ramón, you've ruined our lives, you've already avenged yourself, you've already avenged your mother, what more do you want? Ramón thought it over for a second and said, I want to see you, Soraya, that's all, I want to see you for a second and maybe my anger will pass.

The proposal surprised her. And why do you want to see me, Ramón? A lot of time's gone by and I'm fat, when I was pregnant I gained nearly sixty pounds and I still have twenty I can't get rid of, I don't look like the girl you used to go out with anymore, don't think I do. But he said, that doesn't matter, Soraya, I only want to see you for a second and look you in the face and ask you if you really wanted them to kill me . . . You don't need to look at me to ask that, I already told you, they told me you were in the FARC and were going to kill

Hernán. You can believe me or not. To believe you I need to see you, Soraya, that's why I'm saying this. She thought about it for a while: if we see each other, will you leave us alone? Well, Soraya, that's not up to me anymore, it's up to the law. Yes, but the law can be handled, what matters is that you stop stirring things.

Come to Bogotá on Saturday, Soraya. Bring your cell phone. At three in the afternoon I'll call you and tell you where, O.K.? O.K., but call me straight away, don't make me wait. Don't worry, I'll call you straight away, make sure you have a signal and swear to me you'll come alone. She said: after all this trouble who do you think I'm going to come with? The Virgin Mary?

Ramón traveled to Bogotá on the Friday, to get ready. He had made enquiries about private security and hired four bodyguards for the weekend, and he met them at the Hotel Charleston. He went for a walk with them, got to know them, and invited them out for a nice meal to get them on his side. Then he visited a fashionable brothel called La Piscina, and went into a private room with two women. The bodyguards protected him well and he got back to the hotel at three in the morning safe and sound.

The next day, he called Soraya about eleven in the morning and said, are you already in Bogotá? Yes, she said, tell me where you want to see me. He told her to wait at the entrance to the Carulla on Calle 85 and Carrera 15, and he would send for her. Then he changed hotels, moving to the Radisson in Santa Bárbara, and waited until two of his bodyguards informed him that they were already with her. Señor? The lady's with us. Good, put her on. Hello, Soraya, the security measures are for me, but nothing's going to happen to you, O.K.? Do what the men tell you, you can trust them.

The bodyguards brought her to the Radisson and he waited for her in a suite with a very nice view of Bogotá. When they came in he made them take her into one of the rooms in the suite and, before seeing her, he told his men to check the whole floor and take up positions, two inside and two outside the door. He dressed slowly and well, and at last made up his mind to enter the room.

Oh, thank God, she said when she saw him, I was starting to think this was a wasted journey. Ramón was silent, his eyes started to water and he had to bite his tongue in order not to sob. It was true that she had changed, but she was still pretty. She had put on a few pounds and her hair was dyed, which made her look older, but he recognized her, she was just the same. He saw her smile and remembered that last night, on the eve of his departure from La Cascada. He hadn't gone with her to the Rey de la Pachanga because he had wanted to get up early in order to go to Villavicencio to talk to the police. She had stayed in La Cascada, with Jacinto and her brother Hernán.

Ramón asked her about that night, saying, tell me what happened exactly, I want the details, did you go straight to Jacinto or what? No, she said, I wasn't with Jacinto, but with my brother Hernán. We were in the disco and Jacinto arrived there with Dagoberto. They talked for a while, and then Hernán said to me, Sorayita, there's something important we need to ask you, is it true Ramón is going to Villavicencio tomorrow to inform on Dagoberto to the police about the business with the car? I went red and didn't say anything, I didn't want anything to happen to you, but Dagoberto looked at me and said, I already know what he's going to do in Villavicencio, I only want you to confirm it, that's all, you're the man's girlfriend and I respect you, but it's only right you should know that Ramón is working for the FARC in La Cascada and Villavicencio and that's why he's against us, and what he wants is for them to capture me and then fuck things up for Hernán, that's why it's important that you confirm it for us, Sorayita, because things could get nasty. I asked them what they were going to do to you, and they said, just question him, tell him to let us do our work and not interfere. That's what they told me. So I said, yes, Ramón is going to talk to the police, he's a good man because he covered for you when you were trying to extort money from him for the car, but they said, what do you mean, extort, the truth is the man is working for the FARC, we ought to go and kill him right now, tonight, said my brother Hernán, who was already drunk, and then Jacinto said, don't worry, Sorayita, you know Ramón and I have been friends since we were children and I wouldn't let any harm come to him, but we do have to stop him because otherwise this town is going to become a hell for us. I believed them.

She said these last words with tears in her eyes, and Ramón felt the impulse to console her, but he did not approach her. He said: and were you so stupid you believed they weren't going to do anything to me, when they'd filled La Cascada with bodies in ditches? Oh, Ramón, what could I do if the three of them were in agreement and convinced me? Nothing. Ramón looked at her angrily and said: and then you went off to screw Jacinto! She continued crying and got down on her knees. Look, Ramón, I hurt you a lot, but now I'm paying. My daughter is with her grandmother, my husband is in prison, they've taken away the two farms, the restaurants, and the house, they've confiscated everything, and here I am, on my knees, begging your forgiveness, what more do you need to be able to forgive me?

Ramón looked at her and said: there's nothing you can do to make me forgive you, my mother is dead, she died alone because of you. What I wanted was to hear the story of your betrayal and tell you that I was the one who hatched this revenge, the one who got hold of Dagoberto's laptop with the photographs and distributed them everywhere, because you should know that friend of yours was spying on you and taking photographs, of you and me too, maybe from even earlier, don't you see? You've all ruined my life and now I've ruined yours, that's what you gained from being bastards. You can go now, Soraya, I never want to see you again.

Ramón walked to the door but she rushed to him and fell at his feet, embracing him. When he felt her his body quivered, and in a second she was kissing him and taking out his cock to suck it, saying, let me give you something, like any other whore; let me pay back the hurt I did you even if it's with this, O.K.? She took off her clothes and lay down on the couch. He lay on top of her and finished in five minutes. He stood up and said, come, I'll take you to the Carulla, or wherever you want to go, are you going back to the Plains today? No, said Soraya, I'm staying with a friend in La Soledad. Drop me at the Carulla and I'll take a taxi from there.

They rode without talking, without touching each other. Halfway, she asked: did you like it, at least? Ramón looked at her and said: yes, just like before, you're very nice. Soraya smiled. If you like, we can do it again another time, just call me at this number and I'll come wherever you say. Good, said Ramón, and dropped her at the Carulla. When she got out of the car he felt relieved. Then he said to the bodyguards and the driver: to the airport. That night he was back at home. He rubbed his crotch and lifted his hand to his nose, searching for her smell, and said to himself: the bitch, now she's cheating on Jacinto because he won't be out for at least ten years. It's all backfired on him.

The following week he called her and said, I want to see you, can you come? Of course, just like I said, tell me where. He sent her instructions and a ticket for Cartagena on Saturday, and that was where they met. They spent the day at the Hilton, hardly going out at all, because Ramón had not hired any security and he was afraid to walk with her on the street. As they lay in bed together, Soraya ventured to ask: why do you have so much money now? did you win the lottery or what? I owe it to my God, he said, who unexpectedly gives and unexpectedly takes away, and apart from that I work. And where do you live now, in Bogotá? Don't ask me any questions, Soraya, after what they did to me I've become paranoid. O.K., Ramón, I'm sorry, I won't ask you anything else.

They met almost every weekend for a month, each time in a different city. Sometimes he would ask her to come to Cali, and without leaving the airport they would get on a plane for Pasto, without any warning. Then he would leave without telling her where he was going, leaving her a ticket to get home.

Ramón continued to keep a close watch on the legal proceedings against Jacinto and Hernán and hired his own lawyer to process his accusation. One day he went to the Public Prosecutor's Office to make a statement, and submitted to a long interrogation in which he answered questions about what had happened to him. They told him they would give him protection, but he said, I'll accept it only from the airport to here, I can protect myself. One of the questions had been if he had any links with the FARC, which was what the prisoners, Dagoberto, Jacinto Gómez, and Hernán Mora, were saying, but he said, no, they're just the same as the paras, why should I be with the FARC, Prosecutor, if I were, what happened wouldn't have happened! They asked him why he had covered for Dagoberto when the police in Villavicencio had questioned him, and he said, because I was scared, because I was a coward, I had already seen the bodies thrown in ditches along the highway, that was the only reason, Prosecutor. When they asked him to tell them how he had escaped he saw that they did not believe him, it was not a very believable story, but that was how it had been and that was how he told it, and in fact the priest's disappearance and kidnapping and the discovery of his body were all in the records, so they did not ask him again. What he did not mention to them, because he had realized it was not relevant to what they wanted to know, was Father Cubillos's treasure in Barranquilla. Nor did he go into detail about his life in Panama, because he had read that the paras were everywhere and he was scared that someone in the Public Prosecutor's Office would snitch on him.

Fortunately, the evidence on the computer was irrefutable and the police had gotten to Dagoberto's house in Lejanías. Of course when they asked him how he had found the computer he told them the truth; he had to give them the name of the agency in Villavicencio. Later he found out that they had summoned the detective to make a statement and that their versions tallied, so nobody ever mentioned it again.

One Saturday he was with Soraya in Cartagena, eating in the restaurant of the Hilton, when he realized that a man he had seen that afternoon at the pool and later in the hotel shop was looking at them out of the corner of his eye. He immediately stood up, went out on the street, and hired a taxi to take them to another part of the city, the old part. From the taxi, he dialed a number they had given him at the Public Prosecutor's Office, in case of emergency, and said that he was in Cartagena, and he thought he was being followed. They made him wait a while, and then the prosecutor said: don't worry, Ramón, that person is there for your security, we're keeping an eye on you. Oh yes? and how did you know I was at the Hilton? Oh, Ramón, said the prosecutor, you have no idea how much I know, just be grateful that we were the ones who tapped Soraya's telephone.

He went back to the hotel, got his things, and went to the airport, leaving her in the room. You aren't in any danger, stay the weekend if you like. And he left.

One morning he opened the newspaper and was stunned: it was announced that Dagoberto and Hernán Mora were being extradited to the United States, for drug trafficking, and that Jacinto had been sentenced to fifteen years' imprisonment.

Immediately he called Soraya and asked her how she felt. Those bastards ruined my life, even Jacinto, I hope they rot, was what she said, and she added: I hope now you will calm down too, it was what you wanted, wasn't it? It wasn't what I wanted, it was what they deserved, Soraya. Don't confuse the two things. He told her he wanted to see her, to celebrate this victory. She said all right, but that maybe it was the last time, because she had already paid enough.

They met in Bogotá, where he had been taking steps through his lawyers to recover the ownership of the auto repair shops—they had put Arnulfo in prison too, but only for three years—and put them on sale. His idea was to take her to the Charleston, and he had called ahead to book a room, but as they were driving along the beltway, coming back from the center, two Silverados blocked the road and opened fire. The escort from the Public Prosecutor's Office took shelter behind the wall of a building and returned fire. The shootout lasted twenty minutes. Ramón threw himself down on the floor of the car and did not move, because he knew it was armored. When they lifted him out he had a wound in the shoulder, as he had lowered the window a little and had been shot through it. Soraya, on the other hand, was sitting there, bleeding profusely. They changed cars and raced to the Hospital San Ignacio, but she was dead by the time they arrived. She had two bullet wounds in the head and one in the neck. The first shot may well have killed her. That was what the doctors told him. They also told him she was pregnant.

He did not feel like crying, or rather, no tears came, even though he was sad. When you came down to it, they had all been victims.

After he recovered, he had no desire to stay in Bogotá, so he went straight from the hospital to the airport. As the plane taxied to the runway to take off he felt that he was moving away from hell and death, and he said to himself, could they have located me in Panama? It was possible, but it did not worry him. Revenge had been the most important thing in his life; that had been his only reason for living in the last few years, and now it was over, with Soraya dead—even though that had not been his intention—and the others punished. What did it matter if they shot him down now on some street corner? He had accomplished his mission and could leave without remorse, as if he was saying goodbye to a country that had kicked him out, forever, because he also knew that he would never return.

3.

THE GARDEN OF RARE FLOWERS
(AS TOLD BY SABINA VEDOVELLI)

The life story I am about to relate is a harsh and some-times even macabre one, so I hope there are no young people in the room. There are situations that the inex-perienced or the innocent may find disturbing. I'm not sure of the conference's policy on this, and I shall certainly go ahead and tell my story anyway, but it might be a good idea to check at the entrance that all members of the audience are of legal age, at least for today. That's my feeling at least, but of course it's also possible, indeed quite likely, that these young people may simply find my story highly amusing. The world has changed a great deal and even the most atrocious things don't seem to bother anybody. They may bother me, but then I'm from another era. Before tackling my life, with a wealth of detail and quite a few surprises, I should like to put paid to an idea I know many of you may have in your minds, which is that, due to the nature of the films I make, I'm nothing but a whore. You must disabuse yourselves of that, my friends, and I'll tell you why. Sex on the set is a very distinct thing, because for all those involved in it, it's a paid job. Simple as that. In the best spirit of capitalism, it's all done for a third party who isn't there, like a person who cooks delicious dishes for others, or who writes passionate verses for anonymous readers—who will usually reject them—or even the person who invents mortars and grenades that will kill and maim people he can't see, or even imagine, but which will be real enough when the moment comes. My poet friends may not like to hear this. They'll say it's a far-fetched comparison, but then everything that I, Sabina Vedovelli, do is and has always been far-fetched.

I know there are many rumors about me, but what nobody knows is that I myself am the source of them, since they make me seem larger than life, and the idiots who repeat them, thinking they're hurting me with their vulgar comments, are merely inflating the sails of my ego, pushing the boat that little bit farther out. "When they fly I am the wings," as Brahma says in that poem by Emerson. The result is that they keep talking about me. They can't stop talking about me. And that makes me very happy.

But let's get to the story. I wasn't always this woman who so many men today would like to have in their beds and who as she walks earns a string of lustful glances and throats being cleared and husbands scolded by their wives. I wasn't always what I am. I was once a young girl and men scared me. That's true. They scared me because they were as strange to me as bulls or scorpions, seeing as how I grew up among women, being an only child brought up by my mother and two aunts, all three of them abandoned by feckless men, who had moved from Naples to Rome and settled in a first-floor apartment on Via dei Monti di Creta, on the outskirts of the city, a long way from the center, next to a garden of pine trees called the Pineta Sachetti, where I used to play as a girl, until my mother met a short, stout man who spoke with a strange accent, and we went to Mexico City to live with him, and that's why, when I speak Spanish, people think I'm Mexican.

We lived in an apartment on Calle Ámsterdam, near the Parque Independencia, and I attended the Sor Juana high school. By the time I finished school, I was a demure young lady, and that was how I stayed, oh yes, I didn't change until later, in another country, France no less, the land where the storks come from, the land of love, but also the land of the most revolting vice and licentiousness. I should point out that my mother left me to my own devices during vacations, she would give me money and airline tickets to wherever I liked, so as to leave herself free to have a great time in Veracruz or Acapulco with her lover, who was half businessman and half drug trafficker, from what I discovered later, although more the second of those than the first, so I went traveling around the world, almost always with the daughter of one of my aunts from Rome, my cousin Giorgetta, who was crazier than I was and did everything before I did.

When I was eighteen and she was nineteen we went together to Paris, the city of vice and depravity. On the second day, through friends of Giorgetta, we ended up at a party thrown by a group of immigrants in Belleville, a party that lasted three days and where there was a lot of alcohol and drugs right from the start, although not for me, because I was very young and hadn't yet picked up any bad habits. The group consisted of Jamaicans, Senegalese, and Spaniards who, if I remember correctly, were all studying with a Japanese friend of Giorgetta's. It was just like a movie, I started seeing all kinds of strange things, a young guy with a hypodermic syringe hanging from his forearm, a woman lifting her miniskirt and injecting herself in the groin, another who was rubbing her nose against a mirror as she danced and crying in French, yes, yes, with the muscles of her face tense as wires, another man biting off half a pill and offering the other half to his girlfriend on his tongue and the girlfriend gobbling it up like a fruit, young girls wetting tampons in gin and sticking them in their bottoms, their faces all shiny with pleasure, people smoking some kind of brown tobacco from silver paper, tobacco that took the brain to another dimension, everything washed down with strong alcohol and, of course, hours later, when all modesty had been thrown out the window, I saw another kind of image, a young Jamaican penetrating a woman on a small table in the dining room, my cousin Giorgetta, behind the bathroom curtain, putting a penis in her mouth, a penis so black it looked like a clarinet, a man stroking another man's ass as he danced, things like that, but I stayed as I was and only drank beer and a little Coke to keep going, and when I finally made up my mind to leave, and I'm telling you this so you can see the kind of bad influence I had to contend with, I went to look for my cousin and found her naked and bathed in sweat, having sex with her Japanese friend on the same flea-ridden mattress where a Senegalese guy was fucking a Spanish guy in the ass, which was quite a shocking scene for a young girl like me, if you see what I mean.

When the party was over, we went back to the Japanese guy's apartment and Giorgetta slept for something like a hundred hours in a row, and when she woke up she spent another three hours in the shower and then she came out and said, Sabina, let's do something really crazy, and I said, crazier than that party? She looked at me pityingly and said, don't worry, I'm older than you but I began at the age of thirteen, you're too quiet, you know, you need taking out of yourself, come on, let me take care of it. We went to the house of another friend of hers, a Norwegian who was about ten feet tall, and he and Giorgetta talked for a while and he asked her, are you sure? and Giorgetta said, very sure, it's what I want now, so the guy tied a rubber band around her forearm, burned a liquid in a spoon, put it in a syringe and injected her.

Immediately, Giorgetta's eyes rolled back and she started shaking, which got me quite nervous, but the Norwegian, whose name was Kay, said to me, don't worry, she's shaking with pleasure, it's like having a hundred orgasms at the same time, do you want to try? I said no, I can't feel a thousand orgasms because I still haven't had my first, I'm a virgin. He opened his eyes wide and cried, really? and added, please don't move, I want to take a photograph, you're the first virgin I've met since I came to Paris, and then I asked, and what do you do? and he said, I'm a photographer, let's see, stand over there. I heard the click of the camera and then a second click and a third, and then lots more, as many as the orgasms my cousin Giorgetta must have been having—by now she'd slipped off the couch and was lying on the carpet—thousands of clicks from a camera focused on my body, and I knew he desired me, and I started taking off my clothes, first my sweater, then my skirt, my blouse and my bra, and lastly my panties, my white virgin's panties, and when I was naked Kay kept saying in French, *parfait! parfait!* and I could see the bulge in his pants getting bigger, so I said, take that off and let me see what you're hiding there, and he showed it to me, and it was all pink and as big as an elephant's trunk, with yellow hairs, and he said, you should suck it, it doesn't taste bad, so I went to him and sucked it and it wasn't too unpleasant, it tasted like rust or wet wood, so I carried on sucking and feeling his veins swelling until he said, open those thighs, I want to see what you've got, and he opened me with his tongue and I saw stars, he explored me with his finger and finally he put his penis in, which hurt me at first, but was quite nice after that and moved inside me very smoothly. Just as I was about to have my first orgasm he took it out and moved it up to my mouth and said, swallow it, you'll like it, and so I did, and he spurted a bitter liquid that burned my throat.

When he withdrew, I grabbed his arm and said, where are you going? you haven't finished with me, and I put his mouth back in my cunt and said, now suck and lick until I tell you, and he did as he was told, and one or two minutes later I felt a ray of light split my body in two and I screamed as much if not more than the girl in the movie *Carrie* when they tip the bucket of blood over her, and I lost consciousness, and when that huge volcano had stopped erupting and I returned to reality I saw Giorgetta looking at me through half-open eyes, and saying, did he fuck you or did he give you a fix? and I replied, the first, how are you? and she said, with her cheeks covered in drool, this is too much, it's really intense, I can't speak, I'm sorry, and she lay down on the carpet again and as she did so I noticed she was giving off a disgusting smell. I looked at Kay, who was just emerging from between my legs, and he said, don't make that face, it's normal to shit and pee when you shoot up for the first time, you'll have to get used to it.

I stood up and went to the shower and stayed there for nearly an hour, letting the hot water run over my shoulders, directing the jet of water at my pubis and hearing distant drums, everything was very new and the desire I felt for that man was irrational and probably unhealthy, what others call love at first sight or—which comes to the same thing—the intuition that somebody can destroy us, and so I said to myself, Sabina, when you finish your shower you have to get dressed, walk past Kay and take Giorgetta outside, take her away from Paris and back to Rome, where your aunts are; I felt I was on the edge of something very dangerous and on the verge of falling.

But when I came out of the bathroom, what I saw made things even more complicated, because I saw Kay lying beside Giorgetta with the syringe in his forearm. They had both just injected themselves. From her position, it was obvious my cousin had taken another fix, so I went to the kitchen, made myself a chicken sandwich, had a Diet Coke and waited, how long would it last? After a while, I went to Kay's room, which was filthy and was where he kept his rolls of film and developing equipment, and lay down facing an old TV set which was switched on but with the screen blank. I looked for the remote and when I pressed the button saw it wasn't switched to a TV channel but to a movie.

I pressed play and, to my surprise, what did I see? it was a porn movie! A really old movie by Lasse Braun called *Sin Dreamer*, with pot-bellied men lying in a meadow, having sex with plump women with vaginas as hairy as spiders, a really old-fashioned kind of movie. I got very aroused, and when it finished I looked for another, because those two addicts were still lying on the carpet, and the one I found was *Frequence Blue*, by the same director, only this time I put my hand inside my panties and started touching my clitoris, I remember it very well, there was a scene in the country where a woman in an old Citröen sucked the cocks of three gendarmes from the highway police who were going to give her a fine, and at the end I heard noises and saw Kay come into the room, so I jumped on him and we had sex again, really wild sex. Then Giorgetta came in, with her eyelids inflamed and her skin all dirty, and asked Kay for more heroin, but he said, that's enough for today, sweetheart, cool it, sleep a bit, you need to rest, and she said, O.K., and immediately slipped through the door and lay down on the floor again. Finally we fell asleep, with me embracing Kay, the man who had deflowered me, and Giorgetta on the carpet, her habitat for the last twelve hours.

And that's pretty much how the weekend passed, with Giorgetta injecting increasingly large doses and me having sex with Kay, who with each fuck seemed to me more delicious and his penis sweeter. On the Monday, about ten in the morning, Kay had some black coffee, grabbed the bag with his cameras, and said, my dears, I'm going to work and I won't be back before tonight, so make yourselves at home, I don't know what's in the fridge, so feel free to go to the supermarket and buy provisions, which wouldn't be a bad idea anyway, *ciao, à ce soir,* and he left, slamming the door behind him.

No sooner had Kay gone than Giorgetta rushed to the drawers in his night table, the sideboard, the closet, and the kitchen, looking for drugs, and when she didn't find any she said, the bastard's left me high and dry, I'm going out on the street to get some more, wait for me here, and I said, Giorgetta, do you realize what you're doing? Seeing the look of surprise on her face,

I added, you've turned into a junkie in only three days, don't you think that's a bit . . . excessive? but she replied, I told you I wanted to do something crazy on this trip, I didn't say anything to you about the fact that you're fucking Kay, did I? No, I replied, because it's none of your business, and she wagged her finger and said, that's exactly what I was thinking, so let's make a deal, we each mind our own business, what do you think? I said yes, and she left. That night, when Kay got home, she still hadn't returned. She came back three days later in a very bad state, with staring eyes and her skin all greasy, smelling of excrement and with blood in her anus. I bathed her without asking any questions, only ventured to say, have you had enough yet? can we go back to Rome? We did go back, in fact, but against all expectation I was the one who immediately got on a plane and returned to Paris, because I had fallen in love with Kay. He promised to make me a big star and I believed him, how could I not believe him when he allowed me to fuck him every night and suck his cock and lick his balls? Love at first sight and the bond with the first male who goes on the prowl between your legs did the rest.

Seven months later, Kay left me for a Norwegian model he was taking photographs of, and set off for Oslo. But I went after him. I wasn't going to allow a junkie in a silk bra and G-string to take my man, however languid and rich she was. When I got to Oslo, I went to stay in his brother Stef's apartment, because I'd known him in Paris and got along well with him, and devoted myself to waiting for Kay outside the front door of his girlfriend's building.

The whore would do drugs with him and give him five-hundred-euro bills, and I realized that for somebody like Kay, a child of the Scandinavian middle class, a left-wing activist and enemy of globalization, an opponent of Norway's joining the European Union, she represented something special, a way of touching something distant and desired with his fingers or his

foreskin. I waited for them for about a week, but in vain. Stef
didn't know his brother's whereabouts, at least that was what
he told me.

I was already on the verge of going back to Paris when Stef
invited me to a party, saying, a group of my friends is playing
tonight at Yellowstone Creek, which was a trendy techno bar
in the city, so I went with him. But on the way back home he
raped me. I don't want to go into details, I'll only tell you that
first he tried to drug me, then to seduce me the natural way,
with laughter and alcohol, and when he didn't get anywhere he
resorted to violence, first beating me up and then, when I was
on the floor, fucking me as much as he wanted and forcing me
to suck his ass. When he'd finished, he called two friends and
invited then to fuck me, which they were happy to do, the bastards. When they were all satisfied, they left me lying in one of
the side entrances of the railroad station in Oslo, at four in the
morning, where I almost got raped again.

As you might have guessed, Kay returned to Paris when the
bitch got bored with him and threw him out on the street. I
was in his apartment waiting for him, because in the meantime
I had threatened my mother that I'd go back to Mexico and so
her boyfriend from the Tijuana cartel decided to send me a few
dollars a month, which allowed me to wait for my man calmly
and, above all, with my resentment intact. I was also able to
analyze my rape obsessively, and I say "my rape" because it was
a painful baptism into life, as if somebody had said, hey, you,
do you want to be really free? do you want to be able to stroll
through the world as you please with drug addicts and punks
and alcoholics in a highly altered state, not only that but walk
around in miniskirts and your belly button in full view, open to
the dirty air of the cities? Well, this is what happens, this is the
price, they raped you and now you'll be someone else, someone stronger, the tribe inevitably reprimands women who
resist being confined to the female role that males have created

for them, and that's why whoever abandons that way of thinking is violently punished, in a way that is tantamount to amputating her arm or her clitoris, something like that.

Thinking that, I understood "my rape" a little better, although there's no point in deceiving ourselves, understanding doesn't mean overcoming—because the other thing I couldn't get out of my head was that the rapist was none other than Stef, my God, a young man who had been in Paris, looking at museums and going to concerts, a young man I'd cooked pasta in tomato sauce for, all that kind of thing—I said to myself, men have sex when the prey reveals her fragility, and that was what I had done. I must never appear fragile again. I didn't feel guilty, as sometimes happens to women who are raped, which makes them go to psychiatrists, or sometimes kill themselves, or turn into avengers, these last being the most interesting, because in general, before they end up in some provincial prison, they manage to mutilate a few male members, even pulling them out by their roots, savagely interrupting the trunk-foreskin continuum or the even more complex trunk-testicles continuum, which usually results in a geyser of blood.

I am aware of the injustice that some innocent foreskins may be presumed guilty and cut to shreds, but what we can do if the tribe is cruel, cruel in a different way for each tribesman. The rules of a mob devouring itself, penises still throbbing with life on the floor for having forced themselves into vaginas or anuses that didn't want them, oh, what are we going to do, the world is crazy, we are all crazy: this was what I was thinking as I sat there smoking, wrapped in a blanket, by the window of Kay's apartment, which I haven't mentioned was on Rue Oberkampf, near République, in the eleventh arrondissement, and that was why when I dared to go a bit farther than the corner, where the Monoprix supermarket was, I walked as far as the Canal Saint-Martin and kept myself amused watching the brown waters flowing past, laden with garbage, shit, and plankton. The river that was flowing inside me was the same, a stream of black waters, filled with rats, excrement, and semen, because that night in Oslo they didn't only rape me from the front but also from behind, which was something Kay and I had had a taste of without going all the way, preferring to wait for the right moment, and now that heavily guarded treasure had ended up in the ravine, lost and abused. Take note, girls.

After many days at the window, having already abandoned hope, I saw him coming. His tall, stooped figure, in a blue coat and scarf, stood out among the passers-by on Rue Oberkampf; on one side he was carrying his camera case and on the other a small bag, and I said to myself, there he is, the bitch got rid of him, she must have gotten tired of his snoring and his farting and his sour breath in the mornings. I felt a gigantic flower growing in my throat, because I loved him madly. Of course I made him pay. He had to do things, things that would never have occurred to him, before I would give him the first embrace or have sex with him, which was what he had been longing for from the first second. And so our relationship started up again, rebuilt like a house after a fire, never the same as before, with traces of soot on the ceilings, but still standing. There only remained the matter of my rape by his brother, but I preferred not to talk about it, we could see about that later.

I was young and I felt that my strength was infinite, that I was still able to bear a lot of things, so he went back to his work in Paris and of course continued with the drugs. His months with the Norwegian whore had strengthened his addiction and he increased his daily dose to keep a steady pulse, so he had to work very hard. Heroin is expensive and I was a spoiled little girl who liked exclusive things, fashionable clothes, scents.

And so things went on for nearly six months until one day

Kay suggested taking a few nude photographs of me. He said that kind of thing paid very well and we'd be able to take a vacation in New York, so I agreed, I went to his studio, and we did them. The poses were fairly artistic, though with a touch of spice. In fact, some were a bit too suggestive for my taste, although there were no close-ups of genitals. Kay took them with him the next day and in the evening came back with a lot of money. We packed our bags and went off to New York to live it up for a while, with a room booked at the Mandarin Oriental on Columbus Circle and friends who took us to MoMA and to see the view from Brooklyn Bridge, but of course, there's also plenty of heroin there, it's cheaper and very different, so one night I had to take Kay to the hospital after an overdose, which was pretty unpleasant. When he came out, we had to go back to Paris, as all our money was gone.

Back on Rue Oberkampf, I started to ask myself questions like, what is life? is it worth living? what sacrifices are justified in life and why? questions connected with what I saw in front of my eyes every day, and one afternoon I don't know why the idea came into my mind, but I decided to call my mother in Mexico City. When she heard my voice, instead of being genuinely pleased she sounded anxious, maybe she was worried I was going to announce my return, since by this time it was obvious that my presence bothered her. I quickly told her that everything was fine in Paris, that I was living with a Norwegian fashion photographer but that I wasn't very sure what to do with my future. In other words: I was calling to ask her advice. She liked that and said, listen to me, Sab, I've always believed that what makes people noble and useful is studying, so you ought to study, darling, and in fact something just occurred to me: if you study, you won't be able to work, so I'd like to help you, send you money to cover your expenses, how about it? I thanked her and thought it over for a few days, until I decided I'd study acting and phoned her to tell her.

On the phone, she sounded really moved, Oh, how proud you've made me, she said, a Gina Lollobrigida in the family, a Grace Kelly, a Julia Roberts, hey, Fito, come and hear this, and she immediately sent me a decent amount of money to start my course, and I enrolled in drama school at the Sorbonne, doing a little audition at which, in all modesty, I left the judges in raptures, and not only because I finished my monologue by taking my pants off and walking around the stage with a lilac-colored G-string stuck between my buttocks, but because my talent expressed itself openly, in a direct, transparent form.

A new period of my life began. I felt really active. An inner fire consumed me. Very soon I got together a group of friends from among my classmates from the school and we started going out, day and night, to see plays or hold rehearsals, and it was around that time that Petra first put in an appearance. Petra was a Romanian, and taught Expression through Movement. He was one of those Francophile Romanians like Ionesco, Mircea Eliade and E. M. Cioran, and well, it all happened very rapidly.

One afternoon, Petra asked us to interpret with our bodies something that made us feel afraid, and I evoked my childhood, which for me was the grimmest thing in the world. The one thing I could come up with was to sit down in a corner of the stage with my face covered, get down on my knees, pull my pants down and raise my backside; it was my way of expressing the fragility of childhood, transposing it to the sexual fragility of woman, my rape. Naturally, my male classmates, and some of the women, got a bit distracted, so Petra came up on stage and said, mademoiselle, can you explain your position?

I told him about my childhood and the horror of the rape and how all that formed a whole that generated all the greatest fears in my life. Petra asked the others to go and get changed. We were alone on the stage, and he said, can you get back in that position? I'd like to try and understand it in the light of what you've just said.

I got back on my knees, lowered my head, lifted my ass, and waited in silence, one minute, two, until I felt his hands squeezing my hips and his mouth sinking into my buttocks; I was surprised and uncomfortable, but just as I was about to protest I had the first of at least a dozen orgasms, and I said to myself, here I am again, I looked for it, I guess I really wanted it, so I turned and opened his zipper and took out his penis, the penis of a man of 55, which was another novelty for me, and put it in my mouth, *tout doucement*, as Édith Piaf says in her famous song, and started sucking it with such relish that Petra began breathing heavily and his heart started pounding, I could hear the heartbeats from down there.

Then we moved to an exercise mat and had a spectacular fuck, the kind that, when you finish, you're like the first human must have been who trod the earth after the first time he got laid, a feeling that reality had exploded, as if everything had been sucked into a black hole and all that remained in the world was that stage, Petra's penis, and my desires as a woman; that night, when I got off the metro at Oberkampf and walked to the front door of our building, it hit me, should I tell him or not? Kay was hardly entitled to blame me and I wanted him to know that, wanted him to know I was no longer the innocent young virgin he had seduced one night, and, having decided that, I went upstairs, but when I entered the apartment I found him lying on the couch with a syringe beside him, and I said to myself, O.K., another night alone, enjoy your drug, you don't know what's waiting for you when you wake up, and I went to the window again, with a pot of plain yogurt and a French loaf and looked out at the light of the city and listened over and over to the electronic music of Cyder Bang Bong, the musical essence of what it means to live in one of those soulless cities where all worlds collide.

I thought about the words I would have to use to tell Kay, and I looked at him, heard him making those gurgling sounds the drug forced from him every now and again; it was then that I saw a scribbled piece of paper under the syringe, a sheet torn from a notebook, which said, Dear Sabina, I know everything, I know what you did today with your drama teacher, I followed you, I've been following you for weeks . . . at this point the letter broke off, he must have put it aside to prepare his fix . . .

Although I'd been pumping myself up to remind him of the fact that he had run away with that Norwegian whore, I felt guilty and stroked his forehead, and as I did so I screamed. It was freezing cold! His sweat was so cold, his forehead felt like a salmon in a distant fjord, so I started slapping him and crying out, wake up, Kay, for God's sake, wake up!

I called the emergency service and asked for an ambulance, while at the same time giving him a cardiac massage, which was something I had seen in a movie, but to no avail. The Sapeurs, Pompiers arrived and took him away, also taking the syringe to analyze the dose he had given himself, and I tagged along behind them, crying and on the verge of hysteria, an image nurses must know well, there can't be an overdose that doesn't have a heartrending scene to go with it, and this was no exception. When we were all in the ambulance, they looked at one another, extremely disturbed. Then they tried electric shock and cardiac massage, but nothing worked. I didn't dare look, at any moment one of them would turn around and say, mademoiselle, this man is dead, is he a family member, your husband, your boyfriend, or just your roommate? And I would take all the blame on myself: I'd killed him, it was all my fault, and I knew in advance that the psychologists would say, listen, Sabina, a person only does something like this when he's been carrying it inside him for a long time, there's no such thing as a sudden suicide, you mustn't blame yourself.

Everything was very strange. Nobody had announced his

death to me and I was already hearing words of relief; there were many difficult moments before we reached the hospital and there they took him out without saying anything to me, only the laconic words, wait there, sit down, fill out these papers, and that was all; the worst of it is was that my crotch was still quivering with the memory of Petra's mouth, his tongue separating my inflamed labia, and I thought, how the hell did he know, if Petra and I were alone on the stage? Of course, the curtain had folds that could easily have hidden the spy, the traitor, the informer who had told Kay, who had whispered the terrible words to him, nobody could have come in without my knowing it, it's a small place and I know everyone, that must have been it, I wouldn't rest until I'd learned the name of the traitor, my God, there were words that could kill, yes indeed.

As I was thinking this a doctor came out and walked toward me, Mademoiselle Vedovelli? I found it hard to look at him, my hands were shaking like wires, and he said, the vital signs are slow and there's a loss of motor functions, but his brain is still working. In other words: your friend is in a coma. Now I need you to tell me exactly what happened, but I started crying again and said, he did it deliberately and it's all my fault, I was unfaithful to him and he found out, that's the truth, doctor, he's been injecting heroin ever since I met him and he already had an overdose in New York a few months ago; he knew the right quantity to take to be safe, he wasn't some street junkie, no, monsieur, he was a refined addict, believe me, but the doctor interrupted me and said, mademoiselle, don't talk about him in the past tense, he's still alive, and my hands started shaking again, the doctor had noticed that I was burying Kay, finishing him off, maybe because of his responsibility in my rape or because he had abandoned me, I don't know, there are ways of hurting someone, resentment is the strongest thing that can unite two people, even two people who love each other and because they love each other they mistreat and destroy each other, which is something we have in our cells, like the need to reproduce or to feel pleasure, anyway, the doctor said that the best thing I could do was to go home, it was three in the morning, if there was any change they'd call me on my cell phone.

I left the hospital and walked as far as the Gare d'Austerlitz. Opposite, I found a *brasserie* open and ordered a glass of Sancerre. Then I walked down to the banks of the Seine. It was raining and the brown water was churning under the bridge and I thought about how good it would be to jump, once and for all, to leave behind the contradictions and the guilt, which was like ivy that had attached itself to my skin and was about to choke me. I stayed there for a while; then I carried on as far as Bastille, which at that hour was full of drunken young people coming out of the *boîtes de nuit* on Rue de la Roquette, and from there to Rue Oberkampf, where the memories, Kay's smell, and the most terrifying solitude were waiting for me.

That night I couldn't get to sleep. I drank part of a bottle of tequila and smoked a little grass, but they didn't help. My hands were clammy with cold sweat and my heart was racing, so, in desperation, I had an idea to take myself away from the horror . . . I knew where the heroin was, so I prepared a line and snorted it, calculating half of what he usually took. Immediately the apartment disappeared, and so did Paris, and so did I, and at last I felt calm.

I woke up the next day feeling strange. I was on the carpet, like my cousin Giorgetta, and I could see the view under the couch, which was something I'd never seen before. Dust, rusty springs, old cigarette butts and, right at the back, two tiny antennae, moving. It was a cockroach. I watched it tenderly and followed its rapid movements across the dust, and I said to it, little animal, help me settle a question, will you? The cockroach did an about-turn, retraced its steps, and stopped, moving its antennae, and I said, where do you think we go after we die? have you ever thought about that? The cockroach gave another complete turn and again stopped, this time closer to my face, and I said, do you think there's life after death? do you believe in reincarnation and that kind of thing? and I said, I'd like to believe in something, I'd really like to believe that we get a second chance, and I mean that, my friend, sometimes our intentions are good but it's the lack of experience that ruins us, or other people's wickedness, oh, little animal, I don't know if these things happen in your world, under the armchairs and in the drains, but I tell you this, that in my world wanting a little joy sometimes leads you to do harm, it's hard to believe, I know, if you tighten a rope at one end it may break at the other, which is absurd but true, anyway, I'm boring you, I don't know anything about you, I don't even know if you have feelings, I'd like it if you did because I think you might understand me, right now I feel that I'm like you, that I'm walking in the dust and the rusty springs, moving my antennae alone, very alone in this world, just as you must be . . . The cockroach, disturbed by the air shifted by my voice, stood up on its hind feet, did an about-turn and scuttled off to the wall, and before I could say anything disappeared through a crack and I was alone again, so I dragged myself to the table, where the bag of heroin was, and prepared two more lines, and in this way three days passed.

Every time I woke up, the anguish and the guilt overwhelmed me, they were waiting for me, like the couch and the dust on the floor. But what never came back was my friend with the antennae, which really upset me, and when the drugs were finished, there was a moment of anguish, but I overcame it and went to the shower, gave myself a good wash, dressed and went to my drama school, but unfortunately the door was shut, and I thought, what could have happened here? I started knocking, louder and louder, until somebody opened and said, it's Sunday, mademoiselle, the school is closed. I stepped back, incredulous, as far as the curb. Something very bad might have happened if a passer-by hadn't grabbed me by the arm and said, be careful, there are cars passing. I looked at him and realized that my brain was far away, I could see he was young, but I couldn't focus on his face.

Instead, I thought I saw Fito, my mother's Mexican lover, a little devil leaping around me in a purple cape. I pushed him away, crying, let go of me! and ran to the corner, but no sooner did I take two steps than I bumped into a bicycle and fell to the ground. Another man approached, only now it was Stef, Kay's brother, with the other rapists; I cried out desperately and hugged the bicycle to stop them hurting me, until some strong hands lifted me and I closed my eyes and lost consciousness.

I woke up two days later in the Pitié-Salpêtrière hospital. A fairly young doctor asked me how I was feeling and I said, where am I? what happened? He leaned toward my ear and said, you can't continue taking so many drugs, young lady, you had the DTs but it's stopped now, your blood test shows you're new to this, so I'd like you to stay with us for a few days, because we don't want you to relapse when you leave here, and I said, that's good, I only want you to help me to call somebody; I gave him the number of the doctor in the other hospital, where Kay was, and when I called that doctor he said, there's no change, he's still in a coma, try to think of something else and I'll keep you informed, and I replied, that's what I'm trying to do, think of something else, but it isn't easy, I'll call again.

I left the hospital two days later and returned home, but as I entered my throat filled up again with something sour and foul-smelling. I threw up in the bathroom, expelling a yellow liquid the smell of which made me retch even more, so I opened the faucet and put my head under it.

Then I went to the drama school, looked for Petra, and

asked him for money. He gave it to me in return for a blow job in the bathroom. He said he would like to see me in the evening sometimes. He was married but we could go to a hotel, and I said, sure, whatever you like, as long as you pay me. I gave him my cell phone number, returned home and called Joel, Kay's dealer. I asked how much a gram of heroin cost and he said, for you a hundred and twenty euros. Bring me a gram and a half, I said.

Four days later, I called Petra on his cell phone. I told him I urgently needed five hundred euros and he said, look, I'm just a university teacher. I told him he could save on a hotel if he came to my apartment. I opened the windows and took out the garbage, which was already reeking. In the refrigerator the tomatoes were growing fungus and there was some margarine that had turned green. I threw everything in a plastic bag and took it down to the trash. I looked for clean sheets and as there weren't any I ironed one I'd been using for a while. I cleaned the bathroom.

An hour later Petra arrived, gave me the five hundred euros and said, I don't have much time today, promise me that for the same money I'll be able to come here twice more. I said yes and lay down on the bed. I took out his penis and sucked it. Then I said: I'm your slave, do with me as you please. He sucked my clitoris and my anus and my tits, sodomized me, and finally came in my mouth. He went away well satisfied. As soon as I heard him go out, I called Joel and said, bring me two grams, and on the way drop by a supermarket and buy ham, bread, and a Coke.

Kay was still in a coma.

I went to see him every two or three days, sat down beside him, and thought about the miserable life we had and how much I loved him. Being by his side, I remembered an old movie and decided to tell him the story of it, which I did to ease my guilt about the drugs and everything else.

Time passed, and one day Petra approached me with rather an unusual proposition. A job for which I'd be paid a thousand euros, but I wouldn't be told what I would have to do until I got there, and I thought, a thousand euros? who would pay a thousand euros for a fuck? what will it be? a gang rape, a lesbian scene, sex with a donkey or a chimpanzee? Anything was possible, but by now nothing fazed me anymore, so we went to a building in the sixteenth arrondissement, climbed the stairs, and Petra greeted an elderly lady in Romanian, but didn't introduce me to her.

We walked along a dark corridor and I started to notice strange things. Although the building was respectable enough, the apartment itself was old, with peeling walls; I wondered who the lady was and why we were there, but as I was about to ask, Petra looked at me and lifted a finger to his lips, quiet! he said, we mustn't talk too much, you'll see, it'll be over very soon. We walked through a hall and reached a bedroom in which there was an adjustable bed, the kind you find in hospitals, and Petra said, if you don't want to do it we'll leave immediately, it's something quite simple, a forty-year-old man suffering from Down's syndrome, the lady is his mother, don't make that face, there's no danger, it's only a mental condition. Like anyone who has a penis between his legs, he needs to find an outlet for his sexual impulses, and that's why you're here, if you accept the mission and the thousand euros.

So I said, O.K., you want me to have sex with a mentally retarded man, is that right? Yes, said Petra. Alright, I said, but for a thousand euros I could only give him a blow job, it's all a bit awkward, I'm young and it might affect me psychologically, so it's going to cost more, and Petra said, O.K., wait, and he went to talk to the old lady. After a while they both came and asked me how much I wanted and I said, two thousand euros, not a cent less. All right, I'll go and fetch him, said the lady. The thirty seconds it took for them to bring him were the longest in my life; at last he arrived and I saw him: a mongol with gray hair and squinty eyes. They had undressed him, and a nurse was nudging him forward. He was making these desperate sounds, and it was quite a while before I realized they were words and not just noise. He was also waving his arms and trying to hide his face in his mother's breast. You can get undressed now, mademoiselle, we're ready, said the nurse; as I started to take my clothes off, with my back to the group, I thought of Kay and of the scribbled note and I told myself that this was a punishment, and that after it I would feel clean again.

A cry from the man brought me back to reality: I had taken off my panties and he had seen my ass. His mother and the nurse were struggling to subdue him. His penis was already erect, so I kneeled on the mattress, with my back to him, and said, I'm ready, but his mother whispered in my ear, wait a minute, young lady, I'm paying you two thousand euros, so you'll have to do more than that, and she pointed at his penis. I understood what she wanted and moved my mouth closer to his body, which was hairless, like a giant baby's, and started sucking, closing my eyes and repeating in my mind, I'm not here, I'm not here, but the man's cries were fierce, as were his gestures. The mother and the nurse were finding it hard to restrain him. After a moment, the nurse touched my shoulder and said, mademoiselle, you can change position now, turn your back to him again. It would have been worse face to face, this way it was easier. They moved him closer, the nurse guided him, and they helped him put it in. Mother Nature did her job, since no sooner did he feel that he was inside than he began to rock backwards and forwards. It must be an instinctive reflex of the species, like sucking your mother's breast, and so he went on for a while until his cries grew in intensity and he ejaculated outside of me with the help of the nurse, who had taken his member out first to avoid problems. Then he collapsed on the mattress, as if his muscles had deflated; within a few seconds he was fast asleep and snoring.

They took me to another room with a bath, and said, please have a wash. If you want to take a shower there's no hurry, take your time, when you're finished come into the living room. By the time I was dressed, Petra was waiting for me with the money. Before we left, the old lady said, thank you, mademoiselle, if you like I can ask for you again in a month, and I said, ask for me, and I'll tell you if it's possible at the time. The woman handed over ten two-hundred euro bills and squeezed my arm saying in a low voice, I know this can't be easy for a young woman, but you have to understand, they're human beings, too . . . I understand, I said, I'll wait for your call, and went back down to the street with Petra.

The next day was Saturday so I went to the hospital, I had a tremendous desire to be with Kay. I told him everything in his ear, whispered to him that I had had sex with a mentally retarded man for money, although I didn't tell him it was for drugs; I said it was to arrange our apartment, to fill the vases with roses and the closet with wines from Bordeaux and Burgundy and fill the refrigerator with vegetable, and fruit, which was what the doctor had said he would have to eat when he woke up, and I said, I'm preparing for your return, my love, I feel you close to me, I know you're there, you just have to break one thin membrane, I can feel it, you come and I'll be ready, and so Saturday went by with me lying beside him, I had managed to sneak in some of the drug, so I snorted it in small doses, just to keep calm, and I felt happy, I swear, very happy in that room with a view of a parking lot and the overhead section of the metro line that goes from Charles de Gaulle to Nation. Through the window I could see the train passing in the distance, surrounded by smoke from the chimneys, and I imagined anxious women traveling in those carriages, longing to get home and have sex with the men they loved and cry out with joy between four dirty, peeling walls; and I also imagined disillusioned young girls looking for some kind of direction in their lives, girls who might have been raped, and might be thinking and thinking and feeling abused and guilty, the poor things, some of them might well be savoring the idea of sticking a needle in their veins to escape this den of iniquity; some might be looking up at the sky in the hope of seeing an igneous ball that would destroy everything once and for all, devour the city in a hurricane of fire, the colossal towers leaning and falling in clouds of dust and terrified people running through the rubble, choked by the smoke and the waves of heat, pushed toward nothingness by the winds of destruction, yes, a few lost young girls must be thinking all that, and things even worse that that, which the mind did not dare imagine, let alone say; I imagined them coming and going in the metro trains I could see from the window, with Kay breathing artificially beside me, and I felt protected, as if the world and its miseries could not enter this little room that smelled of disinfectant, this room where death prowled.

When dusk arrived I was filled with a sensation of emptiness and silence, so I went to the bathroom and set up my two gray lines on the wash basin, and when night fell I started seeing the lights and thinking again of my young girls, how many of them must be fucking their men, listening to music by the Fugees and drinking tequila or gin from a bottle, and how many were hugging a telephone that wouldn't ring and they knew it, with the bottle of pills open and a bottle of Vittel ready to swallow the lethal, liberating charge of fifty sleeping pills; and there must also be happy women leading clean lives, writing doctoral theses with the remains of pizzas or Chinese food beside them on their desks, and women cooking and looking after babies and watching the clock, calculating how long the sliced chicken and the potatoes and the leeks have been in the oven, and as they look at the hands of the clock trying to imagine what metro station their husband has reached on his way home, and thinking all these things I fell asleep, hearing these voices emerging from the lights of the suburbs, and when I opened my eyes again everything had already gone black and all that remained was the weight of the night, the oppressive darkness, and the silence, and I could almost hear Kay's blood flowing in his veins and I started again to put a little powder in my nasal septum and already the night was going and when I opened my eyes again it was Sunday morning and a nurse was coming in to take his blood pressure, to give him injections and change the serum; this activity disturbed me, so I left the room with the hope that this week would be the last and that very soon Kay and I would be reminiscing about it over laughter and a glass of wine.

I don't know how much time passed, I really don't remember, but one day the doorbell rang, and when I opened it, with my heart leaping at the idea that it was Kay, I gave a cry of surprise, because it was . . . my cousin Giorgetta! and I cried out because she had changed a lot: her pink cheeks had turned glassy, with just a little flesh left around the bone. I was pleased to see her and we opened some of the bottles of wine I had been keeping for Kay, until she said, listen, you wouldn't have a little…? I handed her a syringe and my case, and immediately we had a fix, although I only snorted, and we spent the night drinking and doing drugs, talking about the divine and the human, with long moments of silence, and the next day, already recovered, she said, Sabina, I've come to stay, there's no work in Rome and my mother can't stand me, she's put me in clinics three times, I can't go back, I've been so alone, you're all I have.

I looked at her and said, then you don't have much, almost nothing in fact, I don't have a job, the money from my mother's boyfriend isn't enough to live on, I have to go out looking for work, and Giorgetta asked, intrigued, and what is it you do? I told her about the mentally retarded guy and she thought it was an excellent solution. Of course, she said, that kind of person has the same needs, dips his wick just like the others, only they pay more, help me to find something like that, but I said, you have to take care of yourself, Giorgetta, you mustn't give the impression you're a mess, this is done with the patient's mother and a nurse, so image is important, know what I mean? It's a medical matter, the crazy guy has sex with you, you empty his testicles, and then you go and change, just as if you were a physical therapist. The mother may even invite you to have a cup of tea.

Giorgetta looked at me enthusiastically and said, okay, I get the idea, call your friend and tell him you need to increase your clientele, an Italian cousin of yours has arrived who wants to conquer Paris, tell him if he wants to pay to fuck me, to try me out, I'd be delighted, tell him I scream a lot and I love S and M and do Greek and French, and even swallow, that'll excite him, tell him. I called him with her standing there and of course Petra, who was sex crazy, asked if he could come that very night.

He arrived at ten and when he saw Giorgetta, who had had a good shower and put on some make up, he said he had a better idea, which was to do it with the two of us, a threesome. We looked at each other dubiously, but he immediately added: I'll pay double, of course. We agreed. I had never felt either desire or repulsion for a woman, so it didn't bother me having Giorgetta naked beside me, because I had known her since she was a girl. When he told her to suck me and she approached, I didn't feel any disgust. Petra had a great time. He cried out, sang in Romanian, quoted Shakespeare and Sophocles as he penetrated me and Giorgetta sucked his balls, and afterwards, to round off the evening, he took us out to eat couscous at the Royal Maroc, a restaurant in République. We drank three bottles of rosé wine from Boulaouane and then, quite merry by now, ended the night drinking cognac in a bar in Bastille. At dawn, we went back to Kay's apartment to sleep.

A week later, Petra called about the job with the mentally retarded guy. When I'd finished I said to his mother, madame, I assure you that I do it with a lot of respect and consideration for the patient, so please, if you have any acquaintances with similar cases you can call me, I have a cousin who needs work, a very healthy young woman, and the mother said, of course, Sabina, I'll talk to the people at the special help center and if there's anything I'll call you, of course. Three days later, the telephone rang and the first job for Giorgetta arrived. A young man of twenty-five suffering from something very serious, dementia, mental handicap, Williams syndrome, I don't quite remember. The young man was bedridden and obese. When Giorgetta saw him, her first impulse was to jump out the window, but then she thought of the money, so she undressed and did the job, telling herself, these are God's mistakes, people who also feel, and even if it disgusts me I have to think that for them it's much worse, I can take a shower and go out and back to normal life, the streets and the metro and the parks are waiting for me and I'm free, and that should give me strength, this is what she told me when she got home and prepared herself a good fix, pleased with the two-hundred-euro bills she'd come away with, and as we took a dose she told me that for her to give him a blowjob, two nurses had had to support his belly, he was that obese, and that his penis was small and flaccid, like a child's.

We clung to each other all night and the next morning the telephone rang, and it was Petra, announcing a good job, something that could be really important for both of us. I asked him if he wanted to drop by and he said, no, this is something different, I prefer to talk to you face to face.

The appointment was in a café near the Belleville metro station, a neighborhood where everyone is black or Chinese or

Arab, and Giorgetta was getting quite nervous by the time we met with Petra, who greeted us and said, come, it's this way. He led us down a side street and we entered a building that wasn't too dirty, in fact it was the least dirty in the block. We went up to the fourth floor. On the door was a sign saying *Eve Studios*. We were received by a man with a businesslike look who, when he saw us, cried, at last I've met you. Petra has told us all about you, and he was right, come this way, I want to see you properly, my name is Dimitros, I'm the head of the company. He explained that he published porn magazines that sold well in Europe, and that he now wanted to make the leap into movies, which was why he needed two actresses. He had studied the market and had worked out that he could make two films a month, which would mean approximately five thousand euros a month for each of us, and that would be just the start, because if the company grew the income would increase, what did we think?

Giorgetta was about to say something but I gestured to her to be quiet; she had never had much of a head for business, so I spoke up and said, first we'd like to see something of what you do and to know what kind of films you want, and he said, of course, the thing is, I only do normal stuff, fellatio, Greek, sodomy, DP, facial ejaculation, all the classic stuff, no fornicating with donkeys or eating shit, and then Giorgetta, intrigued, asked, what's DP, and Dimitros replied, double penetration, darling, two penises in your body simultaneously, if you've never done it before you may find it uncomfortable at first but you'll get used to it, it's a difficult position, you have to have good abdominal muscles, how's your physical condition, girls? and we both said, very good, so Dimitros continued: as I said, I only film the traditional porn themes, because what I'm interested in is art, eroticism, I'm a disciple of Lasse Braun, you may not know who he is, but I said, yes I do, I've seen his movies, my favorite is *Sin Dreamer*. Dimitros looked at me wide-eyed, and said, that's amazing, girl, that's the best porn movie ever made! tell me, what's your name?

We began two days later with a fairly simple scene. I played a nurse in the house of an elderly man. To give him something to eat, I phoned out for a pizza. The young man who delivered it, a fairly well-built Yugoslav named Yarco in real life, was helping me to divide the pizza into triangles in the kitchen and used the excuse of a few olives that had rolled onto the floor to start stroking my legs, my nurse's skirt being short. That developed into a scene of oral sex and then penetration on the table, at which point the cleaner arrived. That was Giorgetta's role. When she saw that Yarco had me on the table with my legs open and was thrusting into me, she started masturbating herself with the mouth of a wine bottle. This scene, of course, Dimitros rehearsed many times, because he wanted the reflection of my legs beating in the air to be seen in Giorgetta's bottle. That was his art, he said, through the camera he was expressing his anger at the world and his nihilistic vision of life, which he had no faith in.

We patiently repeated the scene. The next thing to happen was the miracle, which was that the old man, played by Petra, alerted by the noise, managed to drag himself to the kitchen to see why he was being left alone and once there, seeing Giorgetta sticking a bottle of Burgundy inside her and his nurse lying on the table, being sodomized by the young man, a ray of light from the window fell on his forehead and filled him with newfound strength. He threw off his pajamas, took out a fairly respectable penis, and set to with Giorgetta. In the climactic scene, which was the most difficult, I took Yarco from the front and Petra from behind while Giorgetta sucked their testicles in turn, and at the end came the great ejaculation, which hit Giorgetta's cheeks and mine and which we pretended to savor with relish.

All this took the whole of Saturday and Sunday, but at last

Dimitros congratulated us and told us that even though we were beginners we had a lot of talent and a keen sense of art. He was sure he had pulled off at least three or four shots that showed his stamp, the mark of the artist. We left with three thousand euros in brand new bills each, so we decided to treat ourselves. We bought new clothes, went to the hairdresser, had dinner in a good restaurant, and of course, a good fix and a snort, a full dose, not the half we took to feel good during the filming. After three days of excess, I suddenly remembered Kay, and it was as if the sky had fallen on my head. I rushed to the hospital with my heart pounding, and the premonition that he had died, that they had been calling me but my phone had been off or mislaid, and when I got to his room and saw him there, lying on his back in bed, I felt the soul come back to my body, and I cried and cried, falling to my knees, and spent the night telling him about Eve Studios and the plot of the movie and how the fact that I'd seen his Lasse Braun movies had helped me, because the director was a very artistic and demanding person who didn't just hire beginners. You might earn more having sex with mental defectives, but this is a real job and gives you the opportunity to learn a trade. I told him everything until day broke and the bustle of cleaners and nurses returned and I went home, with the impression that he approved this new development.

Two weeks later we saw the movie and laughed our heads off. Neither Giorgetta nor I had ever seen our vaginas on screen, let alone from such daring angles. The name of the movie was *Home Delivery*, and, from what Petra told us, Dimitros managed to sell it quite well, so the next week we got down to work again. Before introducing the new actor to us, Dimitros got us together and gave us a little speech, saying, the porn world is going through a great revolution and it's necessary to meet its demands, which means there are some changes in this new production, beginning with the actor I'm about to introduce to you and who, I hope, will be to your liking, girls, and I said, what's with all the mystery, Dimitros? and he said, it's just that, you know, the buyers really liked the performances and the artistic shots, but they also said, it's a very white movie, not very politically correct, Dimitros, how about something African, of exceptional size? and well, darlings, that's what I did, and now I have the pleasure to introduce Clarence, a son of post-revolutionary Liberia, and with a theatrical gesture he opened the door and brought him in, a man of about thirty-five, quite strong and well preserved, with a broad smile and bulging eyes, who said, hello, shyly, without looking us in the eyes, which made me immediately want to be his friend, so I stood up and gave him a kiss on the cheek, hello, how are you, it's going to be a pleasure to work with you, and he returned the compliment. Giorgetta greeted him less effusively, and then we started reading the scripts, it took us a while to learn our parts while Dimitros and his crew prepared the shots and arranged the lights. When we went to the bathroom to give ourselves our little shot to calm us down, Giorgetta said to me, are you going to have sex with the black guy? and I said, well, I don't know if that'll be me, in the script it only says I have sex with First Man, but if it's me I'll do it. Giorgetta didn't think the idea was right, and said, don't you think they ought to pay us more to have sex with a black man? and I said, don't talk crap, all human beings are the same, but she said, if we're talking about the soul or the spirit maybe yes, but not the dick, black men have huge dicks, you'll see. I tried not to take any notice and said, don't think about that, we're built to take any man.

Giorgetta never forgot that day, she probably still remembers it, because what with talking to me and taking her shot she forgot to sit on the toilet and empty her rectum, so in the first anal scene with the African, when he withdrew an avalanche emerged from her orifice, drawn out by the suction, which was all the bigger because of the size of his cock, which really was king size. There was a loud laugh and Giorgetta gave a scream. Clarence was covered from head to foot and had to take a shower. The cameraman, who had been filming in close-up, spent an hour cleaning his glasses and his camera with sponges and cotton balls, while Giorgetta was in the bathroom, hysterical with shame.

What happened next was that Giorgetta, who, as you will have already noted, had a certain tendency to fall into the abyss, started to take more than she should in the syringe before filming and one day the scandal broke, when Vidiadar, the Pakistani actor, stopped the scene and said to Dimitros, look, how can I work with a woman like this? I'd feel more heat if I stuck my dick into a gimlet. Dimitros cursed, because delays cost him money, and went up to Giorgetta. He noticed that her eyes were open and her mouth was emitting moans, but her brain was as far away as the rings of Jupiter. So he lost his temper and said, you fucking junkie, how dare you come to the set like that? I have nothing against the fact that you fill your brains with shit, but if you want to continue with me you have to be clean, do you understand? the streets of this old continent are filled with cunts begging for an opportunity to get into movies, so think about it, that's if you're even listening, is there anybody in there? I had to take Giorgetta to the bedroom.

The next day, Dimitros brought in a Romanian named Saskia to replace her and as a punishment put Giorgetta with the fluffers, the girls who are on the set to suck the actors' cocks before they go on and leave them erect or arouse them in case their tools undergo a sudden shrinkage. It was that night, after the fight, that I told myself for the first time: you have to give up drugs.

My cousin stayed on in Paris, but sank into one of her heavy depressions. She tried to contact the family of the mentally ill guy to offer her services, but when they saw her they almost slammed the door in her face, because she was in an awful state, so one day I said to her, listen to me, I'm giving you a week to get your things together and leave, I know you have nobody but it's time you got a grip on yourself, I've done what I could. Giorgetta cried and told me I hated her and had always envied her and wanted to destroy her, but I said, Giorgetta, you're the destructive one, you're the one who wears out the people who protect you, do you know Murphy's Law? well, you're one of the people Murphy's Law was invented for, any situation you find yourself in, if you can make it worse, you will, and you drag the people closest to you down with you, which in this case means me, I'm just as young and inexperienced as you and just as hooked and alone, but I have a tremendous desire to live and succeed, so you have to understand, I'm not asking you to disappear, but I am asking you to let me breathe a little, I need to think and I can only do that when I'm alone, Giorgetta, don't hate me for this, goodbye.

Giorgetta left and I spent three days in the hospital, beside Kay, who was my source of consolation, and I told myself, I have to be good for when my love wakes up. I decided to go into detox. The heroin had protected me over the past year, but now things had turned around and I was its hostage. I got up courage and went to a rehab center. I assume everyone knows what detox is, so I shan't expand. It's a painful experience, which you remember only vaguely, because the brain blots most of it out as a defense mechanism. Nobody likes to hoard horrible images or such extreme feelings of pain, as if a thin knife slashed right through all the nerves in your body, which becomes your main enemy, that body you become tremendously aware of because every pore in it is screaming, and so the minutes and the hours pass, with all the slowness of pain, and you know that at the end of time, there in the distance, behind a chain of Himalayas and on an invisible horizon, is that morning when you slough off your old, sick skin and your body wakes up and your blood flows clean and you can go out because you've been reborn, that's the challenge, there are those who can't stand it and their brains melt, they blow a few fuses, and they are the former addicts who wander the world with a stupid smile and dribble hanging from their lips.

That didn't happen to me, because I hadn't been addicted for long. I suffered unspeakable pain but came out the other side, unharmed. When I felt well, I called Dimitros and he immediately hired me again, this time for a shoot in Brussels. I liked the idea of traveling so I agreed and it was a great experience. I got to know some Hungarian actors and two very pretty Russian girls, who looked so innocent you'd have thought they were virgins, an impression, obviously, that I forgot when I saw them sucking cocks as if they were eating candies and cream. It was a very professional session, from which I returned with four thousand euros in cash. Then, in the hospital, I told Kay all about the horrors of detox and I said in his ear, you don't know how lucky you are to have been spared that, when you wake up you'll be fine, your body will be as clean as a baby's.

I also told him about the filming of *Vixens in Heat*, which was the name of the latest Eve Studios production. I said: you'll get along very well with Dimitros and Petra, they're fantastic and make a great team. We could work together, you're a terrific photographer and, you know, during filming they take photographs, that way they generate more income. It would be a brilliant deal and we'd be together, what do you think, my love? But Kay was still silent, breathing softly. Suddenly the room filled with shadows and I went to the window to watch night fall. The city was drifting like a bank of seaweed toward the brightly lighted cafés. It was Saturday. I felt nostalgic for a normal life. I missed what I had, in fact, only experienced with the man lying by my side.

I carried on working and the year ended. I traveled to shoots in Budapest and Prague, and once in London, and the fees were always good, because Eve Studios was doing very well, Dimitros and Petra and other girls like Laura and Saskia and Valérie and Delphine, and guys like Bruno and Anatoli and Hervé and Alec, who worked on most of the movies, were becoming my family. One day the telephone rang and when I answered I almost fell to the floor with emotion. It was the magazine *Hot Vision*, asking if I would agree to an interview. They had seen *Vixens in Heat* and seven other Eve movies and thought I had a lot of talent. I put down the telephone, feeling really moved. I had an appointment with them at the Banana Café in Châtelet the next day. I couldn't believe it. *Hot Vision* was the best known magazine of its kind in France and every two years awarded the Golden Hot, a prize for the best porn actress. Of course that was a dream, but an interview opened the doors to a possible nomination, oh, I felt so happy that I went with Alec and Delphine to the Casbah Bar and drank a bottle of champagne all by myself. They were all happy about the news and we celebrated in style, until seven in the morning, which confirmed, in passing, that my body was cured, because I didn't feel at any moment the desire to snort.

The next day—in terms of perception, because it was actually the same day—I got up at three in the afternoon. I still had two hours before the appointment with *Hot Vision* so I emptied the closet trying to choose what to wear. Delphine had slept over at my place so she was there to help, thank God, and in the end we decided on a combination of garter belts, navy blue nylon stockings, and a shimmery silk dress of the same color, an extremely light outfit that, according to Delphine, brought out my strong personality and a melancholy eroticism. The makeup session lasted forty minutes and at four-thirty exactly we went out on the landing to call the elevator, both nervous and dying of laughter. As the elevator door opened, I heard the telephone ring in the apartment. Delphine said, leave it, you'll be late, but I said, I'll only be two seconds, what if they're calling to cancel or change the appointment? I opened the door and said, hello? who is it? It was the hospital. Kay had woken up.

I collapsed. I was speechless.

A mixture of fear and happiness swept through my body, like some strange contrast liquid. Delphine had come in behind me and when she saw me on the floor she screamed. After a few minutes I got my breath back. I had to make a decision. Delphine went to the Banana Café in my place and I ran to the hospital. What I had waited for for so long had just happened and now I was scared, is he all right? will he remember me? I got to the room and saw him, he had his eyes open. He looked at me and an expression of doubt came over his face, but then he said, Sabina? and burst into tears. I kneeled beside him, kissed his hand, and thanked God. He had come back, and he remembered me. He was alive. The world had started turning again for the two of us.

The first thing he asked was, why are you dressed like that? I told him that I had made myself beautiful for him, but he didn't seem to believe me. I explained that it was by chance and that I had to bring him up to date with everything. There have been many changes, darling, things are going very well for us now, you'll see. He still had to spend another week in the hospital, for tests, and the best thing was that there were no serious lesions in the brain. The only thing he had lost was the sense of taste; things tasted neutral, like cardboard or a blank page, that was how he described it. He could bear the fact that he couldn't enjoy food, but what he found very sad was that he could no longer savor the taste of my body. But he was alive and remembered everything.

Gradually I told him what had happened during the year he had been absent. About my addiction and subsequent detox, and the main reason I told him all this was to dissuade him from falling victim to heroin again. He didn't feel the need, his body was cured, but in his mind he remembered the pleasure and the sense of calm. All the same, he didn't relapse, and after his "rebirth" he stayed clean. With time, of course, we did do other drugs, but nothing really serious. Coke, to hold up under the relentless pace of the work, and sometimes hashish to fight stress. We did, though, drink rather a lot. It's really hard to live in this rotten world without having at least one damn vice, given how hard and inhospitable reality can be, but anyway, let me carry on with my story. Kay quickly got used to my work. Once he had gotten over the blow of that thing with Petra, which he barely remembered anyway, he started to work in the photographic department of Eve Studios, which was no longer based in that dirty building in Belleville, but had taken over a large apartment near the Opéra, almost thirteen hundred feet of studios and offices.

We left the apartment on Rue Oberkampf and moved into a more spacious, light-filled one on Rue Pascal, in the vicinity of Boulevard Arago and Place des Gobelins, which meant that on Sundays we could go to the little market on Rue de la Contrescarpe and eat oysters and drink Chablis and read the newspapers, which was one of Kay's great pleasures. Kay had opinions and ideas on everything that happened in the world. Thanks to him, I stopped being some kind of selfish animal who only cared about acting and making money. Thanks to him and all those newspapers I became aware that the world had a lot wrong with it and that the bad things that happened to other people could happen to me one day. That was what I thought as I listened to Kay commenting on the news, the wars in Iraq and Afghanistan, terrorism, all the victims of violence, in other words, reality in all its glory. I really took notice of what he said, but at the same time I thought to myself, it's curious, when I was on the floor, like a fallen gladiator about to receive the fatal spear, who cared about me? Nobody, I went through that ordeal alone, and I say alone because calling my cousin Giorgetta company would be like giving a human identity to bedbugs and lice: the lice I sometimes got, in those first movies, from my *partenaires* on the set. The world is cruel to small things, and I was one; a weak flame that needed to be kept alive by protecting hands and could only become a substantial fire with a great deal of effort and sacrifice.

Our beautiful apartment on Rue Pascal became our bolthole. Large and silent—an increasingly rare thing in the lawless cities where we live today—it gradually filled with shelves and books, histories of the cinema and biographies of directors, my own favorite director being, of course, John Cassavetes, while Kay's was Blake Edwards, especially his amazing *Days of Wine and Roses*, with Jack Lemmon and Lee Remick, a movie that reminded him of what he had been through and what we had both suffered. For anyone who knows Cassavetes, I have to say that being with Kay I felt like Gena Rowlands in *Faces*, I'm sorry, I put that in for the fans. You'll notice that my references are to normal cinema, auteur cinema, and you may think that's a contradiction, since I've devoted my life to porn. Well, my answer to that is that the cinema is not divided into good cinema and porn, but good cinema and bad cinema, period. A porn movie by Lasse Braun or Othar Bill James can be as good of its kind as a film by Kubrick of its kind, that's my opinion, anyway. Porn has its Olympus, fantastic actors like John Holmes, who died of AIDS, but who had one of the most extraordinary penises ever captured by a camera, or Ron Jeremy, a really funny man, a man without any great qualities and rather comical-looking, but great at fucking and an exceptional actor, who even did a few things outside the porn world, a short role in *Jesus Christ Superstar* and another in *Reindeer Games*, with Ben Affleck.

I come back to what I was saying before: our apartment on

Rue Pascal was filling with beautiful things and artistic friends who came and went. As I said before, Kay started to make a career for himself as the photographer for Eve Studios, which then sold his work to magazines, *Hot Video* or *Stardust* or *Plaisir xxl*, for good prices, sometimes for more than they paid me, which was strange, but didn't shock me, since Kay was talented and by this stage we were sharing all our income.

One night, after a bottle and a half of gin and lemon, six hashish cigarettes and an intense session involving three of my seven bodily orifices, I made up my mind to tell him the last secret I had kept from him, in other words, my rape. I don't know how I found the strength. I told him the story in minute detail. Kay looked at me, stunned, and said, Stef? He went to the window in silence and after a while said, he was always an idiot, trying to imitate me in everything and never succeeding. What he did to you was unspeakable, and he'll pay for it, he and his lousy friends, I already know who they are.

The next day, much to my surprise, Kay dragged me out of bed at nine in the morning, which was early for us, and rushed me to Charles de Gaulle airport. We got on a Norwegian Air plane and two hours later we were in Oslo. We took a taxi, didn't even drop by his family home, but went straight to a lawyer's office, where a formal complaint for rape was drawn up. Then we went to a police station and lodged the complaint with all the requisite details. From there we went to a hotel to rest and the next day we flew back to Paris and waited for proceedings to begin.

A week later, the telephone rang and it was Stef. He had been informed of the complaint and wanted to know if his brother had gone crazy, but Kay replied, you're the crazy one and you're going to pay, you and your lousy friends, where do you keep your brain? in your ass? you might think more clearly if you did, you idiot, what was going through your mind to make you do something like that? did you think I'd never find out? Well, you screwed up, not only did I find out but it so happens that I'm a civilized person, and I believe these things should be dealt with by the law. You'd have preferred to settle this with a couple of punches in the nose, like you do with your cronies, which just shows what an idiot you are, because this is different, this is the worst thing you can do to a person, somebody I trusted you with, and for that if nothing else they ought to put your balls between cubes of ice and puncture them with a drill. That woman thought she was safe with you and you took advantage of her weakness; now stop sniveling, don't dare call this house again, as far as I'm concerned you're no longer my brother. The lawyer has orders not to stop until you and the scumbags you call your friends are in prison with long sentences, far from the people you contaminate with your stupidity, if you did it once it's because you've done it other times, God knows with what poor women, so I'm going to do the human race a favor, a favor that consists in giving you a kick up the ass and making sure you all go to prison for most of what remains of your useless lives, with plenty of time to just breathe, eat, and shit, which will be the noblest thing you can do. Goodbye.

That was how Kay spoke to his brother, and in fact, eleven months later, they were sentenced to nine years in prison and a fine of 170,000 euros, including 120,000 to me as damages. To collect the money they auctioned everything those bastards owned. My revenge was to waste it on pointless things. I bought ten Louis Vuitton purses and gave them away to the girls I worked with at Eve Studios. I bought Kay a navy blue secondhand Porsche. I bought myself a John Galliano dress. I invited Kay, Dimitros, Laura, and Petra to dinner at the Tour d'Argent. The best thing I did was give away two-hundred-euro bills to those young gypsy women you see begging on the streets with children they claim are their own. It took me four days to spend everything, until I only had a few coins left, which I threw in the Seine. And I felt liberated.

I forgot to mention that the magazine *Hot Vision* called me again soon afterwards about the interview, as some clips from my movies were already showing on Canal+, which gained me a few points. The interview was excellent, and we were able to include Kay's photographs, which were of outstanding quality, and the following year, for my role in *The Tsarina of Sodom*, I was nominated for the Golden Hot as best actress. Kay did everything he could to find out what kind of chance I stood. Through Eve Studios he discovered that seven of the thirty-five judges would definitely vote for me, but there were at least ten who leaned toward the lead actress in a movie by Wolfgang Brothers Productions, so when we arrived at the Cannes Festival, where the prize was being awarded, we had no idea what was going to happen.

The prize show began with the best American actors and actresses in the various categories: oral orgasm, heterosexual scene, anal orgasm, etc. Some time later, with the atmosphere heating up and cameras trained on the stage, the legendary Rocco Siffredi read out the nominees for the most promising European actress. I closed my eyes and when my name was called as prizewinner a warm wind lifted me above the audience. I went up to the platform while flashbulb popped and the music from the movie *Rocky* played, I don't know if you remember it, the music that plays as he runs up a flight of steps.

When I received the statuette I cried, and said, I want to thank the organizers and the judges, and I want to dedicate this award to my love, the photographer Kay Staarsed. Also to the production company who made the movie, Eve Studios, to Petra Nove and Dimitros Aulica and all the colleagues who have worked so hard to make this distinction possible. I don't suppose that in this kind of prizegiving it's common to have someone mention their mother, but I will, wherever you are, Mamma, and I think you're a long way away, in Mexico, I hope you feel proud of your daughter, because today she achieved something important, both in her profession and as a woman, many thanks, I dedicate it the women of the world who have had to fight to survive.

There was an ovation, and people came and hugged me. There I was, rubbing shoulders with Jade and Jenna Jameson, with Fred Coppula and Briana Banks and Kris Kramski, my God, the jet set of porn, I could never have imagined anything like this. That night we drank so much champagne that we forgot the name of our hotel, which of course wasn't the Hotel Martínez or anything like that, but a modest Sofitel on the outskirts of the city, but we finally remembered it the next day, when Kay, I don't know how, managed to find the key card to our room on the floor of the Porsche.

The next important change came soon afterwards, when Eve Studios joined forces with Pussy Films, in Los Angeles, and the budgets started growing, as did the sales figures. At that point Kay and I became partners and co-owners of Eve, with a 35 percent share.

We started to make pictures in San Francisco and Los Angeles, where there are more means, and a common language, and a more open attitude to the genre. Some films we made in two versions, one commercial, the other a "cult" version, as was the case with *Morgana*, in which I played the lead, and which was a hit in both versions. In sales, the commercial version exceeded all expectations, and the cult version, filmed in Épinay-sur-Seine, earned me a second nomination for the Golden Hot, which I didn't win, obviously, as it's not the done thing for somebody who isn't already a legend to win it too often.

Morgana is the story of a young woman with mental powers that allow her to put ideas into the minds of men. She seduces them and does as she pleases with them, but although this seems just an enjoyable game at first, it gradually turns into something more dangerous. Morgana has a sister, Jessica, who has always been her rival and competed with her in everything. When they were younger, Jessica had better marks, men always fell in love with Jessica, treated her better, and although outwardly Morgana hadn't minded it had made her suffer. There is nothing worse than competition between women, especially if they are sisters. So when Morgana becomes aware of her powers she's happy, because it means she can stand out, but once she has gotten past that and starts to remember how bitter she felt as a teenager because of Jessica, she decides to plant in a particular man the desire to kill her. And that's what she does. The strongest scenes are when we see Jessica being penetrated from behind by her murderer while her partner penetrates her from in front and two illegal immigrants from Liberia and Burkina Faso give the murderer a double anal fisting. I don't know if any of you have seen *Morgana*, but I can assure you that the tension achieved in those scenes is incredible, when Jessica is penetrated by her murderer and on the other side of a two-way mirror Morgana watches everything with her lover. She is so excited at seeing her sister sodomized by a man obsessed with the idea of killing her, that she straddles her lover's penis and they perform a truly amazing scene on the table.

This film made me feel that we ought to do more daring things, to innovate, and it was it this point that we met Kim Ji Lu, a screenwriter who had been fired by an American studio for writing things that were too complicated. For us, that was an excellent calling card, and we immediately started reading his screenplays. They were fantastic. There were sci-fi stories, westerns, comedies. We invited him to Paris and when he arrived we were amazed to see that he was really obese, at least 330 pounds, bald, with an ugly ponytail, and wearing a Hawaiian shirt that showed the sun rising over the Pacific. The type of person who doesn't exist in Europe. Kim was an eloquent speaker. He told us about his origins in Asian cinema and his love of Wong Kar Wai and Kim Ki-Duk, Ang Lee, Zhang Yimou, and Takeshi Kitano. His literary influences included Philip K. Dick, Thomas Pynchon, and the poetry of e. e. cummings and William Carlos Williams, and he also admired the techno-erotic paintings and images of H. R. Giger. Anyway, no sooner had he arrived than we spent a whole night listening to him, drinking martinis that he made himself, astonished by how highly cultured he was.

The first thing we did together was a really impressive piece called *Vaginaland*. It begins with a huge close-up of my cunt, filling the whole screen, which is then penetrated by a penis and as it does so turns into a curtain that opens and begins the story. The action takes place in a kingdom situated inside the vagina, where everyone worships the goddess V. and makes ritual sacrifices to her, which consist of outrageous orgies. Every inhabitant of Vaginaland has to offer at least one orgasm a day to the goddess V., and those who don't are punished and sent to hell. And where is this hell? Again there is a full-screen shot of my vagina, but this time my body turns and what we see in close-up is my anus, which again is penetrated by a penis. This takes us into Anusland, the Country of the Damned.

Those who don't do their duty in Vaginaland are sent to Anusland. It's a change of atmosphere or, as Kim Ji Lu put it, a new solar system around a black star, where the objective is to conceal, to plunge everything into darkness. But the queens of both systems decide to fight each other. There is a final battle in which all the women soldiers are possessed in DP, and peace is declared in the absence of a winner.

We shot the movie and it was a critical hit in Europe, which brought Eve Studios some much-needed prestige. In the United States, we shot a lighter, comic version that lived up to our financial expectations. But the important thing was the prestige that *Vaginaland* brought both us and Kim Ji Lu. One funny thing about that was that many people, seeing the two names, assumed that Kay and Kim were brothers or at least from the same city, an assumption that could only provoke laughter if you saw them together, one huge, with his platinum-plated dark glasses and his palm-tree shirts, and the other thin and discreet, dressed in gray or black. Anyway, that was my little family, and the truth is that business was prospering. One afternoon Kay called me into his office and showed me a bank statement. I could hardly believe it, we had a million euros. It was the first time in my life I had seen that amount, and it was mine, or rather, ours.

During those years there was a kind of storm. I had such a strong will, it was like a small plane flying through rain and thunder, but always managing to reach a lighted airfield. Things happened every day, every week and year. We shot dozens of movies and each time Kim went a bit further. One day he came to us with a new project. A horror movie. Horror and sex, he said, it's brilliant, read this. He took out a script and I saw the title, *Deflowering*. It told the story of a young woman deflowered by the devil, who, like the God Zeus, uses different disguises to seduce her. Along the way, she witnesses other deflowerings and a couple of exorcisms, which were supposed, at least in theory, to make the audience's hair stand on end. We read it, and for the first time there was a disagreement between Kay and Kim. Dimitros claimed that there was no feeling more diametrically opposed to sex than fear, because fear inhibited erection and without an erection there is no porn. Kim disagreed, saying that art was the true genital organ to which we ought to aspire and that, once it was achieved, then penises would rise like stalagmites and vaginas melt in their own juice.

I didn't want to give my opinion, but told Kay that, as Kim's screenplays had given us prestige and success, we should show solidarity with his talent and support him, even if the movie turned out a failure. Not everything a genius does is perfect, or, as I read somewhere, "we cannot be sublime without interruption." We did the movie, and again it came out well, perhaps because the scary parts weren't all that scary, but simply gave the movie a sense of darkness and mystery that helped make the sex scenes stand out more.

In those years, at the beginning of the Nineties, a very large number of artists went to Sarajevo, in Bosnia, to express their solidarity with the civilian population trapped in the siege of the city, victims of that stupid war that had its origin in the desire for independence of those republics that had previously been part of Yugoslavia. Theatrical groups from Germany, Austria, France, and Poland all went. The writer Susan Sontag and her son staged a version of Beckett's *Waiting for Godot* there, which stirred international opinion and gave the Sarajevans, at least for a time, the feeling that they weren't alone, and I say "the feeling" because in reality they were indeed alone, more alone than a stone thrown in a river, which was proved by everything that happened later. Faced with that horror, Kay said, we have to do something, we can't just fold our arms while people are dying. We decided to do a stage show that could be taken and presented there. We started working on that and once again it was Kim who came up with the best idea, which was to do an adaptation of the Marquis de Sade's novel *Justine or the Misfortunes of Virtue*, the idea being to showcase a work that had survived intolerance. That was the message Kim wanted to give the Sarajevans. When it was ready, with six actors and a small technical team, we applied to the United Nations for entry papers and they gave us visas as artists within the humanitarian aid program. We traveled from Paris to Zagreb, spent the night there, and the following day flew to Split, on the Dalmatian coast, from where UN flights left for Sarajevo.

My God, what an experience that was.

We went in an old Hercules with wooden seats, which flew at a very high altitude and carried incendiary ammunition, in case anyone fired a missile at us. After an hour's flight the plane went into a nosedive and our skin stuck to our bones. Then, just as it looked as if we were about to crash, the nose lifted, the plane returned to a horizontal position, and we landed. We could see the roofs of burned and demolished houses at the sides of the airfield.

After taxiing along the runway, the Hercules opened at the back and a UN soldier yelled at us, run to that hill and take cover, they're shooting from over there, pointing to the other side of the runway. We grabbed our bags and the boxes with the props and ran behind the hill. The airport's control tower was leaning to the side, not directly out of the ground like the Tower of Pisa but on top of a horizontal building. The walls were full of holes, and there wasn't a single window in good condition. In their place were sheets of steel intended to stop bullets from snipers.

The French UN soldiers checked our baggage meticulously and after a while let us get into an armored car that was to take us to the city. The city. A euphemism for that vast mountain of rubble that Sarajevo had turned into. On the night of our arrival, we could feel it on our skin, because there was an air raid. Grenades and shells plowed across the sky, leaving green vapor trails. It was a macabre spectacle that, in spite of its dramatic quality, contained a certain beauty. I crouched on one of the upper floors of the hotel, looking out through a crack in the wall, because the hotel had been hit early in the fighting and now only the first six floors were in use. The atmosphere was bleak. The corridors were like caves, the rooms side grottoes covered in dust and rubble. In one of them I found a girl's shoe. A little patent leather shoe with a low heel. I picked it up and dusted it off a bit. I lit my cigarette lighter and saw it had been pink. It was some consolation that at least there wasn't a foot in it. Then I remembered the fantasies I had had in Paris, when I was taking drugs and Kay was in hospital. Images of women who saw destroyed cities, and a caravan of hooded men making their way through the rubble to a temple on top of a hill, before being massacred in a shower of black bullets, in the middle of an even blacker night. And I said to myself: it wasn't a fantasy. It's happening here.

The next day, the sun was radiant. We went with our props team to the Opera House and put up the lights and the set. One of our colleagues, Yarco, was Yugoslav, so there was no problem in making ourselves understood. The only sticky moment was when the director of the theater, a man of seventy who had agreed to our participation as a gesture of solidarity, was disturbed by some of the imagery and asked for a summary of the play. Yarco explained that it was a modern adaptation of the Marquis de Sade; the man was enthusiastic, but said, I don't want any explicit sex scenes, my audience would find that quite sad, so we did as he said, limiting ourselves to simulating the couplings, and it all went very well. It was a wonderful day.

But days that are too wonderful scare me, because after them there comes a little voice announcing that a tragedy is on its way. I can hear that voice. It's a metallic tone beneath the wind or behind the light, which suddenly manifests itself, and when it does you have to hide or flee. We didn't flee in time, and two days later our Volkswagen was attacked by snipers. The driver was shot three times in the head and died instantaneously. A cameraman had a lung perforated by a bullet and had to stay in hospital for nearly six months. Kay's right shoulder and shoulder blade and the bones of his arm were shattered in the gunfire. Fortunately for me, I had stayed behind in the hotel. The bullets went in one side and out the other of the car and its occupants. That night we flew back to Zagreb, where everyone was hospitalized.

After three weeks, and six operations, I brought Kay back to Paris, where they did more tests. There was nothing to be done: he had lost his arm, by which I mean, not that it was amputated, but that it had lost all mobility. A dead appendage. He had to reeducate himself and his whole body changed, like a boat with a broken mast. Now he walked bent over, which he tried to hide out of vanity. We spent hundreds of thousands of euros on miracle operations and mechanical arms, but it was impossible. The nerves and tendons had been destroyed. The arm was dead.

One day we were introduced to an expert in occult cures, related to old legends of the blacksmith's trade in central Europe. It was the one card we hadn't yet played, so Kay said to me, I'm going to try. The man, whose name was Ebenezer Selle Trimegisto, had an office in the elegant Parisian district of École Militaire. According to Doctor Ebenezer, Kay could recover his strength by invoking the old medieval blacksmiths, and putting his arm in a splint with various qualities of metal. As he explained it, the earth was the great midwife and every metal was in transition between carbon and gold. Then he said that the bones were the carbonic and solid structure of the body and that the proximity of certain metals could revive the shattered pieces of the inert appendage. We believed him because we wanted to believe him and a few days later Dr. Ebenezer Trimegisto presented Kay with a long leather glove that went from the fist to the armpit and had to be filled with iron and other metals. A Brazilian storekeeper adjusted it for us and that was why Kay started walking around with that strange prosthesis. He looked like a medieval falconer with his arm covered to receive a falcon or a goshawk. Of course, it wasn't long before Kim—who hadn't come with us to Sarajevo, which might have been why he was still alive, because given his size he wouldn't have escaped the bullets—used the idea in one of his screenplays, which he entitled *The Flight of the Vagina Falcon*, and which reaches its climax when, in a tower at the top of a castle, as I'm on my knees giving a blowjob to one man while two others are penetrating my available orifices, a goshawk descends from the sky and comes to rest on his gloved hand at the very same moment when the man's penis shoots its load over my cheeks. It was a very vivid scene that greatly impressed the critics, and again there were hundreds of thousands of euros and a brace of excellent articles.

One day I was walking through the Marais, looking in fashion shops and making unnecessary purchases, when I saw a hideous-looking woman, filthy and haggard. Her eyes looked familiar and her name emerged from my mouth in a cry: Giorgetta! Her skin was all cut and raw, as if she had been sleeping for many years under the sun of the Sahara. I looked at her and it took her a while to focus, but finally she opened her horrible, almost toothless mouth, said, Sabina, and fainted at my feet. A thousand images hit me like a storm of meteorites: playing in the swimming pool at the Circeo, near Rome, when we were very young, or going to parties thrown by our uncles, when she would swig all the dregs left in the glasses to get drunk. She was always precocious, the poor thing. I felt responsible, so I called my driver, a black Dominican named Jenofonte, who had been waiting for me in a nearby square, drinking beer and watching the girls swinging their hips as they passed. Seeing me with Giorgetta, he jumped out and said, Madame Sabina, is anything wrong? Help her into the car, I said, she's my cousin.

When we got to our apartment, which by now was a penthouse on Rue Bonaparte, near Place Saint-Sulpice and the Jardin du Luxembourg, Giorgetta was incapable of stringing a sentence together. The only thing I understood was when she said: I went to a party with you years ago and I never saw you leave, when did you leave? I didn't remember anything, but I didn't think it was necessary to tell her that. The circuits in her brain had snapped and she couldn't catch my words. I gave her something to eat, and during the night, when she asked me for money to buy heroin, I didn't know what to do. Kay was in Los Angeles and wasn't answering his cell phone, so I decided to give Jenofonte a two-hundred-euro bill to go out and buy some and come back as soon as possible. My cousin gave herself two fixes one after the other, sticking the syringe first in her foot and then in her neck, because she had no veins left. When she fell into the abyss, I told Jenofonte to pick her up and help me take her to a private hospital just outside Paris, and there I left her, with a check for twenty-five thousand euros to pay for the best possible treatment.

Two days later, I went to visit her and was told they had been doing tests. Not surprisingly, she had tested HIV positive, and also had the beginnings of hepatitis B and a heart murmur. I contacted my aunt Gerarda, her mother, in Rome and persuaded her to come to Paris. She was a nice, gentle old lady, who burst into tears when she saw me. On the way to the hospital she whispered in my ear, have you seen Beatrice? It hit me like a bombshell, because as I'm sure you remember, Beatrice was my mother. I told my aunt I'd lost touch with her years ago, because we led very different lives. But she said, call her, she's been wanting to see you for years, and she slipped a folded piece of paper into my pocket. I felt a knot in my throat and didn't reply, only looked through the window at the French countryside and gripped my cell phone, longing to call Kay. If Aunt Gerarda had said that, it was because she had talked to Mamma, and Mamma was somehow waiting for me.

We spent the afternoon with Giorgetta, who didn't look as corpse-like as she had on the first day but still left her mother speechless and crying for a good couple of hours. She spent three months in the hospital, and I paid for it all, even for Aunt Gerarda to stay a few times. When the program was over she came out in a fairly decent state, so I went with them to Charles de Gaulle airport and we hugged and agreed to meet again soon. All three of us cried.

That night, while I was sleeping beside Kay, I heard him say: how odd, I feel a strange tingling in my arm. I woke up and said, wait, I'll scratch you, but he said, no, not that one, the other one. We were both stunned. Can you feel your arm? I asked, rubbing my hand against him. Yes, he said, I feel your hand, the pressure of three of your fingers. He tried to move it and couldn't, but it was an omen. Something was telling me that the loose or badly sewed threads of my life could be put back together again.

The next day I looked for the piece of paper my aunt had given me and dialed the number. It was a Miami number. When the phone started ringing at the other end I found I couldn't breathe, so I hung up and waited a little. I poured myself two glasses of gin and the alcohol cleared my head. Then I gave the number to Jenofonte and told him to call from the next room, ask for Beatrice, then tell me. I had quickly downed another gin when Jenofonte said, Madame Beatrice on the telephone. I was unable to speak, but she heard my breathing and started speaking, daughter, I knew you were going to call so I'm ready, Gerarda told me you're living in Paris and you're rich, I know the kind of work you do and you mustn't feel ashamed, what matters is that you had the courage to call, so speak now, tell me something . . . I said hello in a thin voice and we both cried for a while then we started chatting and didn't stop for three hours. At one point I said, Mamma, wait a second. I put my hand over the mouthpiece and told Jenofonte to call the travel agency and book a ticket on the next flight to Miami, and I said, Mamma, tell me your address, I'm coming straight away.

Our reunion was a happy one, if a little tense. She was sixty, but still elegant and beautiful. It was obvious she looked after herself, went to the gym every day, had had a few facelifts, and made a lot of effort to slay slim. She lived alone in an apartment near Coral Gables. She had separated from her Mexican lover more than seven years earlier, and although he was a fairly nasty and cynical individual, he had left her that apartment and enough money to give her an above-average monthly income. I waited nervously for the right moment to talk to her about my work, but it came very naturally. Do you know why I separated from him? she said, and I said, no, tell me, what happened? Mamma poured herself another dash of V8 with vodka, which was what we were drinking on her terrace, and she started her story, which wasn't very long and basically fairly predictable.

I always knew he was cheating on me, she said, but I'd reached the age when a woman gives up and prefers to close her eyes. His meetings and business trips to Acapulco and Sinaloa and the Bahamas were getting longer and longer and seemed to be less and less justified, but I didn't care because it all happened far away, in that great nothingness made up of all the places we haven't lived and know only as dots on a map. Until one day he started to seem strange, nervous, exhausted. He would get home in the evening or at night and go straight in the shower claiming he was hot or tired. His mouth smelled of alcohol. One day he traveled to Chicago and I got into his office and gave it a complete once-over. That was a serious mistake, of course, because what you look for, you find. It's something you should never do.

Well, I found it. A key ring with an address and two keys. 1587 Tijuana Drive, Apartment 6D. I went straight there, and it turned out to be a respectable-looking building, not luxurious but quite clean and well-maintained. When I got to the door of 6D I took out the key, but just as I was about to put it in the lock I heard a voice inside saying, can't you get back before tomorrow? will you be here by noon? She was talking on a cell phone near the door. Then she said, bring me something nice, darling, different than what you always bring me. I felt jealous. I dialed Tony's cell phone and of course it was engaged. I waited until the conversation was over and dialed again. This time he replied immediately and said, did you just call me? I was talking to the office, I'm going to have to stay until Saturday, it's freezing cold here, but there's no way I can get out of it, the Abbotts want to meet with me on Friday and it's too much bother to go and come back.

The next day I found an observation post, a coffee shop on the corner of Tijuana Drive and Anchorage Street, just opposite the entrance to the building. Of course I saw him arrive at noon, right on time, with a bag of gifts. It made me angry, but then I cooled down and plotted my revenge. The first thing I did was make copies of the keys and leave them in their place so that he didn't notice anything. Then I started keeping an eye on the bitch, who was a Colombian named Dorys. She was a stylist in a salon near Fito's office, which was where he'd met her. One day I went in to get my hair done and studied her. She was an attractive woman just under forty, that idiot Fito had good taste. It was obvious she didn't know who I was, because there was nothing nervous or uncomfortable about the way she behaved. On the contrary, she was very friendly and attentive. I started to make plans. My idea was to get her to dump him, or to make him believe that she had a lover. Something like that. One day, while Dorys was in the salon, I got into her apartment. It was quite nicely furnished, the home of someone who was neat and tidy but also romantic. A painting of a stormy dusk in the Caribbean, two heart-shaped red cushions, things like that. I looked through her underwear and was surprised not to find daring panties or garter belts, the kind of thing that appeals to older men going out with younger women. I wasn't there for very long, I knew they'd be coming back together that night. Before I left, I put a pair of men's socks beside the bed. That was part of my strategy.

Leaving things that would incriminate her. Another day, I left
a half-full bottle of eau de cologne, which I'd bought and half
emptied, of course, like everything I left. And it worked,
things started to go sour between them. One day I entered the
apartment after they'd spent all weekend together, and saw
that they had moved the TV into the bedroom. There was a
bottle of rum, cigarette butts, and various DVDs strewn on
the floor. I picked one up and saw you in the photograph on
the cover. I recognized you in spite of the make-up and all the
ways you'd changed, and in spite of the fact that you were
naked. I sat down on the bed. My god, my husband has erotic
parties with his lover and gets off on watching pornographic
videos of my daughter. I felt really disgusted by the time I left,
and when he got home I told him I knew everything and
didn't want to see him anymore. He gave me this apartment
and a decent income. So I separated from him and found out
what you did. Then I investigated a little and discovered that
you were a great professional in that kind of thing and had
even won prizes. I'm not going to tell you I was pleased, but I
thought, if a person chooses to do something in life, however
strange it may be, they should do it well, and that's exactly
what you're doing, daughter.

I told her about my life, about Kay and Kim and Eve
Studios, I talked about my experience with drugs, about
Giorgetta and how hard things had been, but how that hardness had become my greatest treasure, an inexhaustible source
of strength, and probably of talent. She felt guilty: if she had
been closer I wouldn't have suffered so much, but I insisted and
said, Mamma, I repeat, those difficult years are my resource, I
wouldn't change them for anything.

I stayed for a week and found out about her life, which was
quite simple. She had a group of women friends she played
cards with every Friday in a restaurant called Sapori di Sicilia,
and she was a member of an evangelical church led by a

strange Latino, a handsome, muscular man with tattoos all over his body, who would certainly have had a great future in the porn industry. A few days later, Kay traveled to Los Angeles, and that was where we all met up. I think they got along well, because after four days Mamma invited him to Miami and later he bought her an airline ticket to Paris so that she could come and see us.

We are already coming to the end of this eventful life, full of highs and lows. Having now recounted how the only family I had was reunited, and how my professional success came about, it only remains for me to tell you about the last great idea of Kim, our brilliant screenwriter, something he wanted to call "left-wing porn." His screenplays started to depict sexual situations in which selfishness was combated and the collective ownership of the means of production was advocated. The first one, *Orgasmic Integration*, was a founding document. It includes an amusing scene in which a Mediterranean fisherman, hard at work, catches his wife in the hold of his boat, being given a double penetration by two Senegalese immigrants with very large cocks, who had gotten on the boat the night before after drifting in on a clandestine raft. The fisherman takes off his rubber boots and his leather apron all smeared with scales, looks straight at the camera, and says, maybe having her with them will bring me new pleasures, through a combination of all the means of arousal I'll be able to have better sex, because my pleasure is inseparable from everyone else's. Having said this, he throws himself into the fray, displaying a fairly reasonable cock, although, as if to prove certain cultural myths, it's smaller than those of the Africans, and everything ends in a double facial ejaculation accompanied by ejaculation over the buttocks, three cannons shooting their load at the same time, a sublime image intended, according to Kim, to recall the cannons in *The Battleship Potemkin*, which was the inspiration for the scene.

We made a new series of twelve movies to illustrate the theory of left-wing porn, and they were very successful, although, as often happens, we were soon attacked by those envious of us, who said that our esthetic approach was opportunistic, that we were jumping on the bandwagon of the new currents then transforming European socialism, and other nonsense like that. As often happens, instead of damaging us these diatribes gave our work a stronger impetus and helped to spread it. Some even started working in the opposite direction to ours, for example, a Danish production company introduced "center-right porn," although the concept wasn't very clear, because in the end it was all just routine humping and geysers of sperm, with no real significance.

In spite of its difficult beginnings, my story actually has a happy ending, which, of course, is something our screenwriter Kim hates, being an advocate of open and slightly incomprehensible endings, à la Bergman. Our company is one of the biggest in Europe and the movies we make are sold in America, Africa, Asia, and the former Soviet Union. The latest, *The Clitoris and Its Forms*, has sold 680,000 copies on DVD. A real hit.

I haven't mentioned the books I've written, because that probably isn't the part of my life you wanted to hear about, and it's the least important anyway. Lives are like cities: if they're too neat and tidy they don't have a story. The best stories come out of misfortune and destruction.

I have told you mine.

PART THREE
NECROPOLIS

1.

OTHER VOICES

During Edgar Miret Supervielle's lecture, I kept peering anxiously around at the audience, hoping to recognize the guest from Room 1209—looking, in fact, in order to confirm my theories or, rather, my vague conjectures, for Walter. But the auditorium was poorly lit, the ICBM favoring subdued lighting to concentrate the audience's attention on the speaker, and I did not see anyone who looked like him. In response to the applause, Supervielle made a series of athletic bows at the front of the proscenium, bending almost double as he did so. Marta Joonsdottir announced to me that she was going to her date with the doctor: she had no wish to arrive late. Then she gave me an imploring look and said, I have rather a big favor to ask of you, which is that when I get back I'd like . . . to sleep in your room, can I? I left my cell phone there and I can't get back to my hotel. I told her she could, and added: remember, I owe you one.

Things were a bit chaotic on the way out, with people pushing and shoving to get from the hall to the corridor. Many lingered in small groups to pass comment on the lecture, stopping the others from advancing. I was making my way through the crush when I heard a familiar voice saying, my distinguished compatriot, what a pleasure to see you, come, let's have an aperitif together. It was Kaplan. Reluctantly, I said yes. What I really wanted at that moment was to keep an eye on the people heading for the lobbies and staircases, but as I was unable to think of an excuse, my reflexes still being slow, I accepted.

In the first-floor bar, Kaplan ordered two whiskeys and said, what a tragic thing about that preacher, my God, who knows what sins he must have committed in his life, and what pangs of remorse he must have felt! Well, he certainly paid for those sins with his life. Kaplan sipped at his drink and asked me if I had left Colombia for political reasons, but I said, no, I left because I needed a change of scenery and wanted to know the world, but the world just seems to be getting bigger and bigger, and I still don't really know it, that's why I keep moving, and that's the only reason I've stayed away . . . It's an excellent reason, my friend, and how long do you think it will be before you go back? I don't know, I said, sometimes I think what I'm looking for is a way out, but that has nothing to do with the world or even with our distant country, to be honest, I don't really understand it myself.

There was a rumbling in the distance, and the floor shook slightly. Soon afterwards sirens sounded, and Kaplan said, they're pounding Talpiot, what a shame, it's one of the most beautiful parts of the city, the writer S. Y. Agnon, the uncle of the novelist Amos Oz, used to live there, on Joseph Klausner Street. So many trees in the area, pines, eucalyptus. I hope they don't destroy it. I spent some time there, in Bet Hataava. The houses have been evacuated and they're putting up a strong resistance, with Patriots to destroy the enemy missiles in the air, mobile hospitals, chains of evacuation, oh yes, it's a real war all right. We both fell silent for a while. Then I said: why hold a conference here, in the middle of this chaos, with people dying on the outskirts of the city? Kaplan downed his whiskey in one. Oh, my friend, I'd say the opposite, I think right now this is the one place in the world where an event like this has any meaning.

There was another silence, then I said, don't forget you still owe me the end of your story. Kaplan ordered two more whiskeys and said, that's right, my God, so much time has

passed, I can speak about it now as if it had happened to someone else, the pain and anger have worn off; it's like when you
walk away from a fire and stop feeling the heat.

I told you last time that my family had decided to fight
back, well, after our warnings the paras counterattacked, setting fire to my brother's house, and killing the guard, who was
only twenty-two; one of our agents called New York and they
said to us, you have to respond, and we have a number of suggestions. One was to kill one of the politicians linked to the
paras, but I said we weren't murderers, no, let's bring them
down, I said, let the shit hit the fan, I want everyone to know
what they're doing and raise a fuss about it. It'll be more difficult, they said, but we'll try. They followed these people,
tapped their phones, and finally managed to catch some very
interesting conversations: one of the politicians, for example,
demanding the head of a mayor with the words, "get rid of that
Communist for me"; another call where a paramilitary phoned
a governor and said, "I need eighty million pesos, I'll send for
them tomorrow," and the governor replied, "Yes, chief, I have
them ready here, send for them whenever you like." My agents
informed the press and there was a big scandal, the men were
arrested and forced to give up their seats in parliament, now
they would have to face the law and see if they could bribe and
threaten ordinary judges, but that wasn't our problem anymore, it was the country's. Of course, they told the press it was
all a set-up orchestrated by their political enemies. One day I
sent their lawyer the following message: "Tell your client, yes,
we Jews do all have the same sense of humor." We found out
that they had asked the paras to kill us, but by that time we had
already left.

He finished his account with a burst of laughter and
ordered another drink. Then he said, let's change the subject,
friend, shall I tell you what most impressed me about
Maturana's story? It was that, in the end, the famous savior

that everyone believed in was just a wimp! A real wimp, to screw up a business like that through pride! I put my glass down and stood up, pretending that I was expecting an urgent call. Thanks for the aperitif and your stories, Señor Kaplan, the next time it's on me. He gave me his hand and said, it's obvious you're a writer, oh, by the way, if you have any of your books here I'd like to read one, do you have any? I was thinking about his request when he himself said, if you have a spare one leave it in reception in my name, I'm in Room 1211. I stopped dead, 1211? He was next door to 1209! I went back to him and said, excuse me, but have you noticed anything strange about the room next to yours, number 1209? But Kaplan said, I haven't even seen the person staying there, has something happened? don't frighten me. Nothing special, I'm right underneath, in 1109, and I heard noises, that's all. My friend, this city is full of noises. That's because of all the spirits hovering in the air.

I said goodbye to Kaplan and headed for the elevators. Twelfth floor. I crept to the door of Room 1209 but could not hear a thing, nor could I see if there was a light on inside. Apart from Walter, the second likeliest guest, in my opinion, was the black man, Jefferson. As I stood there, I saw a hotel employee coming with a tray, delivering room service; I looked at him out of the corner of my eye and saw that he was carrying a chicken sandwich and a Diet Coke. I thought he might stop at 1209, but he walked right past.

I decided to go back down to my floor, the eleventh, and take another look at the ex-pastor's room. Again, the door was open! I pushed it cautiously, stood in the entrance, but could not see anyone. Suddenly, I heard a moan. On the other side of the bed, a young woman in the hotel uniform was writhing on the carpet, with her legs apart. A man, also in uniform, had his head under her skirt. Seeing me standing there, the young woman froze. When the man's head emerged, I recognized Momo, who said: I'm sorry, sir, I'm so sorry, as you can imagine, working in a place full of beds it really makes you want to . . . The young woman leaped to her feet and ran out the door. Then Momo said: you have to understand, these beds just seem to be saying, sex, sex . . . Her name is Mel and she's my girlfriend. We usually meet in 2918, which is a suite, but Mel is studying cinema and sociology and wanted to see the place where that man killed himself, are you going to report me? Don't talk nonsense, Momo, the only thing I might feel is envy, what's her job here? She works in the snack bar on the third floor, she's Brazilian but her family is from Belarus, these Russian women, my God, they're stunning, and with this war all around it gives you a hard-on all the time, I'm really sorry, sir, it's not my fault.

The room was in perfect condition, ready to receive new guests. The cleaners had done their work well. Momo said that a police team had come that morning and taken everything away, even the dust and the water in the vase. We're used to it, these things happen quite often, was that telephone number I gave you any use to you? Yes, I called Tel Aviv and got hold of an address. I was thinking to go tomorrow. Momo snapped his fingers and said, if you like I can take you, it's my day off and I always go to Tel Aviv. I thanked him. We agreed that he would pick me up outside the main entrance of the King David at eight in the morning.

Back in my room, I grabbed my notes again, but it was hot, so I opened the window and breathed the night air. It was very cool, even the noises of war seemed distant. Marta had left a bunch of newspapers on the table, which she must have picked up from reception. The international news agencies had reported Maturana's suicide and a few papers had picked it up before they went to press. I looked at the headlines: *Suicide at the ICBM*, or *Death Hovers over Conference*; one of the more sensationalistic was *Death Gatecrashes the Feast of Life*. The most succinct was in a French-language newspaper: *Death of a Biographer*. The item mentioned that the marks found on the body "would seem to indicate suicide." I was looking at this when I heard a conversation coming from the terrace of the floor below. Somebody was saying: what bad luck to give my talk after Maturana's suicide, and how ironic, after I'd e-mailed and telephoned the organizers and managed to have the program changed so that I could go before Sabina Vedovelli, it's like a bad joke, pour me a little more of that. The voice was Supervielle's. Then I heard Kosztolányi say, don't be so negative, people were really pleased and interested to hear your story, you told it really well and it'll stay lodged in their brains, I assure you. Maturana's story may have been loud and attention-grabbing, and made even more so by his subsequent suicide, but yours was a slow burner, you'll see, very soon everyone will be praising the sober manner in which you conveyed the narrative, the vividness of the metaphors you chose, the convincing way in which you handled time, with a highly original *mise en abîme* that cracks open and leads to an equally original anagnorisis or recognition, my God, yes, Edgar, and if one adds the stenographic accuracy of the dialogue, your discretion in dealing with burning issues, and your firm control of the emotional content, I don't know what else to tell you, I don't think you should have the slightest worry about the result, it was impeccable, don't you see that?

Thanks, Leonidas, replied Supervielle, you're a friend and what you say is some consolation, although you might be exaggerating a little, I don't know, do you really think he came to hear me? did you see him at the talk? There was a silence. Perhaps Kosztolányi made a gesture asking, who are you talking about, who was supposed to be there? because Supervielle replied, who do you think? the head of Tiberias! Ebenezer Lottmann! Did you see him? My agent sent him two of my books a couple of weeks ago and he's considering them, didn't

I tell you that? Kosztolányi said: oh, well, there's no need to worry about that, he was there, and I'll tell you this, he was taking notes and he had a rectangular object in his hand that might have been . . . I don't know, a Palm, a cell phone or even a miniature tape recorder, yes, something like that, I can see it now, and that's good, isn't it? it means he was interested, he wasn't only there as a member of the audience but as part of his job, and guess what, now that I rack my brains, I can remember there was one moment he spoke into the machine, yes, there's no doubt about it, it was his cell phone, putting two and two together we may assume he was calling his office, he might have been saying, find those books by Edgar Miret Supervielle, check if there's a chapter about two chess players named Osloski and Flø, put them on my table, take them out of the pile and give them a place apart, and he might even, my dear friend, have been giving instructions to draw up a draft contract to send to your agent, perhaps this very day, now that would be tremendous news, wouldn't it?

Supervielle must have been soothed by his friend's words, because he interrupted, saying, do you think he used the telephone for that? wait, I'm very nervous, if that were the case it's possible that my agent has already received something, mother of God, let's find out immediately. Then I heard him on the telephone, saying, Supervielle here, now listen to me carefully, Ethan, did you receive anything from Tiberias this afternoon? no? how strange, I have reason to believe that Lottmann is thinking of making an offer at any moment, whatever you do keep your eye on the fax machine, and for the love of God, check to see if that damned piece of junk has paper and is connected!!! Make sure you don't miss any calls, Ethan, I wouldn't ask it if it wasn't VERY important, what did you say? yes, of course the war is still on, but who the hell cares about that now?? keep an eye on the machine, sit by it till that damned contract arrives! Am I making myself clear?

He hung up and said to Kosztolányi, there's no offer yet, at least according to my agent, who of course is an idiot, why must we always be in the hands of idiots? May God forgive me, Ethan is the son of a friend, but the poor man never gets things right, I must change agents as soon as I get back to Paris, phew, there's no offer so far, that means if he called his office from the hall it wasn't because of that, a false alarm, don't you think? what if he called the publishing house to say exactly the opposite, to tell his assistant, put everything in an envelope and return to sender?

Anything's possible, said Kosztolányi, but if that was the case your agent would already know, why send back manuscripts if he can write an e-mail? you can never tell with somebody whispering on the phone, he might even have been calling his wife, Edgar, or his young mistress, I don't know, a female writer of the new generation anxious for recognition, why not? it often happens, he might have been calling to say, listen, darling, I know I promised I'd be there at seven but I'm listening to one of the best talks I've ever heard in my life, please wait for me, ask room service for whatever you like, clear out the minibar, but wait for me, don't you think it could have been something like that?

You're right, Leonidas, anything's possible, my contract, his wife or mistress, but I prefer to be optimistic, to believe that at the end of the conference he'll get in touch with my agent and make an offer, I truly believe that's what will happen, come on, let's have a drink, we have to celebrate in style.

I fell asleep.

Marta got back just after two in the morning and went straight to the bathroom. When she came out, I noticed she was drunk. Well? I asked, how was your romantic dinner? She turned to look at me and said: there are no words, phew, let me try and tell you . . . Where should I begin? He took me to Jaffa market, or rather, a place near the market that's badly damaged but still functioning. Delicious, spicy food, and a bottle of wine from Mount Carmel that tasted divine. Then we went to an apartment to have a drink, it wasn't his place. He said he would count the beauty spots on my body and that when he got to number twelve he would give me a kiss in that spot, and then he would say a city corresponding to the first letter of the part of the body he had kissed. A bit complicated, but he turned out to be an expert. Arm, Amsterdam, belly, Brussels, thigh, Tallinn, and so on, are you following? When he did that I had to say the country that it was the capital of, or imagine another city where I would like to get married to a Korean or get divorced from a Korean. Each time I failed, I had to take off one garment. When he'd finished explaining all this, I said, my dear Amos, the object of the game is to fuck me, isn't it? so come on, let's get down to it, because that's what I want, too.

We had a fantastic fuck, I don't think I've ever screamed like that before or had so many orgasms. We did it three times in a row and I thought of a great idea for an article, let's see what you think: the life of a military doctor in a city under siege, don't you think that's a great subject? I said yes, and asked if she had found out anything new about Maturana. She stood up again and went back to the bathroom. She returned after a while, naked, with a damp towel in her crotch. I'm sorry, it burns a bit . . . I haven't fucked so hard for ages and Amos has a huge penis, what were you saying? Maturana, did you find out anything new?

She lay down beside me and said, yes, Amos saw the tests, apparently he had drugs in his blood, heroin, highly concentrated, in anyone else, Amos said, a quantity like that would have caused an overdose, but he was strong. Then Marta lit a cigarette and said, Amos is married, that's why he wouldn't stay the night with me, but he's coming to the hotel tomorrow. Here? I asked. No, my hotel, I didn't want to take advantage of you.

She stood up, walked to the window, and looked out at the night sky, which was again filled with storm clouds. I know it's wrong to get involved with married men, but what can I do, he might die tomorrow and he really wanted it, I could sense that, so why not please him? I'm also going to die. He's attractive but I'm not planning to fall in love, I'm not stupid. They promise to leave their wives and never do, especially if they have children. When we finished fucking, he lay down beside me and talked to me about her, can you believe that?

He loves and respects her, but doesn't feel desire for her anymore. Her name is Esther. He saw her from a distance in a university cafeteria and knew she would be his companion, knew that he loved her and wanted her by his side all his life. You know, I feel sorry for people who say things like, "when I saw her I realized . . . " or "it was at that moment that I knew . . . " That's all bullshit. Nobody knows or realizes anything, certainly not so suddenly.

She lay down on the bed again, covered herself with the bedspread and gave a big yawn. Before falling asleep she said: dear Esther, tomorrow I'll have sex with your husband again, and I hope you'll forgive me; he has an amazing penis . . . If you have sex with him tonight, don't suck it, I know what I'm talking about . . .

The next day, Momo arrived at the hotel nice and early. He was driving a beat-up old Toyota station wagon. The bodywork was rusty, one of the rear windows had been replaced with a plastic sheet, and there were springs sticking up out of the seats. I got in and we set off. We drove along the side of the street where concrete and steel barriers had been set up to protect passers-by from snipers. Then we turned into a maze of narrow alleys. It's the shortest route to the highway, he said, wait and see. On the corners, there were overturned cars being used as barricades and old sandbags with holes in them. Why aren't you fighting? I asked, and Momo replied, I'm in the reserve, I'm an only child and I look after my mother, who's sick, and my grandmother, who has a number tattooed on her forearm, know what I mean? I suppose if you take a good look at my life, it's fairly lousy, but just like in the story of the Zen master, what's good luck and what's bad luck? that's why I don't have to be out there killing people or waiting for them to kill me, I'm a pacifist, you know? well, a realistic pacifist, because if they come to my home I'll die fighting.

The street narrowed until we could almost touch the walls from the car. Two Orthodox men in torn suits, sitting on the front steps of a building, looked at us indifferently. A woman who was chatting with her neighbor from a window shouted at us angrily as we passed. What did she say? I asked Momo. That we weren't at the front and her son is. A bit farther along, the fenders of the Toyota hit an empty cardboard box and a hen squawked as it dodged away from the car. I said to Momo: are you sure this is the way? Trust me, the highway is straight ahead. And indeed, we were soon descending through Bab el-Wad toward Tel Aviv.

Didn't your girlfriend want to come with us? Momo asked. She isn't my girlfriend, only a friend, she's a journalist, she's covering the conference and I met her in the hotel. How strange, he said, I know women and I can assure you she looked at you as if you were her boyfriend, I can seen that in women; pardon me asking, but have you fucked her? No, I said. Momo turned in his seat. If you want my advice, sir, tell her something sad, it never fails; sadness always finds a kindred spirit. I have a bit of experience in this.

As we passed the Monastery of the Seven Sorrows at Latrun, a jet with the star of David on the back passed over our heads, flying very low. Fumigation, said Momo. What did you say? Fumigation. When the enemy is so close, we can't shoot too much shit at them, because if the wind changes it falls on our heads; instead they fumigate with a burning liquid that only works for a few seconds but drives anybody who doesn't have a protecting cream crazy; they have to fly low to spray it, and that has its dangers, they've already brought down a couple of planes. But it's worth it. Their operations are becoming less frequent, which gives us a bit of a respite. We've been at war for many years, and we know each other well.

The streets of Tel Aviv were filled with pedestrians in shorts and sandals. It was summer in the Middle East, something that did not seem to exist just forty miles away, because the perception of reality was different there: as if the world's tribulations had come to an end and only one fortress remained to fall. We entered the noisy, traffic-clogged streets. Momo said: my mother's place isn't far, we can have a cold drink and you'll meet my family, then I'll take you to your address. Momo's mother lived in the northern part of the city, near the harbor. The smell of the sea filled our nostrils as we got out of the car. I took a deep breath and felt slightly dizzy, but I was fine otherwise. My health was holding up in spite of all these excesses.

You're the writer, said Momo's mother. Come in, please, you must be hot.

The living room was a small space filled with rickety furniture. On the table was a tray with two glasses and a jug of lemonade with ice and mint leaves. The lemonade was really delicious. Mother and son said something to each other in Hebrew and Momo went out into the corridor. Then he appeared from another room and said to me, come in, sir, just for a minute. His grandmother was in bed, with her eyes open and an anxious expression on her face, as if fearing that something was about to happen. She hadn't spoken for months, but she could hear, so I greeted her with a nod and told her my name. She turned her face to me and a shudder went through me. Her eyes were like two windows through which all the horror and madness of destruction, the proximity of death, could be seen. She raised one hand and I saw the number tattooed on her wrist. She put her hand on mine and smiled. She stayed like that for a few seconds and closed her eyes. That's enough, said Momo, she's tired. We went back to the living room and finished the jug of lemonade. Momo gave his mother an envelope (money, I assumed) and she gave him a bundle of fruit and canned food. I said goodbye to the woman, walked back out onto the street, clambered into the Toyota, and waited for Momo.

The Universal Coptic Church was located on Rothschild Avenue, a tree-lined boulevard whose sidewalks were overflowing with people at that hour, toward noon. The address I was looking for was on a corner, in an old Bauhaus-style building that curved toward the adjoining street, giving a lovely feeling of flow. On either side of the entrance were other businesses, a video rental store and a dry cleaner's called Salonika.

As I got out I made a mental list of what I was looking for, or rather, what I assumed I might find out: whether Miss Jessica was indeed now attached to this organization; the possible links between the Coptic Church and the Ministry of Mercy; and how everything had changed since the destruction of the Ministry as Maturana had told it. Of course, I had no very clear idea of what the Universal Coptic Church might be. From somewhere deep in my memory, I recalled that one of the characters in *The Alexandria Quartet* was a Copt and that in Egypt it still existed as an official Christian sect, would it be the same here? It hardly seemed like it, to judge by the building.

When I entered the reception area, I noticed how bare the place was. No large crucifixes or altarpieces, just a dilapidated wooden desk, a first-generation IBM computer, and a few posters with images of Christ.

Can I help you? asked a woman sitting behind the desk. I told her I was looking for a woman named Jessica, and added, she's an American friend of mine, of Latin origin, when I knew

362 · SANTIAGO GAMBOA

her she was called Jessica, although I realize that names change when people have a religious vocation, I haven't seen her in quite a while and then I heard she was is in the Coptic Church, she's a woman of about forty.

A sly look came over the receptionist's face and she said, wait here, I'll see what I can do. Momo, who was by my side— I forgot to mention before that he had come in with me—had not opened his mouth yet, but now he said: this looks like the complaints department of an industrial complex in a Communist country, I bet they won't tell you anything, sir. I looked at him and shrugged. What else can I do except ask them, this is where the call you received came from, the one Maturana had in his book before he killed himself, obviously they may not know anything about it, we have to be discreet. Momo gave me a knowing look and said, O.K., I understand, my lips are sealed.

Behind the desk there was a window that looked out on an inner courtyard. A fat man was shifting some garbage pails and putting them together near the door. When he had finished, he lifted the flap of his coveralls, took out a bottle, and had a couple of good swigs. Then he looked up at the sky with an expression of gratitude and cleaned his mouth with his sleeve.

At this point the woman came back and said, would you come with me, please? the Metropolitan's secretary would like to see you. We followed her along a corridor, past a number of prayer rooms, and up the stairs to the third floor. A man of about fifty was waiting for us in an office. Sit down, he said, without getting up or holding out his hand to us, merely indicating the leather armchairs with both hands, would you like a glass of water, iced tea, coffee? Nothing, thanks. The man stood up, turned his back to us, and said: I'm Eddy Peters, at your service and God's, welcome to our church. Now that he was standing I could see how fat he was, but in a strange way, with a small, thin face, thin arms, and sunken chest, and then a very large potbelly. I noticed the surprise in Momo's eyes and thought he might be on the verge of committing an indiscretion. I would have to watch out.

So you're looking for somebody, eh? he said, sitting down again, theatrically. Yes, an American friend, I haven't seen her in years, but then some friends of mine told me she's a parishioner of this church and had mentioned to them that she was coming here, that's why I've come to look for her. Oh yes, he said, chance, chance is the ink in which God dips his pen in order to plot the destinies of men, and what leads you to believe that she's here in this particular branch of our church? I looked at him and said, absolutely nothing, just my intuition.

The man scratched his neck and caught a bead of sweat as it trickled down behind his ear.

The fact is, there's nobody of that name here, you'll have to give me more information. As I said before: she's of Latin origin, forty years old, and has worked for other evangelical churches . . . And why do you imagine she may be with us? He was nibbling at the cap of a ball pen. I repeated: because of what our mutual friends told me, that's the only reason. I paused and added, I'm a writer, I'm used to doing research.

When he heard that, his face changed color, and he spat the pen cap from his mouth and said, you aren't one of those filthy opportunists who write about the crimes of the church and crap like that to fill their pockets by deceiving people? No, how could you think that? I'm not even writing, in fact I haven't written anything in more than two years, I only mentioned it to . . . But the man was beside himself. And what's to guarantee that after this visit you won't recover your inspiration and start slinging all kinds of shit at us? The scene was starting to be grotesque, but I was enjoying myself, so I said: I've never done that, I mean sling shit, I only want to know if among your parishioners there's a woman who fits the description I gave you, from what I know the Coptic Church isn't a secret society or anything like that, its followers don't have anything to hide, it doesn't do anything criminal or shameful, or does it?

He went to the window, put his hands on his hips, thrust his body back, and let out a big breath. All right, my friend, I think it's time we put our cards on the table, don't you? let me tell you how I see things: you're a writer and you came to this country for the conference in Jerusalem; you say you're looking for a long-lost friend but that wasn't in your mind at all when you first arrived; but then a tragedy occurs, and one day later you get it into your head to come here and inquire after your friend, don't you think that's a rather curious coincidence? I looked at him in surprise and said: maybe so, but that's all it is, a coincidence. The woman I'm looking for worked with the dead man years ago in an evangelical church in Miami, don't you find that a bit disturbing?

By Christ and his cross, said Eddy Peters, I can see it now, you *are* writing a book, I can see it in your eyes, the way they're shining. Let me see if I can guess the plot: you think it wasn't suicide but murder and that the Coptic Church may be involved? My God, I can just see it: millions of copies, you and your publishers are denounced, there's a great scandal, but then it all fizzles out and everything goes back to normal . . . Do you have a title yet? I looked at him with a neutral expression. There is no title, because there is no book, but if you insist we could call it . . . *Death of a Biographer*, what do you think?

He played with the ball pen in his fingers and said, quite catchy but there's something missing, I don't know, maybe it should mention the Church in the title, don't you think? Then he stood up and said, even though you clearly have no scruples I like you, I must confess. The Coptic Church has nothing to do with that man's suicide, and it's not our fault that it happened; you must surely know that suicides are the work of individuals, and that they're all different? How many reasons can there be to give up on life? To me there are none, because life doesn't belong to us, it isn't ours; you may be obsessed with finding out what happened, but you mustn't lose sight of the fact that the truth doesn't have to be known by anybody for it still to be the truth. Write your details for me on a piece of paper, how long you're going to be in the country, and your full name, and if I come across her, I'll be in touch, now good afternoon.

When we came out, the sun was still beating down. It was a bit early to go back, so we crossed the avenue and went into a café to have a drink. As we were about to sit down at one of the tables, I noticed a woman putting a bill down on the counter and picking up a package. Her face seemed familiar, and a voice told me: talk to her, it's her.

The woman turned and looked at me in surprise.

Seeing her full-face like that, I realized that it was not from the photographs that I recognized her but . . . Was it possible? She was the woman I had seen at the opening cocktail party! Yes, it was her, but it was also Jessica, because she stopped when she heard her name. I asked her if she was who I thought, but she shook her head and headed for the door, so I said, in Spanish, I'm a friend of José Maturana, I have to talk to you. She stopped again and gave me a searching look. Look, let me buy you a coffee, please. We walked to a table. A friend of José? she said, her voice was soft and beguiling, and I replied, yes, I've come from the conference, I didn't know that José was sick and I was impressed by his story, I was the first to reach his room when . . . when that happened, you know, I saw his body with the cuts on it, I found his notes, anyway, are you, Jessica?

She put her bag down on the table and said, I know who you are, you're the writer, aren't you? I saw you at the conference. I told her I had gone to the church to look for her but the Metropolitan's secretary had said he did not know her and that there was no Jessica in his church, had she changed her name? No, she said, I asked them not to give out any information about me, that's why, but why were you looking for me? why are you interested in Maturana? I told her there were things about José that I was trying to understand. I'm not an investigator or anything like that, nor am I, as Peters thought, planning a scandalous book, at least I don't think so; it's a very human story and for some strange reason I'd like to find out more, to get to the bottom of it, it just seems the right thing to do.

They brought two coffees in big cups.

Jessica looked at the steaming liquid with an anxious expression, and said, all right, all right, let me tell you a few things, you're a writer and if you're going to put this in one of your books it's best you know what really happened, anyway, it'll be better if I talk but don't tell me you're not going to do a book—I had been sincere, I did not know it yet—I've lived surrounded by people who say they won't do this or they won't do that, and then it's the first thing they do, so don't come to me with that.

Having said this, she began her story.

When he first arrived at the Ministry, José scared me. He was a tall, strong man, with a face pockmarked from smallpox or acne, swollen veins on his arms, bulging muscles, and those horrible lacerations he called tattoos, which he'd gotten in prison. If Walter was an angel who walked preceded by a ray of light, José was the king of shadows. Everything in him was an expression of evil, starting with his eyes. I had seen murderers, really perverse, cynical people, and I knew what was in a cold look like that. But Walter's affection for him made me lower my guard. Maybe I was wrong, maybe José was like one of those mythological creatures who are all dried up but still have a few drops of life in them, and if somebody can extract those drops they revive, and I imagined that was what Walter had done.

But it was Walter I felt most afraid for, not me. As I said before, I had seen it all, I'd swum all my life in turbulent, shark-infested waters. According to the story José told at the conference, Walter was a violent man who had beaten him up in the penitentiary and as a result of that he had found God. I heard this story many times and the truth was that in the cell-block, when José was pushed, he slipped and hit a hot water pipe, which not only knocked him out but also caused burns, because a nut on the pipe came loose and the water gushed out in a kind of geyser; I assume the mixture of all that led him to see God. Walter wasn't capable of hitting anyone, let alone like that. He was an angel, as I said before. José, on the other hand, was a tough, violent individual. One day he confessed to me that he had killed a man with his bare hands, that he had never been brought to trial for it, and that it weighed on his conscience. He told me that on one of our excursions to spread the word, when Walter had asked us to work together. He mentioned it in his talk, a dive called the Flacuchenta Bar; of course the things he said about it I don't remember that way at all. One night, he went to the bathrooms in that filthy place and when he came back he was very pale, and he said, did you see the face of the man who just came out of the bathroom? I hadn't seen anyone, because I was listening to the music, and he said, oh, Jessica, it's like a zombie movie, I just saw a dead man come out of the bathroom, you have to believe me, are you sure you didn't see anyone? and I said, José, if there had been a dead man we would all have seen him, dead people attract attention, but he'd already stopped listening, he was just looking out at the street, very pale and very scared. Then he said, Jessica, that man who just came out of the bathroom is dead and I know because I killed him myself more than five years ago in Charleston. You killed somebody? I said, and he said, with a look of shame on his face, I don't think he was a great loss to the human race, and I doubt that anyone mourned him, I killed him because he was hitting a woman who wouldn't let herself be raped in a crack house, you know, one of those places where people go to do drugs; there are women who shoot up and then they're anybody's, but even in a place like that there are rules and if the woman shouts, you go away; usually they don't even realize what they're doing, but if they push you away you have to respect them, anyway, this man tried to have sex with this woman, this junkie, who had a crying baby next to her, and she resisted, so he started hitting her, but not the way a man hits a woman, with his open hand, but as if he was hitting a cop or another black guy as strong as him. I got up from my chair and grabbed him by the neck, and said, hey, nigger, are you so stubborn you haven't noticed that she's a woman? have you already forgotten that you wanted to have sex with her, which, even with a brain like yours, ought to tell you that she's a woman? The guy tried to punch me, but I caught his hand in mid-air and squeezed it hard until I heard a couple of bones cracking, then I grabbed him by the hair, and before pushing him against a table, I said, you don't treat a woman like that, let alone a mother, didn't you see she has a child? I hit him a few times; when I picked him up to look at him he spat out a lump of blood, and I said, the next time I'll fuck you myself, you son of a bitch, then I grabbed hold of his head and banged it against the wall about five times, as hard as I could; then I slammed it into the screen of a broken old TV set, which smashed into a thousand pieces, and I left him there, blood all over him, with his head stuck in an old TV. Then I walked out onto the street with the woman, who was pushing her stroller and rubbing her swollen cheekbones. I gave her some money so she could go away and that same afternoon I left the city for a while, but the police never came looking for me. One junkie less in the neighborhood, who gave a shit, but now I saw him in the bathroom, Jessica, and I thought, José, if you left him bleeding maybe he didn't die, maybe that's why the police never came looking for you.

That was the kind of story that José told, but he also talked about private things, how he felt about other people, his love affairs. The first time he slept with a woman was with the mother of a neighbor of his, who was thirty-two and an alcoholic; he and his friend were eighteen and they smoked grass, drank, snorted cocaine, and occasionally gave themselves a fix. José had sex with her one day when he came looking for his friend but his friend had gone out; the woman was drunk, she invited him to have a few beers, then took him to bed and taught him what to do. Having sex with his friend's mother made him feel like a big man, and very soon he was picking fights with everyone. He never saw the woman again. Then he was with a Colombian girl and got into more trouble with drugs, getting closer and closer to the edge, until he became a real addict and started his love affair with smack.

Are you sure José didn't know anything about his origins? He didn't talk much about that, said Jessica, and it may be true; maybe he did have somebody in his childhood but prefers not to remember, like many people do, if something traumatic happened it's better to distance yourself from it and invent a different story. He told me all kinds of stories; about an orphanage, a reformatory, an old woman who sold him, a man who forced him to beg with a plaster on his arm so that it looked as if he had a burn, and a group of children he used to steal fruit with from the trees in the neighbors' gardens. In fact, José remembered a lot of things, but anyway, that's beside the point, let me go back to what I want to tell you, which is the real relationship between José and Walter.

It's true that Walter took him out of prison and that he did it because he believed in him and realized that, with his physical strength and his experience in the lower depths, José would be his ideal companion in his crusade among prostitutes, drug addicts and murderers. He was his first companion, which explains why Walter was so loyal to him, why he was always prepared to indulge his demands, to support any of his ideas or whims, however crazy or even dangerous they were. In his talk, for example, José didn't say anything about the Mobile Ministry, which was one of his brilliant ideas; it involved adapting a large RV, a very expensive one that cost a hundred and seventy thousand dollars, with a chapel inside, so that we could drive through the neighborhoods and spread the word more quickly. We bought it and had a prayer room, a little religious library, and a confessional built in it because José's idea was to position ourselves on the corners in troubled neighborhoods and provide a service to the young people, instant confession and repentance.

But his methods were very violent and one day, in a red-light district, he hit a young man who had refused to get down on his knees, and forced him to ask forgiveness of Christ, which the boy finally did but only when he was already bruised and bleeding. The next day, when José arrived in the RV, he was met with stones and even a couple of gunshots; he had to run away and the RV was torched. The insurance company didn't want to hear about it, what was he doing in such a dangerous place anyway?

The story about Jefferson and Walter being homosexuals is false, I really want to make that clear. I don't have any proof, apart from my word, but I want you to understand that Walter was a creature from another world and sex didn't interest him, either with women or with men, not that he had anything against it, on a number of occasions he said it was a healthy and necessary thing that should be practiced with joy, because God had given it to man precisely it order for him to be happy. But he was very ascetic. Denying himself pleasures was a form of holiness he aspired to, one that he wished for fervently, and that was his life; the parties in the tower and the way José described them, my God, I can't imagine what José had in his head to imagine such things; there were young men around, yes, and they did meet in Walter's rooms, not to have orgies but to talk and exchange experiences, Walter always wanted to know what real life was like, what happened beyond the walls of our chapel; those orgies happened only in José's imagination, I can assure you; when I heard him I said to myself, why is he inventing all that? I have to admit it hurt me, not because of what he said about me, although that was quite disparaging, but I was never a saint and God knows that. It hurt me for another reason. We'd been very honest with each other those times when we'd talked at the Flacuchenta, I'd really opened up to him and told him a lot of things about my life, and he betrayed me. The "Miss Jessica" of his fantasies could only have been invented based on the things I'd confessed to him. As you know, the past is fragile, a very thin layer over the things that surround memory and sometimes give it meaning. But anyway, let's go back to the beginning.

As I was saying, those first years in the house, I'd lock myself in my room at nights and tremble at the thought that he might be aware of my fear, that he might smell it and come and harm me. Then I started to see him as someone lost in the fog, just as fragile as I was, and I started to feel a kind of affection, and let him get close to me. You'll say I'm defending myself, but all I want to do is contradict what he said. You can think what you like. This is the truth, although I repeat, not everything he said about me is false, because he knew me well. It's true I'd been one of the gang, that I'd mixed with good-looking young men who didn't have any feelings. They didn't know anything about love, their hearts were like baseball gloves that supplied dirty blood to their bodies. I was with them and loved them, and then I ran away, though the path I took was just as twisted as before, what else could I do, that was my world, my

little world. People who've never been there will never understand, it'd be like trying to imagine the taste of a fruit we've
never eaten.

Miss Jessica was speaking slowly, and had stopped looking
at me. It was hot and I thought to call to the waitress to bring
us something cool, but I did nothing, I was afraid that any gesture from me would wake her from that hypnotic state. A number of questions were jostling in my head: had she spoken to
José before his death? who did the plural refer to in that message, that mysterious *we've found you*? had she gone to the
morgue to see the body? As I was thinking this, I noticed she
was not wearing high heels but low shoes. Marta had mentioned the sound of high heels receding into the distance.

You're probably assuming I loved Walter to distraction.
That's what people usually say, isn't it? My love was twofold, I
loved him as a woman and as someone devoted to God, which
I still am. Through him, I loved the dispossessed, people ship-
wrecked by life, who had never known love or affection, like
me, like José too. For people like that, the heart becomes dry
until it's as hard as a coyote's tooth or ground baked by the
sun. The heart turns into pure silence. Walter made life spring
up where before there was only dust and old bones, damage,
hatred. That was why I loved him, but not José. José had something dark and terrifying inside him, a stain on his soul that
sometimes appeared in his eyes. And I saw it right from the
first day.

That was why José betrayed him.

I shouldn't tell you this, but both are dead and very soon
you and I will also be dead. I'm a woman who believes in and
loves God, even though she has never seen Him, and if there's
one thing I know it's that José was Walter's Judas. José threw
him to the sharks, he was the one who invented the stories
that led to the downfall of the Ministry. Only he could have
gotten into his tower with those young men and taken those

absurd photographs while Walter wasn't there. The incriminating photographs that turned the Ministry into a heap of ashes. When the first accusations were made, the police investigated and didn't find anything, but then, as if by miracle, evidence came pouring in, all from boys identical to the ones José dealt with when he was spreading the word, don't you find that too much of a coincidence? He instructed them, told them what to say, bought their affections, I don't know with what, maybe with the Ministry's own money, which was a horrible, disgusting thing to do, I'm sorry, a religious woman shouldn't talk like that.

Sometimes I ask myself, when exactly did José start to plan his betrayal? why did he betray him? what on earth did Walter ever do to him apart from drag him out of the gutter, give him his dignity, show him a path to follow, and provide him with a home? Great men are always betrayed by their disciples or their favorite sons, who are closer to the light, the light they want to have all to themselves, and if they can't have it, they don't want anyone to have it. They want it so much, they prefer to destroy it. This is what I believe happened: José wanted the whole logistical apparatus of the Ministry to disappear, he wanted Walter to again be a fragile young man treading the sidewalks of the world, with José by his side, protecting him, keeping the beasts off him, giving him warmth. I believe José betrayed Walter because he loved him.

José talked about a fight that never took place in Moundsville, but what he did describe very well was that when he came to, they both wept. That image reduced me to tears: two men who had lost their way, suddenly realizing that something unites them, and that they will have to be together for the rest of their lives. That's very beautiful, and it only happens to the disinherited. It happened to me, too. But then comes the rest of your life. What starts well gradually acquires a bitter taste until somebody goes crazy. And that's because inside love, hate resides, a nasty animal waiting to hatch and take flight. That happened to José, and his wings never stopped growing. He wanted to take his revenge, but on what? He probably didn't even know that himself.

Walter's fall had to mean that the crown would pass to José. Walter disappeared, and that was his victory. But you must be thinking, what kind of victory is it to spend the rest of your life wracked with guilt, constantly harking back to the paradise you destroyed, the paradise you lost through your own selfishness and hate? That's how it was, José wanted to be Walter, to possess him completely, to be the only person who received his love, and in order to do that he had to destroy him. It wasn't for the luxury or the money, in that at least José was a true follower of Christ.

The one time I went into his cabin I realized how pure his hate was, and I said to myself, it is as devoid of greed and reasons as the blindest love, it is a clean uncontaminated hate. His hut was a bare space filled with books, an easy chair, a stool, a writing table, a mattress, and nothing more, no decoration, no reminder of the beautiful things there were in the world, in the lives of the common people. Nothing at all. Only austerity and discipline. It was obvious that the person who lived there was concerned only with his own soul. A strange silence seemed to hover in the atmosphere. There were no mirrors, only a single light over the chair. José's hatred for Walter is one of the purest, most uncontaminated things I've ever known. A motiveless hate that asks only to be exercised.

As the afternoon wore on, it was becoming increasingly more humid, so I asked for a lemonade. The noises of the street seemed to be carried ever more clearly on the air: scraps of conversation, horns, cars accelerating. Jessica did not seem to hear them. She lit a cigarette and continued her story.

José spent his days in his cabin in the garden, far from the everyday life of the house, and that protected him. It served his purposes. All that resentment would have been visible in the eyes, there's no way you can hide something like that every minute of the day, but with him being at a distance we just didn't see it. What happened in Colombia was another example. I don't know if you remember. José mentioned a party at a hotel, when Walter was depressed and I gave them drugs. Well, I'll tell you what really happened. It's true that Walter was sad, but not because he'd turned into a prima donna, as José's story suggested, but because he was genuinely hurt that his word was not being heard after so much effort and so much traveling, especially as, for him as for José, Latin America was the territory of his dreams. You can choose to believe me or not, but that night the drugs came out of José's bag. Half a kilo of cocaine and three bundles of twenty-four crack cigarettes. The three of us drank and snorted. Remember, we were children of the streets, all that was part of our environment. It was the first time I'd seen Walter taking drugs, and I confess that the reason I did it was fear, fear of being left behind, abandoned, like someone running through a maze afraid to let go of the hand leading her. That night something took possession of us; I remember hearing some kind of construction work going on in the distance and feeling that I was being buried alive. That fear drove me to look for strength, just as it did them. It wasn't a pleasant night, the fear didn't go away, it was there in our words, in our glances, and, of course, in the silence. I stayed out on the balcony, in case they started fighting. We were on the twelfth floor and it wasn't worth taking risks, anything was possible. They talked about the future of the Ministry. José said we should continue working in Latin America, expand, but Walter said no, better to carry on in our own territory, where we know what we're doing, this attempt has been a lesson to us, we should listen to God, hear what He's telling us through these failures. The same thing always happens when two men try to change the world: one prefers to stay within his own territory and the other wants to go out and knock down barriers; one of the two ends up badly, usually the one who goes outside, but in this case it was different because there was another element: resentment.

That night José felt frustrated and slit his wrists in his room, but they found him in time. Exactly as he told it, although I don't know if his motives where those he said. José was ready for anything. It's hard to see the danger when it's disguised as love and lives with you, when you see it every day and have stopped recognizing it and it doesn't surprise you. I never stopped seeing it, which is why one day I made up my mind to talk to Walter. I had to warn him and tried to find the words, but couldn't. I wasn't good at putting the blame on others, or speaking out of turn. My love for Walter was too strong. But in order to protect him, I was ready even to do that, so I talked to him on the plane during a trip to Charleston. I told him what I thought of José, how scared of him I was, how sure I was that he would end up hurting both him—Walter—and the Ministry; he let me speak without interruption, looking straight at me, his eyes like two letters blazing in the darkness, *a* and *f*, for example, standing for *always* and *forgive*, two words he used a lot; when I stopped speaking he hugged me in a fatherly way, and said, poor Jessica, what you must have suffered, feeling all that, being scared without my knowing it, without my being able to help you; he hugged me tighter and said, listen, listen carefully. What, Father? and he said, my heart, Jessica, do you hear it beating? Yes, Father, I hear it. Then remember, those little heartbeats are the life that you give me, through your love and faith. You are the one who protects my heart. While there is love in you, it will continue beating in my breast, whatever happens. He closed his eyes and we both cried. I felt relief for a few days, but then the fear returned.

When José started writing the book, there was a lull. We'd stopped going to the Flacuchenta together, so I was able to devote myself body and soul to Walter, to him and to prayer, because the call that God made to me was great and my answer a genuine one, although you may find that hard to believe. My devotion and my vocation are as strong as ever, do not doubt that for a second. The same could have been said of Walter, who was a pure soul; that was the only thing his burnished, muscular body had ever expressed, yes, it may have been a beautiful wrapping, but his strength came from inside, from his will and his love and his word. I don't want you to think that I'm some kind of fanatic. In talking of him I talk of God. Many people accused the Ministry of being a cult, like the Moonies or the Davidians; they accused it of stealing from believers, of selling false dreams to the working classes. Poor accusers, what ignorance and what wickedness, what energy expended on wickedness. Why don't they accuse the Church of Rome, with its marbles and alabasters and artistic salons? Churches are powerful because they represent something powerful: the faith of those who believe in them.

After the Ministry was destroyed, I devoted myself to study, I took two university courses, in theology and philosophy. For more than ten years I've been reading, learning about ideas, examining the images of devotion from the inside. When I first arrived at the Ministry I was seventeen, I was a scared girl, and in twelve years of spreading the word with Walter I turned into a good priest; today, with twelve years of university studies behind me, I still believe in Walter. I'm a monotheist. Nothing of what I learned in all those years has made me doubt what I felt about him, and if I could put the clock back and see the house in South Beach reemerge from the dust, I would renew my love and devotion to Walter, who represents the supreme idea of holiness.

I realized that she was about to finish, so I ventured to say, to ask rather, if Walter was so holy, why did he suddenly turn into a soldier and open fire when the police came for him?

Jessica cleared her throat and took a sip of coffee. She looked around, nervous again, and said: there were weapons in the house, I don't deny that, and the reason is that there was always money, a lot of money in cash. I never agreed with all that, but there were weapons and money. The way José tells it, it's as if Walter was a sniper or something like that, but it wasn't like that. José was in his cabin and didn't see anything, he imagined it all. But I was in the tower and I know that the people who kept shooting right up until the end were Jefferson and the bodyguards. There were bullet casings clattering on the floor, the boys were jumping from one window to another and throwing each other cartridge clips, everything was filling up with smoke but they carried on; remember they came from the underclass, the school of the street. A shoot-out was a game to them, and better still, it was against the law. While this was going on Walter was kneeling on the floor, with tears in his eyes and an expression that had stopped being human. When fire started to engulf the house, he ordered us to leave and he stayed behind. In my last image of him, he is silhouetted against the flames, bare-chested and with his arms open in the shape of a cross. The Lord decided at that moment to come and take him back and that is why nobody found any traces, of his body or anything. He vanished into thin air.

Having said this, she looked at her watch anxiously and said, it's getting late, now it's your turn to tell me why you're looking for me, and especially how you found me.

I hadn't expected that question, so instead of replying, I took the message out of my pocket and threw it on the table. *We've found you.* She looked at it in silence and nodded, then said, so it's because of this. I thought I saw, deep in her face, the beginnings of a smile. You traced the call back to the Coptic Church? I assume the answer is yes, otherwise we wouldn't be sitting here. Let me ask you another question, why are you interested in this story?

I came across it by chance, I said, a thread flung down in front of me that I decided to follow. I could have decided not to, but I did it for no other reason than that it was there. I did it because I could.

Jessica read the message again, and this time she did smile. Poor José, maybe he never even read it. Yes, I said, he did. I found it in his room, inside his book, *Encounters with Amazingly Normal People*. By the way, who was with you when you made the call? why the plural?

She left the paper on the table and said, I don't know what you're talking about. I insisted: if you'd been alone you would have said, "I've found you" wouldn't you? Jessica seemed confused and looked toward the door. That's none of your business, let me remind you I'm under no obligation to answer your questions, this is a pointless conversation, do I have to justify myself? well, I won't, but I will answer your question, the reason I used the plural is that I was referring to God, who is always with me. And now I have to go, they're waiting for me at the church.

She stood up, looking nervous, and walked toward the door. Before she reached it, I said, is God the guest in Room 1209? As I uttered the question and saw her turn, something welled up in my memory: her voice. I had heard it before. It was the voice from the first night. She came back to the table and said, what else do you know about me? I looked her in the eyes. I know you went to the morgue at the Notre Dame de France hospital to see José's body—actually I was starting to have doubts about that—and that you went there with somebody, I don't know who, perhaps with the mysterious William Cummings, is that his real name? For the first time she looked at me with a defiant expression, and said, the person you're referring to is a companion in faith, who's been with me on and off over the years. He has nothing to hide and has no connection with José, so I would ask you not to call him "mysterious";

he's no more mysterious than that young man who came in with you and is waiting for you at the back there, throwing those very crude glances at us, trying to figure out where our conversation is heading, do you think I didn't see him?

That's Momo, a young employee from the hotel. He brought me here because today is his day off, and he was coming to Tel Aviv to visit his mother. Why didn't he come and sit with us? asked Jessica, but then she snapped her fingers and said, I know why, he was the one who told you about my calls, about the message, about Room 1209, tell him to come here. I refused. He doesn't speak Spanish and he doesn't know anything about this story. She paused again, then asked: what do you find so strange in the message?

It's quite a coincidence that José decided to kill himself after reading it, don't you think? But you didn't know that. Why didn't you put your name on the message? did you think those three words would be enough to tell him it was you? Jessica's eyes filled with tears, and she said, I don't know, I didn't want to leave my name, maybe I felt scared again, I don't know, you said people do things without knowing why, just because they can, well, this was like that, believe me, there is no puzzle, I simply didn't want to.

Knowing you'd found him wasn't sufficient incentive to stay alive, I said, why do you think he killed himself? and another thing, from the message I assume you hadn't heard from him in quite some time, why were you looking for him? what was José running away from?

Miss Jessica took a deep breath and looked toward the door again. There are many things I haven't told you, she said. In the last years of the Ministry, José used a power of attorney signed by me to steal large sums of money. He would put some little phrase like "miscellaneous expenses," "contribution for Oregon Street," "infrastructure," and nobody asked any questions; at first it would be amounts like seven thousand dollars, but then they crept up to twenty-five thousand, and once even fifty thousand. He must have had someone advising him, because after a while it became very difficult to understand what he had done, and impossible to trace. Of course there was still money left in the Ministry, but it was all very strange. So I told Walter and he summoned José to the tower one night, just the two of them alone. He asked me to listen from behind the door, because he wanted me to help him figure it out afterwards. Walter said to him, are you taking money out, José? what do you need it for? He said he wasn't taking it out for himself but for charitable works, and he didn't know he had to justify himself. But Walter insisted. Look, brother, there are days when you withdrew seventy thousand dollars, why? what do you need so much money for? I want you to know something, José, if you want money just tell me straight out and I'll give you all you want, this is just between you and me and all you have to do is ask, you know that, but don't go taking out money here and there like that, it makes everyone nervous.

José didn't own up, he denied it, saying that these sums of money were not for him but for charitable works, that Walter could go out on the streets and see what he had done, everything was there, invested in young people and in reformed prostitutes who were worth more than that money. Walter wouldn't listen to him anymore, he sat down on the floor and asked José to leave him alone. A week later the police arrived, doesn't that seem strange to you?

I was about to speak, because I still had a lot of questions, but she raised her finger to her lips and said, that's enough now, we've talked for a long time, I suggest you go back to Jerusalem and think about everything I've told you. In a couple of days I'll get in touch with you and we'll continue our talk. But I want you to know that I didn't go to the morgue. The last thing I want is to see a dead body, let alone José Maturana's. I saw him from a distance at that cocktail party, and left again immediately. Then I saw him during his talk. Actually I just heard him, because I was sitting at the back of the room with my eyes closed. It hurt me just to look at him, anyway I can't go on, goodbye. She left the café and crossed the street without once turning back.

The highway to Jerusalem seemed shorter now, in spite of the fact that the army stopped us several times. The Jerusalem number plates helped Momo to get through, but he constantly had to give explanations and show his safe conduct. We soon arrived at the military checkpoint on Jaffa Road and passed the hillock that leads into the valley.

There again was the tortured face of the city.

On the horizon we saw the skeletons of buildings that had burned after the first explosions and were now black and covered in dust. Eviscerated apartment blocks, twisted girders, towers turned into huge torches, heaps of broken glass, soot-blackened windows like empty eye sockets. On the corners, mountains of garbage from which foul-smelling streams flowed and buzzards pecked in search of food.

The whole city was laid out before us, and Momo pointed it all out to me. There was the Jewish district of Mea Shearim, with its synagogues and its Hasidic population; there, Bekaa, which had previously been Arab; to the south, Ohel Moshe; the elegant Rehavia and Kiryat Shmuel, near the hotel, and farther out, Talpiot; then the Arab districts, Katamón, Beit Safafa, and East Jerusalem, the German, Greek, and American colonies, and in the middle, like a giant jellyfish run aground on a coral reef, the Old City, that much sought-after treasure.

All this, said Momo, is no more than the entrance to a place that can't be seen from here but is down there, the Valley of Josaphat, where the trumpets will sound for the Last Judgment, because this city, basically, is made for death. Everyone's death. That's why it's the great necropolis, the cemetery of East and West.

I looked with interest at the stumps, mutilations, and pustules of that capital still under siege, which seemed to keep reserves of strength in its centuries-old memory that might allow it to rise again. The sun was setting.

The sharp crack of a grenade broke the fantasy and Momo started the engine. Let's get out of here, he said, and may God protect us.

It was after five in the afternoon by the time we got back to the hotel. As I crossed the lounge on the first floor, one of the organizers of the ICBM approached and said, my dear friend, are you all right, we missed you at the round table this morning, I hope you weren't in any kind of accident? I looked at the board with the conference schedule and read, *11:00 A.M. Round table. On the manifold forms of remembering, evaluating, understanding, and transmitting a life.* My name was on the list of speakers. How embarrassing, it had been at eleven in the morning.

I'm so sorry, I had some urgent business to attend to in Tel Aviv and got back late, but to tell the truth, I didn't know about this, I forgot to look at the program before I left, you must forgive me, please add my name to any of the remaining round tables, I beg you, but he said, don't worry, my friend, life is full of imponderables, we just have to carry on with the conference, we'll wait for your next contribution, he said, adjusting his glasses, and added, I'm sure it'll be worth the wait, in fact, I can tell you that there's a great deal of expectation building up among the public and the specialized press.

I took my leave shamefacedly, how could I have forgotten something like that? Then I ran to my room, eager to get my encounter with Miss Jessica in Tel Aviv down on paper.

When I got to my room, I found a note from Marta saying, take a look at these papers, I'm going out with Amos, don't wait up for me. It was the medical report on Maturana. I didn't understand most of it, but a few things caught my eye: Kaposi's sarcoma, pustules in the liver, *pneumocystis carinii*, fungus in the mouth and the wall of the esophagus, dying lymphocytes, presence of the HIV retrovirus in the ganglions, plus a series of figures I couldn't make head or tail of. He had AIDS! I immediately went to the table and started writing.

The next day, the telephone jolted me out of my sleep, like an arm grabbing me by the neck and pulling me out of deep water. It was Rashid, and he was in the King David, he had come to hear Sabina Vedovelli and suggested we meet down in the bar. I told him to wait for me. I threw water on my face and walked to the elevators, but when I got downstairs I found that Rashid was not alone. He was with Kosztolányi, Supervielle, and the head of Tiberias, Ebenezer Lottmann.

When I arrived, the three men looked at me.

Rashid rose to greet me and said, I think you all know each other? I felt somewhat ill at ease. The only one who seemed pleased to see me was Kosztolányi, who said, my dear colleague, what a pleasure you can be with us, would you like a coffee? we were talking about the latest events. I assumed a surprised expression and asked, which events, exactly? Supervielle threw me a sardonic glance and said, which events? well, Maturana's suicide is . . . striking, wouldn't you say? I'd go so far as to call it outlandish; perhaps the ICBM should suspend the scheduled sessions and host a panel with the title *Interpretations and Variations on a Suicide*, what do you think? and he added, in an irritable tone: everyone's interest has shifted away from the lectures and debates because of this unfortunate event, and obviously a suicide deserves our attention, but . . . isn't it, when you get down to it, merely the story of a man reaching the limits of his contradictions? In France, nobody would hesitate to call that famous Ministry a cult, and of course, between ourselves, what they did would be considered a crime; both the pastor, may he rest in peace, and his guru, may he also rest in peace, if they were French would have been put behind bars and nobody would think of them as heroes. Anyway, sighed Supervielle, poor man, although I'm not sure his tragedy is worth the incineration of a conference like this.

As he spoke, Supervielle observed Lottmann out of the corner of his eye to see his reactions, but the publisher, who was apparently used to having his face scrutinized like that, did not move a single muscle. Then Kosztolányi said, of course, a conference of this kind, with international delegates and in a city like this, with all that it symbolizes, has enough going for it to sustain such a blow, and that's what will happen, I don't have the slightest doubt, in fact your talk, my dear Edgar, was an example of how the public's interest did not fade at all, don't you all agree?

Rashid and I nodded, but Lottmann still sat there, motionless and hieratic, until he raised his hand, moved it to his glass of mineral water, and said, what I think about the subject has more to do with my work as a publisher, I believe that if Maturana's story can be well written, it would make for a very good book; anyone, however poor his instinct, would be able to recognize that and it's a pity that the protagonist did away with himself so early, although his own final suicide is excellent, it gives the story an incomparable romantic aura, a perfect ending for a narrative on modern violence and the role of faith in social redemption, something very shocking and very contemporary, a strong, hard-edged urban narrative, almost a piece of narrative journalism tracing the lives of each of the characters up until the conference starts, and then, bang, the suicide, the mystery of why he took his own life and the endless questions this creates in the others, in those who remain on the side of life, and of course the different interpretations, and what if, instead of being a suicide, and this is just for the sake of argument, it turns out to have been a murder, then we would get into the territory of the noir novel, an extraordinary noir novel in which the same sociological elements would become the natural theater for a tragedy, the story of a solitary man who is redeemed by God and who in the end takes a secret to the grave to him, because somebody, who? has eliminated him to stop him divulging it, who could be the killer? I found myself interrupting him: it wasn't a murder, Mr. Lottmann, I thought that too, at first, but now I'm sure Maturana committed suicide. He was very sick, and he also felt guilty for a whole series of things he did in the past and his relationship with the Ministry. It was a suicide, believe me.

Lottmann looked at me in surprise, and said, ah, my friend, obviously as a writer you weren't going to let such a story get away ... I see you've been doing some research, am I wrong in thinking you've been making notes on the subject with a view to a future book? I was not sure what to say, but I nodded: yes, it's possible I will do one, I don't know yet, but I have been making notes and thinking a lot about the subject.

They all looked at me, waiting for me to say more. Fortunately, Ebenezer Lottmann spoke again: well, if you write the book, I'll be more than happy to read it, my friend. I thanked him. Then he added: it would also be interesting to find that book Maturana mentioned, what was it called again? I told him the title, *Encounters with Amazingly Normal People.* Lottmann took out a notebook and asked me to repeat it; thank you, my friend, I'll ask my office to find a copy so we can get some idea of it, now that the author has died it could be a real hit, I can see it now, I think I'll buy the rights anyway, you never know.

I had a copy of the book in my room, and knew details of the story that nobody else at that table knew, but I kept quiet. Supervielle spoke again, and said, the world is full of good subjects through which we can gain a deeper understanding of the human soul, just look at our old continent, filled with anonymous gestures and heroic lives that are not always recognized but nevertheless form the true profile of the century; that's what comes to my mind when I think of my two chess players, Oslovski and Fiø, characters who may appear insignificant in the light of History, with a capital H, but in whom a profound truth is lodged.

Deeply moved, Kosztolányi said, you're right, my dear Edgar, it's in that kind of simple adventure that we find the small print of history. Rashid and I nodded again without saying anything, and Lottmann remained silent. Then he said, excuse me, gentlemen, took out his cell phone and called his office; in front of us, he asked his assistant to look for *Encounters with Amazingly Normal People* by Walter de la Salle, and to make an offer for the translation rights. Supervielle's lip started trembling, as if he were holding back a fit of anger, but all he said was, it's nearly eleven, gentlemen, Sabina Vedovelli will be starting soon.

2.

STORMS

fter Sabina Vedovelli's talk, Eve Studios invited those present to a cocktail party in the third-floor bar—the most exclusive—at which clips from her films would be shown, along with an exhibit of photographs and videos of important prize ceremonies, and a documentary on her tours around the different film festivals of the world, from Cannes to San Francisco, from Tokyo to New York, with the title *Sexocalypse Now!*

On the invitation poster for the cocktail party was a picture of a very young Sabina in the position known as "the mountain range"—or "looking at Constantinople"—about to stick a carrot inside her. It was the front cover of her first feature-length film. To tell the truth, her story had left us all both surprised and captivated. To my mind, the way that young woman had found her way out of her many difficulties and transformed herself made Sabina Vedovelli, in spite of her eccentric costumes and her body pumped full of Botox and silicone, seem like one of the most fragile people at the conference. Unlike some of the others, I did not have a moment's doubt as I entered the Heroes of Masada room on the third floor of the hotel, to see some images of her work, have a drink with her, and congratulate her on her lecture.

I was one of the first to arrive, which might have been why I found her at the door. She gave me a kiss on the cheek and said, thank you, my dear colleague, thank you for coming to this modest reception, which we are holding as mark of affec-

tion; I have to tell you that my husband and I would like to talk
with you later, if that's possible, there's a subject we'd like to
discuss with you. This greatly surprised me. I confessed my
admiration and said, whatever you like, Sabina, after hearing
your talk I admire you and have even grown quite fond of you,
so of course I'm at your disposal to talk about anything you
want.

Next up was her husband, Kay, who gave me an affectionate handshake (I looked closely at his arms and it was true that
one of them did not move). He was a tall, impressive-looking
man, elegantly thin and slightly snobbish, wearing a silk scarf
and a casual but very elegant suede jacket, the very image of a
wealthy fifty-something left-leaning European intellectual. A
screen at the back of the room was showing images of Sabina
performing various kinds of sexual acts, stunning views of her
buttocks, legs raised, close-ups of her vagina, huge penises, her
face twisted, lips sucking, expressions of pleasure . . . As the
images were silent, I had to imagine the moaning; her acting
was so magnificent that it echoed in the mind, and the sounds
she made could be heard perfectly, and so, with a glass of
Glenfiddich in my hand, I was letting myself be carried away
by the images, unworldly and obscene at the same time, when
Sabina approached and said, I assume you speak Italian? I
read in your biography that you live in Rome. Yes, I said, of
course I speak Italian. She took me aside and said, let's talk a
while in that delightful language, come, have another drink.

She was wearing torn jeans, which made her look very
youthful. I told her I had been impressed by her ability to fight,
come what may, to find the strength to overcome everything,
and she said, thank you, my friend, who better than an artist
can appreciate what that means, living to please other people
is worse than riding a tiger, and just as dangerous; I'm sure
you'll agree with me that living for your art requires you to
weave a net that will catch you when you fall, to catch you

every time you fall, making sure you don't hit the bottom but stop somewhere halfway, from where it's easier to get back up again, but tell me, what kind of subjects do you write about? I took another sip of my whiskey and said, somewhat shamefacedly, I write about things I consider important, friendship and separation, solitude, the past, betrayal and love, the same old subjects, I suppose, the ones you find in writers like Andreas Stiflit, Chekhov or Piotr Bordonave, and even in less well-known writers like Péguy or Bernanos. She said, and do you like Italian literature? Well, I said, we could spend several days talking about all the wonderful things in Italian literature, where do I start? Carlo Emilio Gadda, Bufalino, Carlo Levi and Primo Levi, the poetry of Ungaretti, that remarkable poem by Salvatore Quasimodo that says: *Everyone stands alone at the heart of the world / pierced by a ray of light / And suddenly it's evening*, I may have gotten it wrong, I don't have a good memory; and Calvino and Sciascia and Boccaccio, who wrote about people sheltering from the plague who get together to tell stories, rather as we are doing in this besieged conference, anyway, I said, Italian literature has always been with me, I should say that I learned your language when I was a child and it's always been close to my heart.

As I said this, I glanced out of the corner of my eye at one of the plasma screens and saw what she would have called a "multiethnic and multiracial double penetration," because one of the penises was black. Noticing that my attention had shifted away from her, Sabina exclaimed, oh, I can't believe it! that's *Shadows of Lust*! I'm sorry, my friend, this documentary is a gift from Kay and I don't know what's in it, so it's a constant surprise to me, look at those images, we shot them more than fifteen years ago and I still remember the arguments we had about the message of that scene; one of the associate producers thought it would be more commercial if the African penis, which for anthropomorphic reasons is larger, penetrated the anus, but Kay and I thought that would be sending out the wrong message, as if the anus was the dark part of the body and therefore the natural place for a black man, which didn't satisfy us from the political point of view, so we said, let's take a commercial risk for the sake of an idea that's not only esthetic but also ethical, an idea of social harmony, and so the anal penetration was done by the Caucasian and the one from in front was given to the African, a way of saying to the world, let's have done with preconceived racial ideas, let's respect each other's differences, and well, I think we made our point, we've never been like other producers, who are ready to do anything to be commercial, no, we've always been consistent and perhaps that's the key to our success, anyway, I'm sorry if I changed the subject somewhat, but now I'm going to come to the point and ask you a question, do you think José Maturana's suicide was premeditated? do you think he had been planning for some time to do away with himself in the middle of the conference in order to give his death an esthetic dimension by turning it into a theatrical *mise en scène*? The question took me by surprise and I did not know what to reply, I had assumed that I was the only person trying to make sense of José Maturana's act, at least the only one thinking about it beyond the typical banal comments on his motives and so on.

My husband and I, said Sabina Vedovelli, have talked a lot about it and we see that final gesture as something highly poetic; Kay has been making notes for a possible screenplay dramatizing his life, and that's when we thought of you, because after all you are the only genuine writer at the conference and we're very interested in your vision of what happened. We'd like to make you a formal offer and that's why I'm inviting you to have dinner with us in our suite tonight, could you come? you don't have any other engagement? I said that, unless I had some unexpected appointment with my Maker— like that character in Somerset Maugham—I was free and ready to oblige. She laughed and said: oh no, touch wood! Come and see us then, it's in the right wing of the hotel, third floor, Suite 9D, we'll expect you at eight tonight. I'll be there, Sabina, and she said, excellent, now enjoy our canapés, I'm going to greet our other guests.

One minute before the hour, I was knocking at the door of 9D, the Judith and Holofernes Suite.

It was Kay who opened the door, still dressed casually, but so exquisitely that it made me regret my commonplace costume of blue shirt and khaki pants. He invited me into a luxurious apartment. In the middle was a sunken area covered in rugs and cushions and lit with indirect lighting. Soft music was playing, a concerto, I thought, possibly by Handel, although I was no expert. There was a glass dome above us, through which the stars looked down, indifferent to what was happening below. Scotch? he said, opening a drinks cabinet with dozens of bottles glinting agreeably in the light. Sabina will be here in a minute, I know she's already put you in the picture about what we want and why we've invited you here tonight.

Then he asked me to choose a whiskey, so I looked at the labels and selected the bottle of Lagavulin, which I had discovered years ago in a novel by Vázquez Montalbán. Please sit down and make yourself comfortable while I bring some ice. The large cushions were really welcoming. The windows were closed and covered with prints of the city.

Before coming to the conference, we looked at the biographies of the delegates, including yours of course, and now, in the light of what happened to Maturana, we believe you're the perfect person to write his story. You can write it as fiction or nonfiction, whichever you prefer; then our team will adapt it as necessary in order to turn it into a terrific movie. Sabina and I had been thinking, even before coming here, of writing something about this city, but the best things are always the most unexpected, and bang! the story just turns up, like an animal poking its nose out. That's why we always have to be alert. The pastor's life, reaching a masterly climax with his suicide: what a fantastic subject! I know we shouldn't talk that way about somebody who's died, but I suspect he wanted to make his death a ceremony, a theatrical performance, so I applaud, well done, reverend, excellent work! It made such an impression on us that we went to the morgue to see his body, just to make sure it really was a suicide, and there was no doubt about it, those vertical cuts in his veins said one thing very clearly: dear friends, I'm not joking, this is it. On hearing this, I thought: so it was you . . . Marta, I don't think much of your powers of observation if you couldn't recognize Sabina Vedovelli!

Suddenly Sabina appeared from one of the corridors at the far end of the room. She was wearing thigh-length white leather boots, a miniskirt, and a white latex top, an aggressive Seventies-style outfit in sharp contrast to her cobalt-blue eye makeup and lipstick. Seeing her gave me a sense of calm, like the blue domes in certain towns in the Mediterranean. What are you drinking? she asked, and Kay said, whiskey, shall I pour your martini? it's ready. She drank two tiny sips and went to the door. The dinner had arrived. A bellhop came in, pushing a trolley with silver trays. He arranged everything on the table, lit two candles, uncorked and poured the Sancerre wine, leaving the bottle in the ice bucket, and withdrew with a little bow. Only then did Sabina greet me with a rapid handshake and we sat at the table.

The discussion started immediately. I'm sorry to be so direct, my friend, but I'd like to ask you a question by way of introduction . . . What's your favorite part of a woman's body? Without thinking I said: the buttocks. I love touching them, sinking my fingers into them, sucking them, feeling their girth, appreciating their hardness, resistance, and volume, finding architectural similes, domes of mosques, vaults, opera houses, stupas, ziggurats, coliseums, and pantheons, I love reciting poems by Pietro Aretino to them and proclaiming myself their slave, looking at the sky and finding likenesses in the clouds or in the mountains, anyway, the buttocks, without doubt.

Sabina cracked a smile and said, I like your style, for a moment I was afraid your answer would be: I love the outline of the hands or the delicate shape of the instep or even the shadow of a beauty spot on the cheek, which is what hypocrites reply, even if while they're saying it they're looking at the crotch of the woman walking past. People say empty, stupid phrases that reflect their fears and that insubstantial vision of the world that's so common today in so many groups, the dictatorship of verbal, ideological, and physical asepsis, God, that desire to smother the animal nature of the body, ugh, I also like Pietro Aretino, do you remember any of his poems? Of course, I said, I know a lot of them, and she refilled the glasses and said, let's hear one, tonight should be filled with poetry.

> *Open your thighs, my darling mine,*
> *That I may see your wondrous rose,*
> *That lovely hole where soft hair grows,*
> *Gate to my dreams! O honey fine!*
> *And having made that journey south*
> *And tasted fruit of such delight*
> *Then turn I must, to end the night,*
> *And plant my tool within your mouth.*

Sabina grinned with pleasure and raised her glass: to Aretino, the poet of the cunt and the pleasures of the ass! As we clinked our glasses, a drop of Sancerre spilled on the tablecloth, and she put her finger in it and crossed herself. Ah, how I love the love that is sincere and human, the love of the body, the clitoris and the cavernous textures of the penis and the labia, that's the most important, most daring revolu-

tion in the world today, and it's what Kay and I try to demonstrate through the stories we tell at Eve, stories that both
entertain and convey models of thought, stories that are
instructive and, at the same time, real, performed by men and
women who sweat and ejaculate and shit, the last bastion of
a truth that's on the verge of disappearing from the world forever, and not because of a war, the kind threatening this city
and of which this city is a symbol, but because of something
worse, the war of infinite human stupidity, a siege just as
cruel, just as terrifying, as those waged with bombs and guns,
Eve is fighting that war in hand to hand combat, or should I
say "body to body," because it's in the body that it must be
won, and I tell you, my friend, that we are prepared to use all
the resources we have and even die in the attempt, we will
save and spread that profound truth of the body, my God, we
are made of blood and bones and flesh and the juice that
moistens our vaginas, not only of prayers and empty words
and polite phrases; our heads are in our crotches, setting off
a ruddy geyser of sperm; there is no art or doctrine uncon-
nected with those liquids, because much of art, basically, is an
immersion in those liquids, a series of blind discoveries in
primitive waters, like the harmonious wandering of nomadic
fish, for example, everything that an artist can extract from
that dark cave and bring out into the light, making others see
it, that is great art, my friend, but there are fewer and fewer
of us, hence the importance of going as deep as possible, into
the essence, rejecting the light and frivolous, fleeing anything
that lacks that patina of brilliance that the parthenogenesis of
the Earth gives certain metals, anyway, it is urgent to act, this
civilization is mortally wounded and the duty of Eve, our
duty, is to be the guardians of that ancient nobility of ideas
and feelings that once allowed great art to exist, that is the
only thing we possess, as I'm sure you will already have noted
at the conference, it is we who are really under siege, a small

group of men and women telling stories in the midst of disaster, convinced that in doing so we are protecting something essential, something we can't lose and for which it's worth risking all, with all our strength and talent, we are knights of something that's about to die, an order or lodge in the greatest poetic sense.

Sabina paused and sipped at her wine. Her cheeks had flushed as she spoke and she seemed dazed. She again looked me in the eyes and said, I suppose you must be asking yourself why I'm telling you all this, aren't you? I was about to agree, but noted that, like the others, her question was rhetorical, a prolepsis, because she went on, obviously I didn't ask you here only to tell you about our battles, but because we want you to join us, to fight at our side, to join Eve Studios as a creator of stories, beginning with the story of José Maturana, a story with great potential. We've imagined a movie that tells that adventure, that goes back to the beginnings, to the great secrets of life, that asks questions about the divine and the human and shows us a way, do you follow me?

I said yes, and Sabina filled my glass again.

Before I could say anything, Kay spoke up, saying: we are willing to give you a check for two hundred thousand euros, right now, so that you can start work on something that could be called, as a working title, *The Passionate Pastor*, something like that, I even think it would be a good idea to include the word Christ in the title, what do you think, darling? and she said, I don't know, I like "pastor," or even "priest," it would arouse more morbid curiosity because it includes the idea of pedophilia in its semantic field, which would allow us to make it more combative and accusatory, but there'll be time to discuss that.

Kay continued: anyway, we're interested in the story and we believe you're the best person to write it, given that you were here and saw him. By the way, did you have the opportunity to meet him? I said yes, I had spoken with him at the opening cocktail party, but did not say anything about Jessica or the book or of course the message. We could see about that later.

Good, said Kay, you knew him, you remember his voice, his figure, his style, that will make it possible for you to recreate him in verbal and at the same time philosophical terms, and I say to you right now, don't worry about inventing sex scenes, we have some very talented people who specialize in creating them from any text, I assure you you'll be surprised, they would be capable of making a sex scene from the opening chapter of the *Critique of Pure Reason*, that's why what you have to provide is a literary version that holds up by itself, that's all we need; the publication rights will be yours, all that matters to us is the adaptation rights, and if it turns into a box office hit you'll receive royalties, do you understand? We only ask that you deliver it within six months, do you think you can do that?

While I was thinking of a way to accept the commission that would not reveal my precarious situation, Kay interrupted me: we know you've been out of circulation for more than two years for health reasons and haven't published anything in quite a while, but contrary to what others might think, in our eyes that makes you an even more attractive proposition for this project, since we assume you're less influenced than the others by all the shit that's been dumped on us in the last two years when you were absent, and believe me, there was a lot of shit; and as far as the previous shit is concerned, I assume that being alone will have allowed you to cleanse yourself, and that's important, it means that in your subsequent work that wisdom you've acquired with distance will manifest itself, that translucent condition of the soul, do you accept our offer?

It was the first contract I'd had in front of me since my illness, one related, moreover, to something that had already become an obsession. I accept, I said, I'll write the story of José Maturana within six months.

Kay stood up, went to his study and came back with a folder. He took out a contract with my name printed on it and said, please read it, and if you agree print your initials on each page and sign the last. He handed me a pen, I wrote EH on all the pages and signed at the end. When I had done that, he opened a checkbook from Citibank and wrote me out a check for two hundred and one thousand euros, explaining that the extra thousand was to cover bank and postal charges. He blew on it to dry the ink and handed it to me, then shook my hand. Sabina gave me a kiss and again filled the glasses for a toast.

Then we ate herrings and smoked salmon with vodka. We talked about cinema and literature, Cassavetes and George Cukor, the epigrams of Svellenk, *Kristin Lavransdatter*. I asked Kay if there really was a newspaper in Norway called *Morgen-bladet*, as mentioned on the first page of Knut Hamsun's *Hunger*, and he said, of course there is, I read it every day, it's the national newspaper.

As he talked about a film version of a book by Daphne du Maurier we started to hear explosions, with increasingly shorter intervals between them. The fifth one made the building shake and Kay said, damn, that fell close to here. The sky lit up and its glow entered the room through the glass dome. The suite was flooded with bluish electric light, which made our faces look ghostly.

The subsequent explosions ruined the atmosphere of the dinner, so I put down my knife and fork and announced that I was going back to my room, which seemed to relieve them. It looked as if it might be a difficult night. When I was already at the door, Kay handed me a card with all the information I needed to contact them, and said, call any time you need something or have any doubts, our way of working is based on trust and friendship. I thanked him. When I said goodbye to Sabina I saw two purple rings around her eyes, and an inflamed vein or nerve just under the skin throbbing in her face like a small uneasy heart.

As I walked out into the corridor, the explosions continued.

The lights were flickering so much that it was impossible to walk more quickly. I passed marble-clad reception rooms, wide staircases with handwoven carpets, polished doors, but there was not a soul about. The hotel was one huge abandoned house and from outside came the noise of the bombs, as if a loudly howling wolf was eating what remained of the night.

My body is torn to shreds and my skin red-hot, said Marta when I entered the room. She was dancing about naked, completely drunk. But I'm happy, I want to spend my life with this burning, these pains that emerge after pleasure, oh, I want to sing, I want the walls to let my voice through and everyone to hear me and know about my happiness, I want the angels of this holy city to celebrate with me, instead of the bombs and the fires, I want the last judgment to find us singing, let's drink, the world is going to end! I feel calm and fulfilled, I'm sorry, I think I'm in love . . .

She went into the bathroom and from there called out, don't wait for me, I need a long restorative shower, then you can tell me where you were and what you've been doing, what time is it? what does it matter where the hands of the clock are, the important thing is where we are, don't you think? I said something but she had stopped listening, so I started making notes on my dinner with Kay and Sabina, trying not to think about the explosions. To cheer myself up I looked at the check from Citibank, a figure I had never before seen in relation to money, let alone money that would soon be mine. I was doing this when something novel and unforeseen happened. Another shell roared, the building shook, and the electricity went out. I stood up and went out on the balcony. There were a few flashes still visible, but the whole city was in darkness. I gazed for a while at that thick blackness, feeling slightly dizzy, and heard voices from the lower floors. People were opening windows and, like me, coming out on the balconies.

I went back into the room and heard Marta calling from the bathroom, why did the light go out? has something happened? I opened the door and said, we have to go down to reception, there's a lot of bombing tonight, let's go, hurry up.

She put on one of the white bathrobes and we went out into the corridor, where others were lighting the way with cigarette lighters. We ran to the stairs and found a swarm of frightened guests. I was sure the light would come back on or that the hotel's generator would start working before we got down to the first floor, but neither happened. Marta looked for my hand and squeezed hard. I hate the dark, she murmured, which you may think is stupid coming from a country that's in darkness most of the time, but that's how it is, my analyst says it's related to sexual fears, he may be right.

I saw the backs of the people moving in front of me in rhythm with their steps. Whenever one lighter went out another flared up, and so we had light all the time. By the time we got to reception I felt that I was in the bowels of the earth, the gallery of a mine dug centuries ago. Outside, the explosions were increasing in intensity and we were asked to keep calm. The manager stood up on a chair and said, we'll go down a few floors to the sports club. We'll be safe there because it's an air raid shelter, but in any case there's no danger, it's purely routine, the light will come on again any minute now, could I ask you please to form groups of twenty and carry on down, it's vital that everyone stays calm.

Near us somebody said: I know what happened, the defenders cut the lights off because a squadron of enemy planes has gotten through the antiaircraft batteries and anti-missile radar and is on its way here. The defense planes are already flying overhead. There's going to be a battle in the sky, planes will crash onto the roofs and there'll be fires, may God help us. Marta got scared and squeezed my hand hard. Another voice said: a missile of enormous power is heading straight for us from long range, that's why they cut the electricity and made us go down, but a second voice rejected that, saying, long range missiles with nuclear warheads move according to pre-established GPS systems, and just turning the lights out won't save a city from the impact, that might have been true in the days of biplanes and the Red Baron.

The sports club, with its sauna and Turkish baths and muscle-building machines, was covered in tiles. The groups advanced slowly, somewhat inhibited by the funereal atmosphere of the place. Marta and I sat down in a corner, on the track of a treadmill, and waited for everything to pass. It was only when she laid her head on my chest that I realized she was crying. Nothing's going to happen, it's just routine, in a minute the light will come back on, relax, but she said, that's not why I'm crying, I wish my sadness were only fear, no, I'm crying because of Amos, I'm crying because I've realized that I love him with all my soul and because at this moment, when a woman needs her lover's embrace, he's embracing another woman, protecting another woman; I know he would be capable of putting himself in front of a grenade to save her, and here I am, wrapped in a bathrobe, with my body still trembling because of him, but I'm alone, in a poetic sense I mean, please don't take it badly.

I interrupted her and said, I understand you but don't think too much, and don't keep going on about it, any moment now the generator will come on and everything will be the way it was. Then Marta said, you're an angel, why the hell didn't I fall in love with you? it would have been simpler. To tell the truth it never even occurred to me.

And what about your planned article on the life of a doctor in a city under siege? I don't think I'll do it, said Marta, I'm too involved personally and I wouldn't be objective; I don't want to violate journalistic ethics, that was one of the first things I learned in this fucking profession, ethics, and I'm not going to throw that overboard now. I think I'll go with my earlier idea, something on Maturana and his tragic death, a summary of his life and the circumstances of his death, all that spiel, of course I'll have to rely a lot on you, my dear, I'm a bit of a disaster when it comes to organizing my work. By the way, how did it go in Tel Aviv?

I told her about my encounter with Jessica, adding something I forgot to include in my notes, which is that she had been with the Universal Coptic Church for ten years, first in Miami, then in Bolivia and Ecuador, then in Nairobi, and finally in Tel Aviv; she had donated the property she had inherited from the Ministry to the order and thanks to that had been allowed to jump the queue in being assigned to the Tel Aviv branch, which was closer to the tomb of Jesus, where every true Christian longed to be.

The story seemed to calm Marta down, so much so that she stopped sobbing and was now making circles with her finger, saying, Amos is turning into an obsession, I can't stop thinking about him, I feel his warmth and his smell, I feel his touch, being a woman is the dumbest thing in the world, always falling in love at the most inappropriate time, damn it, I'd rather be a male who fucks and forgets, so I said, but Amos hasn't forgotten you, as far as I know, he simply isn't here, that's all, don't think too much, don't let your imagination run riot, think about your life just forty-eight hours ago, isn't that too short a time to be making such a big thing out of this?

Marta looked at me with a hint of annoyance: you're talking like an attorney, someone who analyzes and dissects, not like a writer, don't you know that literature is filled with cases like mine? cases of women who turn their lives upside down overnight for love, without looking back? have you forgotten *Twenty-four Hours in a Woman's Life* by Stefan Zweig? I mean, that woman took half the time I did, and I have more of an excuse than her, because I'm in the middle of a war, where love affairs are common because the fragility of life is so evident, have you forgotten Malraux's *La condition humaine*? You should know all that.

Look, I said, I've just come out of a long period of silence and illness, surrounded by people with greenish skin and eyes bloodshot with hatred. People sick with emphysema, the swelling of the pulmonary tissue, who think they can't breathe because of the others, and that's why they look at them with the silent hatred of the weak, who can't act on their hatred but only feel it. Having been there I've developed strong nerves. My sensors are covered with a layer of what might be ice, like a plane in a cold airport, and I react slowly, like those who've been in this siege for a long time. Don't ask me for tears I don't have, don't ask me to screw up my eyes in anxiety. At the moment all I feel is tired and sleepy.

Murmurs could be heard. The shadows around us were engaged in agitated discussion. Suddenly there was a movement, the arrival of another group of guests in the protected cave of the gym. Some came and sat down with us, no doubt haggard and resigned. We could barely see them, until a woman said: we're going to lose everything, who had the terrible idea of holding the conference in this dead city? When the light comes back I'm going up for my things and getting out of here, I should have done that earlier. Damn it, this is all my fault.

She was a woman of fifty, slightly weather-beaten, but still proud and beautiful. She was wearing tight jeans and Texan boots. As she bent, her backside protruded over her pants and part of her buttocks appeared, revealing a triangle of black thread and a tattoo with the opposing signs of the yin and the yang. Her hair had been dyed thousands of times in different shades and the roots were iridescent lines; her nails were purple half moons, with white tips.

Seeing her distress I said, don't worry, the generator will start up again any moment now, in no time at all we'll be back in our rooms. She looked at me angrily and said, this is a cold, inhospitable place, without windows or ventilation, ugh, I hate enclosed spaces, look how my muscles are tightening, look at my pulse, don't you see I'm shaking like a jelly? I suffer from claustrophobia, I don't know why the hell I'm here, so I said, come, let's chat a little, are you a delegate at the conference? She shook her head and said, no, I came on my own account, do you think I can smoke here? oh hell, I'll make an effort not to smoke, pleased to meet you, my name's Egiswanda but everyone calls me Wanda, it's easier to remember, the truth is, I've been very alone in the last few hours, so alone, you can't imagine how much . . . So I said to her, you have a lovely accent, you're not by any chance . . . ? Yes, she said, I'm Brazilian, I was born in Sao Paulo but I grew up partly in New York and partly in Miami, my parents emigrated when I was a girl, I've been many things, but mainly a nurse at the Marieldorf Memorial Hospital in Detroit, anyway, I'm sorry, I don't want to bother you.

Marta, who had been silent so far, said, don't worry, what we have to do while we're in this hole is tell each other things, rather like the conference but on a lower level, that way the time will pass and the light will come back, then Wanda said, you're very kind, and she started crying bitterly, as if all the sadness in the world were in her eyes. Marta hugged her and said, concentrate, imagine you're a stone at the bottom of a river: the water passes over your sides, the fish brush past you, the vegetation on the river bed caresses you from below; gather those sensations in a single pleasant image, put it in the center of your mind, now you're fine, your face is already calmer and your eyes aren't darting about, breathe from your stomach, one, two, breathe out, think of your talisman and . . . once again, one, two, again fill your stomach with air, deep breath, press the plexus when you breathe out, do you feel a little better? Wanda opened her eyes and said, yes, I need professional treatment, you can see that a mile away.

Marta said to her: this is a surefire method for controlling anxiety attacks in enclosed spaces, I suffered the same way all through my adolescence and after a thousand psychiatric and hypnotic treatments I had myself treated with tantric reflexology, and well, there you see the results, I've forgotten what an anxiety attack is like.

I'm very grateful, said Egiswanda, it did me a lot of good as far as being in an enclosed space goes; the problem is, my anxiety goes much farther, I could say it goes beyond this room, beyond the conference, out across the city . . . Anyway, there's no point in my saying more, not that it matters if I tell you my secrets, it's all over, nothing matters anymore.

We looked at her curiously, what's all over? Wanda seemed to realize something and said: nobody knows it, but I'm the wife of the man who killed himself; or rather: his widow. Shit, I'll have to get used to that strange word; don't look at me like that, surely you were both at my husband José Maturana's talk, weren't you? let me tell you.

When she said that, my hands started shaking. Maturana's wife? Once again the story had come to me, and I said, please, tell us, how can that be, we didn't know José Maturana was married, did you meet him after he left the Ministry? Marta put a hand over her mouth and said, oh, Wanda, my sincere condolences, your story must be very, veeeery interesting. I nodded, as if to say the same, but Egiswanda appeared not to notice and started talking.

I met him in Detroit seven years ago, she said, and the fact is, I didn't know anything about his past until much later, when I'd already fallen into his arms, if I can put it that way, and even lived with him, on and off.

Where did I see him for the first time?

It was when he appeared at the Lampedusa Palace Hotel to sign one of his books. The book was called *My Life with Jesus*, and I'd bought it by chance only three days before at the Taylor Mall and had already finished reading it. That book came along at a very hard time in my life, I'd just lost custody of my daughter at a court hearing where I was accused of being irresponsible and all kinds of unpleasant things, and I was in the eighth month of detox. Among other things, I'm a passive alcoholic. It's a monster I have inside me, constantly waking up and trying to devour me. José's book said that the one way to defeat monsters like that is with the cloak and sword of Christ, because His words are stronger than muscles, vanquishing through faith that force that pushes us to the abyss, to the deepest abyss of all, which is our own conscientiousness, where there are spaces as terrifying as those there must be at the bottom of the ocean, with mountain ranges and silent valleys that are simply there, waiting, but whose presence disturbs us, anyway, José's book, which describes all this with metaphors, was a rope to cling to, a last hope for somebody about to drown, do you understand?

Saying this, Egiswanda leaped to her feet and said, this damned place must have bathrooms, don't you think? I'm going to look for them, and she walked in the darkness to the door. A minute later she came back and said, my God, the bathrooms are lit with candles and they're rationing the water. Somebody asked me not to go unless I was doing "number two." Marta had been looking at Egiswanda curiously, now she bent toward her ear and said: you have traces of powder on your nose, best clean it. Egiswanda lifted a finger to her nostrils, then pulled it away and rubbed her gums with it. She gave a sly smile and said, seriously, I'm on the verge of a nervous breakdown. Anyway, let me carry on telling my story.

After I'd finished reading *My Life with Jesus* and was getting ready to start it again, pencil in hand, I saw by chance in the *Telegraph Post* that the author was introducing and signing the book that very afternoon. I went there and sat down in the front row. I don't know if you know that at that time he wasn't called José but Cyril Olivier, that was the name he used for the book, and the name they'd used to advertise the event. I listened to his words, which were eloquent, José was always a good speaker, and I felt a road opening up in front of me, not a road but a five-lane blacktop, with signposts and neon lights and side barriers, or something even bigger, a solar system with the heart of God throbbing in the center of it, I listened to it all and I was stunned, and that's why when he finished I went and joined a short line with my copy of his book, there weren't many of us there that night in the Lampedusa Palace, and I asked for his autograph, but something happened: when he was halfway through signing I was overcome with a terrible feeling of emptiness and I fainted, and when I opened my eyes again I was in a room in the hotel attended by a doctor who was saying, take a deep breath, Egiswanda, look at the light, do you remember the number of your cell phone? what drugs did you take today, Egiswanda? and so it went on for a while until José, or rather, Cyril, said, that's enough questions, she's fine, you can go; we were left alone, and he was looking at me with that disturbing, icy expression of his and I could feel my blood exploding in my veins and starting to flow through my body again, and I said—and I don't know how I found the strength to tell him this—you changed my life, Mr. Olivier, I'm very alone, your book was a revelation and today I became a different person, and he asked, and who or what were you before? and I said, not very much, a student nurse having problems finding her place in the world, a frightened woman feeling small and scared in this universe of noisy meteorites, and he said, even frogs carry weight in the world, that's in the Bible, come with me, let's go eat something, you must be hungry, a burger and a Coke, and then you can tell me again that you're nothing, O.K.?

So that was how I met him. We spent the evening together and that night I slept by his side, and I mean, by his side, without touching, let alone screwing, and also the following night and so on all week, together with him, in silence most of the time or else telling him about my past, but he wouldn't tell me about his, whenever I asked him a question he'd simply look up in the air, so I finally realized it was better if I kept quiet, but I was ready to do anything as long as he let me stay with him.

At least five years had passed since the end of the Ministry, according to my calculations, because he never said anything. He was very silent. We had a very strange relationship, I don't think a man and a woman have ever had a relationship like that before, at least not on this planet. I don't know how to explain it, it was as if every day we started again from scratch; as if every day we had to spend hours and hours breaking a thick, grimy pane of glass that covered his heart. After that, slowly, the man he'd been the day before might emerge, though not always. Sometimes he didn't surface for several days and you could wear yourself out looking for him, and when he appeared he never appeared completely. Life with José was a constant process of loss. There was always less there, nothing seemed to accumulate. We lived in anonymous hotels, changing every now and again; by the time I'd started getting used to one, we already had to leave. What are we escaping from? I would ask, and he would say, we aren't escaping from anything, we simply have to go, come on now, hurry up. We took with us two small beat-up cases and some plastic bags from Dalmart. Sometimes, when they saw us walking by the side of the highway, police cars would slow down and they'd look at us very suspiciously. José didn't care, he'd say: let them stop, we have nothing to hide. I don't know why I decided to stay with him. I didn't want to lose him, I longed to be by his side and get away from the dizziness, the cold, the solitude. I'm a typical Aquarius-Pisces cusp, the silent fish staring out from caves of coral. For me, José was like the sun he saw on Walter de la Salle's tattooed back, one of those eyes of God that shine brightly and burn; I burned up in that fire, but I clung to the man, and I was his woman, although he never let us live together properly, he never even wanted me in the same room as him, never, he'd pay for my accommodation and food separately and leave me banknotes in the pages of the Bible; he never registered with me, as if being together was an offense to God or that young Christ he worshiped and was always talking about, night and day, so much so that I ended up drawing my own conclusions about their relationship, but anyway, that was my life during those years, although I must also tell you that I was happy and that there were many times he made me feel fulfilled as a woman. A woman pursuing a man who basically was never there or who never loved her, although now I'll never know. I was never able to demand anything of him, except when I fell sick. Then, yes. Then he'd come and give me shelter and care, and I swear I managed to feel happy when my throat was overrun with platelets or ganglia, or when my ovaries hurt or I had infections. I'd get down on my knees to the doctor and beg him to diagnose horrible things and take a long time to cure me, because when I was sick I meant something to José, like the poor in my country, who only matter when they have epidemics or they die of nasty things.

That's how things were for me with José, who was still Cyril at the time.

By the way, let me tell you how I found out about this whole name-change thing. He'd gone to Delaware, to a little place called Zinc Town, where they'd invited him to talk about his books and about God. Zinc Town is a stretch of earth and stones with nothing beautiful about it at all. It's like hell. Most of the people worked in the mine, whole families. They'd set up a platform for him opposite the church, with chairs in front. I sat down in the front row and waited for Cyril to come out with the local bigwigs, but when I took a close look at the flyer they'd left on the chair it said:

> Presentation of the book *A Star in the West*, by its author, Silas Ebenezer Burnett.

I thought Cyril would be coming later, but suddenly I saw him come out with the mayor and the priest and sit down at the centre of the table. The mayor blew on an old microphone and said: please give a warm welcome to the great religious authority Silas Ebenezer Burnett, who has been kind enough to travel to our humble town to talk to us and introduce his book, and imagine my surprise when I saw Cyril stand up and lift a hand to his heart, in a sign of gratitude, and then raise his clasped hands, like the black leaders did; I sat there petrified, watching him saying a prayer to Christ the Redeemer before beginning his talk, and I said to myself, this man is a real mystery, and then just laughed, but in time Silas Ebenezer Burnett, author of *A Star in the West*, turned into Uriah Tennyson, author of *Builder of Hearts*, and then into Sean Méndez, whose work *Gods of Mud in the 18th* analyzed violence from an evangelical point of view.

José was so schizoid, he even had names for other genres. His poetry he published as Iván Arabi, and incredible as it may seem it was very successful, almost more than his religious and self-help books. His poetry book *Bullets from the Night against the Last Man* won a prize in San Francisco and was translated into Spanish and French. At a conference in Minneapolis somebody compared his poetry with Bukowski, and this wasn't a young guy high on crack but a university professor. His poetry had depth because it came out of the filthiest, most foul-smelling parts of the city, out of the lines of coke laid out by pale women on lavatory seats, and out of newspaper pages smeared with shit, and out of the frenzied couplings of immigrants scared of being deported back to their grim cities, oh God, all that fed into José's poetry, or rather, Iván Arabi's, I don't know where the hell he got that strange name from, and it also fed into his life, which was also mine because I was his guardian; I'd get down on my knees and beg him to let us spend a few days in a cabin by the sea, or in a little house in the mountains, or go fishing by the lake or go camping, but there was no point, it was impossible to get him away from those shabby motels with people having loud sex in the next rooms and breaking bottles against the walls; he never explained why he was so afraid of happiness, why he was so disturbed by light, or the centers of towns, or a settled life; maybe he thought he'd be betraying his origins, out of his old loyalty to Walter from all those years ago, which was a lot stronger than his ties to me.

We'd spend the days in those motels, on the outskirts of towns, most of the time in silence because he'd be writing a lot, or reading one book after another, so I'd kill time listening to music on my iPod or going on Facebook and chatting day and night with invisible friends and even having steamy affairs on the internet, because I couldn't spend one whole day without talking to somebody, without finding out about other people's lives, without somebody asking me things, and while I was chatting I'd be making imaginary journeys, looking at photographs of countries, cities, lost towns. Once I looked up the motel where we were staying on the internet and when I couldn't find it I had the feeling we were already dead and none of what I saw around me was real. After a time I became like him. I preferred to stay in the room, sitting on the carpet, with the laptop on my knees and my headphones on.

The only thing we shared was prayer, and the hours in

church, with him on his knees, in an attitude of supplication and penitence, and me behind, pressing my hands together, and asking God, or rather, imploring Him to explain why He had given me such a strange destiny, why, Lord? why, when you know that I'm a woman like any other, with human desires and rages? That was what I asked God, over and over again, without any hope, because my prayers were never answered, I don't know why, maybe because of the sins I'd committed or the things I'd neglected, there were certainly plenty of those. A few years passed and one day he said: I'm going on a journey, Wanda, I'll be back in six months, I have to go alone, wait for me in the Comfort Inn on Sausalito Drive, I'll be there the first week in September. When he said this, he already had his things on his back, and he just walked out without looking back. I couldn't ask anything, only listen and obey. I saw him getting smaller in the distance. I'd never before felt so unhappy to be his companion, so I begged God: make him turn around and come back, let him be by my side when I open my eyes, let me see him sitting on the balcony when I wake up. But it didn't happen. What I did find was a book he'd wrapped for me. On every page there was a hundred-dollar bill and a note saying: *Wait for me on Sausalito Drive.*

I collected my things and went to a hotel in the center, near the bay and with a view of the sea. From there I called my daughter, but when they wouldn't put her on to speak to me I went out and bought her a whole lot of gifts and asked for them to be delivered to her. Then I had dinner in a nice restaurant, and had Mexican tacos, and without thinking twice ordered a margarita with a double shot of tequila. The first led to a second and then a third, and then five more; then I went to a bar I'd often been to when I was a teenager and drank three more, one after the other. In the bathroom, I bought two grams of coke. I started taking it right there, and drank some more. It was like I was seeing my life coming back in the opposite direction. I fell into the darkness like a body falling in water and sinking, hearing reality in the distance as if it was a bus I'd missed that had left with all my bags on it.

When I opened my eyes I was in a bed next to an unknown man who was snoring. My legs hurt. I slipped out without making a noise, and that was when I saw that my money had been stolen. Fortunately, the book was still in the hotel and there were still lots of pages, so I went back to tequila and cocaine, a long party that never ended, I'd go from one bar to another, from one mirror to another, mirror, mirror on the wall, until one day I looked at the calendar on my cell phone and saw that it was September 3, six months had already passed! I drank a million coffees, swam in the pool and took a little more coke until I could remember what José had told me, the Comfort Inn, and that was where I went. When I'd paid the taxi, all I had left was three ten-dollar bills, one of five, and a few coins, but it was enough. I rented a room and sat down on the carpet to wait. When I looked at myself in the mirror, I screamed.

He arrived two days later, as if everything was normal. Hello, Wanda, are you sick? He looked after me for about a month, stopped me drinking and taking drugs again, but then our life resumed its old rhythm: silence and motels, journeys on Greyhound buses, walks on obscure back roads, long mornings in local churches, and the occasional book signing. One night I found a snake in the shower and fainted. Thanks to that, José agreed to go up a category and we started staying in slightly better places; he also got in the habit of inspecting my room before he went to his just in case.

One year later, one morning before breakfast, he again said the same thing: I'm going on a journey, I'll be back in six months, the book is in your case. This time, though, I managed to say, why don't you take me? but he replied, I can't, not yet, wait for me at the Comfort Inn, first week of March, and again he disappeared into the crowd; as I watched him getting smaller and smaller I felt my legs go weak and my brain was like a railroad station in New Mexico, filled with confused immigrants. I opened the minibar and drank all the little bottles one after the other. Then I went to a 7-Eleven and bought three bottles of JB, as green as emeralds, and drank them over the next two days without leaving my room, eating nothing but yogurt.

In the book there was a large amount, twenty thousand dollars, so I made another attempt to contact my daughter. The result was the same and again I jumped into the void, submerged myself in an ocean of alcohol, but when I came up again I felt disappointed. Only three weeks had passed. What was I going to do with the rest of the time? I'm sorry to be telling you all these sordid details, but I decided to add something to the drugs and the alcohol and hired two male prostitutes, two Spanish guys who were really depraved and did things to me like the things you see in Sabina Vedovelli's movies. I have only vague images of that, because to tell the truth I was so out of it I can barely remember. Better that way. José kept his promise and came back on the date he had told me, stayed with me for another year and then left again. His journeys were becoming a ritual, and I was also starting to get used to that plunge into dark waters that left me exhausted, ready for his return.

Two years later, something new happened, which was that his laptop got damaged and he had to buy a new one. I managed to get hold of the old machine and tried to get into it, but I couldn't so I hired a specialist. The man charged me seven hundred dollars, but anyway now I could get into the files and see what was there: his drafts of books, his rejected poems and the final versions, his personal pages, which didn't really have much. It was when I connected it to the internet that things turned good, because that was when I saw all those e-mails from a travel agency confirming flights from Miami to Johannesburg via Sao Paulo, the first leg on Continental Airlines and the second with Varig.

I was puzzled, what on earth was José doing in Johannesburg? And worse still: why didn't he take me with him if his route took in my native country, Brazil? why did he go every year? who did he have there? Through the e-mails I found out that whenever he arrived in Johannesburg he would rent a hotel room for three days and then disappear. Where did he go? My theory was that he was going into the jungle to spread the word of God, he wouldn't have been the first to do that with native tribes. The next time he left on a journey I was prepared. After saying goodbye to him I went to the travel agency and asked to speak with the employee who had done the ticket for him. The man received me in his office, but said he couldn't reveal Mr. Burnett's itinerary—that was the name on his passport—unless I could prove I was his wife by bringing in a marriage license. I changed tactics and stroked his penis through his pants. I said that if he gave me that simple piece of information I'd give him a blowjob in the bathroom of the bar across the street. The man agreed to give me a copy of the complete printout: flights, hotel, times, everything. When he'd finished I changed my mind and said, listen, wouldn't you prefer a hundred dollar bill? My gums are bleeding and I wouldn't like to get blood on you. Then I went and called the hotel in South Africa and asked for Burnett and they said, he's arriving tomorrow, madam, would you like to leave a message? Yes, I said, there are problems with the transportation to the jungle so he'll have to wait. There was a silence at the other end, until the person said, what jungle are you referring to, madam? I thought it was weird that somebody in Africa should ask me that, but I had to keep up the lie. Mr. Burnett hired transportation from his hotel to the jungle, but there have been some problems and he'll have to wait. Another silence on the line.

There must be some mistake, he said, Mr. Burnett can't have rented any transportation, because on Friday he's taking the Tupolev to Tristan da Cunha, we booked it for him.

I hung up, and went and looked up Tristan da Cunha on the internet and, to my surprise, it turned out to be a tiny island in the middle of the Atlantic, halfway between Africa and America, with a population of three hundred. Why the hell had José been going there all these years? I confess I still don't know.

A strange silence descended, interrupting Egiswanda, and at that moment the lights came on.

Immediately a voice announced that the danger was over and that we could go back to our rooms. The light from the generator had started working and reality, after that horrible flickering, seemed to have returned to us. But we weren't the same anymore. In the light I recognized some of the shadows: there were Kosztolányi and Supervielle, and I even thought I saw Kaplan in the distance. Our faces were haggard. Marta was so pale she worried me, and Egiswanda, who I had never seen in the light, looked really grim-faced. From the way they were both looking at me I assumed they were struck by my appearance, too.

It was clear that the situation was moving quickly, that our days at the conference were coming to an end.

We went up in the elevator, after a long wait for our turn. When we reached the floor where my room was, Egiswanda looked at us anxiously and said, can I stay with you a while longer, I feel a bit scared. Marta hugged her and said, of course, our room is also yours, I think we should drink something. We sat down on the bed with some gins from the mini-bar and Egiswanda continued her story.

One day José himself said to me, why do you never ask me where I go? to which I replied: because I know perfectly well you won't answer and I'm not stupid. José was silent for a long while, lost in thought, and finally said: you'll come with me soon to live in another country, I'm getting everything ready for that; it will do you good, you and the people who need you, the moment is coming, you just have to wait.

Time passed and one day he said, get your bags ready, we're going on a journey. I thought he was referring to a change of motel, but he said, no, we're going to travel together, bring your passport, and that's how we came to this conference. Of course he didn't want us to share a room and asked me not to be close to him. He said: stay in your room and think about important things like your destiny or the destiny of the world, I'll come for you when I need you. The day of his talk, he asked me to go and hear him, saying: only by listening to me will you finally understand who I am, and that was what I did, I went to hear him. I listened to him eagerly, drinking in his every word. I cried. I got goose bumps. I got wet. I felt all that, listening to him. It was what I'd been waiting to hear for years and I assumed there would be a change in our life. First the journey and then his words, why wouldn't I have imagined that everything was about to change? Men like José, who love humanity, aren't capable of loving one particular person; that's something they have in common with the prophets. When he finished his talk I met him in the corridor and tried to speak to him, but he brushed me aside, saying we would talk later, he would come and find me.

I was in my room waiting for him, with the TV on, and had no idea what had happened. I found out in the most brutal way, because I kept calling his room until the switchboard operator answered, and said, we're terribly sorry, the guest in that room has just had an accident. I went to reception and that's where I heard the news. I almost fainted. They also gave me a letter, they said they'd been going to take it up to my room but had been distracted. A letter? I recognized José's handwriting on the envelope and when I opened it I found another envelope inside, with these words written on it: *Don't read this today, wait until tomorrow.* I went into a corner to cry, trying to hide my grief from everyone, but then I said to myself, if he's not here anymore there's no reason for me to hide, I'm not harming anyone and I deserve to be able to cry for him, after all the sacrifices and the sad, solitary life I'd lived with him. I deserved to cry rivers of tears in that lobby where nobody knew I was his wife, which was why nobody had a kind word, nobody bothered to talk to me with any kind of tact, it was just: the man slit his wrists, they took his body to the morgue; I tried going to his room but, as I walked toward it, I felt his presence and got scared. I thought he was watching me and was going to fly into a temper, seeing me break the rules: never approach him, only wait for him to come, so I went back to my room and lay down on the carpet to cry, I wanted to drink but I couldn't swallow the alcohol, I'd lost even that, and besides, he wouldn't be there to take care of me anymore, so I cried and cried until there were no more tears left, until the last cell of grief left my body, and I was empty, and this city and this destruction and all that's happening here seemed to me the ideal place from which to go away, and I even imagined that if I slit my wrists I could still get to him, get to where he was before he moved off and squeeze his hand and fly together to who knows where, I don't know what there is after death, because deep down I'm not very religious. The world hurts me without him, the light and the air, everything hurts me without him. This conference and its delegates hurt me. The world is still turning, as if nothing had happened. I can't believe it, José's death can't go unnoticed, like the fall of a dead leaf in a forest. It can't be. I've read the letter about ten times or perhaps a hundred, and I know parts of it by heart. I have it here, would it bother you if I read it aloud? Marta wiped the tears from her cheeks and said, no, please, Wanda, read it.

Before doing that, Wanda asked if she could go to the bathroom to wipe her tears and freshen up, but what we heard were two loud snorts. She came out looking a little better, and said, you two are special, you're the only people in all this mass of vanity who really care about José's death. She picked up the letter and read:

Wanda,

My purpose isn't to explain to you what happened to me, and notice that I'm speaking in the past tense, not in the future, even though as I write this nothing has happened yet. But it will happen. There are no reasons for certain things, and there doesn't exist the slightest possibility of transferring experiences that are untransferable. Within three hours at the most, I will leave this frozen planet for good, and unlike Jesus Christ, my master, I won't be coming back on the third day, because despite your admiration for me and the books I've written I've never been anything other than a total shit, a swindler. I'm not coming back after three days, among other things because nobody is waiting for me, with the possible exception of you. I am going to the world of the shadows, where I lived curled up before I was born, before somebody put their hand in that bag and pulled me out by the scruff of my neck and dumped me in the world, a hand that left me defenseless and in the most terrifying solitude, or, which amounts to the same thing, said, aha, my brother, I saw you, have a nice stay in this shithouse, you're going to spend a few decades here, you already know that, the rest depends on you, you will see whether after a while you will be the grain that appears in the shit or the paper that cleans it or the stream of water that pushes it through the pipe, I give you those three possibilities, I'm feeling generous today—the hand continues—because, my friend, we'll meet again during the race, and then the hand withdrew from the world with a nervous

420 · SANTIAGO GAMBOA

and rapid gesture, like someone pulling their hand out of a snake pit, and there I was lying on the street, bleeding and weeping, covered in entrails and shit, more alone than the first man on earth, without a trace of a past and without a history, my memories are the dirty walls of an orphanage, the concrete floor of a kitchen, the garbage piled up in the corners, a leaning lamppost filled with pigeons, anyway, I tried to do something in life and I don't know if I succeeded, but it's over now, what's going to happen to me, in fact what's already happening, can't be changed, and that's why I'm writing to you, let's hope by the time you read this letter the situation in the city hasn't gotten worse, because this is a farewell and a request, but let's take things one at a time; first I'll say goodbye and thank you for all the suffering and the deep faith you always had, accepting those silences and those abysses of mine, you were the strong one and I was the absent one, you were the island of air and clouds and me the nothingness; you knew how to respect my silences, which climbed all over yours and were harder to bear, and I say thank you, seriously, thank you, Wandita, my queen, what I am saying comes from the heart and there is something important: together with this letter there is a smaller blue envelope and a yellow one. Open the yellow one, you'll find the details of a bank account into which I've transferred all the money I have, which now belongs to you, because you will have to carry on without me.

The request has to do with the other envelope. Look for God in the deep, say the gospels and that is what you are going to do; you are a rock on a cliff, strong, tough, I never told you these things but today I am saying them and writing them, so that you know they were inside me, so that you remember them, I leave you these words; being so close to death leads me to say them to you, I don't know, in any case you deserve them and they are yours, in the end, I am leav-

ing many things but not you or your company, my own life
has finally caught up with me and now I can only escape by
flying, like the birds or the souls, oh, the past never ends
and is unpredictable; one of the first things I think I will ask
the Big Enchilada, if he forgives me and I can see him even
if only for a couple of minutes, is why he puts us to live on
the tightrope of time, which brings us so much anguish and
makes us act wickedly sometimes as long as we forget that
sensation of emptiness, which is why we seek instant pleasures and put coke in our veins and look for ways to escape,
but it doesn't work, time is relentless and is always there in
the corner, that's what I want to ask the Big Boss, not even
about my origin or about this shithouse where he made us
live, but about the mystery of time; anyway, I'm finally getting to the point, because I don't even understand myself
anymore and I don't want to write this letter again: in the
blue envelope there is a map with an island marked on it
and directions on how to get there, like in stories about
treasures, except that in this case the treasure is the whole
island, the one place on Earth where peace exists, a rock
remote from the world where I would have liked to take
you, I really had planned to take you there if this emergency
had not come up, so the request is that you go and settle
there; you can go whenever you like and move into our
house, ask for the chaplain, his name is Talisker, he will help
you because he knows about you and knows you'll arrive
sooner or later. You have to go there to be pure and clean
and then, when that day arrives, you will make the leap into
the infinite where the Big Enchilada and I will be waiting
for you; but in the meantime go there and stay, that island
is how I was when I was born, something small and solitary,
lost in the world; on it you will be protected by millions of
tons of water and you will be happy, because it is an emanation of the soul of God; my last gift is more solitude,

Wanda, but what can I do, I was born alone; when I look at the world it will be to imagine that you are there, on that solitary dot, and to tell me that that pure uncontaminated place is Wanda's island.

When she finished reading, Egiswanda brushed away a few tears, and said, thank you for listening to me, being with you has been a real consolation; José's death is slowly becoming part of my life, and that's how it must be, a grief that very, very slowly turns to resignation. Then she swallowed two pills out of a bottle, closed her eyes, and laid her head on one of the pillows, saying, let me sleep here, I beg you, I don't want to be alone.

Marta put on one of my T-shirts and lay down next to her. I sat down on the carpet, thinking about Maturana's words, José Maturana's life. I was slowly drifting off to sleep, but before sleeping I asked myself: what kind of island is that? is it true you can find peace and tranquility there? I had a strange dream. I dreamed I had woken up in a clinic in ruins. My room had a hole in the wall and part of the roof had blown away because of some kind of explosion. I opened my eyes and looked up at the sky. There was nothing in it apart from a faint tinge of color, but I felt calm. From the bed ran cables connecting me to machines to check my heartbeat, my blood pressure, my breathing. There was nobody around. I heard the sound of the wind blowing through the dusty, rubble-filled corridors. The medical staff had left and I was the last patient, but my bandages were clean. How quiet it is, I said to myself, is this what death is like? There was no way of knowing. Suddenly a bird came to rest on the back of my bed. It looked at me in surprise, moved its head rapidly from side to side, and flapped its wings, stirring the air, and again I felt alone. The sickness had disappeared and I breathed in the air with relish, I could feel its sweet taste, the joy of its clean, fresh taste.

My temperature was fine, below 96 degrees. The coolness of my body was transmitted to my soul. I was alone but I had recovered.

The next day the city woke up to silence.

After the night's explosions the air seemed even thicker with mist and smoke. It was hard to see anything beyond a few yards. We were advised not to leave the hotel and to avoid the windows. Marta was asleep beside me and Egiswanda had gone, so I decided to go down and sit at one of the tables in the coffee shop, with my notebook. I drank two very black coffees. I put down in my notes what had happened the night before, the appointment with Sabina Vedovelli, her proposition, the air raid, and Egiswanda's long story, all these things seemed to be finally putting an end to my period as a writer who does not write, so I immersed myself in my notes with a concentration close to what I had before my illness.

An hour later, the explosions started again. Every now and again, you could hear the unmistakable whistle of a grenade crossing the sky and how it was intercepted by the defense system, creating an area of conflagration. But I carried on with my notes. One can get used to anything, believe me. As Hemingway might have said: outside they are fighting for a city or for a world, but at this moment I belong to this pen and this notebook.

Some time later, I went back up to my room. I had to get ready for the round table at noon, *The Soul of Words: A Look Inside*, for which I had brought a number of short texts I could read in case the muses of inspiration did not lend me a hand. It was my first contribution to the conference and I wanted to make a good impression, especially after that had happened with the first of my round tables. By the time I got to my room, Marta had gone. Her laptop was open at a page with the heading *The Body of a Suicide*, but the screen was blank. Instead of writing she had been chatting: I saw various windows open with answers sent twenty minutes earlier: are you still there? are you coming back? What to say in my talk? I would talk about literature and life, I thought; I felt the desire to compare it with other artistic disciplines and also to tell human stories. I wanted many things but only had twenty minutes. The texts I had prepared had been written for other conferences or for short story anthologies, so I had to find a way to adapt them to the debate.

After a good shower, I dressed in a newly ironed suit, although without a tie; I combed my hair as best I could and went down scented and ready for my performance, which was in the Heroes of Masada room.

My companions at the table were all intellectuals specializing in the subject. Elsa Goudinho, from Mozambique; Dionisio Bumenguele, from Kenya; Itamar Machado, from the University of Oporto; Shé Kwan Mo, from Singapore; and, much to my surprise, Rashid! Rashid Salman. Seeing him at the door, I said, what a surprise! I didn't know you were here, I didn't see you on the program, but he replied, I asked them not to announce me for security reasons, as you know, these days there are a lot of weird people on the streets, the smell of gunpowder makes everyone go crazy, but here I am and you'll see, I'm the best, the audience will take me in their arms and the most beautiful women will ask for my cell phone number and e-mail address, others will say with sly expressions on their faces that they're waiting for me in the bathroom, get ready, I'm a tornado.

The debate was being chaired by Professor Emma Olivier Dickinson of Cornell University, and the first question she threw out was, "Can we get to the bottom of a life through the word?" As Professor Elsa Goudinho replied, skillfully improvising, I looked around the hall, which was quite full in spite of the bombardment. I saw the publisher Lottmann in the fourth row and a little farther back the inseparable Kosztolányi and

Supervielle, watching him, obsessed as they were—especially
Supervielle—by the Tiberias publishing house; they were cran-
ing their necks in their desire to see what he was writing in his
notebook, but as I was close to him it was obvious to me that
he was drawing circles or sunsets or sailboats, not taking notes
on anything connected with the words of Professor Goudinho.
Farther back I saw Kaplan, who on seeing me looking at him
raised his hand and waved.

I continued looking for a face that would tell me something
concrete. A face that would say: I'm Walter, you found me, let's
have a talk after the event. Even after my conversation with
Jessica, I still believed—at least that was what I wrote in my
notes—that Walter could not have died in the shoot-out at the
Ministry; to escape, he must have used a ploy similar to that
used by the guerrillas of the Polisario Front, which consisted
in burying yourself alive in the sand with a straw sticking out
just above the surface to breathe through, and in that way
tricking the enemy. Then Walter must have gone looking for
José and Miss Jessica in order to recover his money and move
to another country, clandestinely, to begin a new life, but for
some reason José must have betrayed him, taking part—or
all—of those funds; all this was possible, and I was hoping that
it was, because, to tell the truth, my mind was already on what
I was going to write about José Maturana, and that seemed like
the most convincing and dramatic ending.

After reading the letter to Egiswanda, I had completely
ruled out the idea of a murder, but I kept thinking about the
unknown person in Room 1209. The guest was a man and had
some kind of relationship with Jessica, but I did not know who
he was or, rather, I had been unable to confirm whether or not
he was Walter under a new identity. The idea that he might
simply be a lover of Jessica's, without anything to do with the
story, refused to lodge in my brain. As I thought about this, I
realized that Jessica and Egiswanda had very similar voices: a

slightly accented Spanish, an underlying sense of nervousness, which of the two had been the woman waging that terrible battle of love the first night? The voice was the same, but whose voice was it?

I was still scrutinizing the audience, row by row, when the door at the top opened and a slim female figure entered the room. The light was dim but I recognized her immediately: it was Jessica. She was alone and I assumed she would look for her companion and sit down beside him, but that did not happen. She simply looked for a free seat at the back of the hall. As she sat down I noted something incredible: the person beside her was none other than Egiswanda. The two women had never met, and Jessica could not possibly know that Egiswanda even existed. It was strange. There they were, sitting side by side, not knowing how much they had in common. They were linked to one another by men who were now dead, and I, who had not even lived through those events, was the only person who could have revealed that fact to them. I vowed to do so after my talk. Each woman had a piece of José; their descriptions and experiences revealed different, contrasting men.

Sabina Vedovelli and her husband were not in the hall, but it was well known that they did not attend events, not for the reason that might have been imagined, a lack of interest in anyone's activities but their own, but in order to avoid becoming the center of attention and stealing someone else's show. This was what Sabina had said at the cocktail party when she was asked why she had not attended other talks. She said that she followed them through the hotel's closed circuit, and she demonstrated, by quoting accurately from them, that this was indeed the case.

After Elsa Goudinho's contribution, the chair asked Rashid to speak. I put aside my reflections and got ready to listen to him. Rashid cleared his throat, took a sip of water, thanked the chairperson for her words of introduction and the organizers of the ICBM, and said: allow me to tell you a story, which is after all what we are here for. My story is this:

I have come to tell you about an old Palestinian who once traveled throughout this region as a driver of trucks and buses. His name is Jamil Abu Eisheh, he is eighty-two years old and was born in the city of Hebron, on the West Bank. But let us take things one at a time. Hebron is the most densely populated Arab city in Palestine and of course the capital of the West Bank. Hebron is a white city extending over a number of hills, whose center is the mosque, built over the tomb of the patriarch Abraham, worshiped by both religions. We Arabs call him Ibrahim, but he is the same man as the Abraham of the Jewish tradition, the father of Isaac and Ishmael.

It was there that Jamil Abu Eisheh was born, in 1923, when the West Bank was known as Transjordan, and the whole of Palestine was part of the British Mandate. Jamil still has his British identity papers and his British driving license, which he had when he started working as a driver, like his father, who owned a bus that did the route from Hebron to Jerusalem. But those were other times. Today, sitting in his house on Ein Sara Street, Jamil has talked to me many times about his childhood. "Our neighbor in the old city of Hebron was a Jewish woman. When my mother had to go out, she would leave us in this woman's house and if it was for a long time the neighbor would breastfeed her son and then my little brother." That was what life was like between Jews and Arabs in those days. It was the British who created the problems, the old man says, when they gave the power and the government buildings to the Jews. They set the two sides against each other and then just left.

Jamil remembers his journeys by truck. He has thousands of stories. For example, when he traveled alone along the edge of the Red Sea to get to Jedda, in Saudi Arabia. Six hundred miles without roads through the desert, praying to Allah that the engine of his truck would hold out and he would not have to abandon it in some solitary place through which other truck drivers rarely passed. He finally reached Jedda, the city of the white towers, and then, after another forty-five miles, Mecca, the holy city of Islam, the pilgrimage to which he has done seven times, which gives him the title of "Hadji," and that's why, whenever he talks about Mecca and remembers his pilgrimage, the old man gets down on his knees and touches the floor with his forehead. What's Mecca like? I asked him once, and he replied: there's nothing like it in the world, it's the holy city, it's the center of the universe, it's the first and last city, it's a prayer made of tile, white walls, and towers. Jamil knows all the distances in the Middle East in miles, which is something that everyone has forgotten now, because of the borders and the barbed wire fences. Today most of the roads are either closed or can only be driven along if you have a safe conduct. "From Jerusalem to Amman is seventy miles," he says. "From Amman to Daria, on the border with Syria, another seventy, and from Daria to Damascus, seventy." At this point he opens his eyes wide and exclaims: "And from Damascus to Beirut, another seventy!" If the region were at peace a person could have breakfast in Jerusalem, lunch in Damascus, and dinner in Beirut.

Then I decided to ask him an uncomfortable question, which I hated asking him but if I hadn't done so, I would never have been able to round out his portrait. I said to him: what do you think of life these days in Palestine? The old man shifted in his chair, frowned, and lifted one of his arms. "Let them go and make their Palestinian State in Gaza, they and the crazy fundamentalists, and leave us alone. The best thing that could happen to the West Bank would be to revert to Jordan, and be ruled from Amman." There was not the shadow of a doubt in his words. "That would be my dream, because in the past, when we belonged to Jordan was the best time." Between the wars of 1948 and 1967, the West Bank had been under Jordanian control, and Jamil had driven a bus that did the route from Hebron to Amman, there and back every day. "I know that road like the back of my hand," he says, "and I would give my life to drive it again, freely." Then he was silent for a moment before adding, slyly: "more than anything else I'd like to go back to Beirut, with its movie theaters and its nightclubs, its women with eyes as black as caves who take you back to the first day of the world, with its neon lights in the night that seem to say to the visitor: you've just gotten here after a long journey, now just enjoy yourself."

Jamil still has his Jordanian documents, his passport and driving license. After the 1967 war and the Israeli occupation, he had to change documents again. He was living in Israel now and couldn't go back to Amman. The border on the river Jordan, which before had been only a small bridge, had now turned into an unbreachable wall. The region had become smaller and he had to limit his journeys: to Jerusalem, to Nablus, to Haifa. After a few years, with the Oslo Accords and the new maps, he had to change documents again for those of the Palestinian Authority and the territory became even smaller, so he decided to retire, sell his truck, and open a store selling cold drinks, ice cream, and candy.

The story of this old driver is the story of a whole region, with a past that is cruel, intense, and beautiful. A metaphor for life in the world: Jamil has lived in four different countries without ever moving house.

Rashid was applauded, and I looked again at the back of the room, where Jessica and Egiswanda were. They were still sitting side by side, without talking. I felt like getting up and going to them, and revealing to them something of what united them, but I could not leave the table. In this, I must confess, there was also a slight erotic charge: I wanted to know which of the two had been the voice I had heard in the darkness.

Suddenly I heard my name and, looking at the chairperson, saw that she was smiling at me. In my distraction, I had heard neither her introduction nor the question with which she had handed over to me, so I had to rule out the idea of improvising, especially because, as I now realized with horror, I had completely forgotten the theme of the round table.

I thanked the chairperson and the directors of the ICBM, apologized for having missed the first event at which my presence had been scheduled, and announced that, as a writer, the best thing I could do would be to read a story. And I immediately grabbed the first of my papers and started to read:

The story I am about to tell you is rather sad, and the truth is, I don't know why I should tell it to you now and not, for example, in a month or a year, or never. I suppose I am doing it out of nostalgia for my friend the Portuguese poet Ivo Machado, who is one of the main characters, or perhaps because I recently bought a model plane made out of metal that I now have on my desk. Excuse the personal tone. This story will be extremely personal.

The protagonist of my story is, as I have already said, the poet Ivo Machado, who was born in the Azores, but what matters to us now is that his everyday job was air traffic controller, in other words, he was one of those people who sit in the control towers of airports and guide planes along the air routes.

The story is as follows: when Ivo was a young man of twenty-five (in the mid-Eighties) he controlled flights in the airport of the Azores, that Portuguese archipelago in the middle of the Atlantic, an equal distance from Europe and North America. One night, when he came into work, the chief controller said: "Ivo, today you will direct a single plane." He was surprised, because the normal thing was to guide the flights of a dozen aircraft. Then the chief explained: "It's a special case.

An English pilot taking a British World War II bomber to Florida, to hand it over to a collector of planes who has just bought it at an auction in London. He made a stop here in the Azores and continued toward Canada, because he has to follow a strictly laid down route, but he was caught in a storm, had to fly in a zigzag, and now doesn't have much fuel left. He won't reach Canada, and he doesn't have enough fuel to turn back. He's going to fall in the sea."

Saying this, he passed the headphones to Ivo. "You have to keep him calm, he's very nervous. A Canadian rescue team has already left in boats and helicopters for the spot where he's expected to fall."

Ivo put on the headphones and started talking to the pilot, who was indeed very nervous. The first thing he wanted to know was the temperature of the water where he was going to fall and if there were sharks, but Ivo reassured him that there weren't any. Then their conversation became more personal, which doesn't often happen between an air traffic controller and a pilot. The Englishman asked Ivo who he was and what he did in life, he asked him to talk about his tastes, even his feelings. Ivo told him he was a poet and the Englishman asked him to recite something. They were talking in English and luckily Ivo knew by heart a few poems by Walt Whitman and Coleridge and Emily Dickinson. He recited them and thus they continued for a while, commenting on the sonnets of life and death and a few passages that Ivo remembered from *The Rime of the Ancient Mariner*, the story of another man struggling against the fury of the world.

Time passed and the pilot, already calmer now, asked him to recite his own poetry, and so Ivo made an effort and translated some of his poems into English just for him, just for that pilot battling a storm in an old bomber, in the middle of the night over the ocean, the clearest and most terrifying image of solitude. "I sense a deep sadness in your poems, and even a certain disillusionment," said the pilot, and they talked about life and dreams and the fragility of things, and of course about the future, which would not be a future full of poetry, until there came the dreaded moment when the needle of the fuel gauge went into red and the bomber fell in the sea. Then the chief controller told Ivo to go home, because after such a difficult experience, it would not be a good idea for him to handle other aircraft.

The next day Ivo found out what had happened. The Canadian rescue team had found the plane intact, floating on the water, but the pilot was dead. Part of the cabin had came away and struck him on the back of the neck. "The man died at peace," Ivo said to me, "and that's why I still write poetry." After a while, IATA held an investigation into the accident and Ivo had to listen, in front of a jury, to his conversation with the pilot. They congratulated him. It was the only time in the history of aviation that the frequencies between a plane and a control tower had been filled with poetry. The whole thing created a very good impression and some time later Ivo was transferred to the airport in Oporto.

"I still dream of his voice," Ivo told me once, remembering him, as we drank whiskey in Póvoa de Varzim, where the great writer Eça de Queiroz was born, and I understand him. All of us who write should do it like that: as if our words were for a pilot struggling alone, in the middle of the night, against a raging storm.

When I raised my eyes, the audience realized that I had finished, and I received some timid, uncoordinated applause. The chairperson looked at me again, not with a smile as she had at the beginning but with a touch of incredulity, which suggested to me that my text had little or no connection with the theme that was being discussed, or at least with her original question, which unfortunately I had not been able to hear and which I had been too embarrassed to ask her to repeat. Anyway, she took the microphone and said, very good, we thank the writer for his imaginative words, a truly original and unexpected way of dealing with the subject of words and life, which recall, as he himself said, the deep links that exist between poetry and aviation, between the fragility of existence and our idle words, thank you again for your contribution, at the end of the first round there will be questions and comments and we may ask you to expound a little more on these literary ideas.

After this, she turned her attention to the other side of the table, and the poet Dionisio Bumenguele, with these words: dear bard, you are one of the most exalted sons of Africa, an intellectual bathed by the springs of that fascinating continent so full of stories. In the talk we have just heard there was mention of the sky and the hurricane winds, which is the most common meteorology in lyric poetry, and that is why I now give the floor to you, so that you can give us your own testimony of how you remember and evaluate a life.

The poet gave a huge smile that seemed to cover his whole face, cleared his throat, gave the microphone a couple of little knocks, and said: a very good afternoon to all of you, ladies and gentlemen, it is an honor for a modest poet like myself to be in this distinguished place, surrounded by such remarkable personalities. Before reading my text, I should like to tell you that it is dedicated to the memory and legacy of the great African patriot Patrice Lumumba, some of whose verses I want to read by way of epigraph and as a kind of prayer for hope:

> *Music: you have allowed us too*
> *to raise our faces and see*
> *the future liberation of the race.*
> *May the banks of the great rivers that transport*
> *your living waves toward the future*
> *be yours!*

May all the earth and all its riches
be yours!
May the hot noon sun
burn away your sorrows
May the rays of the sun
dry the tears spilled by your ancestor,
in the torment of these sad lands!
Our people, free and happy,
will live and triumph in our Congo.
Here, in the heart of great Africa!

The audience greeted the poem with thunderous applause and somebody at the back cried out: "Freedom for Lumumba!" The poet Bumenguele raised his hands to calm the enthusiasm and announced that he would now read his text. When the audience had fallen silent he brought the microphone closer and began reading:

It might not be entirely pointless to tell you something about myself, but for now I shall refrain from doing so and will only tell you that little of myself that truly matters to the narrative. Indeed, I should like to create a wall of smoke around my own life, a wall that might be of bamboo or of sand, or even of ice, something to separate me from the person of whom I am going to talk to you this afternoon, about whom I have written and thought so much and who justifies this introduction, as you will see, none other than the great poet Elmord Limpopo, one of the greatest that post colonial Africa has had, in the opinion of many, worthy to stand beside such outstanding figures as Joseph Yai Olabiyi Babalola, from Benin, or the Nigerian Nobel laureate Wole Soyinka, and without any doubt the best poet in Kenya, may God place him, not at His right hand, but in the darkest of His dungeons.

Although I am quite aware that it is inappropriate to use this kind of expression at the beginning of a biographical speech, I will say that these are words that express the purest of truths, which after all is the objective of any scholar of life, whether a biographer, a philosopher, or simply a citizen, which is why I repeat, they are an expression of the truth, which is a way of saying, they come from my own truth and experience, and in spite of the fact that they presuppose an adverse moral posture, I want to make it very clear to you, from the start, that I was one of Limpopo's most devoted followers, that I have given the best years of my life to his work and that, in some strange and inhuman way, I still admire him. I write about him because I know him, in that always imprecise way in which one may know a life, including one's own, that is to say, as an interested and in no way impartial observer, because any life that is close to us usually has serious repercussions on one's own, I know what I am saying and so do you, given that as one's life, the life of any one of us here, including the honorable audience, is a block of marble that is shaped by circumstances, our times, and the corner of the world in which we chanced to arrive, as well as the people we meet, and that close contact, that drumbeat whose rhythm never varies and never stops, helps a figure emerge from the stone, an imprecise silhouette that is born inside the block and gradually acquires depth and volume until it forms that unique, irreplaceable being that is each one of us, as unique and irreplaceable as the circumstances of each life. It is the immaterial and intangible tam-tam of life that makes us different, but anyway, some of you may already be saying to yourselves that I was not invited to this golden conference to come out with polished reflections on existence, which is something that should be done in privacy, or is more appropriate to a written essay or a bohemian disquisition. I am aware of that, and I beg your forgiveness in advance. I assure you that I am as suspicious as you are of those philosophers who constantly practice the vain exercise of great ideas on their audience. In any case, we shall see how these introductory reflections acquire their full meaning as we find out about the terrifying life of this man, or rather, of this unusual human case, and now we are indeed coming to the point.

I shall begin by telling you that Limpopo was born in Kilimani, an area of Nairobi that we could define as previously middle-class and now definitely well-off, close to Ngong Road and Argwings Kodhek Road, and although his young mother could have chosen between the National Hospital and the Aga Khan, both very close, she decided to give birth in her own home, a two-story wooden building with a porch, facing north toward the famous hills of Ngong so often spoken of by Karen Blixen, whose mansion, as you know, is today one of the attractions of the capital. In the mornings, a very cool air blows through the city from the mountains and is one of its subtler vices. Whoever has breathed it, enjoying it in silence, will find it difficult to leave it behind and Nairobi will be impregnated forever in his memory, he will remain irrationally trapped in that plain and his imagination, his pleasures, will be marked by the memory of those cool mornings, still damp with the night rain, when a slight mist rises and the red earth of the streets is like a mirror in which the children sink their feet as they run to school. It could also be the image of a lost innocence that refuses to disappear.

During the 1960s, one of those children was a boy running to the Presbyterian school of Newshenwood with a bag tied around his neck and his head seething with dreams, with constellations of dreams that might begin with the most distant star and end with one of the hummingbirds he could see from his window. His father, Clarence Limpopo, was

Professor of World History at the National University of Kenya, and his mother, Evelyn, who had studied to be a teacher, taught biology at the English College. Young Elmord was an only child, so the attention of these two intellectuals, fascinated by independence and the socialist ideal of a dignified, self-sufficient country, as represented by Jomo Kenyatta, was entirely focused on him.

When he was nine, his father read to him aloud from the poetry of William Blake and Milton's *Paradise Lost*. He explained to him why Africa had to unite in a single great nation and recover its dignity before the white man, who should not, however, be hated, because what was hateful was the system imposed by a series of white nations which, with the shameful complicity of Africans, had come to Africa to steal its wealth, rape its women, and confine its men in labor camps or, in the best of cases, to give them ridiculous uniforms, with epaulettes and boots, and make them serve in their houses and clubs.

But according to Elmord's father, all that was over. With Jomo Kenyatta at the helm, his country could lift its head high and look with dignity at the other nations of the globe. Now they were independent, masters of their lives and destinies. They had to educate themselves, work hard to obtain the benefits of freedom, and make sure these reached the whole population, not only a few privileged people, as used to happen, and as had happened to him, Clarence Limpopo, who had gone to university and graduated in contemporary history, a destiny that had come about by chance, as he had been born on a farm owned by an old Englishman who had decided for some mysterious reason to give him an education, perhaps out of philanthropy or a feeling of guilt, he never knew which, because his mother, who might have known why, died when he was a child, so Clarence Limpopo had gone to university and was now a professor, and that was why his son, Elmord, had to have the best, had to be privileged so that he could be first in line and show the way to his countrymen who had not had the same luck, those Kenyans who died of malaria or typhoid, who lived in the slums of Nairobi, near the railroad tracks, feeding themselves on something similar to *ugali*, but without proteins, a crust of hard bread in water, hence the huge bellies of the children, the absent eyes of malaria, the high fevers, anyway, that was the great luck of Clarence and later of young Elmord, who by the age of ten was already mentioning in his poems the grave injustice of God, so grave, he wrote, that it deserved human judgment, a Nuremberg trial, or at least the same legal process that was given to any of his brothers when they were caught stealing or killing, because that serious crime had caused death and humiliation and was the midwife of great violence. "My God, I don't know how anyone can still believe in you," was the conclusion of young Elmord Limpopo's poem.

At the English College, his poems were regarded with a degree of anxiety, but because he was the son of a teacher none of the staff took much notice. Not even when at the age of twelve he presented in the English literature class a poem that said:

> *Yesterday, in the midst of sleep,*
> *I saw trees on fire in Nairobi,*
> *rivers of forest where before there were streets*
> *and specters of ash weeping on the sidewalks.*
> *A group of lone men were climbing a hill*
> *crowned by a church,*
> *climbing in the midst of pain,*
> *death and ashes*
> *led by a strange being.*
> *But before reaching the church,*

all the way up there,
something exploded in the blackest part of night.
A burst of gunfire stopped the silent group
and threw it in the dust,
in the ashes.

It was pure chance that this and other poems came to the attention of Dr. Growsery, an elderly English entomologist now retired from the university and a great lover of poetry, who read them with great interest up to a dozen times and finally delivered his verdict: a great poet has arrived, but I don't know if we are ready for what he has to say.

It is worth pointing out that this had all come about by chance. On Wednesdays, Dr. Growsery would come to Westlands to pick up his grandson from the English College. He was waiting in the cafeteria when he found a small case that somebody had left behind and, in order to find out who it belonged to, opened it and found the young man's poems. Then, when he had located the owner, who of course was Elmord, and went to give it back to him, he said, I saw there are poems in your case, whose are they? and Elmord replied, they're mine, sir. Although surprised, the old man asked, but are they yours in the sense that they belong to you or in the sense that you are the author? The young man said, I'm the author, sir, I wrote them.

That was the beginning of the friendship between Dr. Growsery and young Elmord Limpopo. Growsery decided to send a selection of his young friend's poems to London and eight months later his efforts bore fruit and a university review, *Literary News*, published three of them on a page devoted to Africa. Two weeks after this a package arrived, addressed to Dr. Growsery, with five copies of the review. Elmord's poems were on page 76. It was a very emotional moment when the young man first saw his work in print, and it made him feel dizzy. It is such an extraordinary thing for a human being to see his creations on display, a beautiful, complex thing that can determine the future course of a life. After the first impact, Elmord looked at the page with his poems and it struck him that they would have been better if instead of being arranged horizontally across the page they had been placed one above the other. He also had objections to the typeface used and the size of the capitals. A young poet writes to get close to the center of his soul, and the graphic appearance of his work is the packaging of that search . . .

At this point, a loud explosion interrupted Bumenguele, and the amphitheater, where the audience had been listening with delight, filled with cries, smoke, and gas.

Such things can happen in a second.

The building shook. The lights flickered and went out. Only one of the walls remained illumined by the glare of a fluorescent tube, giving the hall a marmoreal appearance. Glasses of water fell to the floor and a shower of dust and fragments shrouded the air.

Then came a second explosion which must have hit the hotel full on, and almost immediately there was a third, which made part of the ceiling come crashing down on us. Not the structure, luckily, but a stucco vault and a few lamps.

The air filled with the smell of fuel, of chemicals. Also with smoke and the smell of burning plastic. A cloud of dust hit our heads like hail.

In spite of being on a mezzanine, with windows that looked out on an inner garden—which luckily had shattered, letting the air in—the people clambered over the rubble to reach the main doors at the top of the semicircular auditorium. I looked toward where Jessica and Egiswanda had been, but could not see them. It was darkest in that area of the auditorium, and a layer of dust and smoke hung in the middle.

I was under the delegates' table. The first explosion had thrown me to the floor, and that sturdy table seemed like a good place to wait; I had been in bombed cities before and I knew that the best thing was to stay still, like a hunted animal. I was not the only one under there: farther back I could make out Elsa Goudinho, Bumenguele, and Rashid. I went to Rashid and asked, are you O.K.? Well, I've been better, said Rashid, but I'm not complaining; I think I have a few pieces of glass in my underpants, but no cuts, how about you? I'm fine, I said, but there are some wounded people in the hall.

Above the cries of those clambering over the rubble, I thought I could hear moaning from people lying on the ground, unable to move. I thought of Jessica and Egiswanda, had they managed to get out? or were they on the floor, bleeding, hit by one of the lamps or trampled by the others? Some of the bodies seemed strangely motionless. Marta was not there, but that did not worry me too much as I had not seen her earlier either, perhaps she had gone to meet Amos? It was highly likely. In the upper part of the hall, dozens of desperate people were piling against the doors, since only one was open. They finally opened wide and there was a stampede. A powerful beam of light invaded the hall and everything appeared to come back to life.

I thought of Ferenck Oslovski, trapped deep in a well. That was how it had been in the hall, although now we were about to leave, and, of course, we did not have the slightest idea of what awaited us in the lobby and the other floors. Outside, a war was raging, and it had finally reached us, in spite of all our words and theories about words. Even language had its limits. The barricade of language. Our refuge was as exposed as the rest of the city and our luxurious bedrooms might even now be in flames. I thought of my notes, but saw that I had them in the notebook and felt relieved. The check from Eve Studios was in my billfold. The rest might as well blow up.

With the return of the light, things became clear. Nobody had died, fortunately, but many were wounded. The most serious was a Norwegian poet, Sven Tellegar, who had suffered a heart attack; he was already under observation in the hotel's infirmary. Others had been hit, there were bruises and a few broken bones, but nothing really serious.

Rashid and I went out together and found out that three mortars had fallen in a cluster and hit floors nine and ten. A team of firefighters were at work in the left wing. I thought of Sabina Vedovelli's elegant suite, now reduced to rubble. I ought to take an interest in her fate, we had a contract and I would hate to have to give it back.

The management asked us to go down to the gym, like the previous night, but I decided to slip away. Rashid went out onto the street, saying that he was going with his family to Tira, his Arab town. The moment had come, and he knew how to get out. We hugged. I told him that I would go to see him before I went back to Rome, and he thanked me, but we both knew it was impossible.

On my way back to the coffee shop, I found Jessica in one of the wide corridors on the first floor. She was standing there looking at a tapestry on the wall, as calmly as if she were in the Kunsthistorisches Museum in Vienna. The tapestry depicted the destruction of Jerusalem as described in the prophecies of Jeremiah. The city in flames, gray creatures escaping from the smoke and destruction, an old man looking on with sorrow. I greeted her and she looked at me gravely; she had been crying, but I considered it impertinent to ask her the reason. There were reasons to spare. I'm surprised to see you here, I said, and she replied: I came to look for somebody who's already gone and could have said goodbye. Walter de la Salle? I ventured to ask. No, she said, he died many years ago, in the ashes of his house. You don't need to keep looking for him, that's the truth.

Then I asked her: was the person you were hoping to meet the guest in Room 1209? She shot me an angry look and just when I thought she was going to either burst into tears or hit me she said, yes, he was a kindred soul, a friend pure and simple, somebody who experienced what happened at the Ministry from a distance and decided to write a book about it; I met him in Miami, or rather, he came looking for me. He was the one who investigated and finally tracked down José, who had changed his name and had been invisible for years. I don't know how he tracked him down to this conference, but he decided to come and see him, and talk to him; as I was nearby, he suggested we meet here. He registered in the hotel under a false name, he didn't want to attract attention. His name is Mario Zambrano, although he signs his work Mario Simonides, he's a writer and journalist of Latin origin. It's a pity you never met him, he's a lot like you.

And don't you think he's coming back? I said. No, said Jessica. Mario is like José: always with his jacket on and a knapsack over his shoulder, ready to disappear, I know he won't come back. He spoke to José after his talk, told him I was here and wanted to see him. That day, I had to go straight back to Tel Aviv, but Mario told him I would come back when he wanted; José asked me to leave him a message to confirm that, and that was what I did. Then he killed himself.

Why did he kill himself? I asked. Jessica looked at her nails, scratched her forearms hard, and said, I'll tell you what I think: he killed himself because he didn't want to show his face, he wasn't capable of looking me in the eyes after what he had done, all the lies he had told; he killed himself out of cowardice. We're all of us cowards. Even Mario. All those who leave are cowards.

The ground shook and there was another violent explosion.

Pieces of stucco fell from the ceiling. Jessica sought protection in my arms. A cascade of earth and rubble rained all around us. From outside came the clear sound of a siren. So I asked her, what do you mean when you say José hurt you? Jessica did not look at me, but clung tighter to me. Again she was crying. She took two steps back and looked around, as if trying to find a way out, so I said, I'm sorry, Jessica, I don't have a right to ask you these questions.

A smaller explosion shook a column, and as it fell it shattered. We had to either get out of there or take shelter in the basement.

Then Jessica said in a low voice, almost in my ear: José raped me on three occasions, I want you to know. I've never told anyone, but I think we're going to die here. He did it three times, three long and painful times, you know what that means for a woman? I took her hand and said, I can imagine, Jessica, now let's go, nobody's going to die today.

Wait, she said, wait a moment. Things weren't so simple. He raped me on three occasions, but there were other times when I consented, I was young, I felt terribly jealous, I loved and hated him at the same time. Those years are over and José is dead, Walter is also dead, and I'm dead too, anyway, that's all over; I've survived a world that doesn't exist anymore and has no place in this one; nothing of what we were then can be understood by anyone today, nobody believes in what we believed in; the things that were important to us provoke laughter or curiosity, do you understand? We're dead, we're all dead.

Two more explosions blew out the large windows of the terrace and a splinter lodged itself in my forearm. We ran to the door and found several hotel employees there. Among them was Momo, who said, come with me, sir, I can get you out of here, there's an airfield just outside the city and a Hercules plane to evacuate you, but we have to go now. I asked him to stay with Jessica and went down to the basement.

When I got there, I looked around at the various groups, but could not see Egiswanda. At the far end, on a bench, was Marta. I rushed to her and said, where were you? are you O.K.? She said yes, indifferently. She was worried about her laptop and wanted to go up to my room. I told her that was absurd, her newspaper would give her another one when she get back, but she said, I'm not going back, I've decided to stay, I was thinking of using your room until the end of the conference, if you don't mind, it's in your name, right? I looked her up and down. Are you crazy? I'm not crazy, she said, nothing too serious will happen to this building and I already brought all my things, my best clothes, my most daring underwear, do you forgive me for not coming to hear you this morning?

Another explosion shook the building, so I grabbed her hands and said: let's look for Egiswanda and get out of here, Momo's waiting outside to take us to a plane we can leave on, but she said: I'm staying, please don't insist. Her attitude exasperated me and I said, where's the sense in staying? you'll be in grave danger in return for very little; as far as I know, you haven't written a single line so far, about the conference or anything else, so what reason do you have to stay, apart from Amos, who's married and has a life he has no intention of giving up? I don't understand.

Marta moved to the wall and said, obviously Amos is part of my decision, but he isn't all of it, don't you see? don't you understand? Egiswanda's story was a great revelation. It filled me with questions, things like: would I be capable of giving up everything for something I believed in or for something I wanted without thinking about the risks? have I ever believed in anything or anybody intensely enough to do that? You'll say that's simplistic, but these are the questions I'm asking myself right now and they seem important to me, and I think most people ask themselves these questions all the time, in every foot of this overpopulated planet there's somebody asking themselves things like that, that's the truth of life, and I tell you something: if in your books you dealt with this subject and imagined answers, you'd be more successful, you'd increase your loyal readership, you'd be translated into Icelandic and I'd be able to read you, anyway, to go back to what I was saying, I'm staying in the city, I decided last night, while I was trying to sleep. I realized that I'd never believed in anything seriously and that's why I never made a radical commitment, not even to journalism, which to be honest I couldn't care less about, like almost everything right now except the questions I'm asking myself, which I want to answer and which have to do with the fact of being more or less European and white and being born in that rich protectorate that's the north of the world, where everything's arranged so that nothing ever shocks you, and where life ought really to disgust us.

That's what many of us feel: disgust or shame or uncontrollable anger. When I heard Egiswanda, I felt ridiculous, poor, disgustingly poor in spirit. I felt an infinite sadness, having it all and at the same time having nothing. It's contradictory, isn't it? The things that stifle me today are the result of wars and destruction and learned books and terrible peace treaties; many people have died so that we, the grandchildren of the century, can have what is crushing us today, as if we were on the verge of falling into a deep sleep, an opium sleep. Coming to a place like this is a way of waking up completely, opening your eyes and, once they are wide open, you can't let them close; beyond the borders of our beautiful countries there is a terrifying outside world filled with life, a black sun that stretches over a number of continents, only revealing its beauty after the first impact. What you see on the surface is horrible and cruel, but slowly the beauty emerges; in our world, on the other hand, the surface is lovely and everything is bright and shiny, but with time what we see is the horror. I don't want to go back to that opium dream that's our paradise of the north,

I'm staying here, with real people and real problems, where everyone has to go up on the trapeze without a net and the struggle for existence is real and not a metaphor; I've found life here, I've understood the value of that miraculous, fragile thing called life and that's why I've developed an overwhelming desire to live it, to exhaust it to the last drop, what a miracle. This I discovered thanks to Amos, with his pink fingers and sweet penis; the best way to live life to the full is to take it to the limits, putting your face in its deepest depths, its edges, its caverns and ruined palaces, only that way will we keep our bodies hot and our heads boiling with dreams, I'm staying here and I'm in love with Amos, I love him with all my heart and with my vagina, both throb for him, my chest is bursting, I'm wetting my panties, everything is happening because of him.

That's fine, Marta, I understand you, I said, you'll be part of that smaller stream of contrary immigrants, those who go from the north and its wealth to lose themselves in the tropics or the deserts or the jungles of the south, you see, that demonstrates that paradise isn't in any one place and everyone paints it with the color of his own needs, because you have to be aware of the fact that this boring, predictable, overprotected life you curse is the dream of millions of poor Africans, Asians, and Latin Americans; the dream of all those who see their children die of typhoid or malaria in the slums of Khartoum or Dar Es Salaam, the young people who fall asleep in their rickshaws in broad daylight because of malnutrition in New Delhi; the dream of those who grow up without schools or health and have to make do later on with picking up a rifle or a package of drugs in Burma or Liberia or Colombia; the dream of those who, because of poverty, lose their humanity and are capable of cutting throats, decapitating, lopping off arms and legs, castrating. You want their smiles and their dances and their freshness and their contagious optimism and they want your schools and libraries, your hospitals, your thirty-five-hour weeks and

448 · SANTIAGO GAMBOA

your paid vacations, your labor laws and your human rights, and of course they also want the abundance and the glitter. You want their soul and they want your money. The difference is that they can't choose and you can. You can have both worlds just by wanting them. They can't. Their world is a prison from which they can only escape by knocking down a wall or jumping into the sea or digging tunnels as if they were rodents; you just have to buy an airline ticket, you don't even need a visa. To get what you despise, they risk their lives, you know what the fundamental difference is? that the rich can choose to be poor if they want, or pretend to be poor, but never the opposite. I was silent for a second and then said, what's going to happen to your articles?

Marta gave a weary gesture and slapped the air. I'll carry on writing, she said, but differently. Not to satisfy that daily appetite for the latest news, but writing non-topical articles, things the newspaper can give more of a spread when it's less rushed, and I said, surprised, I didn't know you were involved with news, I thought you were already doing non-topical articles, and she replied, I know, don't remind me, I was going to do articles but they had to be connected with current events, do you understand? the proceedings of the conference, the debates, after all, that was what they sent me here for, but being here I realized there was something more important and that's why I want to write real human-interest articles, something like Oriana Fallaci, do you know her? yes, I said, and she continued: a bit like that, but the truth of something that's being lived through real people, which here means all those linked to the war and its victims, not the biographies or the literature of the conference, and I'm really sorry if saying that offends you, but I'm convinced that what's important is happening outside, on the streets and on the walls protecting the city and not in these conference halls; it would be idle to devote my time to literary topics when half a mile away the destiny of one or several cities is being played out. The night I met Bryndis, my newspaper's war correspondent, meant a lot to me. Hearing her tell her stories of brave men who leaped into the fray, the courage with which they went on the attack and fell under the crossfire of the tracer bullets, hearing those really profound adventures, I felt empty, without anything to give her in return, and I realized that what was happening in the conference was only words, nothing more.

Then I said: don't you think the death of Maturana and the mystery of his life is something profound? Yes, perhaps it is, but not enough. It was because of that story that I met Amos, I can't forget that, but believe me, there are times when literature has to take a back seat, and this is one of them; maybe you don't like what I'm saying, but I respect you and I'm only trying to be honest.

I thanked her for her honesty and asked her about Amos, did he know she was planning to stay? what did he think about that? When she heard his name the blue fishbowls of her eyes shone.

He loves his wife and children and that's something to be proud of. I came later and I have to respect that, but I've seen his eyes looking at me and heard his voice and seen how his skin quivers and his penis rises like a sunflower toward me, I can't live as if I didn't know that, as if I hadn't seen it; to be honest, I don't know how important I am to him, but that doesn't really matter. You can love someone who doesn't love you, can't you? Literature is full of cases. It's the beautiful and terrifying thing about love, a prison of pleasure with bars that vibrate and punishments that give us spasms and fluids, addictions, anyway, love doesn't always expect anything in return; in this city people love gods they've never seen, gods who don't love them and of course don't repay them, but they still love them, and have done over the centuries, isn't that the supreme proof of love? I'll love Amos and I'll be his secret lover or his whore or whatever he wants; I told him that yesterday: wouldn't you like to gather every whore together in one single whore? He didn't answer, there are questions that don't require an answer. Amos looked at me in silence and smiled, then turned me over on a cushion and entered me from behind, and we both enjoyed it a lot, I swear to you, I saw stars, not only the star of David, but the western star and the star that lit the wise Kings and the fleeting stars of this war, this war that will do away with all of us, even with this passion I feel for him, a passion that expects nothing but to be lived to the full, and that's what I think and want, to take command of my own ship and steer it as I wish, and if it sinks to sink with it, as captains used to do in the old days, those who had a high sense of honor, and what about you? are you leaving already?

The building shook again, and I realized that a lot of time had passed. Yes, I said, the conference is over, the sessions are indefinitely suspended, so I'm going. Marta gave me a big hug and said: thank you, take care, think of me, and now go, I hate long farewells, the kind of farewell you see in movies is for movies, I'll look for you in a chat room or on Facebook, and remember this, joonsdottir73@livadia.com . . .

When I got back to the lobby, I saw that Jessica and Egiswanda were standing side by side. I felt relieved. Momo signaled to me from the car and I said to the women: come with me, please, I'll introduce you on the way, hurry now.

As I got in the car I saw the female employee I had caught him with. I know how you can get out of here, said Momo, they've organized a shuttle from an airfield near Rehavia. All entrances to the city are closed because of the continued attacks, the only way to get out is by air.

Thank you, I said, but as you can see I'm not alone, there are three of us, do you think it'll be possible? He looked and seemed to make a calculation, that doesn't matter, if there's enough space in my car then there'll be enough space in the plane, now let's go. It's better if we don't talk on the journey, I have to concentrate.

A cluster of grenades fell near us, setting off a chain explosion. The ground shook. According to Momo, an international intervention force was forming, but the people from the conference needed escorts to get out of the city, which was not easy. The wall around the city, which had once protected it, was now strangling it.

The residents could only go in and out through the checkpoint on Jaffa Road, which was the target of fierce attacks. The enemy armies had advanced as far as the walls, and from there they could easily control the siege.

We went out through the back gate of the parking lot and on reaching the street we were overwhelmed by the smell of smoke and gasoline. Sirens could be heard, and simultaneous detonations in places now distant; there were people seeking shelter, dragging cases and plastic bags. Momo accelerated along the street, dodging fallen trees, charred automobiles, and craters in the middle of the asphalt. A little farther on, we came across the body of an old man hugging a shopping cart; two young Orthodox men were reciting Kaddish and trying to separate him from the cart in order to put him in a van where other bodies were piled up. It reminded me of the plague.

Suddenly there was a blinding purple light and Momo had to brake abruptly.

The explosion shattered our eardrums.

What was around us disappeared for a moment and there was an infinite emptiness, a terrifying silence . . .

There came another explosion, and a third.

Everything disappeared from our sight, everything was illumined by that strange light . . .

Egiswanda and Jessica, who had been talking in whispers, hugged each other. The wave passed over our heads, stretching the tops of the trees, as in a painting by Munch, bringing down roofs and antennae. The rubble fell in front of us, but the mortar exploded in the street parallel to ours; the force of the blast reached us through courtyards and houses whose windows had been blown out.

Once the conflagration had passed, Momo accelerated up a slope and we reached one of the highest points. From there, between the columns of smoke and the thick air, we saw the gleaming silhouette of the Old City, a heart of jade in the middle of the night, a jewel in the black earth of a cemetery, a beacon amid the chaos. Nobody dared to say anything, such was the impact of the vision.

A second later, Momo and I got out on the opposite side of the hill, just as the sky again became an electric cloud and a new explosion could be heard.

I was starting to get nervous and I asked Momo, are you sure of the route? Very sure, sir, in a few minutes we'll be at the airfield; if we aren't hit by one of these bombs, of course, but don't worry, I'm taking the long way around to avoid the most dangerous areas. It won't be long now, relax. He accelerated again, zigzagging between fallen walls, charred skeletons of buses, trees turned into columns of charcoal.

Suddenly Momo cried: We're there!

In front of us, we saw a huge hangar that had so far escaped the grenades. There was a helicopter parked next to it; on the sides of the building were antimissile protection systems and nests of cannons pointing at the sky.

Entering the improvised air field, we saw a group waiting with cases to be taken on board and recognized some of the delegates to the conference. There were also wounded people on stretchers and a half-erased inscription saying *Alqudsville*, that word that had so intrigued me when I arrived. A hand waved at me, it was Edgar Miret Supervielle, who said, my friend, this has ended badly but at least I had the opportunity to present my story before they chased us away with cannon fire, that was my victory against barbarism! I'm sorry you weren't able to present your main speech, because I greatly appreciated your words at the round table, a good story, very human. I'll read your speech at the next conference of the ICBM, if they manage to repeat it.

I told him I would keep my story, and added: I'll take away with me many of the things you said in your lecture, which were enlightening and profound. Superviclle smiled and said: there's no need for you to say that, my friend, although I appreciate it, my story had a good reception because, basically, if we analyze it in detail, we find a novel philosophical aspect that perfectly fits the present moment, in spite of coming from another time; although sometimes one feels as if one is plowing in the desert, my friend, because, as you have indicated, many people aren't capable of seeing such a clear message, or what is worse: they refuse to see it, and I say this because most of my colleagues, among whom I do not include you, seeing as, strictly speaking, we aren't colleagues, anyway, most of my colleagues refuse or simply pretend not to see that importance and enjoy maintaining their silence and ignoring me, condemning my work to ostracism out of envy or even, in some cases, because I'm Jewish, you know the attitude in certain intellectual sectors on that subject, it's a never-ending story, but anyway, why do I need to say that to you, you were present at the tasteless spectacle provided by that former pastor who bamboozled everyone and who, along with Sabina Vedovelli, gained the greatest honors at the conference, the greatest applause, although I'm referring to easy applause, that programmed applause that does not celebrate a strong idea or an accurate touch, but the amusing and empty phrase, the *boutade*, an ingenious remark that means nothing beyond itself; that kind of demagoguery gets good results, what can we do, verbal pyrotechnics like that seduce isocephalic minds with a flat neuronal spectrum, and that's why nothing remains after-

454 · SANTIAGO GAMBOA

wards but a huge ontological lagoon, and that's even without mentioning the suicide, although this has to remain between you and me, I know it's politically incorrect to say so, all that pseudo-humanist verbiage, that crude style of his, was carefully calculated, I'm not deceived by these miracle workers; what I can't understand is how he ended up at a conference as serious as ours, he should have been giving advice in women's magazines or attending minor events, not the most distinguished assembly of analysts of the past, as was the case; if I were a little sharper in my conjectures I might even think that some rival had slipped him into the program before me in order to put a spoke in my wheels, do you understand me? you know that once one has reached a point of international recognition playing tricks or tripping one up is the order of the day, and the saddest thing is that it sometimes happens between close colleagues, those who through that closeness are more exposed to your lucidity and therefore more confronted with their own contradictions, and what immediately happens? resentment, the desire to restrain and outshine, to bring down.

Supervielle paused, so I said: the fact that others envy you is a confirmation of your talent, it shows that you're on the right track, don't you think? from that point of view it's something positive, trust me, although I'm unacquainted with envy, nobody plays tricks on me or puts a spoke in my wheels, which must mean that people are indifferent to me.

It seemed strange to be involved in such a discussion in that huge hangar, with the sound of bombs in the background, and waiting for a plane to evacuate us.

An interesting point of view, said Supervielle, and one I have already considered, but I confess, one gets tired of the fact that time and time again the results we hope for do not come, it has happened too many times in the history of thought and culture that the genius of exceptional people is unrecognized because of the stupidity and limited vision of their contemporaries, but what can we do if we live surrounded by idiots and simpletons? I know that poetic justice will save us eventually, but when we are already ash and mineral remains, as might happen to this city if things don't change, but at least let me tell you that although I was dissatisfied, I do have one reason to be happy, and that is the promise of a contract with Tiberias, one of the most important publishing companies, in whose catalog any student of the past, indeed any writer, dreams of appearing, given the range of subjects it handles; he is a hard but upright man, in love with knowledge, sensitive and with good taste, in short, a true Renaissance man, so at least I will have that consolation.

I said: that's excellent news that cancels out the other things, I know perfectly well what it means to be with Tiberias, it's a privilege to share a publisher with so many great men, but I'm curious about one thing, which of your titles is to be translated and published by Tiberias? and Supervielle replied, well, I'm still not very sure, several of my books are being read in his office, but I assume it will be the one that tells the story of the chess players, because that was what finally made Mr. Lottmann's mind up; he was very impressed with my talk and before I had even finished, he had already called his office from the hall, to tell them to put my books in a special place, because he wanted to consider them personally, so there you are.

Momo had stepped forward to talk to one of the soldiers in charge of the evacuation and tell him that our group was from the ICBM. Jessica and Egiswanda sat down on a bench. They continued talking in low voices, with their heads very close together, which made me think that they had already discovered what united them, so I preferred not to disturb them. Suddenly a Hummer appeared in the hangar, advanced to the middle of the runway, and parked next to a small private jet I hadn't seen before, which had three letters painted on its back part: EVE. Immediately, Sabina Vedovelli and her husband got out of the Hummer and walked up the steps, and the plane left.

In the next transport, Kosztolányi and Kaplan arrived, together with other delegates who had decided to leave—others preferred to wait, to stay a little longer. Kosztolányi came over and hugged Supervielle; he said that on the way they had seen horrible things, an inferno of destruction, pieces of bodies flying through the air, people running in flames, human torches, wounded people lying on the streets, mutilated bodies. That's war, said Supervielle, nothing more, nothing less.

The soldiers had told us that there were two possible destinations for the planes: one was the city of Haifa and the other Nicosia, in Cyprus. I assumed we could get in either, because the important thing was to get out, so I wrote our names, mine, Jessica's and Egiswanda's, on a piece of paper and gave it to the lieutenant.

I went to say goodbye to Kaplan, who was standing in another of the lines, looking very pale. When he saw me, he said, oh my God, these things follow you all your life. To think that what I most like is to have lunch in peace with my family and spend the afternoon reading history books, I don't know what brought me here, or rather, yes, I do know and that's why I came, but now I'm glad to be leaving, I never thought I'd say that about leaving this city. But I'm accustomed to departures, my friend.

Can I ask you if your story is true? I said, and he replied: Oh, all stories well told are true, that's my motto, but please don't think I'm arrogant; to be honest I don't know if it was all right and I don't even really want to know, I like that story and that's why I tell it. Don't forget it and, if you can, tell it one day yourself. It'd be a pleasure to come across it in one of your books. I'll try, I said, although I think it's already been told, isn't it *The Count of Monte Cristo*? Ah, I see you're a good reader, you may have been the only one to realize that, yes, it's my version of Edmond Dantès, but based on reality. I hope life smiles on you, my friend. You too, I said. Good luck.

Momo approached and said, sir, the next flight leaves in five minutes and is going to Nicosia, do you want to get on it? I went to ask the women. Both agreed to go to Nicosia and Jessica said, it's a good time to leave, Egiswanda and I have decided to spend some time together. Supervielle and Kosztolányi were still waiting for the next transport. They preferred to go to Haifa and try to get back to Tel Aviv from there to catch their flights.

I gave Momo a big hug and said, you saved our lives, next time you get under your girlfriend's skirt make sure you lock the door first, O.K.?

We got on the Hercules and sat down on one of the side benches, between the stretchers carrying the wounded. The plane started moving with the ramp still open. The soldiers of the intervention force asked us to adjust the harnesses and keep our luggage between our legs. Through a round window we saw the roofs of the destroyed houses, the walls punctured by shrapnel, the metal twisted by fire.

Goodbye, Jerusalem.

Many stories had died and others were just beginning. It had always been that way in this city. The plane rose into the air and we were off, leaving behind that battlefield where I had been on the verge of recovering part of what I had lost. I looked down and saw the rocks, the aridity. From the air the city seemed to merge with its surroundings. A vast ocean of sand.

3.
WANDA'S ISLAND

After two days in Nicosia, in the Greek part of Cyprus, near the military airport at Lakatamia, Jessica and Egiswanda decided to come with me to Rome, a nearby destination where it was possible to resolve practical matters. Egiswanda, for example, checked her account in Citibank, on which she had a Visa card and an American Express card, and was able to confirm that José Maturana had transferred a large sum of money to her, although she was too embarrassed to tell us how much it was. All I found out was that she gave five hundred thousand dollars to Jessica, who in turn donated half to the Universal Coptic Church. She wanted to give me a similar amount, but I refused.

All this happened in a very short space of time.

In the nights, the hot nights of the Roman summer, we gathered together in the living room of my apartment or in my library to chat, listen to music, or simply sit there in silence, the three of us together, drinking tea or even a last whiskey. The two women settled into the room at the back. It comforted me to know that they were near and that nobody had an urgent reason for the situation to change.

And so the evenings passed.

The air seemed so clean that it hurt our nostrils. There were no bombings or smoke, or the acrid smell of garbage; there were no burning tires or flame-lit sunsets; no lights turned blue by the din of mortars or violent explosions. The city was not under attack from enemy armies, only from banality and indifference. The horror wasn't in the air filled with dust and chemicals, but in the anonymous looks of the passers-by, their frozen pupils, the gestures of the younger people, the men and women walking indifferently across the cobbled squares, the defeated attitudes of the elderly. There was the horror. All of the cities we came from seemed to us, suddenly, equally cold and inhuman. Equally cruel. How to explain that profound rejection? how to convey that certainty that something in them was wrong, profoundly wrong? what to call that feeling that everything was empty and insubstantial? We just had to look at each other to be in agreement and we very soon came to a decision. We were going to the island where José had fled, and where he had chosen to establish his residence.

When Egiswanda pointed it out on the map I was impressed. That rock in the middle of nowhere perfectly represented what his life had been, or his situation in life: a small boat in the middle of a storm, lashed by surging waves and storms. He, like me, was a small boat. The fact he had found in such a place a refuge for his soul was a great lesson, and I did not doubt for a second that I should go.

We flew from Rome to Johannesburg, stopping in Jedda and Nairobi. From there we went to Cape Town, where we had to wait three days. We rented two rooms in the Winchester Mansions, facing the Atlantic, and killed time walking around the city, as if we were three tourists rather than fugitives.

Finally the Friday came, the day when the Tupolev flies out provisions, mail, and equipment. The only quick way to get to Tristan da Cunha.

Our arrival was a highly emotional moment.

After flying over those limpid skies so common in the south of the world, with the sea shining bright red and ocher, we saw that awesome dot in the middle of nowhere, the smooth, volcanic surface, like a lunar crater or a dry, chapped old nipple. Then the plane nosedived toward that tiny planet until it was almost swallowed up by the waters or the wind, so fragile did it seem from the air.

The little airfield had the same name as the colony: Edinburgh of the Seven Seas, and lay in the foothills of a huge volcano. It could hardly be described as a town, not even a small town or village. It was a collection of large houses beside the headlands. A settlement.

When we got off the Tupolev, it was cold and there was a strong wind. A group of people was waiting at the military base, and on seeing us getting out, a man with a white beard, in his fifties or sixties, approached and said, are you visitors? I handed him the envelope with José Maturana's letter and the old man read it, screwing up his eyes. His neck was red and rough, like a rooster's, and his long hair was gathered in a ponytail. Without looking at us he called to another of the old men, a man nearly seven feet tall, and showed him the letter. The giant took out his glasses and read. Then they nodded and came toward me. Welcome, the three of you are welcome, and they introduced themselves:

Reverend Ebenezer Talisker, said the first. Reverend Silas Folkes, said the second. As they said their names, they put their hands over their hearts and gave theatrical bows.

They hugged me and greeted the two women effusively. Reverend Talisker called something to the others which I did not understand, and then said to us, come, it's cold and the wind will rise in a few minutes. I'll take you to your house so you can settle in as soon as possible. Two young men picked up our bags and put them in an old Silverado rotted by the salt and sea breeze. Talisker motioned me to get in, with Jessica and Egiswanda, and drove for about ten minutes along a coast road in the foothills of the volcano, until we saw the first houses. A few people came to the windows to see us and smiled. Most were more incredulous than anything else.

José's house was on the other side, near the post office and the cliff. It was a two-story house of wood and slate, with wide balconies, reminiscent of British houses in the Caribbean. On the front there was a plank hanging from two chains on which the words *Black Sparrow* could be read. Talisker explained that for the construction of the house they had used the rigging from a ship of that name, which had run aground here.

The house looked out on the ocean on three of its sides. Does it get very windy? I asked. The two men laughed. Instead of replying, they took out their pipes and filled them with tobacco.

In one of the side naves was the chapel. A modest cross and an inscription that said: *Chapel of Christ the Redeemer*. At the back were two rooms which communicated with the living room and the dining room on the first floor. The chapel had about twenty wooden benches, an altar, and some images of the Virgin Mary, St Antony and St Paul. And at the front, behind the vestibule, a huge and very modern image of Christ with a heart of alabaster fixed to the wall, which appeared to throb in the sunlight.

The young men helped us to unload the things, of which there were not many, just a few cases and some hand luggage. Jessica said she would live in the rooms that adjoined the chapel. Egiswanda took over two of the rooms on the first floor and I settled into those on the second floor. I unpacked my case in the bedroom and occupied the adjacent study. Everything was furnished simply and in good taste. Tables and chairs of wood and leather. Fitted closets. There was a good library, with literary classics and philosophical works. I assumed that Maturana had slept in what was going to be my bedroom and I approached the large windows, which were like the mouths of caves facing out to the heart of the ocean. I connected my laptop on the work table and arranged the few books I had brought with me: the *Complete Plays* of Tennessee Williams, *Old Masters* and *Frost* by Thomas Bernhard, *Marcel:*

First Dialogue on the Harmonious City by Charles Péguy, *Diary of a Country Priest* by Bernanos, and the *Diaries* of Léon Bloy. Then I discovered that Maturana had them in his library, with annotations. I also placed my old chessboard on a side table, and a *Book of Openings*. I was complete.

We rested for a couple of days, each engaged in his or her own activities and walks. At night, we would get together for dinner in the huge oak dining room—did it come from another shipwreck, like the rest of the house?—and Jessica or Egiswanda would explain the dish they had cooked. The provisions we obtained at the administrative office, although soon after settling in a very silent man brought two boxes filled with food. A gift from the reverend, he said before he left.

The second night I went to the only pub in the village and saw three fishermen sitting at the bar, having an animated conversation. On the wall there was a huge stuffed swordfish and a white and red life preserver. I asked for a whiskey, and then another. The men smiled at me and very soon I received two free rounds. They invited me to go out to sea with them whenever I wanted; only it would mean going to the harbor at three in the morning. They went out early to catch banks of fish farther south, past the other two islands in the archipelago, Nightingale Island and Inaccessible Island.

308 people lived in Edinburgh of the Seven Seas.

One night some time later, Egiswanda also came to the pub. The men were surprised. She drank three whiskeys with them and reminded them that continuing in a straight line westwards you would reach Brazil, her home country. They already knew that, but were delighted to hear it. We played darts, drank a few more whiskeys, and got back home after midnight. Jessica was already asleep.

After four weeks, I felt strong enough to start writing about José's life, and I asked myself, should I tell the two women who were now sharing my life? They were leading characters in the story, but I preferred not to say anything. I started by making a fair copy of the notes I had made during the conference, which were a whole notebook. One day I asked Egiswanda to let me reread José's letter and I copied out the section that referred to the island, which said this:

The request has to do with the other envelope. Look for God in the deep, say the gospels and that is what you are going to do; you are a rock on a cliff, strong, tough, I had never told you these things but today I am saying them and writing them, so that you know that they were inside me, so that you remember them, there I leave you these words. (…) In the blue envelope there is a map on which is marked an island and the way to get there, like in stories about treasures, except that in this case the treasure is the whole island, the one place on Earth where peace exists, a rock remote from the world where I would like to take you and I really had planned to take you there if this emergency had not come up, so the request is that you go and settle there; you can go whenever you like and move into our house, ask for the chaplain, his name is Talisker, he will help you (…) You have to go to be pure and clean and then, when that day arrives, you will make the leap into the infinite where the Big Enchilada and I will be waiting for you; but in the meantime go there and stay, that island is how I was when I was born, something small and solitary, lost in the world; on it you will be protected by millions of tons of water and you will be happy, because it is an emanation of the soul of God; my last gift is more solitude, Wanda, but what can I do if I was born alone; when I look at the world it will be to imagine that you are there, on that solitary dot, and to tell me that that pure uncontaminated place is Wanda's island.

Two weeks later I attended a service in the chapel, organized by Jessica and Egiswanda, with help from Reverend Talisker. From what Jessica told me, they had tried to follow the model of the Ministry of Mercy, but it was difficult, because she now realized that all that had been entirely based on Walter's personal charisma, and without him it did not work. But they prayed and listened to contemporary music and talked about people's problems in a simple, direct way.

I had not exactly acquired a new faith, but I did believe in them and was starting to love them. I have to confess that I also desired them, and some nights my brain filled with voices, the ones I had heard that first night at the conference, which one of them had it been? Those voices made me imagine them and desire them even more.

I also decided it was time to recover my health completely, so I started doing exercises in the meadow and taking long walks over the mountains that climbed to the volcano. Later, I installed a gym in the garage and my muscles responded well to the exercise. My back got stronger and my arms swelled. On my walks I went farther each time and was able without too much effort to reach the terraces where the peasants planted potatoes. At other times I went down to the harbor and plunged into the swelling waves of the Atlantic. I never again got out of breath. I was being born again.

One evening I talked in the village with a man whose name was Jonathan, a Maori who had stayed on the island after being found guilty of organizing a mutiny on a factory ship flying the Australian flag. I made a few drawings on a piece of card and said, I want these tattoos on my back and chest, could you do them? He said he could, but needed ink. He would do them as soon as the next boat arrived.

I was growing accustomed to my new life, my two women.

One night, after drinking a lot of whiskeys in the pub, Egiswanda got down on her knees at a bend in the dark road that led to our house and gave me a blowjob. When we got home we went up to my room and made love until dawn. During the day we did not speak and at night we would spend a cozy evening with Jessica, reading poems or articles recently arrived from the continent, and then have sex. I understood that Egiswanda's rhythm was one or two sessions of sex a week, behind Jessica's back. And I agreed to that. I liked the fact that she was in control.

When Jonathan received the colors and did the tattoos on my arms, chest, and back, the two women were delighted. You look really good, you're magnificent, they said. That night I decided to let my hair and beard grow. I felt an urgent need to transform myself.

One afternoon Jessica came to my study and said, I have to talk to you, do you remember Simonides, the writer? Yes, I said, the guest in Room 1209. She rubbed her hands nervously and said: I got in touch with him and asked him to come. I got a reply from him today, he says he'll be here soon. I wanted you to know. The two of you will get along well.

I continued with my walks as far as the foothills of the volcano and along the headlands, breathing in the salty wind. At night I would sit down to write, although I spent most of my time looking at the storms whipping the ocean, our protecting ocean. Storms that recalled the violent siege of the city where the three of us had met. Or perhaps I should say: where Maturana had brought us together.

The fury of the thunder lit up the blackness of the night, which had abolished the boundary between sky and sea. The lightning flashes were like electric vipers sinking their teeth into the water. With each flash, the threatening clouds could be seen. The waves were mountain ranges of water hitting the cliffs of our fortress.

Those terrifying lights suggested a battle, but what battle? The final one, Armageddon, as Jessica sometimes thought, or

a more conventional one, fought with missiles and nuclear warheads? None of us knew, but our little island, lonely and drifting, made me think that all of that had happened in another
time, and that the horror was over now, and that the world as
we had known it was already a distant, forgotten planet.

EUROPA EDITIONS BACKLIST
(alphabetical by author)

Fiction

Carmine Abate
Between Two Seas • 978-1-933372-40-2 • Territories: World
The Homecoming Party • 978-1-933372-83-9 • Territories: World

Simonetta Agnello Hornby
The Nun • 978-1-60945-062-5 • Territories: World

Milena Agus
From the Land of the Moon • 978-1-60945-001-4 • Ebook •
Territories: World (excl. ANZ)

Salwa Al Neimi
The Proof of the Honey • 978-1-933372-68-6 • Ebook • Territories:
World (excl. UK)

Jenn Ashworth
A Kind of Intimacy • 978-1-933372-86-0 • Territories: US & Can

Beryl Bainbridge
The Girl in the Polka Dot Dress • 978-1-60945-056-4 • Ebook •
Territories: US

Muriel Barbery
The Elegance of the Hedgehog • 978-1-933372-60-0 • Ebook •
Territories: World (excl. UK & EU)
Gourmet Rhapsody • 978-1-933372-95-2 • Ebook • Territories:
World (excl. UK & EU)

Stefano Benni
Margherita Dolce Vita • 978-1-933372-20-4 • Territories: World
Timeskipper • 978-1-933372-44-0 • Territories: World

Romano Bilenchi
The Chill • 978-1-933372-90-7 • Territories: World

Kazimierz Brandys
Rondo • 978-1-60945-004-5 • Territories: World

Alina Bronsky
Broken Glass Park • 978-1-933372-96-9 • Ebook • Territories: World
The Hottest Dishes of the Tartar Cuisine • 978-1-60945-006-9 •
Ebook • Territories: World

Jesse Browner
Everything Happens Today • 978-1-60945-051-9 • Ebook •
Territories: World (excl. UK & EU)

Francisco Coloane
Tierra del Fuego • 978-1-933372-63-1 • Ebook • Territories: World

Rebecca Connell
The Art of Losing • 978-1-933372-78-5 • Territories: US

Laurence Cossé
A Novel Bookstore • 978-1-933372-82-2 • Ebook • Territories: World
An Accident in August • 978-1-60945-049-6 • Territories: World
(excl. UK)

Diego De Silva
I Hadn't Understood • 978-1-60945-065-6 • Territories: World

Shashi Deshpande
The Dark Holds No Terrors • 978-1-933372-67-9 •
Territories: US

Steve Erickson
Zeroville • 978-1-933372-39-6 • Territories: US & Can
These Dreams of You • 978-1-60945-063-2 • Territories:
US & Can

Elena Ferrante
The Days of Abandonment • 978-1-933372-00-6 • Ebook •
Territories: World
Troubling Love • 978-1-933372-16-7 • Territories: World
The Lost Daughter • 978-1-933372-42-6 • Territories: World

Linda Ferri
Cecilia • 978-1-933372-87-7 • Territories: World

Damon Galgut
In a Strange Room • 978-1-60945-011-3 • Ebook •
Territories: USA

Jane Gardam
Old Filth • 978-1-933372-13-6 • Ebook • Territories: US & Italy
The Queen of the Tambourine • 978-1-933372-36-5 • Ebook •
Territories: US
The People on Privilege Hill • 978-1-933372-56-3 • Ebook •
Territories: US
The Man in the Wooden Hat • 978-1-933372-89-1 • Ebook •
Territories: US
God on the Rocks • 978-1-933372-76-1 • Ebook • Territories: US &
Can

Anna Gavalda
French Leave • 978-1-60945-005-2 • Ebook • Territories:
US & Can

Katharina Hacker
The Have-Nots • 978-1-933372-41-9 • Territories: World (excl.
India)

Patrick Hamilton
Hangover Square • 978-1-933372-06-8 • Territories: US & Can

James Hamilton-Paterson
Cooking with Fernet Branca • 978-1-933372-01-3 • Territories: US
Amazing Disgrace • 978-1-933372-19-8 • Territories: US
Rancid Pansies • 978-1-933372-62-4 • Territories: USA

Alfred Hayes
The Girl on the Via Flaminia • 978-1-933372-24-2 • Ebook •
Territories: World

Jean-Claude Izzo
The Lost Sailors • 978-1-933372-35-8 • Territories: World
A Sun for the Dying • 978-1-933372-59-4 • Territories: World

Gail Jones
Sorry • 978-1-933372-55-6 • Territories: US & Can

Ioanna Karystiani
The Jasmine Isle • 978-1-933372-10-5 • Territories: World
Swell • 978-1-933372-98-3 • Territories: World

Peter Kocan
Fresh Fields • 978-1-933372-29-7 • Territories: US, EU & Can
The Treatment and the Cure • 978-1-933372-45-7 • Territories: US, EU & Can

Helmut Krausser
Eros • 978-1-933372-58-7 • Territories: World

Amara Lakhous
Clash of Civilizations Over an Elevator in Piazza Vittorio • 978-1-933372-61-7 • Ebook
Divorce Islamic Style • 978-1-60945-066-3 • Ebook • Territories: World

Lia Levi
The Jewish Husband • 978-1-933372-93-8 • Territories: World

Valerio Massimo Manfredi
The Ides of March • 978-1-933372-99-0 • Territories: US

Leïla Marouane
The Sexual Life of an Islamist in Paris • 978-1-933372-85-3 •
Territories: World

Sélim Nassib
I Loved You for Your Voice • 978-1-933372-07-5 • Territories:
World
The Palestinian Lover • 978-1-933372-23-5 • Territories: World

Amélie Nothomb
Tokyo Fiancée • 978-1-933372-64-8 • Territories: US & Can
Hygiene and the Assassin • 978-1-933372-77-8 • Ebook •
Territories: US & Can

Valeria Parrella
For Grace Received • 978-1-933372-94-5 • Territories: World

Alessandro Piperno
The Worst Intentions • 978-1-933372-33-4 • Territories: World

Lorcan Roche
The Companion • 978-1-933372-84-6 • Territories: World

Boualem Sansal
The German Mujahid • 978-1-933372-92-1 • Ebook • Territories:
US & Can

www.europaeditions.com

Eric-Emmanuel Schmitt
The Most Beautiful Book in the World • 978-1-933372-74-7 •
Ebook • Territories: World
The Woman with the Bouquet • 978-1-933372-81-5 • Ebook
• Territories: US & Can
Concerto to the Memory of an Angel • 978-1-60945-009-0 • Ebook
• Territories: US & Can

Audrey Schulman
Three Weeks in December • 978-1-60945-064-9 • Ebook •
Territories: US & Can

James Scudamore
Heliopolis • 978-1-933372-73-0 • Ebook • Territories: US

Luis Sepúlveda
The Shadow of What We Were • 978-1-60945-002-1 • Ebook •
Territories: World

Paolo Sorrentino
Everybody's Right • 978-1-60945-052-6 • Ebook • Territories: US &
Can

Domenico Starnone
First Execution • 978-1-933372-66-2 • Territories: World

Henry Sutton
Get Me out of Here • 978-1-60945-007-6 • Ebook • Territories: US
& Can

Chad Taylor
Departure Lounge • 978-1-933372-09-9 • Territories: US, EU & Can

Roma Tearne
Mosquito • 978-1-933372-57-0 • Territories: US & Can
Bone China • 978-1-933372-75-4 • Territories: US

André Carl van der Merwe
Moffie • 978-1-60945-050-2 • Ebook • Territories: World (excl. S. Africa)

Fay Weldon
Chalcot Crescent • 978-1-933372-79-2 • Territories: US

Anne Wiazemsky
My Berlin Child • 978-1-60945-003-8 • Territories: US & Can

Jonathan Yardley
Second Reading • 978-1-60945-008-3 • Ebook • Territories: US & Can

Edwin M. Yoder Jr.
Lions at Lamb House • 978-1-933372-34-1 • Territories: World

Michele Zackheim
Broken Colors • 978-1-933372-37-2 • Territories: World

Alice Zeniter
Take This Man • 978-1-60945-053-3 • Territories: World

Children's Illustrated Fiction

Altan
Here Comes Timpa • 978-1-933372-28-0 • Territories: World (excl. Italy)
Timpa Goes to the Sea • 978-1-933372-32-7 • Territories: World (excl. Italy)
Fairy Tale Timpa • 978-1-933372-38-9 • Territories: World (excl. Italy)

Wolf Erlbruch
The Big Question • 978-1-933372-03-7 • Territories: US & Can
The Miracle of the Bears • 978-1-933372-21-1 • Territories: US & Can
(with **Gioconda Belli**) *The Butterfly Workshop* •
978-1-933372-12-9 • Territories: US & Can

Non-fiction

Alberto Angela
A Day in the Life of Ancient Rome • 978-1-933372-71-6 •
Territories: World • History

Helmut Dubiel
Deep In the Brain: Living with Parkinson's Disease •
978-1-933372-70-9 • Ebook • Medicine/Memoir

James Hamilton-Paterson
Seven-Tenths: The Sea and Its Thresholds • 978-1-933372-69-3 •
Territories: USA • Nature/Essays

Daniele Mastrogiacomo
Days of Fear • 978-1-933372-97-6 • Ebook • Territories: World •
Current affairs/Memoir/Afghanistan/Journalism

Valery Panyushkin
Twelve Who Don't Agree • 978-1-60945-010-6 • Ebook • Territories:
World • Current affairs/Memoir/Russia/Journalism

Christa Wolf
One Day a Year: 1960-2000 • 978-1-933372-22-8 • Territories:
World • Memoir/History/20th Century

Tonga Books

Ian Holding
Of Beasts and Beings • 978-1-60945-054-0 • Ebook • Territories:
US & Can

Sara Levine
Treasure Island!!! • 978-0-14043-768-3 • Ebook • Territories:
World

Alexander Maksik
You Deserve Nothing • 978-1-60945-048-9 • Ebook • Territories:
US, Can & EU (excl. UK)

www.europaeditions.com

Crime/Noir

Massimo Carlotto
The Goodbye Kiss • 978-1-933372-05-1 • Ebook • Territories: World
Death's Dark Abyss • 978-1-933372-18-1 • Ebook • Territories: World
The Fugitive • 978-1-933372-25-9 • Ebook • Territories: World
Poisonville • 978-1-933372-91-4 • Ebook • Territories: World
Bandit Love • 978-1-933372-80-8 • Ebook • Territories: World

Giancarlo De Cataldo
The Father and the Foreigner • 978-1-933372-72-3 • Territories: World

Caryl Férey
Zulu • 978-1-933372-88-4 • Ebook • Territories: World (excl. UK & EU)
Utu • 978-1-60945-055-7 • Ebook • Territories: World (excl. UK & EU)

Alicia Giménez-Bartlett
Dog Day • 978-1-933372-14-3 • Territories: US & Can
Prime Time Suspect • 978-1-933372-31-0 • Territories: US & Can
Death Rites • 978-1-933372-54-9 • Territories: US & Can

Jean-Claude Izzo
Total Chaos • 978-1-933372-04-4 • Territories: US & Can
Chourmo • 978-1-933372-17-4 • Territories: US & Can
Solea • 978-1-933372-30-3 • Territories: US & Can

Matthew F. Jones
Boot Tracks • 978-1-933372-11-2 • Territories: US & Can

Gene Kerrigan
The Midnight Choir • 978-1-933372-26-6 • Territories: US & Can
Little Criminals • 978-1-933372-43-3 • Territories: US & Can

Carlo Lucarelli
Carte Blanche • 978-1-933372-15-0 • Territories: World
The Damned Season • 978-1-933372-27-3 • Territories: World
Via delle Oche • 978-1-933372-53-2 • Territories: World

Edna Mazya
Love Burns • 978-1-933372-08-2 • Territories: World (excl. ANZ)

Yishai Sarid
Limassol • 978-1-60945-000-7 • Ebook • Territories: World (excl.
UK, AUS & India)

Joel Stone
The Jerusalem File • 978-1-933372-65-5 • Ebook • Territories:
World

Benjamin Tammuz
Minotaur • 978-1-933372-02-0 • Ebook • Territories: World